The Father's Son: A Viking Saga

Norway, 840 AD: A young peasant seeks revenge for the death of his clan's leader and searches for his absent father in a warrior culture of Feudal kingdoms as they clash over limited land, sending their kinsmen across the seas to plunder riches. To complicate matters a Danish Prince attempts to overtake an aging Jarl's kingdom, his scheming effective and despised by the common people. A story of adventure, romance, war, and humanity.

Regards
Thank you
Bill

A VIKING SAGA

The Father's Son

William Jay Taylor

Island Entertainment Media
Sherman, Texas

ISBN-10: 0-9974658-8-3

ISBN-13: 978-0-9974658-8-4

Produced and Distributed by Island Entertainment Media

Printed in the United States of America

Cover Design by Island Entertainment Media

First Edition

16 15 14 13 12 11 10 / 10 9 8 7 6 5 4 3 2 1

Library of Congress Control Number: TBD
Island Entertainment Media, Sherman, TX

Chapter 1

840 AD., Hoanger, on the Sognefjord, Norway

The sun, rising over the mountains, to the south, across the fjord, on this early May morning, suggested a hint of spring; its soft rays, casting their light, gently across the landscape. Seventeen year old Bryan Thorsen opened his eyes. Through the door of his family's room he could see the first sunbeams, streaming into the common room of the longhouse.

His young brother, lying warm against him, under the scratchy woolen blankets, and, not far away, breathing softly in their sleep, his mother and sister. Bryan watched his own breath drift up into the icy air, slipped from under the blankets, the cold stinging his bare skin, quickly pulled on woolen trousers and tunic, scratchy, but warm and comfortable. He would much rather have stayed, under the blankets, with his brother.

In the common room, he stirred together the coals in the fire pit, rekindling the flames.

"Good morning," his uncle said, coming from the opposite side of the longhouse.

"Good morning, uncle. How are you this morning?" He didn't expect an answer. "Is Ari coming?"

"He'll be along soon as soon as he dresses."

"All right, I'll be getting ready then."

From a half dozen horses, standing peacefully in the corral, he picked out one, Fryea, a mare, too old to do field work, but still enough left in her to pull a cart load of fire wood.

5

He was nearly done hitching her to a two wheeled cart when Ari arrived; the two finished harnessing the horse, not a word said, they headed for the foot hills.

Sounds of waking forest surrounded them; breezes, drifting through newly emerged leaves overhead, pine squirrels chattering, looking down from their high perches, the call of birds, a cacophony of noise swirled about them.

Toward the hill top, trees, burned years ago, thinned from harvesting as long as Bryan could remember, a large stand of dead wood still remained to be cut. In the panorama of the valley below, a stream, fed by melting snow, cascading down the other side of the valley, tumbling on rocks below, could be heard in the distance. A road, a footpath really, meandered along the valley floor, the same road running past the clan's homestead; out of sight, it continued up through the hills, over a high mountain pass, east to the next village, the only road to the east, its frequent use keeping it free of vegetation.

"We better get started," Bryan said, "if we don't want to be here all day."

"As slow as you are, it'll probably take that long anyway," Ari said.

Though nothing more than a tease, Bryan accepted the challenge. "We'll see about that," he shot back. They set to work, to prove who could cut the most wood in the shortest time, a sibling rivalry, the competitive spirit, preparing them for battle, the Norse culture of war. The two grew up learning to fight with wooden swords; throwing axes, spirited competition, in everything.

They felled the dead trees, cutting them into lengths, loading them onto the cart, for the better part of the morning, but stopped short, hearing voices; angry, far away, from the valley below.

Rushing to the edge of the clearing, they peered down. On the road below, four men, one by his size, Bryan's Uncle Gunner, arguing with Skjolden, the Danish Jarl, two other men, Skjolden's thugs, stood by.

"What's he doing here?" Bryan exclaimed.

"Don't know, but it doesn't sound like father is very happy about it," Ari returned.

The conversation on the road, animated; arms and heads gesturing in every direction, a long way from the boy's perch high on the hill, the words unintelligible.

Suddenly, the Dane's guards moved behind Gunner, grabbing his arms, in the Jarl's hands, the metallic glint of a sword flashed.

Bryan heard Ari suck air between his teeth.

Skjolden plunged the sword into Gunner's belly.

"Noooo!" Ari's voice rose in a crescendo from whisper to a scream, lunging, toward the road, as if to breech the distance.

Bryan tackled him, landing a-top his cousin, pinning him, clamping a hand over Ari's mouth, muffling the scream; not able, in disbelief, to take his eyes from the horror below, watching the Dane stabbing Gunner, over and over, until he fell to the ground.

Bryan closed his eyes, shuting out his shock and terror, and stop the tears, already flowing, searing stabs of grief, terror, and panic, in his chest, reality forcing itself into his brain.

Ari's face, wet with tears, smeared with dirt, pain, terror, sorrow, helplessness, devastated. Bryan, having difficulty with his own grief, could only imagine the sorrow his cousin felt.

Speaking in a low, deliberate, shaky, voice, between sobs, he said to Ari, "We must be silent, less they hear us, and

7

kill us too. We must remain alive, to tell the others, so that vengeance can be done, it is the way."

They lay arm in arm, a long time, their bodies heaving with sobs of grief and shock. Finally Bryan said, "Come, we must tell the others."

Their descent, off the mountain, seemed forever long; as if slogging through deep mud, the cart heavy with logs, the pony slow, Bryan's head throbbing, his thoughts stunned, slow, tears burning his eyes, his throat parched. He wrestled with his thoughts; what could the Dane possibly want, what was he up to, how could anyone avenge this deed, how could they possibly tell the others the horror they just witnessed?

The longhouse finally came into view, halting, they were, dismayed; the Dane and his men, in the front of the longhouse, Gunner's body on the ground, family gathered around, the Jarl telling them, who knew what, gesturing profoundly, throwing his hands wildly in the air.

"For the sin of gods, I swear," Ari cursed, "The filthy dog has the nerve to defile our own home. By the honor of Thor, I'll take an oath to kill the motherless swine if it's the last thing I ever do."

"We'll both kill him, and Thor will be our witness, when the time is right, but for now we'll not let him know what we've seen, nor give him any hint of what we feel toward him. We must go down there, grieve for your father; bare our true feelings at our loss, and when he's gone, we'll make plans for vengeance. That is what Gunner would do, and what we must do."

"I understand…, I do understand, but I don't know if I can hide my feelings that well," Ari confessed.

"Me neither, but we must."

"Then let's get on with it," Ari nudged the horse, leading the way down the hill.

8

Bryan understood his cousin's outrage, felt it gnawing at his gut too, his skin crawling with the heat of rage. What they had to do, a fate almost as bad as death itself, they must do. Garnering all his strength, his bravery, untested, not sure he had the guts, they moved on. The family, gathered tightly around the Jarl, listening to him, as they approached.

"Bryan, Ari!" someone called out.

They stopped short.

The clan turned as one to face them, an awkward moment of silence. Ari's mother emerged from the group, and ran up the hill to him.

"Son, your father's..., been killed," she said, her voice shaky, tapering to nearly a whisper, "Murdered on the road over the hill," she paused, "The jarl found him dead, and brought him home to us."

Ari looked across to Bryan, the rage on his face, terrifying, Bryan let his jaw drop open, a feign surprise, they stared at one another for a long moment.

"No," Bryan said quietly, then, "NOOOO!" at the top of his lungs.

Both turned, and ran into the circle of people, pushing them aside until they stood over poor Gunner' body, motionless, skin pale and cold as snow. No need to hide their grief longer, kneeling beside him, they sobbed, his arm around his cousin's shoulders, Bryan pulled Ari to him, together they wept.

When Bryan was able to open his eyes again, two booted legs stood on the other side of his dead uncle's body. The Dane, stooped down, reached across to the boys, putting a hand on Ari's shoulders.

In a deep, soft, gentle, soothing voice, he said, "If there is anything that I can do, P-L-E-A-S-E let me know. I am so very sorry. My heart aches for you."

Bryan turned away in revulsion, and vomited, the lying, sanctimonious, hypocrite, how could anyone be so audacious? Hatred seethed, deep in his being; taking all the self control he could muster, to restrain himself from trying to kill the motherless bastard, right there. His arm still around Air's shoulders, his cousin shaking, sobbing, trembling with rage; under his breath, Bryan swore an oath, to his dead uncle, to Thor, and to everyone on earth, this soulless dog would suffer the rage of the gods.

Bryan or Ari unable to say anything, the silence awkward, the Jarl stood, and resumed his speech to the clan. He would leave his body guards with the clan to 'protect' them in Gunner's absence.

"We don't need them," Bryan said in a low, barely audible voice, as he stood, his rage, thinly disguised.

"But, surly Gunner's absence well be felt," the Dane said.

"Yes. He'll be missed more than words can describe. But, there are men here who are capable, and without doubt your guards are needed more sorely elsewhere."

"Don't tell me that you couldn't use the help of a couple extra hands to tend your crops, and bring in the fish," the Dane replied.

Looking at the guards, he doubted they ever saw the back side of a plow, or hauled in a wet fishing net, or bloodyed their hands cleaning fish, or butchering pigs, if so, it was a long time ago. "We won't need them," he said firmly, no doubt in his mind, they would never lift a finger to help.

"What about the rest of you," the Dane said turning to the clan. "Is there anyone here who disagrees with aaa-."

"Bryan."

"With Bryan?"

No one answered.

"Very well, as you wish," he said, turning to the side, his hands on his hips, annoyed. He turned back. "You, aaa – Bryan, yes Bryan," he said, reassuring himself. "You're Thor's son aren't you?"

"Yes Sire."

"A very brave courageous man, your' father," he paused, "I would be pleased if you would join my court. You would be an excellent addition. You'd be educated and trained to fight like a true Viking, an opportunity to follow in your father's footsteps."

Bryan caught his breath; the Jarl just handed him the opportunity, to get close, to gain his confidence, and kill him.

"I would be honored," he said, bowing his head, a quiet murmur rippled through the clan.

"Excellent, when you've settled matters here, come to my compound in Balestrand. You'll be welcomed there, and I will have your training begun."

"I'll be there, M'Lord, as soon as I'm able." Bryan said, in his head, already plotting.

"Are you sure that you don't need any help, with the burial or the farm?" The Jarl wanted his men to stay in the worst kind of way.

"No, we will handle it, you need not waste your important time here," Bryan repeated, with as much authority his trembling voice could muster. He glanced at Ari, his cousin returning his gaze, apprehension on his face. Neither understood why Grunner was killed. Not for a moment, did either trust the Jarl, nor understand why he wanted Bryan in his court? But both grasped the opportunity that had just been presented them.

"Very well then, once again please accept my condolences." The Jarl turned to his horse, motioned to his

11

guards, the three mounted their steeds, and rode toward the mountains.

"What on earth are you thinking," his mother screamed in anger, the moment they were gone.

Chapter 2

"Leaving us alone, going off with that Dane. You've lost your senses, as bad as your father." She shouted over his uncle's body, her temper, fanned by grief, burning deep in her slender body, exploding into scalding rage directed at her son.

Bryan searched frantically for the words to sooth her anguish, his heart breaking.

Ari choked back a blustery sob, and with a gasp of air, blurted out, "Revenge, papa's murder must be avenged. Bryan goes there for vengeance."

She shouted back, indignantly, "What could vengeance possibly have to do with your running off with that scum, leaving us here to fend for ourselves?" "You don't understand, t'was them that did it," Ari sobbed.

"Did what?"

"Killed papa, we saw them do it, with our own eyes, the Dane and his henchmen," Ari's voice cracked, he coughed.

Slow to comprehend what he was saying, followed by suddenly realization, she stood up straight, her eyes big as saucers. "No?" she said in an astonished whisper.

The clan, gathered close to listen, quiet murmuring stirred among them.

"T'is true," Bryan said in a low raspy voice, "We saw them from far above while gathering wood. They argued, angry words, the Dane drew his sword, while the henchmen held Gunner, the Dane ran him through, again and again, till he was dead. By the time we arrived, off the mountain, they delivered the body here, and told you their lies."

After a long silence he said, "I will stay to see to a proper burial of poor Uncle Gunner. Then I'll go serve the

Dane, as much as I don't want to, and make plans to avenge my poor uncle in a proper way. This I've sworn to Thor."

The clan stood quietly. One of the men said, "You're bound then by your oath to do what you've said you would. You must go settle your affairs with this Jarl."

The sun, setting behind the mountains, its soft purple glow fringing the dimming sky, and cool air filtered down off the hills cast a sullen mood over the clan.

"Pick up this poor man, and bring him into the great room," Bryan's mother, recovering from her initial shock, took charge, it was her usual manner. She and Gunners' wife spent the night preparing his body.

In the morning, they excavated Gunner's tome, high up on the hill above the farm house, digging into the mountain, using wooden shovels, metal digging pikes and muscles, opening the earth, lining the bottom and sides with slabs of stone. While they labored, the women gathered the dead man's' belongings; the things to accompany him in his grave. Banks of clouds were gathering atop the high mountains as they headed down to the longhouse.

Daylight broke, cold and foggy, people streamed in from the village and surrounding farms, dressed in black. A goat and a hog were butchered, their meat, carved from the carcasses, and along with vegetables, added to a large cauldron, which was brought to boil, to simmer all day, and be eaten by the funeral party in the evening.

The sun, a ghost in the sky, discernible, only as a blur, through thick clouds, when the men hoisted to their shoulders, the wooden frame, carrying Grunner's body, and with a slow labor of love, hauled it up to the tomb. The funeral party, gathered around, solemn and quiet, as they lowered their fallen leader into his grave.

Grunner's wife, first to adorn the grave, laid his belt of gold, studded with gem stones at his side, followed by the other women, bearing his treasures; a gold embellished drinking horn, his sword in its sheath, a dagger with an ivory handle, a silver chain, eating utensils, a bear skin he had used on cold winter nights to wrap around his shoulders, and a fur hat.

One of the elders, a spiritual leader from a near-by farm, spoke of Grunner, speaking words of admiration, offering prayers to Thor and Odin, asking that when the Valkries fly, Grunner be taken to the halls of Valhalla, followed by a long silence, when finished, broken only by the soft weeping of women.

Ari slowly stood, stepped into the grave beside his father, knelt down; placing a hand over the fur covered man, said a quiet farewell prayer of his own, then picked up his father's sword, and stepping from the grave, held it out to Bryan.

"Ari, I cannot accept this, I am not worthy, it belongs in his grave, beside him."

Ari, with his father's inbred, indignant, stony, resolve, replied, "It is my right and my will that you should have it. Take it, and use it to avenge my father, and the honor of our clan."

Bryan, deeply humbled, that Ari would bestow such a great honor upon him, grasped the heavy sword; on one knee, swore to Ari, "I will carry it with honor, in reverence to Grunner, and it shall draw the blood of the Dane, if it takes the last breath of my life, I swear to Thor and the clan, and in gratitude I shall forever remain your faithful servant."

Gradually the people wandered away, a few at a time, to seek warmth and shelter in the long house, where a warm meal waited. A small group of men, who remained, lifted large flat slabs of stone, placing them across the upright stones

15

surrounding the grave, then covered it with earth, sealing the tome for eternity. A stone pillar, carved with ruins, telling of Grunner's life and deeds, a tribute the stone carver worked on, all the previous day and trough the night, was erected in front of the mound.

Bryan felt heavy, drained, empty inside; much as he'd felt when his father left them the second time; his entire world, suddenly turned on end, never to be the same again, Ari, knelt before the ruins stone, beside him, eyes filled with tears, probably feeling the same. They wept until darkness overcame them; light rain began to fall, the gods too, mourning. Bryan's mother came up the hill, put a hand on the shoulders of each boy, and knelt down between them.

"Come on down to your home," she said ever so softly, "Warm yourselves by the fire, and have a hot bowl of stew and cup of ale. You've mourned enough for this day. It's time to look forward to the heavy burdens before us."

That night Bryan dreamed; while passing through a deep forest, Thor, disguised as a wolf appeared before him.

"Where are you going young one?" the wolf asked.

"I am going to avenge the murder of my uncle," Bryan replied.

"I'm sorry to hear of this tragedy. Who is the object of your vengeance?"

"The Dane, Skjolden, who killed uncle Grunner in cold blood. My hope is that I might find an opportunity to avenge my uncle."

"The Dane is an imposter?" The wolf half stated, half asking.

"Yes, you might call him that," Bryan answered.

"So as an imposter yourself, you go to serve the Dane, and seek to slay him."

"True, my cause is just," Bryan protested.

16

"Beware that in order to kill your enemy, you do not become like him yourself." the wolf chuckled to himself. "Is this not the way of war, whether between two men or thousands?" ThenThor, for a brief moment, reveled himself; the god of warriors and common men, and just as quickly turning into a wisp of smoke, drifting skyward, disappearing into the mist, his laugh echoing through the forest.

Chapter 3

Bryan woke early, his brother next to him, warm under the blankets, he would miss his younger brother, always warm on cold nights, and Ari, who understood his every thought; and he was troubled that his mother was not going to be at his side with her sound, unwavering advice. But then, the reoccurring vision of his uncle's murder, flashed through his mind, an image that would remain, never far from his consciousness, rekindling anger, rage, helplessness, gripping his cousin and him, high on the mountain side, and sitting with Ari by the ruin stone, weeping, suffering the black depths of grief. That anger, would dwell within him, quenched only when the Dane's blood flowed over his hands, and the heart of the foreign jackal stilled by the cold steel of his uncle's sword. Silently, he vowed his oath of vengeance anew.

His mother helped him prepare a pack to carry on his journey to Balestrand, home of the Dane: A change of clothes, a few loaves of flat bread, a bowl, a blanket. His uncle's sword, fastened to the back of the pack, with a cord, a knife of his own, his father had given him on his tenth birthday, its blade two hands long, thin, sturdy, hickory handle, wrapped in leather, a carved wood sheath, stuffed into his waist belt.

His mother and Ari helped hoist the pack to his shoulders.

"This should get you there comfortably," she paused, "Bryan, listen to me now," her voice low and serious.

"Yes, mother."

"You will be missed greatly. Not just because you won't be here to help with the planting and harvest. Your' absence...," a tear came to the corner of her eye, "I shall miss you being here more than you could possibly imagine." She swallowed hard. "Though I know why you must go," her voice quivered, "Please be careful, take time to make wise decisions, affect your vengeance, and be gone from there." She drew something from the pocket of her apron, "I want you to have this," a gold amulet, the shape of a hammer; Thor's hammer, tied to a leather thong. "This will protect you from harm. Never forget the courage of Thor, rely on him for your own courage, strength, and bravery, he'll not let you down." She placed it over his head, around his neck.

"Thank you mama," he said, "I'll be brave and strong and wise, and I'll not forget."

They held each other in a lingering embrace. She looked up at him, weeping silently, the sadness in her eyes, griping him like the claws of a savage beast, ripping at his heart, his father gone, he was her strength, now Bryan himself was going. She knew, and he knew she knew, he might not return.

"You know I must go – what I must do."

"I do. I just wish it wasn't needed."

"So do I, but I must."

He shifted the pack on his back, picked up his walking stick, and kissed her on the cheek one last time.

"Good bye," he said quietly as he turned away to began his long journey.

Ari walking alongside.

"Look after my mother while I'm gone, well you."

"I promise I will."

Ari (pronounced Ah-ree) his cousin, had been Bryan's side kick, and companion since birth. The same age, they were together constantly; fishing, doing chores, playing, bathing, dueling with play swords and throwing axes. They thought alike, even looked alike, could not have been closer had they been brothers, which many, who didn't know, took them for. Separation from Ari, was to be the most difficult.

"It'll take me some time to figure things out. Come see me in the fall after crops are in, we'll make plans then. It would be good if we are together when the deed is done." Bryan stopped, looked Ari in the eye, "Don't forget our vows."

"I'll never forget, you needn't ever worry about that," Ari's anger, seethed, not far from the surface.

They embraced. Bryan walked away.

As his cousin and boyhood home faded away into the distance below, his heart, filled with loneliness, fear not far away, a whirl-wind of emotions, stormed inside him. He struggled for courage; this must have been how it was for father, he thought, when he left.

The trail wound up through the valley behind the homestead passed the blood stained spot where Grunner had been murdered, and up to the tall pines. When he looked back, far, far below, to a view of the farm, sitting above the fjord, the longhouse, a traditional Norwegian home, large, and unlike many other country homes where both livestock and people found shelter in the same building, the Thorsen clan longhouse was reserved for the extended family only. Separate buildings sheltered the cattle, chickens, pigs, and goats. Horses were corralled separately. There was a smoke house, a building for farm implements, a forge, and a grainery where bjoor, ale, and mead were brewed.

The longhouse, a sturdy wood beam structure, set against a hill, half of wood slabs, half of sod and rock, rooms extending right and left of the common room where a central fire burned continuously through the winter, providing warmth and heat for cooking, and around which family activities, weaving, food preparation, and socialization took place, rooms, in the wings, off the central common room, occupied by family groups.

Beyond the farm, the cold deep waters of the great Sognefjord, extended far inland from the coast. On its north shores, the eastern most village on the fjord, Hoyanger, a sleepy, trade and fishing town, home of a few dozen, hard working, decent families.

Bryan's clan's farm, a half day walk east of Hoyanger, on the strip of land between the shores of the fjord, and the foothills, that bordered the great towering mountains of Norway, where the clan's extensive holdings of land, livestock, and cultivated gardens that provided them a good life.

The Viking raids, begun 50 years earlier, expanded by competition between, petty war lord kings, called Jarls, threatened to disrupt the clan, and all of Norway. These raids, just beginning to spread across Europe, terrorized the populaces, and would threaten the stability of Europe's ruling classes.

Danish kings, feeding on the profits of the initial raids, were starting to push their influence into the vast frontiers of Norway, who's many small territories, headed by the petty chieftains, were fragmented, constantly at war with one another.

Bryan turned away, ascending upward into deep forest, the delicate odor of pine drifted in the air, mixed with the even more pungent, sweet, musky, odor of deep debris on the forest floor, now released, from winter's melting snow.

As he walked through the forest his thoughts turned to his father, Thor, who, four years ago, left with other local men to go Viking for Skjolden, returning after a year, with a small fortune of gold, and a slave girl to help Bryan's mother, telling tails of adventure. He had been impatient to go again, gone now for three years, with no word of his where abouts, what he was doing, or why? Since his departure, Bryan shared responsibility and decisions with his mother.

When Thor, their clan chief, left, Grunner took his place, stepping in as Bryan's father figure. A huge man, six feet tall, tall by any standard, for the time, hands like bear's paws, wide shoulders, chest like a barrel, blond hair (Their clan shunned dying their hair red as was fashionable), braided in rows, back to a tail, a full beard. Bryan, emulating him, wore his hair in the same style, and though he could not yet sport a beard, he hoped to one day be as large as his uncle.

Grunner had not favored the new Danish chieftain, in spite of the fact that Bryan's father was Viking for the Dane. Indeed most of the clan, those of the surrounding farms, and the village remained loyal to Innvik, their traditional Jarl, from Torg, north over the mountains, on Forde Torg, the head waters of Stavfijorden. The old Jarl had always been fair; not interfering in their lives.

The new Jarl, the Dane, Skjolden, and an army of thugs, had worked their way into the area, usurping territory not easily defended by Innvik, forcing their will on the people. His home of operations was Balestrand, forty leagues east of Noyanger on the banks Sognefjorden, where small arms of the fjord came together.

Bryan had been having difficulty sorting his loyalties; with the utmost respect for his father, never understanding why he submitted to the service of the Dane, and feeling great trust for Grunner's Judgment. His uncle's death and the actions of the Dane cemented the decision for him.

As the day wore on, the spring sun warmed the air, but in higher altitude, that warmth was fleeting, and by the time he emerged from the high timber unto the tundra, the air was chilling; his breath froze in the air, crystals formed in his nose. Snow still covered the earth here, deeply in places, few trees grew in the high altitude, those that did, stunted and misshapen, the snow broken by dark patches of earth, where thin snow and ice melted away by the sun's rays, broke the monotony of dazzling white.

Across the top of the mountain, the level terrain, eased walking, and breathing became easier, despite the thin air. Pressing on, by late afternoon, the trail, beginning to slope downward, off the top of the mountain, promised to deliver him from the tundra, before night fall. The sun, low over the back side of the mountain, cast long shadows, and objects stood out with great contrast.

High up, on the side of the hill, well above him, he noticed a bear ambling along, unusual, for a bear to venture this high, on the naked tundra, this early, where there was little food. A great distance away, he paid it little attention, bear's vision poor, it probably couldn't see him. He continued on his way, after all, the edge of the tundra wasn't far, the green blanket of forest lay just beyond.

A chance glance back, he was astonished, the bear had closed half the distance between them. Strange, the hairs on the back of his neck stood on end, a tingling sensation running down his back. Picking up his pace, he studied the landscape before him, now, keenly conscious of his surroundings; an outcropping of rock, just ahead, to his left. Another glance back, the distance closed by half again, the bear, extraordinarily large, charging at him, at a dead run.

Chapter 4

Fear gripping him, he headed for the rock outcropping, a hole there, possibly a cave, among the rocks, its opening, big enough for him to squeeze into. Tearing his pack from his back, he tossed it into the hole, the bear, panting, pounding the snow beneath its feet, rapidly approaching; he backed into the hole, as fast as he could. It narrowed much too quickly, to the side, an opening, big enough for him to fit into, quickly he backed into it, his legs doubled up against his chest, and his pack crushed down beside his legs, he fit, with no room to spare.

The bear, immediately at the caves entrance, taking in huge huffs of air, tasting his scent, growling, the rumble from deep within its belly, resonating through the hole, it pushed its great head into the small opening, its shoulders too large to fit. Sensing Bryan in the side tunnel, it squirmed to get at him, with great exertion, turning its head, poking its' nose into the side opening, nearly touching Bryan's face; foul, dank, breath, filled the space, suffocating. Panic and claustrophobia, gripping him, Bryan's head spun, he thought he would pass out. Thor, help me, he prayed, with his free arm, he hit the massive nose with his fist, making the bear roar, snapping blindly at his hand, again it squirmed, not able to get further into the hole, grinding monstrous jaws, full of enormous teeth, crashing together, before his face. Bryan wormed back, trying to make himself smaller.

It backed out of the cave. Bryan heard it pace to and fro, grunting and panting. With its front paw, it tried to sweep the hole, long, sharp claws narrowly missed Bryans face, a moment later the giant head was back, menacing him.

Bryan's thoughts raced, what could make a bear behave this way, had he done something, how could he rid himself of the enraged beast? He tried to dislodge a rock from the wall of the hole, to bash it with, none of it loose, a piece of bread from his pack, what it wanted, once fed though, it would be back for more.

What to do? The dream, came back to him, he chuckled, what irony; Thor had said, in order to defeat your enemy you become like him.

How to become like the beast that was fierce, resourceful, attacking unexpectedly, persistent, and patient in its pursuit? I can be fierce, and I can be resourceful he thought, then, it struck him - his uncle's sword, tied to his pack.

Working a finger between his knees, to the side of the pack, he untied it, drew the sword ever so slowly to his side, only to realize, it pointed toward his feet, not out toward the bear, the beast would grab it from him, in its teeth, the sword would be gone, no room in the hole to turn the blade, what to do?

The bear withdrew once more, frustrated. Bryan seeing his chance, quickly thrusting the weapon into the outside chamber, turning it, angled it back into his little hole, with no time to spare. The bear was back, mashing its teeth, and stretching its long tongue into the hole, trying its best to make contact with Bryan. He had to strike now, the evening light, fading fast, already dark enough in the tiny hole, in no time, he wouldn't be able to see at all. Grasping the handle with one hand, he guided the blade with the other, lying on his side, only able to move it a short distance, thrusting the point of the blade into the bear's nose, with all the strength he could muster, making solid contact. The animal's thundering roar, in the tiny space, made Bryan's head spin. Blood gushed from the nose. It withdrew, hastily, grunting and pacing about outside, no telling what it was doing; probably rooting its blooded nose in the snow. His heart pounding in his chest, hands shaking, he prayed to Thor for help and courage.

In short order though, blood smeared over its face, the beast was back, angrier than ever. This time, he thrust the blade, into the animals gaping mouth; the beast bit down, razor sharp edges, carving deep into its gums, between its teeth, the savage bruit, crunched again, cold steel, slicing a great gash in its tongue, tying to pull the blade, clenched in its vice like jaws, from Bryan's hand. With all his might, holding tight, Bryan slid the smooth blade from its mouth, lacerating its lips deeply. The gigantic beast's withering roar, angrier, louder than before, made Bryan's ears throb in pain. It spat, and sneezed, showering the inside of the little hole with blood, its retreat hasty.

Outside, it continued, growling and snorting. Bryan held the sword ready, and prayed, "Help me, please, Lord Thor."

Then…, in the distance, the cry of a lone wolf; one howl, far off, nothing else. He listened intensely, straining, the bear too, silent for a moment. Had he really heard it, and then, another howl, closer, answered by another, then another, coming closer, a pack.

The bear let out a long, loud, menacing bellow, leaving absolutely no doubt, it meant business. In less time than Bryan could think, a cacophony of wild, vicious, ferocious fighting, exploded outside, dog against bear, fierce, hideous, brutal, the bleating sound of wounded bear, kai-yaying of wounded dogs, going on and on, then as suddenly as it started, it was over. The panting of wolves faded into the dark, silence. After a long while, a lone wolf howled, long, lonely; a victory call?

Bryan lay in the quiet darkness, drained, eyes closed, trembling, weak, and fell into fitful sleep.

Cold air and daylight, seeping into the cave, woke him. The animal had not returned. Through the night, he woke to listen, but heard nothing, except the eerie call of a nearby owl.

Could the beast be gone? Cautiously, he crawled out of the hole, legs stiff and achy. The snow, in front of the hole, covered with bloody bear prints, a trail of blood, lead up over the hill. Diligently searching, Bryan found no wolf prints, anywhere; this whole thing, very strange, spooked him, sending a cold shiver up his spine. He shouldered his pack, fastened the sword to his belt, and made haste, down the side of the mountain, rapidly descending through the heavy forest, constantly checking over his shoulder, vigilant, every little noise causing alarm.

Finally, emerging from the trees; a wide, green, grassy meadow greeted him, a stream of rapidly moving water, running through its middle. Glad to be off the mountain, and away from the threat of bear, but still wary; he reasoned, he could wade the stream for a time, erasing his scent to the bear. Fighting through the dense rushes and cat tail, to the edge of the stream, the broken stalks exuding a minty odor, making him feel good, joyful.

The water, fresh from melting snow, knee deep, cold, bone chilling, frigid. At once, the muscles in his legs clenched in searing pain, like he never felt before, he was sure he could tolerate it, for a short time, surely his legs would numb to the cold. A dozen steps later, the pain, unbearable agony, could no longer be ignored. Making a break, toward the opposite side of the stream, stumbling over rocks, suddenly not sure he would make it, panic gripping him, the second time in two days; after saving myself from a crazed bear, about to drown in a little stream. Torturously forcing his legs to move, one painful step at a time, over rocks, through reeds, searing agony, dulling his senses to anything, but escape.

Finally, stumbling onto the bank, he crawled onto lush green grass, and collapsed. His legs, paralyzingly painful, beyond endurance, sucking the air from his lungs, blinding, he heard himself moan, the sound far away, losing consciousness, everything went black.

Chapter 5

He woke, the pain gone; replaced by pins and needles, the sun high in the sky, warming him. A slight rustle in the grass, to his side, drew his attention, he turned toward it, his gaze met by a pair of gray-yellow eyes, intense, intelligent, crystal clear, surrounded by gray-brown fur, edged in black; a wolf, magnificent, at an arm's length, lying in the grass, watching him, ears erect, head tilted at an inquisitive angle.

Bryan froze, and stared back; frighteningly beautiful, regal, and wild, a thought, flashed through his head, "Are you Thor?" his own voice surprised him.

The wolf jumped back, crouched, wary.

"Can you speak to me?" The wolf didn't respond, probably not Thor, at least in person. He continued, softly, "I'll not harm you. You are far too elegant, I'm just passing through, be gone from here straight way."

The wolf glanced away, briefly, laid back its ears, then, after staring back at Bryan a while longer, it turned and cantered into the forest.

Bryan pondered the moment, feeling as if something mystical just happened.

His legs warmed, and feeling returning, he stood, wobbly at first, picked up his pack, and began walking.

Talking to himself, for company, more than anything, he began, "I've battled a crazed bear, nearly froze myself to death, and drowned, and talked to a wolf, can't wait to see what might happen next." Then after a while, "I was thinking, I would bathe in the stream before turning east to Nassane, but I'm not going to, can't even imagine it, that water so cold, worse than death, it'll have to wait, might be able to bathe in the village.

As he neared the fjord, the meadow became a widened expanse, and the trail turned east, following the ribbon of green, along the water's edge, where grasses and low shrubs, along the shore, extended up for some distance, to the dense pine forest; a transition between meadows and precipitously sheer cliffs, which were the foundations of great mountains that climbed to the sky. This green ribbon, along the shores of the fjord, sometimes very narrow, other times extending far from the water's edge, formed the land, where farms and villages grew, where all crops and livestock were raised, where the majority of people lived; the wealth of the Nordic people.

Always keenly aware of his insignificance in this vast world, a land he knew and loved; the great frozen mountains humbled him, the dense forests, and vast expanses of water, streams tumbling from mountain tops over rugged cliffs, thundering onto the rocks below. The fjord, at times, still and smooth, or whipped by wind, into frothy waves, and on across the water, mountains, on occasion, capped with snow, sea birds, perpetually flying helter skelter, on their own private journeys, and always, the pungent, ever present, smell of the sea.

The trek to Nassame, lending to thoughtfulness, was long, and darkness was fast approaching when he arrived. The village was not unlike other Norse villages; a dozen and a half smallish longhouses, smaller buildings, made of log, the ever available construction material, with sodden or shake roofs, a few people still ambling along the road.

He stopped an old woman along the way, "Pardon me, my lady I've been traveling, and I wondered, can you tell me if there is a place I might stay for the night."

The women looked him up and down, suspicious, "Try the home at the end of town on the left, the one with stables in the back. Sometimes they have a room." Turning she hurried away.

"Thank you mam," he called after her. She showed him no notice.

With the sun long below the mountains to the west, and the hazy, cold, gray light of evening settling across the fjord, he approached the longhouse. Larger than the other homes in the village, a stable in the rear, as the old woman said, holding a few horses and goats, accounting for the faint odor of animal, out buildings scattered haphazardly.

The door to the main building, stood open, a hearth fire, its glow warm, someone bent over, stirring a pot, an evening meal he presumed. Bryan stopped at the door, removed his hat, and cleared his throat.

The woman stood and turned toward him, "Hello," she said, not too warmly, "Do you need something?"

"Yes, M'lady," he said bowing, "I am traveling from Hoyanger, and was told you might have a place for me to rest my head for the night."

The women hobbled toward him, indifferent to her awkward gait, probably that way a long time, wearing a patterned work dress, and a plain blue apron she pulled up, and wiped her hands on. As she neared, she appeared older, than he first thought. Her approach, suspiciously cautious, partly concealed behind her, a young girl.

"Just for the night," She asked?

"Yes, M'lady, be gone in the morning."

"All I've got is the work shed, if that'll do." She turned to the girl behind her, "Signy," she commanded.

"Yes, mum," the girl said, a quick curtsy.

"Take this man to see the work shed. He wants to stay there tonight."

"Yes, mum." The girl whisked by the women and Bryan, to lead the way.

"If I might ask, M'lady, Bryan asked. The woman had already turned away. "I haven't eaten in two days. If you could spare a bowl of stew, perhaps some hot water with which I could bath, I can pay." He shrugged off his pack, and drew out his little money bag, and placed a couple coins in her hand.

She looked at them in the dim light and nodded. "Signy, come back when you've shown him the shed. We fix him a meal."

The shed, a small wooden structure, one of several, away from the animals, was small. In the low gray light, little of the inside was visible; tools hanging about the walls, sacks of grain, stacked in one corner, in another, a raised platform, covered with straw, he supposed was to be his bed. It smelled reasonably clean, like grain and earth.

"Will this do?" the girl asked, her voice high pitched, soft, girlish, he took her to be eleven or twelve years old.

"This'll be fine," he said.

"I'll be right back." She turned and ran back to the longhouse.

Hoping to see more, he looked around, the room, but even darker now, gave up, took his pack from his back, set it beside the platform, stretched, sat down, and immediately heard the girl returning.

She appeared, a bowl in one arm, a small oil lamp in the other. He took the bowl, full of meaty stew, a couple rounds of flat bread on top. While he ate, the girl produced candles from her apron, lit each from the lamp, and placed them around the room. The soft light unveiling the mysteries of the room; a slice of life from a small farm, harness, knives for cutting grain, haying utensils, buckets, stacks of cloth bags, a small goat cart, and butchering utensils.

34

The girl sat down on the floor in front of him, and watched him eat. Curious girl, he thought, he didn't imagine many visitors came this way, but he didn't think his eating that interesting, still, she watched intently, her eyes pale gray, heavy blond eyebrows, brownish blond hair, pulled back tightly, into a single braid, wound into a little bun at the back of her head, plain, unremarkable, small.

"My name is Signy," she said.

He stopped eating for a moment. "Hello Signy, I'm Bryan."

"Where you from?"

"I live near Hoyanger, to the west." He pointed.

"Never heard of it."

"Up over the mountain," he answered.

She nodded, though clearly did not understand.

"I go get you hot water," she said, jumping up, and ran out.

He was finishing the last of the bread, when she returned carrying two heavy buckets of steaming water, clunked them down on the wooden floor in front of him, and smiled.

"I'll take your clothes and wash them. They'll be ready for you in the morning." "That's ok; I have a clean set of clothes with me."

"As you wish," she stepped back. "Well, take them off."

"What?"

"Your clothes, take them off, you can't wash with your clothes on, can you?"

He began, taking his boots off, undoing his belt, pulling his shirt over his head.

"Aren't you going to leave?" He asked.

"I'm not going to leave, I'm going to wash you." She said, nonplused.

35

Feeling a little awkward, he didn't really care, but hadn't been washed by another for years, let alone a young girl. "Doesn't your mother need you?"

"She's not my mother," the girl said, ruefully, "I'm her servant, and I'm done with my duties for the day," She revealed, "You…, are my duty now."

A thrall, he realized with some consternation, not having occurred to him; she was not leaving. He removed his trousers; she stepped forward, and began washing him. It wasn't that he felt self conscious, where he grew up, in his extended family, privacy was unknown, someone was always present when changing clothes or bathing, but this girl so young, touching him so frankly, not missing any part, now drying him off, thoroughly, even helping him put his clean underclothing and trousers on was unusual.

Out through the door he could see the moon, rising above the mountains, south of the fjord.

Before she put his shirt on, he said, "I'm going to walk out to the water's edge. Would you like to join me?"

Her mouth burgeoned into a grand smile, skipped lightly across the room, and out the door, taking his hand, once outside, much as his little sister would, eagerly leading the way.

They walked across the field, a short distance, to the shore, stopping at water's edge; the moon, just risen, floating above the mountains, across the fjord, casting a trail of shimmering, silvery, gems across the inky black water. A warm breeze flowed down from the hills behind them, across the beach, and out over the water, where it formed a ghostly mist, tendrils snaking out to entangle the sparkling gems.

The air across his bare shoulders, cool, his skin tingled with gooseflesh, muscles slightly tensed, a sensation he always enjoyed. He glanced down, she was gazing at him, the

36

pale moon light highlighting his chest, with eyes of a much older woman. She leaned lightly against him, and wrapped her small arm around his waist, and lightly kissed his abdomen.

The night was beautifully romantic, the sweet gesture, wonderfully arousing, had she only been a few years older, her little hand around his waist, ever so gently caressing, but the young thrall, much too much like his little sister, he couldn't allow himself to think about her, in intimate terms. Gently, he took her hand in his, and turned back toward the shed.

Before going inside, he turned to gaze back over the fjord. She slipped her arm around his back again, gently pulling him to her, slid the other hand across his abdomen to his waist, before he knew what was happening, she had eased her wandering hand beneath his waist, down into his trousers, to fondle him.

He gasped, and quickly pulled her hand free, before she could feel him becoming aroused. "No, I - I - cannot," he stammered, "You are…too young, my little sister is older than you. I cannot. I'm sorry." He turned and stepped away, embarrassed and ashamed. He could feel his face flush, the flesh on his chest on fire, erect against his trousers, glad it was dark, she wouldn't see how foolish he was.

"The other men let me," she pleaded. "I can do things for you, wonderful things that will make you feel so good, I can, I would like to, you are very handsome."

He cupped his hand under her chin, and lifted her face up toward him. "You poor, dear, sweet, thing if you were a few years older I would be the one offering to please you. But, I am not one of those men, there's nothing wrong with you, It's me, I just cannot, I'm sorry."

37

He leaned over and kissed her ever so lightly on the lips, turned away, and went inside, removed his trousers, climbed onto bed, and pulled the blanket up over him.

She followed, going about the room, extinguishing the candles, quiet as the whisper of a breeze, then slipped under the blanket, softly snuggling naked against his bare back, wrapping her little arm around him. For a brief moment he was tempted to turn over, inexperienced, yearning to learn what intimacy was about, to fondle her, make her feel good down there, who would know? But she was so like his little sister, the idea, even with a thrall, revolted him.

"It's alright Master Bryan," she whispered. "You are very nice. I stay here with you tonight, you're warm, and you smell good." She pressed her face against his back and kissed him lightly, he soon heard her slow, deep, breathing, her body relaxed against him, asleep.

He woke before the break of dawn, rose from the bed, and quietly dressed. After putting his pack together, he took some coins from his pouch, and laid them on the bed next to the girl. What she offered him, her way of buying her freedom, though unfortunate, she had few other opportunities, to earn her ransom, or to seek affection.

He headed down the trail, leaving the little village behind. The land between the fjord and cliffs, narrowing to nothing, the trail climbed the hillsides, steeply, to high precipitous ledges, through the mist, that lay like a woolen blanket, upon the water. Once above the haze, he could see far across the fjord, to the south and east, where the sun was about to appear, the mountains, silhouetted against the horizon. The land all around him seemed to float above the clouds, surreal, unearthly; he imagined it the land of Thor.

After a time, the trail descended back to the shore, where a narrow ribbon of rocky land ran between the sheer rock wall, and the water. The mist, rising, gray from beneath, formed a ceiling, hovering above the water's glassy surface, eerie, in the light, filtering through the mist above.

Ahead of him, he thought he caught a glimpse of a gray wolf, running, he couldn't be positive. Surely, the gods were about the land this morning.

Eventually, the foggy ceiling rose and thinned, warmed by the sun, and clear blue sky reigned over the fjord. Once again, the road climbed high among the cliffs, and he could see far out over the water. A ship moved eastward, traveling the same direction as he, no wind filling the sail, the crew rowing. Tiny in the distance, at least seven or eight oars to a side, a wide beamed merchant ship, a Knarr.

At this elevation the air was cool, flowering plants clung close to the ground, the trees were just beginning to leaf out, and birds were raucous and bold. The trail continued on the hillside, until afternoon, then slowly dropped to the shore, where the air was warmer, flowers grew on higher bushes, concealing birds among the foliage, only their cheerful song, giving them away.

Late in the afternoon, approaching the quite village of Kvamme, right away he could see the houses were neater, cleaner, and more ordered than in the last town. Buildings lined both sides of the wide road, out buildings to the rear.

The road empty save a wrinkled old man, wandering aimlessly down the road, his gait unsteady. "Good Afternoon," Bryan greeted him. The man looked up with a start, acknowledging Bryan with a nod. Ancient; his leathery face, framed in long, scraggly, grayed hair, nose red, from time, and maybe a few strong ales, taking their toll. Through squint eyes, he scrutinized Bryan.

"I am Bryan Thorson of Hoyanger."

"Well…you don't say. From Hoyanger, been travel'n over the mountains then. Didn't think I'd seen you before," as if he'd actually been looking with any interest. "What brings you here?"

"On my way to Balestrand, have business there," Bryan answered.

"That so, I can think of better places to go for business than that place," he said ruefully.

"I suppose so," Bryan answered. "But, it's important. Do you know where I might find lodging for the night?"

The old man paused, pointed down the street. "Try that little cottage down there with the garden in front, door painted blue, old lady there, Gloa. Sometimes she has a room for a price."

"Many thanks, my friend, may Thor watch over you," Bryan said, gave the old man a pat on the back, and headed down the road toward the cottage.

The little log building, looked as ancient as the old man, added to many times, its sodden roof grew a plethora of flowers, and between the road and house, a plot, overgrown with vegetables, surrounded by a low wooden fence. He passed through a small gate, followed a narrow path through the jungle, toward the door painted blue, light blue, lighter than the blue sky, he'd never seen paint that color, and wondered how it had been obtained; the pigment must have come from some local source.

About to knock, a small squeaky voice came from under the cover of green leaves.

"Don't get your fancy pants in a hurry sonny. There's nobody in thar."

He spun around, a little gray head, protruded from among the forest of leaves, topped by a tiny blue bonnet, and bore an inquisitive old face.

"Afternoon, M'lady, Names Bryan, from Hoyanger, on my way to Balestrand, old fella down the road said you might have a room for the night. "

"He did, did he? Old coot, probably drunk, well...I might if yer cud help an old lady up off her knees," she said, holding her hand up toward him.

"Forgive me," he leaned over, and gave her a lift.

She struggled to her feet, and brushed the dirt from her blue apron. "I'm Gloa," she said, "Pleased to meet you Bryan of Hoyanger. Come this way, I'll show you what I've got." She hobbled into the cottage, motioning for him to follow. Inside, a front living area, and to the rear a place for cooking, though a door to the right, a small room; a raised platform for sleeping, a stool, and table its' only furnishings.

"You can stay here, small, but it'll keep ya warm and dry." She asked a price so low he was almost embarrassed to accept.

"Good," she said emphatically, "Then put your things down, and come along with me."

He followed her, into the garden, she picked up a wooden hoe. "You know how to use one of these?"

He chuckled, "I grew up with one of these in my hand."

"Well then, get to it. You don't think I'm renting that room for free do you?"

He hoed the garden, Gloa following, pulling weeds, then afterward, they picked arm loads of vegetables.

"Have a sit," she pointed to a bench beside the door, and disappeared through the blue door, soon to return, a tankard of ale for each, in her hands. He wasn't sure, been on the trail for a while, but it tasted heavenly, immensely satisfying.

She took a long draught then asked, "Now tell me again, where you headed to?

41

"Balestrand, to work in the service of the Jarl."

"Skjolden? A nice boy like you, I wouldn't serve that Loki, if it were the death of me."

"Well mum, some things we have to do, I've sworn an oath, only way for me to fulfill it is to go there, and by stroke of fortune, the Jarl invited me, don't judge me, I cannot tell you more." He left it rest.

After a long silence, he asked, "Why do you say that about him, the Jarl."

"He's a bastard Dane, for one; got himself a little kingdom, stepp'n on poor folk he threats poorly. Has spies, sneek'n round, th' find out sump'tn, or say they did, then blackmails em into doin' sump'tn on others, goes into a village, makes them swear loyalty to em, pay em tribute, else he sells the poor folks as thralls. His Vikings go over there ta the islands, captures those Irishers, sells em as thralls, gitten rich doin it too. You ask me, that's a bad one, he is."

"You don't approve of thralls?"

"Is not right, those poor folk, have'n ta do, what they have ta, ta get their freedom, all decent folk, at one time, ya know. People have no right, ta own someone else."

Bryan pondered, he'd always felt a little guilty about the thrall his mother kept, but she was such a necessary part of their life, and she was always treated as if she were part of their family.

The old lady went on, "He keeps ask'n for more and more tribute, what do we get fer it, protection, I doubt it; the bugger'is a liar n'a cheat."

"You may not have to put up with him much longer," Bryan said. He caught himself short.

She jerked around, looking him in the eyes, squinting, trying to discern what he meant, "Why? You know sump'tn I don't?"

He averted her gaze, staring blankly out over the fjord, and shrugged his shoulders.

She searched his face, yearning for an answer, trying to read his mind, waiting for him to elaborate. He didn't offer an explanation, sharing her hatred for the man, he couldn't tell her how much he was going to enjoy killing the Jarl, not yet knowing, what all that might entail.

After a long silence, he offered, "The future is difficult to predict, mum, but if something should happen, and I should need your help, it would be much appreciated."

"If it has anything to do with kicking the scum in the arse, you can count on me."

Her face, let him know, she at least thought she understood what he was saying, wanted more, but was'nt going to get it – not this day, his first ally.

"How long have you lived here?" He asked, to change the subject. The strong drink, affecting him, he didn't want to accidentally slip up, revel anything to jeopardize his plans. Their conversation went on till darkness ruled the night, the moon rising. Gloa went inside, brought them both a big bowl of vegetable soup, a large chunk of sharp cheese, and a small lantern. They ate, and talked until late.

Even then, he hated ending their conversation, but needing rest, he begged her leave. Inside his room a small oil lamp gave off just enough light to see what he was doing.

"Thank you and good night mum," He said.

"I'll wake ye at dawn. You'll need a good meal before ya head out."

"Thank you."

The little room, dark, a tiny window, high on the wall, let a trickle of moonlight stream onto his bed. He spread Gloa's blanket out on the platform, laid his own on top, removed his clothes, and lay back on the blankets, gazing up

43

at the tiny square of light, cool air drifting through the doorway, over his body, and up through the window, puckering his skin to gooseflesh, a mildly erotic feeling; soon his thoughts, drifted drowsily to the unknown, trusting the conviction of his vows, and the power of Thor, to see him through, peacefully, slipping into undisturbed slumber. Sometime during the night, he pulled a blanket over him.

As promised the little old woman woke him early, fed him fresh, warm, flat bread, cheese, and rye porridge. "Balestrand is not that far, far less strenuous than yesterday, road quite good, and little elevation, you should make good time." She handed him a package, "Some bread and cheese for your belly this evening."

"Thank you, Gola." He had become fond of the women, she was smart and tough.

"You go now, do what you have to, but don't forget us here. There are many of us who feel as I do about the Jarl."

The path to Balestrand, hugged the coastline, wider more heavily used, travelers toiling with weighty packs, returning from journeys to the political capitol.

Past midday, the air quite warm, the road dusty, horses approached from behind, hooves thundering, kicking clouds of dust into the air.

Chapter 6

Three horsemen, knights, henchmen for the Dane, rode toward him, circled about, pulled up and came to a halt. The dust cloud, stirred up by the sturdy, short legged, Norwegian horses, over took them, and blew away in the breeze.

Although small, these horses, their coats shaggy, and appearance less than regal, were capable of traveling great distances, tolerating heavy loads, their gait, not a trot or a canter, but a rapid, smooth, peculiar walk, they could go all day without tiring. Well respected among men of the north; evidentially the Danes liked them as well.

The knights, in black trousers, tunics to their knees, the Jarl's colors, emblazoned on their chests, helms of polished iron and gold, concealing part of their faces, swords dangling at their waists, confronted him, with as much bluster as possible.

"What's your business, boy?" One of them said.

"I am Bryan Thorson of Hoyanger. I travel to Balestrand to join in the service of Lord Skjolden, at his behest," Bryan said in the biggest, boldest voice he could muster.

"You were asked by the Jarl," the knight said, skeptically.

"Yes, M'Lord, in person."

The knight glanced at the others, a sly smile on his face. "Well then, we had best get you to him as soon as possible, hadn't we?" He moved his horse up beside Bryan with a kick, held his hand out, took hold of Bryant, and swung him up to the back of his horse. Bryan grasped him about the waist, and they were off toward Balestrand.

They didn't believe him, he knew, the leader, acting benevolent, planed to trap him in a lie, for which he and his men would take the pleasure of killing him. He could only hope the Dane would remember him, and he would survive. Odd, his life would depend on the very man he was sworn to kill. The irony would please Thor.

They rode steadily, the road following the shore, around a long gradual bend, toward the north, Balestrand, clearly seen, far across the bay, whenever an opening in the trees allowed.

They pulled up in a clearing, stopped, and dismounted.

"Do you have water?" The leading knight asked.

"No."

"Food?"

"Yes."

The man tossed him a water skin. He drank deeply and tossed the bag back, "Thank you M'Lord." He nibbled at the old ladies' bread, while the knights conferred among themselves in low undertones that he was unable to decipher, occasioning him a suspicious glance. He returned a wary glare; if attempting to intimidate him, they were remarkably effective.

Finally, they mounted up, for yet another long ride, till they approached Balestrand. He felt more secure in the town, for some reason, and at the same time, apprehensive; uncertain what was about to happen to him, this alien place promising possibe dire consequences.

He had never seen such a place, large longhouses in every direction, like his family lived in Hoyanger, small cottages, special longhouses, barracks for soldiers, barns for cattle, corrals for horses, odd sized buildings, meant for purposes he could not fathom. The whole of the town, centered on, and covering a large hill, surrounded on three sides by water. They rode past boat docks where long ships and large merchant knarrs were docked, men busy loading and unloading cargo.

The horsemen turned, and headed up hill. Atop the hill, at the center of the town, a very large long house, to its side, an enormous oak tree, things hanging from its branches, looking like dead chickens. A waddle and mud wall stood as high as Bryan himself, enclosing the area around the tree, many tall slender poles, stuck in the ground, topped with goat heads, their hides dangling beneath; a hoff, an area of worship, where sacrifice was made to the gods. He'd heard of such things, his family did not worship in this manner. He wondered why.

They came to a halt at the entrance of the longhouse, and dismounted.

"You stay here with them," the leader said, nodding toward the other knights, and went into the longhouse. Bryan stood there, gave a self conscious smile, and a nod to the remaining knights who stared back, malicious glee on their faces, sure that he lied, about to teach this impudent upstart, a lesson that he would never forget, if he lived to tell about it. Shifting from one foot to the other, he pushed dirt into small heaps with his feet, flattened them out, then plowed the dust into little furrows, parallel to one another, waiting nervously.

The great door swung open, and from the dark interior the Dane, dressed in royal robes, emerged. "Bryan, my good friend," He exclaimed. "I'm so very happy you decided to accept my invitation. Welcome to Balestrand. You should have brought your cousin..., Ari was it?"

"Thank you, M' Lord, "Bryan said. He bowed down, breathed a deep sigh of relief, glanced at the knights, amused at their astonishment, disbelief, and disappointment.

"Gentlemen," the Jarl turned to the knights, "This is Bryan Thorson, son of Thor Bryanson, our own great Viking. Bryan, these brave men are my personal guards, Vandel, Angar, and Godfred."

Bryan bowed to them, and smiled, careful not to be too derisive.

"Come, let me show you your new home," the Dane wrapped his arm around Bryan's shoulders, as if his long lost son. Though the affection made him uncomfortable, coming from a man he thought he hated, a phony, and a hypocrite; he went along, nervous, tolerating it as best he could.

The Jarl led him through the door, the interior of the building, warm, dark, spicy sweet air enveloped him, lost in darkness, momentarily blind till his eyes adjusted. Almost magically, a huge room emerged from the gloom, constructed like a traditional longhouse, except there were no partitions, just one large open space, higher and wider than any room Bryan had ever seen. At the head of the great hall, a huge chair, the throne upon a stage. They walked among a multitude of well dressed men and women, mulling about the dirt floor. Many chandeliers, full of burning candles, illuminated the room with soft warm light.

"This is where I hold court," the Dane explained, they walked toward the front, "And these are my loyal courtesans, waiting to serve me. All this will be your home, and your charge. You will be instructed to attend to the needs of the court whenever it is being held. When you are not here you will be trained in combat, and schooled in our history and language. Do you know how to read?"

"Well I ... ."

"You'll be taught, all the things you must know, to become a great warrior, like your father." He gave Bryan a pat on the back, a big smile, beckoned one of the pages, the boy, about Bryan's age, moved quickly to the Jarl, and bowed.

"Yes, my lord."

"Ivan, this is Bryan. You will show him around, find him quarters, and see that he is clothed suitable to his position."

"As you wish, my lord," the young man, bowed deeply. "Follow me," he said and walked quickly toward the back of the hall, out to the street. Slightly shorter than Bryan, stocky, with coal black hair, braided in rows, front to back, glistening lustrously, he had piercing blue eyes that flashed brightly. Once outside the page relaxed, "I'm Ivan, been Sjkolden's personal page for two years now. You'll be taking my place, once I train you. Where you from?"

Bryan told him.

"You really Thor Bryanson's son?"

"Yes."

"He's much revered here, a great warrior, sure to go to Vallhalla when he dies."

"They know of him here?"

"Certainly, every one hears stories of his valor. I'm sure the Jarl has high expectations of you."

"Well I hope I can live up to them," Bryan said, unsure.

As they walked away from the great hall Ivan motioned to the hoff. "These are the sacred grounds of the kingdom, where they celebrate the gods. Only shamans go in there except during public celebrations."

The gate to the hoff stood open. Bryan stopped, and looked in.

"It's sacred in there," Ivan told him, "One must never carry a weapon inside, except the priests, when they sacrifice. To kill someone in there is a sacrilege, unless you're a shaman, anyone who does will be hunted to his death by

49

elves, and if the elves fail, the gods will surely put an end to him. At least that's how the legend goes."

Bryan heard stories like this, told by his uncles as they sat around the fire at home, on long winter nights, along with the exploits of gods and men, to a young boy, intimidating, frightening, fascinating, inspiring his imagination, and stirring his yearn for adventure.

The longhouse and hoff, on high ground, overlooked the fjord. The street ran down hill to the dock area, lined with warehouses. The page led Bryan down, to a small longhouse, partitioned into small rooms, a barracks, for soldiers and other men, serving the Jarl. Ivan showed Bryan to a room, just big enough for a sleeping bench, and storage for his belongings, all the rooms alike, no luxury, and no distinction accorded rank, reasonably warm, dry, and out of the wind, his home.

"Leave your pack here," Ivan said, "Follow me." He led Bryan, further still down the hill, toward the docks, pointing out another large building. "This is where you will be trained to fight. The classrooms for learning are in there too. We'll come back here later."

"Do you know how to read the ruins?" Bryan asked.

"No, the Jarl doesn't think I need to know how to read."

Was there an undertone of jealousy, well hidden, in that reply?

"That doesn't seem fair," Bryan prodded, hoping to find out more.

"Yea, well what can I do? He's made up his mind," Ivan said ruefully, shrugging his shoulders.

Near the bottom of the hill, they went into a long low building; Bryan was struck by the musty odor of wool, familiar, having sheared many sheep on the farm; wool clothing, piles and piles of wool clothing, supplies for soldiers, and members of the Jarl's court filled the room.

"Jutta!" Ivan called out loudly. A female voice, returned something, from far back in the building, Bryan couldn't make out what, but after a while a short, fat, old women waddled from the darkness of the building.

"Ivan you Loki, whad'da ya want? Who's this?" She looked Bryan up and down.

"This is Bryan Thorson, Thor Bryanson's son. Skjolden wants you to outfit him with new clothes," Ivan said. Once again, Bryan thought he caught derision in the way Ivan said the Dane's name.

"Humm, Thor's son, you don't say." She examined him. "Quite a prize for his highness, and a bit more fit than some of the riff raff he sends down here, present company included." She winked at Ivan.

"Now Jutta, be nice."

"Humph! Come back in the morn'n, ain't got the time right now." She turned, and disappeared back into the shadows.

The two boys stood, for a moment, silent, looking at each other. "Ok then," Ivan said, "On to the trainer."

Back up the hill, the training arena, another longhouse, sat perpendicular to the street, classrooms in front, with a small library of manuscripts and scrolls. To its rear, a vast open arena; men scattered about, practicing with various weapons, some with swords, others axes, while still others fought with long sticks. Light from open windows, all along the eves, illuminated the interior, shutters stood open, hung on leather hinges, drawn up by ropes.

Ivan took Bryan to one of the men, "Thiorek, this is Bryan, your new student, the one the Jarl told you about."

"Welcome Bryan, do you have any experience with sword or axe?" Thiorek asked.

"I used my uncle's sword on a bear once, I can fell a tree, my cousin and I used to practice with wooden swords, and threw axes at logs, but I've never REALY fought anyone before," Bryan said.

"Ok, be here tomorrow afternoon, we'll start then, I'll teach you to use them all, swords, axes, poles, knives, and spears."

In the classroom, the teacher; Harald, weasel of a man, his voice high and nasally, "Can you read or write?"

"No, I can't," he answered, embarrassed, blushing.

"You'll learn, it will open new worlds for you; history, things you never imagined, politics, and military tactics, things that will empower you, enable you to control your destiny." Foreign, ambitious ideas, to Bryan, but the written word, always magical to him, something he always wanted, appealed to him, and he yearned to know the arts of battle.

Not wanting to seem too eager, with Ivan present, he tempered his response, "I promise I'll work hard."

"Good, be here tomorrow, after your combat lessons, we'll spend several hours every other day, you can work on your own, every day, count on working diligently." Harald said sternly.

Ivan, impatient, interrupted, "Its time for us to go now."

"Ok, Harald, I'll see you tomorrow."

It was dark, Ivan took him to the kitchen, located behind the great hall, an attached, rude wood shelter, rows of benches and tables, oil lamps, provided faint light. They were served boiled mutton, a small loaf of bread, and a tankard of ale.

"The food here is good, and there's plenty of it," the page said, "Makes up for a lot of other things."

"What things?" He asked.

"Just things you have to do," Ivan said rather casually, he shrugged.

What was bothering the boy? What wasn't he saying? He would have to explore it further, Bryan thought, when the time was right.

"I'm going to get some sleep," Ivan said, "Do you think you can find your way back to your room?"

"Sure, no problem."

Before returning to the room, he wanted to wash the dirt and grime of the road off, and thought he had seen a bath, across the street from the barracks; a large building, smoke rising from an opening in the roof, and steam drifting from the windows and doors, a soft glow from inside.

Inside, warm, steamy, and humid, oil lamps hung on the walls at regular intervals, the light soft, inviting, a trail of sooty smoke drifting from each toward the roof. Directly beneath a central opening in the roof, a large oven burned, its smoke swirling toward the ceiling, sweeping the lamp soot with it. Somehow, the water for two large wooden tubs, dominating the room, were heated by the furnace. The lamp light, sparkled off the mirror smooth water, and shimmered through the steam, rising from the hot baths. It looked terribly inviting to Bryan. "What can I do for you," A lilting voice called, from behind the tubs. In the direction of the voice, a slender young man approached, wearing clothing, of light material, understandable in the heat of the room, it clung to his skin, accentuating his thin physique, a peculiar sway to his walk, his light blond hair, not put up, flowed down over his shoulders. Bryan had never seen anyone quite like him before; his face long, as was his nose, a mouth large, thin pale lips, and his eyes pale gray.

"I came for a bath."

"Oh, you're new aren't you?" He said, looking Bryan up and down. "Where did you come from? Just take your clothes off, hang them on one of those pegs." He pointed to the wall.

"Hoyanger,"

"What?" the boy didn't understand.

"I came from Hoyanger," Bryan explained, "Just got here this afternoon, been on the road for four days."

"What on earth brings you to this place? Stand over here." He pointed to a large square of wooden slats next to one of the tubs. Bryan stepped onto the grid. The boy dipped a wooden bucket into the tub, lifted it, full of steaming water, and poured it over Bryan's head, amazing, the boy didn't look that strong, a wooden bucket, full of water, was a heavy thing.

"The Jarl asked me to be a member of his court." Bryan said.

"Oh! Well…I'm impressed." He said, a note of sarcasm in his voice, "And just what did you do to earn that privilege," beginning to rub Bryan down with heavily scented lye soap?

"I don't know, probably because of my father."

"Who's your father?"

"Thor Bryanson."

"OOOh Yessss! That would do it."

"You knew him?"

"No, sorry…, never met him, but everyone hears of his exploits, ever since I've been here anyway." He finished with the soap, dipped another bucket of water from the tub, and rinsed Bryan off. "Now, sit in the tub for a while, relax." He turned and marched to the back of the room.

The water came up to his neck, when he sat on the submerged ledge, very hot, relaxing, luxurious, he nearly fell asleep, not sure how long he'd been soaking, he heard the boy bustle back into the room.

"Ok, time to get out," he ordered. He rubbed Bryan down, "Here, I've got you some clean clothes, your old ones stink."

Bryan chuckled, "I don't doubt it. You should have seen what they've been through." He put the clothes on, they fit nicely.

"Good, Perfect," the attendant exclaimed, his fingertips held to the sides of his cheeks. "You look lovely, here's your old rags," he passed them to Bryan, at arms length.

Across the street in the barracks, except for the glow of a single candle on a table beside the open door, the building was dark. He took a candle from a box on the table, lit it from the flame, and made his way to his tiny room, the light rumble of men snoring filtered from rooms as he passed. Taking blankets from his pack, he made his bed, took off his clothes, lay down, and was immediately overcome by sleep.

Sometime in the night, he woke; something was gnawing at his feet. He pulled his knees to his chest, but in short time the chewing sensation returned. He picked up the candle, lifted it high, peered into the darkness at the foot of his bed, gasped in horror, the Jarl, a mouth full of huge, bloody, canine teeth, and a great tongue, hanging to the side, dripping blood, Bryan's feet gone, gnawed off, the foot of the bed soaked in blood.

"Noooooo.....!" he screamed at the top of his lungs.

In an instant, he was sitting straight up, the room dark, the candle out. He grabbed his feet – intact, no blood, but soaked in sweat, struggling to catch his breath, adrenalin coursing, hot through his veins, his mind racing, where was he, what just happened, he tried to make sense, a dream. Was the Dane going to consume him, like prey? Wrestling with his jumbled thoughts, revenge his duty, sworn, determined to carry it out, no matter how daunting; the way of the Norse; wait, plan, until the time was right. But how could he with the Jarl so cordial to him? He forced his mind to focus on his vows. Finally, sleep again enveloped him.

Shaken awake by the page, early, still dark, he pulled his clothes on, crammed his feet into his boots, tried to smooth his hair, growing long, the yellow braids were loose and frayed, needing to have someone braid them soon.

They went across the street for a breakfast of porridge and fresh flat bread, he savored it.

Bryan remembered the page's earlier comments, were they disparaging, as he first thought; the boy seemed wary, withdrawn, not the right time, he didn't want to arouse suspicion, not just yet.

"Where are you from," he asked Ivan.

"A village, a while north of here, Jarl gained the loyalty of my clan, a few years back, asked me come here; with five older brothers looking for brides, and few girls my age in the village, meant no chance of attaining an inheritance, there was little choice, besides," he said, "I might have been killed for refusing, so here I am," he dropped his gaze to his food, volunteering no more.

Eyes still downcast, Ivan said, "You're going to be fitted for your clothes this morning, don't be late." When he finally looked up, his eyes were teary.

"You ok?"

"Just lonesome for home's all, sorry."

Bryan, very curious, still not the right time, not wanting to embarrass the boy, there would be plenty of time for questions later. "I won't be late," He reassured.

"Good, come see me in the Hall, afterward, wear your dress clothes, she'll give you a set, and we'll get you started on your new duties."

56

"What are they going to be?"

"You're going to be the Jarl's morning attendant, my old job. I'll tell you about it when you get there."

"What are you going to do?"

"Don't know yet," Ivan continued to keep his eyes lowered, as if Bryan were his superior, though Bryan thought there was a different reason.

Breakfast finished, he left the kitchen. The smell of salt water drifting from the fjord filled his nostrils as he reached the bottom of the hill, the first rays of light streaking across the sky.

In the tailor shop, again greeted by the musty odor of wool, the old lady appeared, as the door closed behind him, from the dark piles of clothing, her arms full of fabric.

"Good, you're here on time," she said, "I likes a man knows how ta be on time. Take your clothes off," blunt, to the point, amusing, she disappeared back into the darkness.

He chuckled as he removed his tunic and trousers; quite cool in the unheated building, his skin erupted into a landscape of gooseflesh.

When she reappeared, she growled, "I told you to take your clothes off," wagging her finger at his undergarments, "How do you expect me to give you a good fit with those things on?" She shook her head, "No need be embarrassed, not in front of this old coot, I seen em all, from the pages to the Jarl. I seen your friend Ivan too, now there's a man," she raised her eyebrows in approval. " If only I was a few years younger, I'd be hav'en a piece of him, I'll tell ya. Not real big, but he's pretty, with muscles too. You can tell by looking at em, e's strong as a bull, and that coal black hair, and icy blue eyes, 'll grab a girls heart, I'll tell ya that."

"Do you know, does he have a girl friend?" Bryan asked.

"Not that I knows of, standoffish he is," she shook her head.

His under clothes removed, Bryan stood naked, freezing, while the old lady went to work, using a string, tying knots to mark his measurements; his shoulders, his arms, his trunk, his chest, waist, hips, feet, and groin.

"Ok," she got off her knees, "Wait right here," she told him, and disappeared one more time, into the back.

He shivered; except that there was no wind, he might as well have been standing outside.

The door opened, and a soldier stepped in, looked at Bryan, amused. Bryan, shrugged his shoulders, the soldier chuckled, "See you're getting the Jutta treatment, she just likes to be in control, she does, and really likes look'n at the young bucks, with nothing on."

"And you're none the worse for it now, are you?" The old lady exclaimed as she emerged from the back, her arms loaded with clothes.

"No mam," he answered.

"Then go over there sit down and shut up. It'll be your turn next."

"Look'n forward ta that aren't ye, want me to take my clothes off now," he joked?

She "Harrumphed," and helped Bryan into fresh new undergarments, new wool trousers, black, close fitting, and light, a white linen shirt, long sleeves, and collar. Next she put a long, dark tunic, the Jarl's green emblem embroidered on its front, over his head, and pulled it down, stockings covered his legs, and calf high, black leather boots finished the outfit. "These are your dress clothes, to wear when attending to his lordship, so's you can impress all the pretty ladies in wait'n up there, which you'll no doubt be bed'n, soon enough," she chuckled.

"She's got a good imagination about what happens up there, too," the soldier chuckled.

"Shut up, or I take ya back in the back and teach ya a thing or two."

"Oh, Lord," the boy feigned nausea.

A floppy beret set to the side of his head topped it off. He was not used to clothing that fit so closely, it felt odd, but not uncomfortable.

She stood back, looking him over approvingly, "That should get their little twats in a tizzy. Now," she lifted an arm load of clothes into his arms, "Take these with you. Your work and military clothes'll be delivered to your room later by my man. Let me know if there is a problem."

"There won't be," the soldier said, "Everything she does is perfect."

"Thank ya, Sigured fer yer vote of confidence. Now, off with ya. I've got business to attend to. Sigured here didn't just come fer new clothes now did ya sweetie."

The soldier wrinkled his nose, and made a face. They laughed.

The guards at the entrance of the Great Hall gave him no challenge. Just inside, a crowd of pages, milled about, all dressed like him. All of them having stood naked before Jutta, he chuckled to himself. Ivan appeared in front of him almost at once.

"Come with me." He led Bryan through the crowd of young men. Long, flowing, elaborately decorated tapestries, hung from ceiling to floor, side by side, about three paces from the outside walls, providing a space in which people could come and go, unseen by those attending court. They went up through this passage on the right side of the hall, to the front, past a long line of people, waiting to petition the Jarl. Some half naked, changing to their best clothes, from soiled road attire, still others huddled, in private conference, by twos and threes.

At the front of the hall, the Jarl on his throne, of heavy, oversized, oak, upholstered in copious amounts of leather, and decorated in gold leaf, talking to someone, when he spotted Ivan and Bryan. He excused himself, and motioned for Bryan to come forward.

"Welcome, Bryan," he greeted enthusiastically, wrapped his arms around Bryan, gave him a bear hug, before the court, for all to see. It made Bryan very uncomfortable, he wanted to pull away.

"Thank you, M'Lord," he spat the words out as best he could. His discomfort was about to become much worse.

"Ivan is here to help you with your tasks, not to worry, they're easy. He will acquaint you with our guests, some whom are important, many who are not, but we never let on we know," he smiled, "Many are from important, wealthy, influential families, powerful men who can help you. Of course, there are also, beautiful women, whom you will be delighted to know, are interested in splendid, handsome young men, such as you. You will find them most entertaining, well trained in the art of making a man feel good, if you know what I mean. Like Ivan, you will have the run of the place. Sample them as you please." He winked at Bryan, "Ivan can tell you," his devilish grin, mischievous, but warm, and genuine. "These women belong to families who can bring you fabulous wealth," he paused, then added, "You look just splendid in your uniform."

He reached out and took Bryan's hand, "Stand up here with me for a moment," pulling Bryan up on the platform, beside the throne; raising Bryan's arm high in the air, the room fell silent.

"My faithful patrons, I wish to introduce to you a new courtesan, and my new personnel page, Bryan Thorson of Nagomas, son of Thor Bryanson. Make him welcome as one of our own. We have high hopes for Bryan." Scattered, unenthusiastic, polite applause sounded around the room.

Bryan, embarrassed at the recognition, more uncomfortable than standing naked in front of the old tailor lady, felt his face flush. Now everyone would compare him to his father; what if he couldn't meet their expectations? Although the Jarl seemed sincere, the warm introduction would last until he stepped off the platform. He bowed to the courtesans, and then to the Jarl.

"I do look forward to seeing you each morning," The Dane said then turned back to the man he had been talking to before.

Bryan was suspicious, the man seemed warm, but had he just been set up, what for?

He met Ivan to the side of the room, just behind the tapestry.

"That was interesting," Ivan said, "I've never seen him do anything quite like that before, just for a page."

Bryan's suspicions grew, "You think I've been set up?"

Ivan shook his head no, "He's just patronizing you, making political mileage on your father's good name, it'll soon be forgotten. Everything and everyone is insincere here. They set you up, you set them up, they manipulate you, you manipulate them. It's a way of life. Keep your wits about you, and stay on your toes, you'll be ok."

Over the next days, Ivan would coach him in intricacies of court life, where to find things, the Jarl's preferences, how to behave in and out of court, how to address the Jarl, the knights, and the ladies in waiting.

And there were many ladies in waiting, some very, very beautiful. A fact that didn't escape Bryans notice, nor him theirs; tall and healthy, probably wealthy, they wore wonderfully, beautiful, elaborate gowns. One in particular caught his attention; dark skinned, long, braided, dark hair, eyes sparking in the candle light, as dark as her hair, mysterious and mischievous. Her tall, slender, attractive body was like a magnet to him, and he stole glances, at every opportunity. On several occasions he caught her looking in his direction, and when he did, she would look away, demurely. He would make a point of making her acquaintance, as soon as possible, he thought.

Ivan saw, and warned, "Be careful with them. They're daunting and treacherous…, beautifully bewitching. You'll get your heart broken with the likes of them, you will."

"Do you know any of them, I mean, romantically? The Dane said you did."

"He did?" Ivan laughed out loud.

That morning passed quickly into afternoon, and the midday attendant arrived. "The afternoon attendant usually has less work to do as the Jarl's court rarely continues late into the day," Ivan explained, "Though he does have to stay a while afterward to clean things up."

Bryan looked for the brown haired girl as he left, but she was gone.

Back in his room he discovered piles of new clothing. In all his life, he had never owned but a few changes of clothing, at one time. Now, he had four sets to wear in court, four sets for everyday, and four sets of military clothes, plus under clothing, comfortable socks, hats, three overcoats, and the finest boots he'd ever seen, sitting at the foot of his bed three pairs of felt shoes, and sandals for use during the warm summer days. Back home, he would be thought wealthy.

Due at the sparing arena, he would have to put the clothing away later. Off came his court uniform, and on went his military trousers and shirt.

Thorick was waiting at the sparing arena, when he arrived. Looking Bryan over, "You seem strong enough," he commented. Built of sturdy Nordic stock, Bryan was tall, youthful, heavily muscled, attributable to endless farm work, strong and fit, confident. Thorick tossed Bryan a fighting stick; a long, solid, hardwood branch about as tall as Bryan and hefty diameter.

"Let's see what you can do."

They squared off, Bryan parried Thorick's attack, taking a few blows, first to one side, then the other, the instructor only toying with him; the next blow came, hard, devastating, stinging his hands to numbness, knocking the stick flying through the air. Bryan stumbled back, stunned, Thorick followed, quickly, a blow, to his shoulder, from the side of the stick, continuing to stumble backward, landing hard, flat on his back, a resounding blow, the dirt floor hard, knocking his breath from him. The world went black, stars floated before his eyes, he gasped for air, not able to breathe, clutching his chest in panic, again trying to suck air into his lungs, consciousness quickly fading.

The trainer leaned over him, eyes wide, "Are you alright?" The man's voice, distant.

He tried to answer, no air in his lungs to speak, he gasped again, finally sucking a bit of air in, another deep breath, his panic began to subside, saw light, the instructor came into view. "Yes," he gasped, "Yes - I think so," he said with little conviction.

Thorick helped him up. "We need to work on some basics, starting with footwork drills."

63

For several hours they focused on foot work, attaining greater balance and stability. He thought he was getting the hang of it, but slowed by fatigue, Thorick dismissed him.

"Hello Bryan," Horold, the teacher greeted him, as if a feast to be devoured. Obviously, eager to begin studies with his new student, an empty slate, upon which he could write his wisdom.

"Please come in and sit down. Today we shall commence learning the sound of the different ruins and numbers, boring for certain, but be patient, once learned we can commence reading and writing. You must practice constantly, not just here in class. Until you are able to read on your own I will read to you, and soon enough you will read the tails to me, you'll find them exciting and helpful, I think."

Bryan, eager to learn, not sure he could match the instructor's enthusiasm.

Dark by the time the lesson was over; he headed to the bath to sooth his sore body, and injured spirit. The strange boy was elated to see him in military clothing, "You look dashing." He exclaimed, "I'll bet the fancy court outfits make you look just royal. The Jarl must be delighted."

Bryan asked him if he could braid his hair.

"Of course, I'dlove to," The boy said enthusiastically.

He undid and washed Bryan's hair while bathing him, afterward braided it, tightly, front to back. Where it was long in the back, he braided a tail.

Afterward, at the kitchen, he ate goose meat, boiled in its juice, with turnips. Always fond of goose, the combination with turnips seemed a little strange, sure he would be getting used to many strange new flavors.

Back in his room, he tried to put his new clothing away. There didn't seem enough room to store it all, and after several attempts he gave up and went to sleep among piles of garments.

Again, the page woke him early. He dressed, and they went to eat.

Ivan reviewed what Bryan needed to do before the Jarl arrived, "We'll clean the throne and platform, fill the water vessel, and fetch a breakfast tray to set at the side of the throne. Then the old straw in the front of the hall has to be raked back, and replaced with fresh. Others will rake it the rest of the way back to replace the straw to the back of hall. They throw the old straw out in the street. We'll check to see that everything is in place. If you miss something, and he notices, the Jarl can be most unpleasant."

"Has that ever happened to you?"

"More times than I like to think about."

"Is that why you're leaving?"

Ivan lowered his gaze, speaking low, soft, deliberately, "I've done everything ever asked, sometimes more, something's not too pleasant. At first, he treated me well, like a son. But, lately...," Ivan shrugged his shoulders. "Now I'm going to be sent to Ireland Viking. I asked permission to go see my folks before leaving, but was denied. He says the slaves have to be guarded."

Bryan's heart sank, taking Ivan's place, after the boy was being discarded like so much garbage? A small bit of information, helpful to understand him better, he pitied the boy.

"Do you think he got tired of you?" Bryan asked.

"No. His knight did," his voice tapperd off, the page sat silent, his head bowed, not moving, his face flushed red.

"Ivan?" Bryan prompted.

65

"Sometimes…, after court is over," his words slow and deliberate, "And the patrons gone, he and the knights would gather together. I was asked to serve them, along with other pages. The knights drank his ale and wine, one, when he got drunk, would take me, us, into a backroom behind the throne, and take advantage of us," he was speaking so softly Bryan could hardly hear, the boy trembled.

Bryan frowned, not understanding, "Take advantage of you?"

"Take my trousers down, make me bend over, and bugger my arse."

Bryan horrified, "The Dane knew this?

"He'd be drunk, didn't know, or ignored it."

"Why did they pick on you?"

"Just one, he liked me, I was small, he could make me submit, I guess. There were other boys, didn't seem to bother them, they did't say much, I was his favorite, but, lately I've refused."

"Unbelievable."

"It's nothing, wait till Warpurgis begins tomorrow night, lasts two days, the final celebration, evening of the second day, they gather from all around, in the Hof, for their sacred rights. That's something you definitely won't believe. You'll see."

"Ok." Bryan still uncertain about Ivan, he'd only known him a few days, likable enough, he wanted to believe him, but wasn't sure, opening up to a stranger he'd only just met, could it be a trap? Or perhaps, Ivan was being honest, pushed to his limits, and didn't care anymore.

As they went about their morning chores, the job rudimentary, needing little instruction, leaving plenty of time to keep an eye on Ivan, who went about, eyes downcast, shoulders slumped, his mood dark and lack luster.

Later on, a knight came up to Ivan, behind the tapestry, put his arm around Ivan's shoulders, and whispered something in his ear. Ivan shook his head no, but the knight persisted, shaking Ivan and motioning his head in the direction of the entrance. Ivan brought his elbow up, and pushed the man away. Bryan couldn't hear the page, but he could clearly see him mouth the words, "Leave me alone." A frightening look of rage, crossed the knight's face, he turned away. Afterward there was little doubt for Bryan; Ivan's story was true, he needed help, and Bryan thought he knew how to do it.

That day in court the Jarl sentenced a poor man, to have his right hand cut off, for thievery. A women accused of cheating on her barbaric husband got thirty lashes. A dozen or so land disputes were settled, always in favor of the Jarl, or one of his wealthy patrons. One poor man, a thrall, who had eaten left over crusts of bread from his masters table, was sent away, to be beheaded, by the master.

Finally, the afternoon attendant came to trade off with Bryan and Ivan. Bryan looked about the hall for the pretty girl he'd seen earlier, but she was nowhere. Ivan too, was gone. Bryan dashed to the door and out on the street.

"Ivan, wait," he shouted, and ran to catch up with the page, headed down the hill. "What are you doing this afternoon?"

"Probably go down to the docks, and watch darkness fall."

"Is there a place we can get a tankard of ale?"

"Sure, the inn, it's not much but the drink is good," eager to accept Bryan's offer of friendship.

"I'll buy you one if you join me," Bryan said.

"Sure."

"I have to practice sparing, and take my lessons, but how about we meet there on the docks around dark?"

"Ok." Ivan agreed.

Before sparing, he stopped by the tailor shop, and placed a special order with the old woman.

Thorick, thorough and tough, repeated the lessons from the day before, adding new moves, emphases on smooth flow, from one action to another. Bryan absorbed the teaching enthusiastically, and was sweaty and tired when finished.

Writing class, progressing rapidly, Bryan thought it fun, picking it up much faster than the teacher expected.

When he left the master, darkness fast approaching, he walked down the hill, found Ivan sitting on the end of the pier, swinging his legs over the edge, tossing pebbles into the water, watching the ripples go out in all directions when they landed, ca-plunk. A light mist hung over the water, gulls skimmed peacefully just above. He understood why Ivan liked to come here.

"Hea."

Ivan turned to see him. "Hi." He got up, and they walked back down the pier.

"I saw your boyfriend approach you today."

"Yea," Ivan answered flatly.

"You weren't very cordial. Aren't you afraid of what he might do?"

"What's he gonna do?"

"Kill you. Rape you."

Ivan shrugged his shoulders.

"Wan'a do something about it?" Bryan asked.

Ivan shot him a sideways glance, startled.

They approached the Inn, a large square building, one big room on the ground floor, a second story, looked to be cribs for a number of ladies, plying the premises. In the mix of patrons; sailors, soldiers, dock workers and others in various stages of drunkenness. Bryan found a table, in a dark corner, toward the back, away from the commotion. They ordered a tankard of ale each.

"What'd ya mean, do something about it?" Ivan looked about nervously, "There are spies about in this place, whose loyalty can be to any number of persons, and whose ears are keen. Take care what you say," Paranoia and fear on his face, dubious about what he thought Bryan was suggesting.

"I'm willing to take the chance." Bryan said. He took a long quaff of the strong and actually quite good drink. He looked around to be sure no one was listening. "I've watched you Ivan, I think that I can trust you," he paused, "I have no misconceptions about the Jarl. He used some kind of treachery to get my father to fight for him, he murdered my uncle, and lied to my family about it. He invited me to serve in his court to help cover his tracks. Trust me, I have reasons to dislike him, and don't believe his masquerade, it's as thin as spring ice."

"Wait till the end Of Walpurgis," Ivan said, seething, his eyes flashed, "You won't believe, till you see it, they celebrate all the gods, the sacrifices bloody, like you've never seen."

The only gods Bryan ever knew were Oden, Thor, and maybe Loki, god of trickery, the beliefs here, much different from his clan.

He continued, "I mean to cause as much trouble as I can, I don't know how, yet, haven't been here long enough, have to be secretive, beyond suspicion, I'm asking you, Ivan, to join me, help me, might be dangerous, I won't hold any hard feelings if you say no."

For the first time since they met, Bryan caught a gleam in Ivan's eyes; the Loki in him ignited. "What kind of mischief?" Ivan wanted to know, for the first time, enthusiasm in his voice

"As much as I can conjure up; it wouldn't bother me to kill a few."

"Really, you think we could kill them!"

"I do."

"You know that if you get caught, it would mean a very unpleasant death?"

"How unpleasant could it be? When you die you die." Bryan took a long drink. He was being flippant, he knew.

"Trust me," Ivan said gravely, "The Jarl can make your death long and most painful. He's creative that way."

"Ivan," he stared into the boy's eyes, "I'm not going to get caught."

Ivan chuckled. Looking back at Bryan, said, "You know I despise that son of a ...," he paused to emphasize his contempt. "I'm with you all the way, and I know just where we can start."

They had a long earnest talk.

Walking back up the hill toward the Great Hall, Ivan said, "There's no court tomorrow."

"There's not?"

"No - Walpurgis - Sacred days - no regular court; the Jarl stays secluded, and when the ceremony begins holds court alone, by himself. Symbolically holding court with the gods while they are celebrated outside in the Hof."

"So we don't have to go in to work tomorrow?"

"Not till late, to set up the room for the Jarl, to conduct his sacred court, it'll only take a few moments."

"So, what do you want to do tomorrow?

"We'll go down into the village, visit some of the shops, maybe have a good meal, what d' you think?"

"Sounds great," Bryan was pleased at his new found friendship, another ally.

The page was dressed in his court clothes and hat in the morning when he woke Bryan. Bryan dressed in a like uniform, and they headed down toward the docks, turned left before the warehouse buildings, to a street lined with shops; a butcher shop, a shoe maker, a candle maker, a black smith, a wool dealer, and a bakery, its doors open to the street, emitting heavenly smells.

Ivan took Bryan into a tailor shop, and showed Bryan a green wool suit he liked. They tried on different hats, Bryan, clowning around, picked up a stout walking stick, with a brass serpents head atop, and put on a black cape, lined with dark green cloth, fastened it around his neck with a silver broach, and strutted about the shop.

Ivan laughed, "You look a randy peacock, you should buy it."

"I think I will," he said, "You know," under his breath, "If I dress like this people will think me a ladies' man, distract them from my real intentions, don't you think?"

"Yea, I don't suppose you'd mind if the girls found it attractive either," Ivan teased.

As they were leaving the shop, a group of ladies in waiting entered. With barely enough room for them to get by, Bryan and Ivan, being gentlemen, stepped to the side, making way, and as the darlings passed, their eyes met, those deep dark eyes, a perfectly oval face, dark brown curls of hair, cascading over her bare shoulders, dressed in dark royal blue, the girl from court, stopped even with him.

"Hello," Bryan exclaimed.

"Hello Bryan Thorson," her voice sweet, smooth as honey, alluring.

She remembered his name.

"I've seen you in court, but I haven't had a chance to meet you" he said.

"Well you've met me now. I'm Germani."

He bowed discreetly.

"You look very handsome today," She said.

"Thank you M'lady," he said, bowing again. "And you are stunning as ever."

"Come on," the lady behind her said, irritated.

"I'll see you in court M'lady," he said.

"I'll look forward to it," she smiled sweetly, and went on by, leaving behind a wonderful musky aroma.

Out side, Bryan, all smiles, walking on air, head floating, insides trembling.

"Did you see that?" He asked Ivan.

"I saw."

"I've wanted to meet her."

"I know."

"She said I looked handsome."

"Yes, she did."

"Isn't she beautiful?"

"She is Bryan," Ivan said disdainfully.

"Don't you like her?" Bryan couldn't imagine.

"Oh, she's beautiful. She's also rich, with many suitors. Good luck bedding that one."

"Ivan…, for shame, you're jealous."

"No, I've seen it happen before, many times."

Bryan was sure that he could handle her.

At a street side stand, they bought fresh baked sheppard pies from a village lady. Her business brisk, with all

72

the people in town for the Walpurgis rites, she treated them like royal gentlemen, and her pies, like a little bit of heaven to the pallet, reminded Bryan of food from home. Next to her stand, a rotund man sold them ale, a tankard each, Ivan paid, it was strong, dark, rich, bitter and filling.

After wandering about the town they headed back up the hill, and stopping in at the bath were they were greeted by the attendant.

"Bryan! My, don't you look distinguished, a cape and walking stick," his hand aside his cheek, "You're starting to fit in with the crowd up on the hill, aren't you?" He allowed a sly smile to grow across his face, tilted his head to the side, and wiggled his hips. "And Ivan, you lucky boy you, leaving this lovely place, has he conceded to let you go see your family yet."

The strange boy, in a position to gather valuable information, would make another important ally, but Bryan wasn't sure about his wicked sarcasm. Could he be trusted?

"No, he's not giving in," Ivan answered.

"What a shame, he's such a creep," he waved his hand in disgust in the general direction of the hall. "I'd like to ... ."

"Like to what?" Bryan asked.

"Nothing," the attendant became suddenly sullen, dismissing the question.

Bryan looked at him hard. Caught off guard, the boy looked away, embarrassed.

"Nothing?" Bryan asked.

He hesitated. "Just once, just one stinking time I'd like to do something to get even with the bastard," quickly looking around, afraid someone had heard.

Bryan put his arm around the boy's neck, and pulled him close, walked him to the side of the room, and whispered

73

softly in his ear, "If I should be able to vex the Jarl, would you be willing to help."

"With the greatest of pleasure," He grinned, "I knew there was a reason I liked you."

Bryan kissed him teasingly on the cheek. "Keep your eyes open, and ears to the ground. Let me know if you hear anything special, gossip, something being planned, or the Jarl has done." Bryan kissed him again, lightly on the other cheek.

"Don't patronize me," he brushed Bryan's kiss away, "I'm always listening; I'll be sure and let you know," he slowly turned his head, with a sudden move, kissed Bryan on the lips." Bryan pulled back, startled, the boy smiled, "Two can play that game, don't toy with me."

"Sorry," Bryan said.

Ivan had already washed off, and was sitting in the tub. Bryan stripped down, the attendant quickly washed him, and he joined Ivan in the tub.

"He's with us."Bryan said.

"Yea, looks like he would like to be with you."

"Good luck to him," Bryan tilted his head slightly, "Could be an interesting adventure; I'll bet he's kinky."

Ivan looked at him, then realized Bryan was putting him on. "You're strange too, you know that?" Ivan said cynically.

"Not as strange as he is."

"Got that right."

After the bath, they went to the great hall, and set up the Jarl's throne for his solo reign that evening.

"Want to spar with me for a while," Bryan asked Ivan.

"Sure, but I'm not real good at it," Ivan said.

"That's ok, I'll teach you what I've learned."

When they left the arena, it was dark. They went to the Inn for a meal and a few tankards, afterward they retired.

Bryan found a package, in his room, from the tailor. He examined it, and hid it under his bed.

In the morning, he and Ivan went to the great hall and readied it for another night's ceremonial court. Then went to the docks, played around for a while, and when the towns folk began to celebrate, setting up parties and banquets, in front of their homes, the boys explored the streets, visiting with families, especially those with pretty girls, sampling food and drink, all of it tasty. The village festive, the atmosphere of celebration, contagious, easy to catch, Bryan was in a good mood by late afternoon, when they split up.

"Meet me, in a little while, in front of the hoff," Ivan told him, "Be prepared for the likes of which you've never seen."

Chapter 7

He went to his room, took a nap, then dressed in his military uniform, for no other reason than he thought it looked elegant; black pants of fine wool cloth, a shirt of linen, a black tunic with green and gold trim around the edges, the Jarl's coat of arms embroidered on the front and back. He had sewn a sheath inside his boot, long enough to hold his long knife. He'd heard the superstitions, carrying a weapon into the Hof, a sacrilege; they'd have to find it first, he thought, placed the dagger in the sheath, and put the boot on. He'd spent a good deal of his life in the forest, never having seen an elf; the dangers, in this foreign place, far more real.

Evening closing in fast, torches, strategically placed along the top of the waddle and mud wall cast flickering yellow light about the Hof where he met Ivan. People, from every part of town and every walk of life were rapidly filling the interior.

"Come with me," Ivan led the way, along the wall to where it met the outside of the great hall, a plank atop the wall, reinforcing the wall against the side of the building, just big enough for the two of them to sit on. They scaled the wall to the plank, and took seats, side by side. From this vantage point, they had a good view of the crowd, the altar, and the activity, taking place; a fire already burning beneath a huge cauldron, half full of steaming water, ready for sacrificial meat, shamans in long, gray, hooded, robes gathering about the altar.

In a short time a shaman brought a goat trough the gate, leading the animal among the crowd of people, so as many as possible could touch it. The shamans, waiting at the altar, received the animal, blessed it, using ritual icons of a god, Bryan supposed was Oden; the crowd chanting his name over and over, barely audible at first, just a murmur, rippling through the Hof, quickly rising to a great roar.

The shamans took the animal to the altar, positioned its head over a very large pottery bowl, hobbled its hind legs, steadied it, forced the beasts head down toward the bowl, and the head shaman reached around its neck, a long shiny knife in his hand, quickly drew it across the goat's neck, cleanly slitting its throat open. The animal jerked, its life blood gushing into the bowl, slumped to the earth, gone, the bleeding stopped. The shaman raised the bowl over his head, into the air, and the crowd roared, clapping hands, jumping up and down, dancing about; again, the chant went up to Oden, chief of the gods. A boy dressed like the shaman, carried the bowl to the crowd, people dipped their hands into the fresh warm blood, some painted their faces with it, while others licked it off their fingers.

The priests lifted the goat's body to the altar, it was quickly skinned, it's head, severed from the neck, leaving the hide and head in one piece, and placed it upon one of the long poles, which they hoisted into the air, the bottom of the pole, placed into one of the holes in the earth.

The goat's belly was slit open, its entrails slid out onto the altar, the liver removed, along with kidneys, and heart, sliced to pieces, and placed into the boiling cauldron. The carcass was quickly boned, cut into small pieces, and put into the cauldron. The entrails and the bones were thrown into the flames; a cloud of black, acrid smoke to swirled into the night air, pungent, foul-smelling, adding to the spectacle, and sending the crowd into another dizzying, frenzy.

Another goat was led into the Hof, the chanting rose to yet an even higher pitch, this time to Thor, god of the common man, the pall of burning flesh, gathering, heavy over the hof. A third goat was brought, the chant went to Freya, goddess of

78

love and fertility, then Foresti, god of justice, with each god the chanting reaching an ever increasing crescendo, then Bragi god of eloquence and poetry; the celebration, running long into the night, the crowd hysterical with chanting and dance.

"This is unbelievable," Bryan leaned to Ivan and shouted.

"There's more, just watch," Ivan yelled back.

A true spectacle; the fire burning high, cauldron boiling, the air, putrid with burning entrails, the chanting mob, pressing ever closer to the altar, now covered in blood, surrounded by a semicircle of goat heads and hides. Ivan nudged Bryan, pointing to the entrance; a young man, naked, bound at the wrists, and around his neck, willingly followed a shaman, with whom he spoke, laughing, stumbling in the wrong direction, drunk.

"Oh, god no!" Ivan cried out.

"What?" Bryan asked.

"It's Eric, one of the pages, a little older than me, comes from east of here, been here a long time; one of the favorites, a good friend, it can't be!" Tears glistening on Ivan's cheeks, the color gone from his face, he was trembling.

The page was led through the mob, winding back and forth so that all the people could touch him; women kissed him about the face, caressing his, arms, shoulders, and genitals, men stroking his back and muscular arms.

"They're sending their prayers to the gods through him," Ivan sobbed.

Bryan, mesmerized by the spectacle, slow to realize what was about to happen, became suddenly aware.

The captive young man was taken to the altar, pulled to his knees. The head priest greeted the boy, gave him a drink, a strong one Bryan hoped. Transfixed, not wanting to watch, the scene was so ghastly, unable to take his eyes from it.

The boy's ankles were tethered, lifted high into the air, till he was nearly upside down, a garrote looped over his head, drawn tight, till his body spasmed, then released, the head shaman lifted the boy's head by his hair, with the crowed roaring, the priest reached around the boy's neck, and the same smooth stroke used on the goats, opened the boy's throat, his life blood gushed into the bowl, he jerked, struggled for a moment, then went still.

A wail, inhuman, animal like, came from Ivan, like a wolf, on a dark winter's night, having lost its mate, heard even above the roar of the crowd, an unimaginable pain, from deep in Ivan's heart. Chills ran up Bryan's spine.

Bryan wrapped an arm around Ivan's shoulders, pulled his head to his chest. Ivan was breathing hard, and shaking uncontrollably.

Bryan was still unable to tear his attention away from the horror unfolding before him. With the last drop of the young boy's blood spilled into the bowl, the body was lifted to the altar. The shaman lifted the bowl making an offering to the gods, the crowd wild, eager to get to it, the shamans cutting, their work grizzly, pulling the victims skin from his carcass, leaving it attached to his head, as with the goats, the decapitated head placed on a pole, and raised behind the altar, the skin dripping bloody.

The bowl was passed to the maddened crowd. Everyone's face, already smeared with blood, they eagerly drank the young boy's blood, from hands and fingers, dipped in the bowl. The boy's body was gutted, shamans stripped meat from the bones, and women carried bowls to the cauldron. Bryan felt nauseous, the chanting incessant, barbarians soon to feast on the boiled meat.

Bryan, over-whelmed with sheer horror; the murderous act, the wild crowd, and the sickening, acrid, odor of burning flesh. He needed to get himself and Ivan out of there; jumping to the ground, he turned, extending a hand, helping Ivan, beyond consolation, to the ground, fought his way, leading Ivan, through the crowd, toward the gate. Suddenly, a young woman, a bowl of the boy's blood in her hands, appeared in front of them, offering it to Ivan. Enraged, Ivan struck out, sending the bowl flying, blood spattering everywhere, pummeled the poor girl across the face, knocking her to the ground.

Bryan grabbed Ivan, hauled him, hurriedly, toward the gate, before anyone could realize what he had done.

Outside, Ivan stumbling out into the darkness doubled over, vomiting thick green bile, onto the street. Bryan followed, throwing an arm around Ivan's neck, and guiding him across the street.

"They killed him Bryan. They cut his head off, and now they're about to eat him." Ivan cried like a baby.

"I Know, I know, barbaric," Bryan buried Ivan's head in his chest.

"I told you. I told you it would be worse."

"Yes…, yes you did."

"How can I face them tomorrow without spitting in their disgusting faces, without cutting their throats?"

"I don't know. But we will."

"NO, No I Can't."

"Yes you can, you'll stay with me tonight." Bryan led him across the street to the barracks room, helped Ivan remove his clothes, and they lay down, under the blankets. For a while, they talked about the evening, until Ivan, exhausted, calmed, and fell asleep.

Bryan, unable to stop his thoughts from churning, lay awake, thinking. No court tomorrow; a good day, perhaps, to implement revenge…, for Ivan, to keep him from going mad.

Chapter 8

Brian rose early, the gruesome proceedings of the previous evening, fresh, sour, sickening, heavy on his mind, the odor of burning flesh, lingering in his nostrils. He covered Ivan who had worked his way from beneath the blankets, dressed quietly in his work clothes, and went across the street to get something to eat.

Goat meat, boiled, perhaps left over from last night, page boy and all. One look at it, and bile rose, bitter in his throat, his gut filled with nausea. He sent it back to the kitchen, and settled for a mug of ale, and some stale bread.

The Great Hall, abandoned except for the Jarl's body guard, the knight Vandel, who mentored Bryan in his lessons, teaching him military strategy, sitting on the platform, in front of the throne.

"Well lad, didn't expect to see you here this morning. Didn't you go to the celebration last night?"

"Yes." Bryan said flatly.

"What'd you think?"

"It was… ."

"Grizzly?"

"Ghastly." Bryan replied.

"And pointless?"

"Yes."

"A shameful waste of life," the knight continued, "Of someone who could have become a great soldier."

"Yes, sir," Bryan agreed, surprised at the knight's candidness.

"Don't believe in such hocus pocus, never did agree with it; peoples imaginations running away with them, sacrificing your own, a captured enemy maybe, someone you're going to kill anyway, but one of your own, a loyal one at that. Never did understand that business."

"I can't believe the Jarl tolerates it," Bryan said, impulsively, then thinking it too bold a statement, but unable to take it back.

"Don' think he does, just wants to keep the shamans happy," the knight paused. "What about you. You do'n ok?"

"I'm ok. Thought I'd come in and straighten things up a bit." Looking around, it was evident the Jarl had one of his parties last night, like Ivan talked about.

"You go ahead, won't be anyone in here today," the knight said, and walked off.

Bryan wiped down the throne, swept the stage and around behind, raked back the straw, and spread new in its place, freshened the wine in the decanter next to the throne, and covered it with the carved wooden lid to keep it free of vermin until the Jarl was ready to partake.

When finished he headed back to his room. Halfway there, a female voice called from behind, "Hello there, how are you."

He turned to see Germani, a broad smile on her face, wearing a dark hooded smock, the hood pulled over her head, dark curls, hanging from the sides, around her angelic face, coal black eyes, like pools of ink, caressing his face with her gaze, her teeth strong, white as snow, accenting the lips he wanted so much to part with his tongue. His heart leapt inside his chest. He'd seen pretty girls before, but she was different…, special.

"Good morning," he said, unable to hide the excitement in his voice.

"Did you go the Walpurgis rights last night?" She asked.

"Yes, it was…, interesting. I've never seen anything quite like it," he said, his feelings mixed, excitement for the girl, and loathing for the spectacle. It didn't come out right, he cursed under his breath, his emotions showing, like a little boy, wanting to impress more than anything.

"Don't you celebrate Walpurgis where you are from?"

"Not like that." He hesitated. "Were you there? I didn't see you."

"No, I don't care for it too much."

"I know what you mean, doubt I'll go to another," he said, relieved. "Where are you going?"

"To visit my aunt to do some sewing for her. She's old, blind, and isn't able to do fine work anymore, but I'll be coming back this afternoon."

Good, he thought. She wants to meet me, "Maybe I can walk you home?"

"I would like that," her voice demure, as she smiled.

His heart jumped for joy, "I'll watch for you."

"Ok, see you then."

He watched until she disappeared over the hill. When he turned back toward the barracks, he spotted Ivan emerging from the bath, and jogged over to the page. "How are you feeling, better I hope?"

"Ok, I guess," He said with little enthusiasm, "We need to clean and set up the hall. There's no telling when the Jarl'll show up."

"It's already done. I got up early, and took care of it."

"Well, aren't you just the little royal page, taking care of his favorite king," Ivan teased, "Com'on, let's get something to eat."

"I've eaten, but I'll join you."

Ivan's face paled at the goat stew. They both took some flat bread with honey and ale. While they ate, they talked.

"Do you think you could arrange a meeting with your knight boy friend this evening?"

Ivan hastily looked around to be sure no one was listening, "Possibly," he said, tense, questioning, not sure what Bryan had in mind.

"We'll plan a little surprise party for him, after dark, go someplace secluded where we won't be seen," Bryan said.

Ivan nodded, still not quite sure what Bryan was talking about. "I'll have to find him. After the celebration last night he'll probably be sleeping. It's been a while, I'm sure he'll be eager."

"Eager, and hopefully, dumb."

"Yea that too, what have you got in mind."

"Not here," Bryan motioned with his head toward the street. Once away from the kitchen, Bryan leaned close to Ivan's ear and whispered.

Ivan said, "Really!" surprised. "You're not kidding?"

Bryan shook his head.

"We'll go to his barracks," Ivan said, "Tag along in case he's too eager."

"Ok, lead the way."

They went around behind the hall, between buildings to the next street west, to one of several barracks.

"Shhhhh," Ivan put his finger to his lips.

Past several rooms, Ivan pointed into an empty room, and nodded in that direction. Bryan went in. Ivan entered the next room. Bryan could see Ivan through cracks in the wooden wall, approaching the knight, snoring, loudly, asleep on the bench. Ivan softly stroked the knights shoulder, whispering, "Sir Sigrud, Sir Sigrud."

"Hua, what, what," The knight grunted, slowly waking.

"Ivan, what do you want boy?" Contempt in his voice.

"Sir Sigrid, I've come to apologize M'lord for my behavior the other day. I wasn't feeling well, should not have been so rude, your invitation was gracious, I should not have refused. I was thinking, perhaps, if you would so like, we could meet, and take care of our needs, if you know what I mean," Ivan's voice was soft, enticing.

"Uhhh, why not..., right now?" the knight said, as he threw back the blanket from his large nude, hairy, body.

"Can't right now," Ivan said coyly, "Jarl has chores for me." He ran his fingers lightly through the hairs on the knights chest, down over his belly, to his inner thigh, and massaged him there, his hand brushing the man's genitals, "Had to sneak away, even now, I can see you tonight, after dark, make it up to you, I promise."

The man, becoming excited, reached out, caressed Ivan between his legs through his trousers, "You won't regret it, you are a sweet boy Ivan, I'll make you so happy," the knight cooed.

"Down by the old boat house, back behind, in the grass by the trees, you know the place."

"Yea, yea I know it. I'll see you then my boy." He looked up at Ivan, "Gods, you are so handsome."

Ivan backed away. "I'll be there," turning away, walked from the room down the hallway, and out into the daylight. Bryan followed stealthily.

When they were away from the building, Bryan said, "I can't believe what you just did, had him completely convinced, the way you touched him."

"Yea, well we're not complete strangers." Ivan's face flushed red, "I want him to get what's coming to him, you have no idea, how I had to grovel, him having his way," the boy choked, "I'll have revenge, like you." He looked at Bryan, tears of anger blurred his blue eyes.

"We'll do it, tonight, I promise," Bryan clapped Ivan on the back. "Meet me after dusk at the inn."

Bryan spent most of the afternoon in the sparing arena practicing with Norse broad swords, like his uncle's, used for close personnel combat, and war axes so much favored by the Scandinavian warriors. His confidence, stamina, and strength were developing rapidly.

Reading class was also progressing well. He had learned the ruin letter figures well, and was starting to put basic words together, clumsily reading a few pages, more slowly than he wanted, and Vandel's instruction fascinated him.

Late afternoon, he left the classroom, went back to his barracks, and sat on a bench in front of the building, where the old men usually sat, catching the warmth of the afternoon sun, picked up a piece of wood, found on the street, and whittled shavings from around its edges, waiting.

At long last, he saw, the top of her hood, bobbing up and down, over the top of the hill. Excitement rose in his chest, and his face flushed with heat. He didn't like how his light skin so easily blushed, it showed so, betraying his inexperience, never occurring to him; the flash of red might be attractive to the young ladies.

She walked right up to him, "Have you been waiting long?"

"Not at all," he lied. He threw his cape over his shoulders, and took his walking stick in hand, trying to look as dashing as possible.

"May I?" He took her basket in one hand, and offered her the other. Handling the basket and walking stick with the same arm awkward, but he saw himself elegant, a lovely young lady, on his arm.

They made small talk, as they passed down the hill, through the shopping area, then on to a long row of rather large well-designed homes. She came to a halt in front of one of them.

"This is where I live, the guest of a friend of the Jarl - Nice people, very rich. But, most of the time, I am at the hall fulfilling social obligations, for my father. As lady in waiting, the Jarl expects me to wed one of his knights." She said, rolling her eyes, with a sly smile on her face.

Did she mean me? Does she think I'm going to be a knight? Bryan's thoughts took flight.

"I would very much like to see you again, m'lady."

"That would be most enjoyable," she said, there was that coy smile.

"At the earliest opportunity then?"

"Yes, indeed." She answered.

With a short bow, he took her hand, and pressed it to his lips, her skin warm and soft, smelling of something sweet and tasting even better, his lips lingered.

She blushed ever so slightly, causing his face to flash with heat.

"Good afternoon, master Bryan." She curtsied, and he bowed again, her hand still in his.

Near dusk, at a half run, he hurried back to his room, retrieved the package he'd gotten from the tailor lady, left his cape and walking stick.

"Thought maybe you weren't going to make it," Ivan was waiting for him outside the inn.

"Had some important business to attend to."

"Bet I can guess who she was," Ivan teased.

"I wouldn't miss this for anything," Bryan reassured him, "You can bet on that." Full of excitement, the thrill of anticipation; his throat tight, dry, a rush of warm adrenalin, running through his veins, his breathing quick, at the prospect of what was about to happen.

"We better get going," Ivan sounded excited, too.

At the end of the street, they followed an obscure path, skirting the edge of the fjord, among tall weeds, and through an abandon dock area; a fallen down old building, looming in the distance.

"That's it, the boat house," Ivan pointed, "We should go quietly." Evening, giving way to darkness, difficult to see clearly, Ivan led the way. All was quiet, the old building sat silent; a small open meadow, to the rear, grass grown ankle high, bordered by a thick stand of young trees.

"This is it," Ivan whispered, "I'll stand here next to the building, you hide in the trees, when he comes, I'll take his hand, lead him to the grass, he'll think that natural, and take charge. The rape will happen quickly, don't hesitate please. When he's distracted by what he is doing, make your move, but make it good."

Bryan faded into the trees, changed into the tight fitting black trousers and shirt the tailor lady had sewn for him, a black hood over his head, covering his face, made him stealthy in the dark. Hefting the axe he'd barrowed from the arena, he ran his finger over the razor sharp blade, drawing a trickle of blood, he was ready. He could just see Ivan, crouched down next to the building, waiting.

It wasn't long, he heard the slight rustle of the weeds, a soft male voice, called out, "Ivan, Ivan, you there?" The dark figure, appearing around the corner, "Ivan, my sweet boy, where are you?"

"I am here m'lord." Ivan whispered as he stood up.

"Oh good, little Ivan, my sweet, I was worried you had reconsidered."

"No, m'lord, I'll not deny you; I'm your faithful servant."

"That's my good boy." He ran his hands over Ivan's shoulders, down his arm, then up over his chest, wrapped his arms around him, and pulled the page to him, pressed his lips to Ivan's mouth, and explored inside with his tongue. Ivan wanted to bite it, resisting with as much will power as he could muster.

"Come, m'lord, over here where the grass is soft like a bed."

"Oh, Ivan, so thoughtful."

In the grass, he held Ivan with one arm, slipped his hand into Ivan's pants, and stroked him, a horror Ivan knew well; in spite of himself, Ivan was becoming erect. Forcing back panic, trying to relax, he slipped his hand into the knight's trousers, rubbed the very excited man between his legs. The knight gently pulled Ivan's pants down, sank to his knees, and took Ivan in his mouth, the boy breathed deeply. Unwanted, undeniable pleasure, with it, bad memories, forced to submit, he shuttered, a tremor so slight, had the man noticed. Ivan struggling with his own sexual excitement, forced, but all the same, very real, leaning over the man's back, he pulled his pants down, and began to message him. The knight, engulfed in rapture, grunted an urgent guttural noise. Rising up, he turned Ivan around, forced the boy's head to the ground, spat into the crack of Ivan's buttocks. Ivan braced for unpleasantness, so familiar, and prayed for Bryan to interrupt, soon, please.

The knight, intent on having his way, his beautiful lover, so easily submitting, didn't notice, a shadow, slowly creep up behind him. Strong arms, hefted the axe high into the air, hesitated, for the briefest moment, with all his strength Bryan brought the axe down, swift, noiseless, the razor sharp blade, sliced through the knight's skull, penetrating his head, with a pop, like a hollow pumpkin being split, slicing through his face, and embedding itself, at the top of his spinal column. His head, cleaved in two, folded outward in opposing directions. Without a sound, the man collapsed, limp, his full weight atop helpless Ivan, who left out a yell. Blood pulsed from the ruptured head, in great torrents, washing down over Ivan.

Bryan scrambled, rolling the dead knight's body from atop Ivan. The page sprang from beneath, half naked, drenched in and spitting blood.

"Is he dead? Did you kill the bastard? I was afraid he was going to, you wouldn't get him in time, filthy bastard?" He looked at the head, split open, gasped in horror, and started pulling up his trousers, "Turn him over on his stomach."

"What?"

"Turn the son of a bitch over on his stomach," Ivan repeated, desperation in his voice, pulling at the body. They rolled him to his stomach. Ivan, like a crazed man, ran into the trees, came back, brandishing a stick, round as three fingers, and as long as Ivan's forearm. Quickly, he rounded one end with his knife, grasping the rough end, placed the rounded end between the man's buttocks, with all his might, he crammed the stick into the man's rear, only the handle protruding, Ivan stood, raised his foot, and kicked the end of the stick, forcing in all the way into the dead body.

"Take that you son of a bitch," he sobbed through clenched teeth, there was so much venom in the boy's act, Bryan shuddered.

He put his arms around Ivan's neck, pulled him close, "It's done Ivan, over, he's dead, you're vengeance is complete."

Ivan trembled, the rage he had secreted, deep inside, so long, released, he buried his face in Bryan's shoulder, and sobbed like a baby.

After a tearfully long time, Ivan calmed, Bryan led him away, toward the shore. He stripped the blood soaked clothes from the boy, washed him in the cold water of the fjord, and thoroughly rinsed the blood from the clothing. Then realizing that Ivan would quickly become chilled, in the cool night air, in wet clothing, and not make it back to the barracks; Bryan gave him his dry clothing that he'd removed earlier.

"Let's get out of here," He said.

They hurried back, through the weeds, past the old docks, from shadow to shadow past the inn, and up the hill. Ivan slowed, to a slow walk, the cold, and extreme emotional drain, rapidly taking their toll. Finally, back in his room, Bryan stowed his ax and sword, and changed out of his black suit.

"Come on, let's go get a warm bath," Bryan suggested.

"That's the best Idea I've heard in a long time," Ivan shivered.

The warm water, reassuring, calming, the enormity of what they done, began to set in.

"Don't have to worry about lover boy anymore." Bryan said.

"Yea," Ivan said unconvincingly, unsure they'd done the right thing, or that it would make any difference, or they would get away with it, murder, foreign and disturbing, something he never contemplated, and now a part of.

Bryan moved to Ivan's front, took the boys head in his hands, stared directly into his eyes, and said emphatically, "You're going to be all right, my friend, think what he was doing to you, what he would have done if we hadn't, let's see some anger. "

Ivan nodded, tears, again in his eyes, hugged Bryan, "Thank you, thank you."

Bryan flushed with success, remembering the event, now in slow motion; recalled an electrifying feeling, first in his arms, as the axe did its business, then down his spine, into his groin, for a very brief moment, orgasmic euphoria, the thrill and terror of killing a man, surprised him, and at the same time, gave him great satisfaction; a first step toward revenge, so easy, should he feel guilty, to feel so good, taking a man's life. He wondered, it was so easy he could become careless, overconfident; a dangerous elixir, he would have to be vigilant not to indulge in its toxic allure.

When they finished, ready to leave, Bryan pulled the attendant aside, "Remember our conversation about helping?" He asked.

The boy nodded.

"If anyone asks, we were both here tonight for hours."

"You stayed so long I thought you were going to dissolve in the water. What'd ya do?"

Bryan shook his head, "Can't say, best you don't know." He gave the attendant a peck on the cheek, rubbed him on the back of the head, "That's my good friend." There was a strange affection, building in him for the boy, an inner softness - odd.

Out on the street, Ivan said, "You shouldn't carry on like that with Ole."

"That's his name, Ole, first time I've heard it."

"Aren't you leading him on, unfairly?"

"I guess I am, he likes me, in a way I like him too, but I think he knows where we stand with each other. He's a valuable ally to us right now, in a position to hear all kinds of stuff, and like tonight, be an alibi if anyone should come asking, and what's to hurt, if I show him some affection, doubt if he gets much appreciation from the rest of the bruits go in there."

"I don't know. I don't think I could do that."

"You couldn't? You seemed to do alright a little earlier this evening. "

"I guess, but it wasn't affection I was showing."

"You didn't feel anything?"

"Well," he thought a moment, "It wasn't affection," he said with conviction.

"Maybe so, but where I come from, it's ok for people who care for one another to show each other how they feel. If you ever get to meet my cousin, Ari you'll see how close we are, like brothers. It doesn't mean we're like you and the knight."

"Watch it there," Ivan warned, jokingly serious.

Bryan's dreams, that night, were filled with turmoil; fighting one enemy after another, killing, over and over.

Toward morning,Thor appeared, his hammer held high, lightening flashing in all directions, his voice deep and gravelly, "It would seem you have become cunning, like the gods, ruthless as your enemy, striking unpredictably, unexpectedly. You've chosen your tactics well, keeping your enemy off balance, guessing, suspicious, paranoid. Be sure you remain invisible when blame is meted out." In a flash the fiery god vanished, and Bryan woke with a start. He stared at the ceiling, wondering what would happen when they found the knight.

Chapter 9

Six days later someone stumbled on the body, word of it, whispered about the Jarl's court, causing a great uproar, the scandalous circumstance, mostly kept from the courtesans, made those who knew furious, with no one available to vent their anger on.

The Dane, reserved in public, was enraged away from the eyes and ears of the court, raving at his guards and knights, "How could this happen, why was Sigrid's absence not noticed, who could have done this?" He demanded answers, none were forthcoming.

Over the weeks the furor calmed. Ivan trained with the soldiers, rarely guarding slaves, and little was said of his going Viking.

Ole said nothing about the murdered knight, but Bryan knew, from the look in his eyes, and his knowing smile, he understood what they had done.

As summer approached; the days warmer and longer, evenings pleasant, Viking ships arriving, holds rich with plunder, making court gay and festive, the Jarl jocular.

Bryan was spending more time with the brown eyed girl. He had kissed her often, feelings of growing affection, with each parting of their lips, certain he was in love, and that she bore like feelings for him. Though having never been in love before, he wasn't going to let his lack of experience prevent him from thinking he was; the romantic imagination of a young man, having no bounds.

One warm, cloudless day, after he finished obligations to the Jarl, he donned his hat, threw the cape over his shoulders, picked up his walking stick, and headed from the hall, toward the sparing arena.

"Bryan," he turned to see her run from the hall.

"Where are you going?" She asked.

"The arena, to practice."

"Oh…, I thought, was hoping we might have some time together, maybe go for a walk or something, but if you can't…?" She cocked her head sideways, away from him, looking from the corners of her eyes, a gesture used to get her way. He disliked being manipulated, but still, this once.

I could skip practice, he thought, I shouldn't but.

She smiled her sweet smile, and his willpower evaporated.

"Ok, just this once."

"Oh, that would make me so very happy," she cooed, held out her arm for him the take. They headed down to the docks, watched dock hands, strong men, muscles flexing, unloading large, heavy bundles, baskets of gold, bundles of cloth and furs, glass objects, pottery, knives, from one of the longboats, just arrived from the Ire, all of it Viking booty.

She led him south from there, along the shoreline. Unlike the north shore, overgrown with weeds, littered with the trash of old buildings, the shore to the south was wide, covered with sand and small pebbles, soft green grass filling the void between sand and trees. The fjord, like glass, rolling ripples, ever so slowly crossed the mirrored surface, up to the sand, gulls dotted the sky, floating close overhead, searching for food.

They strolled, holding hands, talking small talk, about the goings on in court. She reveled in the social atmosphere there, and although he found it tiresome, it gave them something to talk about, and he adored talking with her.

They found a small meadow, the grass thick and soft, secluded among the trees, away from the water. Bryan spread his cape, they sat together; he liked being close to her, their bodies, gently touching, her perfumed scent, tantalizing his senses. They kissed. He put his hand on her shoulder, pulled her to him; his tongue explored her mouth, her taste - ecstasy. His hand on her chest, a firm nipple beneath the cloth, the beating of her heart, or was that his? He lay back on the cape, pulling her down with him, she didn't resist.

Eagerly devouring each other, their tongues entwined. Bryan aroused; feeling the pleasure and excitement in his loin, pressing against the cloth of his trousers, his skin tingling, his head light as if gravity suddenly ceased.

He caressed her breasts through her richly embroidered smock, soft and pliant to his pressure. Wanting more, he moved his hand, under her tunic, across the softness of her belly, lightly, ever so lightly, brushing his hand across her naked breast. She sighed, arched her back to him, he cupped a breast in his hand, gently messaging her nipple, firm and soft at the same time, between his fingers, wanting to take it into his mouth, her clothes, too many of them, in the way, suckling her lips instead.

Her hand moved underneath his tunic, caressed his abdomen with the flat of her hand, sliding down into his trousers, he didn't protest. She caressed the inside of his thighs, never touched like this; it felt wonderful, marvelously sensuous. Taking her time, she slowly moved, between his legs, to his groin, cradling his scrotum in her hand, messaging firmly; the sweet edge of pain, shooting between his legs, tantalizing, stingingly sexual. He cried out in the joy of it. Watching him, she smiled at his pleasure, raised her hand, took hold of him, and began stroking.

Their breathing ragged, her face flushed, his own on fire, the heat spreading, over his neck and shoulders, down over his belly, to where she was rubbing his manhood, his desire to be inside her, overwhelming, but this, this, so...

pleasant, like sucking on a comb of spring honey, he never wanted it to stop. He pushed his hand down into her dress, to the soft velvet between her legs, she moaned, her stroking increased.

Long moments passed. The ferocity of their passion, beyond anything Bryan dared imagine. She moaned, as he parted her, gently entered, penetrating deeply, incredibly soft, warm, and wet, her cry; soft, exceedingly primitive, female, and passionate.

Things were happening inside him; too rapidly to control, as much as he wanted the moment to last, he heard himself cry out, his body spasiming, consumed by his release. She made the sound again, her rhythmic contractions squeezed his fingers, very wet.

Long moments of ecstasy washed over them, an eternity, he couldn't breathe, his body convulsed, again and again, hoping it would never stop, for a brief, fleeting moment thought maybe, just maybe..., but finally, his ecstatic contractions slowed. Wonderfully drained, peaceful, holding each other, trembling, their breathing slowed; the heat of love making searing his face, neck, shoulders, and chest.

For the briefest moment he dozed. A cool breeze from the fjord washed over them. He could hear the calls of the birds over head, and her soft breathing in his ear, the wetness between his legs, and on his hand between hers; he thought it, the most beautiful moment he had ever experienced.

Rousing, he looked into her beautiful, brown, watery, sensuous eyes, and they giggled a carnal, knowing giggle. She removed her hand from his trousers, and wiped it on the edge of her apron. He didn't want to, but he pulled his hand from her dress, she wiped it dry.

"That was..., wonderful," He said.

"Yes it was," she replied, "It makes me so happy." The smile on her face was radiant. He kissed her.

They lay there together in the warm sun for a time holding each other.

Getting up to go, he was cool and wet between his legs, there was a large dark wet spot on the front of his trousers.

She noticed him looking. Softly she squeezed him through the wet clothing.

"My man," she said.

"I adore you," he replied.

Giggling like little kids, they walked back along the shore, holding hands.

The world seemed renewed and alive; the birds flying more freely, the trees greener, and the breeze fresher, invigorating. Before today sex was something he so desired, but was unable to attain. Now holding hands with his beautiful lover, walking in the warm sun, satisfaction in his loins, he understood. Thor had been good to him this day.

They took their time on the way to her home; their conversation easy and enjoyable. He liked kissing her, and stopped quite a few times to do it. He watched as she went up the path to her home, and felt certain that she would be his to make love to very soon.

He nearly ran to his barracks room where he changed out of the wet sticky trousers, and went across to the baths. The attendant, always happy and all smiles when he saw Bryan, greeted him, scrubbed him down and left him to soak in the hot tub. His body was particularly sensuous and the warm water relaxed him even further; almost asleep when Ivan came in to join him.

"By the look on your face, something good happened," Ivan said?

"Yea, it's been an unusually nice day," Bryan replied, lazily smiling.

Ivan looked at him, hoping for a better explanation. "What have you been up to this afternoon? Did you go see that girl again?"

Bryan's smile broadened, he stretched back against the wall of the tub.

Ivan's curiosity was eating him up. "Bryan," He said, not sure about what he was thinking, "Are you bedding that wench?"

Bryan sunk down into the water over his head, blowing bubbles. Ivan could come to his own conclusions. He knew it would drive the boy crazy.

Germani was not in court the following day.

Chapter 10

Absent for two days after, Bryan, anxiously, watching, scanning, hoping, disappointed. What happen, had he done something wrong, offended her, hurt her feelings somehow? At a loss, he was perplexed.

As midday approached that second day, searching for an item from the storerooms off the main hall; shelves, full of accumulated junk, lining one side of the long narrow hallway, the other side, a series of seldom used rooms, the Jarl, ministers and knights occasionally use for private meetings, otherwise empty. He heard sounds as he passed one of the rooms. If anyone was meeting there, he would have known, and the Jarl was holding court this very moment in the Great Hall.

Without a second thought, he opened the door, and froze cold; there on a padded bench, on all fours, Germani, her long dark curls hanging down over her bare shoulders, framing her face, red with passion, naked, her legs spread wide, from behind, the captain of pages, an arrogant boy a couple years older than Bryan, on his knees, as naked as she, taking her, his body wet with sweat, face flushed red, intent on his lust for pleasure, rocking, thrusting, about to explode. He was sure Germani saw him; she stared directly at him with no sign of recognition, completely absorbed in her passion. The boy, eyes closed, engrossed in his own world.

Erupting in anger, his fury, instantly and completely consuming every fiber in his body; he slammed the door shut, turned away, fell back against it; searing heat coursed his veins, unable to catch his breath, his head spun. This couldn't be, he was imagining things, on the other side of the door, she cried out, the same cry of passionate he heard out on the fjord, followed by a long, low moan of ecstasy, from the boy. No, No, No, he stumbled, into the hall, eschewing his duties, bolting from the hall, into the blinding sunlight, the heat in his chest, scorching, suffocating, about to explode, gasping for cool air with no relief.

To somehow escape, running, past the barracks, the bath, down the hill, past the tailor shop, through the line of storeroom buildings, and out to the end of the long dock, where the clear cold deep water waited.

Staring down into its depths, to jump in, sink beneath the surface, suck the cold liquid into his lungs, it would be over in seconds, wanting it so badly, but, he didn't, couldn't; to die would be to fail his vow to Thor, oh the misery, sinking to his knees, sobs racking his body, overwhelming, unrelenting. It began to rain, he didn't notice, washing his cheeks of tears, wetting his back, and slicking the planks of the docks, he didn't notice, feeling nothing, but the inferno in his chest.

Then, an arm, around his shoulders. He turned, through tear blurred eyes, Ole smiling his soft gentle smile. "I saw you run by, knew you were in some kind of trouble, needed a friend." He pulled Bryan to his side, "What happened? Did that monster Jarl do you wrong?"

"No, No..., not him..., nothing like that, oh Ole, a wench, Ivan tried to warn me, said I couldn't trust them," chocking on his words, "Said they would eat me alive. I thought I knew better, could handle them, he was right; she led me on, and then she ..., she," he didn't finish.

"Oh Bryan," Ole rocked him back and forth, "I wish I could help, but mending a broken heart is not something I know how to do," his voice, gentle, soothing, "You grieve now, when you're done, Ivan and I are here for you, you can count on us."

Bryan put his arms around the frail boy's body, leaned his head against Ole's chest, and cried, it rained, his head ached with a lovers fever.

Later, he and Ole walked slowly up the hill, through the mud, to his barracks.

"Com'on over, I'll give you a nice warm bath."

"Thank you, no."

"Do you need me to stay with you?"

The offer tempting, but Bryan shook his head, "I want to be by myself."

The boy hugged him gently, and left. He removed his wet clothes and layed down on his bed. His insides hurt, the fire continued to burn inside, unable to cry anymore, his mind numb, he lay awake, listening to the rain, the last light of day inched its way from the doorway, in the darkness, sleep eventually enveloping him in its tranquil arms.

He woke before dawn and dressed. Slightly more at ease than the night before, his stomach still aching, hot like he had a fever, his whole body running at high pitch, his skin on fire.

Stepping out on to the street, the cool morning air, and quiet slumbering village, refreshing.

He was at the kitchen eating smoked salmon and flat bread, and drinking buttermilk when Ivan spotted him.

"Mornin'," the page said cheerily.

"Good morning," Bryan replied with half a heart.

"Valhalla, what happened to you?"

"Why?"

"You look like death warmed over; eyes bloodshot and black and blue, you're pale and pasty, you sound as if you've lost your last friend. Last time I saw you, you were on top of the world."

He told Ivan what had happened, "You were right to warn me. But, I was so cock sure I could handle her. I knew for certain that the next time we met we were going to make love, then…"

"Bryan, look, these ladies in waiting do their best to find a husband who will take care of them, give them the kind of life style that they desire. They try to capture a man with high status, the greatest potential, who will chase after their charms. My guess is she's been servicing this page captain for a while, he had some rank. When you came along, destined to become a knight or something, she decided to line you up, take his place, someone who would do a much better job bedding her than that clown, I know him, he's crude, rough around the edges. With your good looks, you could probably still have her, if you wanted."

"No thanks," Bryan said ruefully.

"That's up to you. But, if you use her to satisfy your own needs no one's going to think any differently of you. That's the way it's played, you use her, she uses you, everyone's satisfied, as long as no one important gets their toes stepped on, everything's just fine."

"You're probably right, you warned me, and were right about that. I'm just angry, angry at her, at him, mostly at myself."

"I'm really sorry you got hurt Bryan, but you'd better perk it up a bit, or the Jarl'l sense something's amiss, ask questions you may not want to answer. If he finds out you're vulnerable on this, you'll lose face, he'll embarrass you in front of everyone, trust me."

"What'l I do?" Bryan asked, bewildered.

"Come over to the bath, Ole'll know how to fix you up. He'll love making you handsome again, a good second mom." Ivan said with an air of derision.

106

"Yea, he helped me out yesterday, you know, or I might have jumped in the fjord and ended it all, he was very understanding."

"Yea, he's just, you know, everyone makes fun of him."

"It's their loss, he's really a decent guy," Bryan said, grateful that the boy had lent him his shoulder when he needed it.

As they entered the bath, Ivan called out, and Ole came running. "Bryan here needs some of your special treatment."

The assistant took one look at Bryan, and said, "I'd say so."

"Thanks a lot." Bryan said.

"Sorry, no offense intended," Ole said.

He gave Bryan a good scrubbing down, soaked him in the hot tub, after drying him off, laid him back, washed his hair, worked some lotion into it, and combed it out, so that it glistened like the sun off the fjord, braided the long yellow curls, put drops in his eyes that stung like fire, but rid them of redness, clear and fresh.

As he did all this, he told Bryan he'd overheard talk, among the boys from the docks, a long ship was expected to arrive, loaded with booty, and thralls newly captured from the Ire. "They said that it was sure to make the Jarl a lot of money. Wa'd'ya think you can do with that?"

"Don't know, have to look into it, ought 'a be some mischief there," the prospect of new adventure, brightened him up.

At the great hall, a gaggle of pages, gathered about the entrance, chatting among themselves, nothing unusual. Almost immediately, the page captain emerged from the group, confronting him. Up till now, the boy hadn't given Bryan the time of day, probably didn't even know Bryan existed.

"Hea, hot shot, how're ya doin'?" he said, disdain heavy in his voice.

"Fine," Bryan said flatly, trying to ignore him, and push past.

"Heard you were upset yesterday," he persisted.

"I'm fine."

The captain strutting at his side, crowding him, bumping against his shoulder, "Well if I can help, let me know, cuze I know my way around here pretty well, you know," his tone condescending, cheep.

'I'm fine," Bryan said coldly.

"Just thought I might be able to help show you how things are done."

Bryan stopped short, turned to the page, irritated, stepped up to him, their noses nearly touching, the young man barley as tall as Bryan, good looking, in a youthful kind of way, slight of stature, Bryan, sure he could best the boy, overcome all the young bastards' bravado, beat him to a pulp.

"I didn't ask for your help, don't need any help, I'm fine - let - me – alone," forcing the words through clenched teeth.

"Ok, just trying to help," the little twerp stepped back, spun on his heels, and headed back toward the entrance.

Bryan went about his morning tasks, angry; the stupid jackass actually had the nerve to try to intimidate him, his anger carrying him through the morning, and when he was finally relieved of his duties he donned his cape and walking stick, left the hall headed to the sparing arena, to venting his frustrations.

Coming up the hill, a group of people, single file, hands bound in front, necks lashed to the person in front and back by rope; newly captured thralls, slaves, on their way to the slave barns, on the other side of the hill, to be kept until sold, peasant folk, harvested from Ireland. At the head of the column, a boy, maybe a year or so younger than Bryan, dressed in rags, an old shirt, barely covering his muscular chest, what was left of trousers, concealing little, brown with filth, blue eyes that blazed hatred, through his dirt blackened face, his youth stolen, beaten and starved out of him.

As the thrall approached, about to pass by, Bryan let his walking stick fall into his path. The boy stopped short, the column behind him, crashed into one another. The bedraggled boy, like a beaten dog, looked at Bryan, Bryan looked down at the stick then back at the boy, the thrall, obedient, stooped down, picked up the stick, and handed it to Bryan, who wrapped his hand over the boy's, so he couldn't release it, and held it. Their eyes met, for a brief moment, two soles; one striving to destroy the Jarl, and one destroyed by the Jarl, pleading for help. Bryan felt his gut tighten, took the stick, and bowed slightly. In that moment, he had a plan.

The column of thralls moved on by. He changed his clothes and went to the arena where he fought so hard the instructor was hard put to defend himself, the effort burning away his anger. In class he read about the Danish Kings, caring little for the Danish, but their strategies, the mistakes they made in battle, he studied closely, the Dane himself, might be vulnerable to the same mistakes, he wanted to be quick to take advantage.

After leaving the classroom, he went to the bath, where he met Ivan.

"The gods are about tonight, and they will have their way," he told Ivan, their code for adventure in the making.

Ivan nodded, ready, not exactly sure what for.

Chapter 11

It was dark when they left the bath. Bryan told Ivan, "Get your black suit, and meet me in my room. Don't let anyone see you."

"What's going on?"

"Later, go get your suit." He had ordered a black suit for Ivan, like the one he'd had made for himself, so they could work together, black, stealthy, invisible.

Ivan was quick about getting back to Bryan's room, the little bundle under his arm.

They changed.

"What are we going to do?" Ivan wanted to know.

"Come with me," Bryan said. He led Ivan over the hill, passed the great hall, down toward the slave barn, ducking behind and around empty buildings. Stopping where Bryan thought no one would hear. "No one must recognize us, or we'll have to be eliminate them, I'd rather not kill someone needlessly."

"Ok, but, what are we going to do," Ivan asked once more.

"New shipment of thralls."

"What about it?"

"We're going to set em free."

"What for?"

"Cause they're just poor folk who were captured by the Vikings. They don't deserve to be thralls. You think it's right to buy or sell people?"

"Hadn't thought much about it."

"Besides, it'll cost the Dane a bundle."

"That makes sense, and how're you going to do it?" Ivan asked as he pulled the hood over his head.

"Not me, we are going to do it. Don't know yet, you got a knife?"

"My carving knife."

"That'll do, come on." Bryan hefted his favorite weapon, an axe, borrowed from the arena. Creeping from shadow to shadow, slipping behind piles of boxes, wood, and straw, like wisps of smoke, unseen by searching eyes.

When a group of noisy revelers, well into their cups stumbled up the street, they ducked behind some trash, at the side of the street. The group, men and their party girls, zigzagged their way past Bryan and Ivan. The street was quiet again, they scrambled forward.

Just ahead the slave barn, oil lamps, illuminated the front of the building. They crouched behind a hay stack, the door open, the interior dimly lit.

"There doesn't seem to be anyone moving inside, there should be a guard," Bryan whispered.

They crept across the street, up behind a large boulder, in front of the barn. Crouching on their hunches, they watched, and patiently waited.

After a long while, with no sign of a guard, the shadows, quietly dashed to the entrance, peered into the darkness of the barn, no guards.

Suspicious, Bryan thought.

Inside many silent eyes watched as one by one Bryan and Ivan put the lamps out except for one by the door, it's light, too dim to reveal them in the shadows. The thralls, lie on straw, on the floor, side by side, on one side of the barn. Bryan walked along the line of bedraggled souls to the last captive, who, dirty and raged, was the boy who's blue eyes seemed to glow from of his blacked dirty face, even in the darkness of the barn. He sat up, frieghtened and suspicious.

Bryan put his finger to the boy's lips, "Shhhhh." The boy stared into Bryan's face, not at first recognizing him from their afternoon encounter, recoiling in fear and uncertainty, and when Bryan removed his knife from his boot, the thrall tried to scramble back away from Bryan, wary, terrified.

"No, No," Bryan whispered, shaking his head, reached down, picked up the rope that bound the boy to the thrall next to him, deliberately, showing the fearful slave the rope, cut it with his knife. He reached toward the boy, took his hand, held it for a moment, slowly pulled the tied hands toward him, carefully cutting them free. The boy pulled his hands back, messaging his wrists, while Bryan did the same for his dirty calloused feet. The young thrall stared at Bryan, the beginning of a smile on his face, more calm, still unsure, but starting to understand what was about to happen. Bryan put a finger to his own lips, the boy nodded.

Ivan had gone down the line, freeing the rest of the thralls. Bryan whispered to him, "Watch the door; there must be a guard somewhere," while he made sure all the rest of the thralls were free of their bonds.

With Ivan in place, Bryan went back to the young boy, who would be the group's leader, as all the others were women and children. Taking the lad's hand, and led him toward the door.

Suddenly, Ivan left out a hiss, between his teeth.

Bryan ducked into the darkness.

A guard lumbered through the door, about five steps in, stopped, and stood erect, realizing the barn was dark, or perhaps seeing Bryan's shadow move in front of him, stepped back, reached for his sword, but Bryans axe, already in motion, arching over his head, a glint of light, flashing along the edge of the blade. The guard reacted, tilting his head away from the on-coming steel, too late, the axe shaved his ear off,

113

and struck down the side of his neck, severing arteries and tendons, continuing downward, cutting through the collar bone, that cracked loudly, embedding itself in the guard's chest. The force of the blow drove the man to his knees, at that moment Bryan recognized him; the captain of the pages; Germani's lover. The boy opened his mouth, to cry out, a warning, or in pain, or perhaps shock, realizing he'd just been killed, but only a trickle of blood came out, his body dropped backward to the ground.

Bryan leaned down close to his ear, and whispered with a sneer, "I don't need your help."

The boy closed his eyes and died, a black pool of blood, quickly forming in the dirt, around his head.

Ivan came up and peered down, "Valhalla, Bryan that's..."

"I know," the calmness in his voice was disquieting. A sharp, cold, thrill stabbed through his groin, and up his spine. He was actually beginning to fear how much he enjoyed killing; the violent, murderous finality of it, he hadn't known it was the page, but it pleased him, it had turned out so interestingly well. What was he becoming?

The page wore a distinctive gold ring, with a green stone. Bryan removed it from his limp finger. "The spoils of war," he exclaimed, but he had other plans for it. He gave the pages' sword to the slave boy, who was looking at him, in stunned horror, as a disquieting silence, permeated the barn. He stepped over the dead page, and motioned for them to follow him out of the barn, into the darkness of the street.

"Bring up the rear," he whispered to Ivan, "Make sure no one is left behind." Taking the hand of the slave boy, he guided him quickly, quietly along the dark street, from building to building, up over the hill, and down toward the docks, the others following. As they neared the water, they slowed, and took refuge, behind a warehouse across from where the long ship was docked.

Bryan and Ivan, cautiously peered around the corner of the building, the longboat the thralls came in on, still there, a good distance away, guarded by two Vikings

"Must be two hundred paces before we can get at them, they'll be sure to see us, we need to cross, without alarming them?" Bryan whispered to Ivan.

Looking around, far down the end of the street behind them, the Inn, an occasional shout could be heard in that direction. He nudged Ivan, motioning with his head, toward the inn, held his hand up for the thralls to stay where they were.

He and Ivan walked toward the Inn, behind the buildings, for a way, then turned out into the middle of the street, between the store houses and the water.

Bryan pronounced in a loud voice, "Iffan, yrr durnk."

"I'm not," Ivan protested, immediately picking up on what Bryan was up to.

"Yesssss...Ya R." He staggered.

"I yam? Naaa."

"N' so'm I," Bryan wrapped his arm around Ivan for support, and the two of them staggered down the street toward the longboat.

"Woll...If'n I was drunk, I wn'd be able ta hald Y'a up."

"Wall ur not doing so good at that."

"I beg ur pardn, am so."

Nearing the ship, they had the full attention of Viking guards, who watched closely.

"Hey, hey," Bryan called out to them. "Take us fer a ride in ur boat, sure is a perrty one." He stumbled over his own feet.

"Yea..." Ivan yelled, "I wanna steer, C'mon give us a ride."

"I think you boys had better go back where you come from," one of the guards said.

"Ahhh, Com'on, won't hurt ta ga'out fer a little tinnney weeney sail. No body'l know, I promise." Bryan stumbled, closer by a few strides.

"Can't do that boys," the big Viking said, "Now, just turn around n'go back ta where ya came from." He was coming toward them now.

Bryan broke from Ivan's shoulder, turned away, bent toward the ground, faking a puk, took a firm grip on the handle of his axe, twisted his torso back, spun around, and let the axe fly with everything he had. End over end it spun, invisible in the darkness, closing the distance, in the blink of an eye, the blade buried itself in the man's chest, with a crack, like a chunk of wood, being split.

The impact punched the guard backward, off his feet, landing on his back, the axe popped out, a fountain of blood, black in the darkness, shot into the air, from the gaping wound, two, three, four, five times it pulsed upward, then died away. The big man was motionless.

The second guard, his sword drawn, was on Ivan in a flash, Ivan's only weapon, his carving knife, Ivan ducked, and rolled away. Bryan drew his grandfather's sword, in two strides the guard was on him. He met the first blow, but the man was strong, Bryan staggered at the power of the assault, parried away a second attack, but was off balance, staggering, he fell to his knees. The guard raised his blade high into the air, Bryan, in an impossibly awkward position, tried his best to get his sword up to protect himself. The Viking poised to strike a death blow.

Chapter 12

At the very top of his stroke, the Viking paused, for the slightest moment, intent on killing Bryan, then gasped, sucking a deep breath, frozen. Ivan had stuck his carving blade deep into the man's back. Bryan immediately on his feet, swinging his sword, its razor sharp blade opened the guard's throat wide, and when he tried for one last breath, coughed; blood filling his lungs, spraying in a frothy mix of air and fluid, and gushing down over his chest. He pitched backward, loosing grip of his sword, and fell to the ground, not to move again. Ivan reached down, and pulled his knife free.

"Thanks," Bryan said.

"Twern't nothn," Ivan said with a nervous chuckle as he wiped his blade on the man's pant leg.

Bryan turned, to motion the thralls forward, but they were already rushing toward him.

"Let's dump these two into the water." He told Ivan motioning toward the edge of the dock. After removing weapons and valuables, which they gave to the Thralls, the bodies were thrown into the icy cold fjord.

They hurried the thralls into the boat. The poor wretches knew what to do, immediately seating themselves at the oar stations, with oars in hand, as they had seen the Vikings do, many times, though most of them women, unafraid of the task. Bryan handed the boy the weapons they had taken from the guards, his eyes flashing blue, in the dim light, he shook Bryan's hand, with a smile, Bryan and Ivan helped push the ship out into the fjord. The ores bit into the water, and the ship surged away, into the darkness.

Bryan and his friend disappeared into the shadows. Like ghosts in the night, flitting from behind one building to another, back to the barracks.

While they changed out of their black suits, Ivan said, "You killed a man tonight, Bryan."

"Killed three men."

"Weren't you scared? I was so terrified I could hardly hold onto my knife."

"Too busy to be scared."

"You really did a job on the Page Captain."

"Didn't think much about it at the time, did what had to be done, how was I to know it was him, till I had done it."

"How'd it make you feel? It was like vengeance almost. Wasn't it? After Germani and all."

"It felt...," he paused, "Sickeningly sweet, a thrill, like sex, kind of perverted."

"You enjoyed it?"

Slowly he shook his head yes, ashamed of his own emotions. "It's not the first time; I felt it when I killed your knight. Do you think badly of me, for it?"

Ivan was silent.

Bryan woke early, had breakfast and bathed. He dressed and went to the Great Hall where he readied the throne, cleaned the straw, prepared a morning food tray for the Jarl, and stood by.

The courtesans and pages trickled in, a few at a time. Germani making her entrance; accompanied by two knights, she called cousins, attending to her bidding. Bryan, dubious of their knighthood though they acted self important, carried weapons, and dressed in overly elegant clothing. He doubted that they were even cousins. Perhaps she was bedding them in return for their loyalty, but then his imagination was probably getting the better of him, knowing she liked a romantic bent to her affairs, these two characters inconsequential tools, or was it fools, to be used. He was anxiously curious to know how she was going react to news of the pages death.

The question of the Dane's reaction was another thing altogether. He bought and sold thralls daily, without thought to their well being, frequently sending soldiers and prisoners alike to their death, with little or no feeling, but monetary loss? The escape of the Thralls, and the theft of the longboat, would take a lot of money from his pocket; he could react violently.

In short order the Jarl entered, strode across the front of the room, sat down on the throne, and began eating; everything proceeding in the usual manor; the court waiting for him to initiate the daily activities, people milled about, and spoke in undertones, with one another.

A slight stir, a mear murmur, from the rear of the hall, among the pages, the first indication of anything wrong. The kings own body guard, Vandel, came forward through the courtesans, approached the Jarl, did a perfunctory kneel, stepped forward, to the side of the throne, and spoke softly into the Jarl's ear. A hush came over the hall.

A slight movement, toward the middle of the room, drew Bryan's attention, one of the pages, making his way to Germani. The page bowed, and began talking to her, his voice, hushed, she gasped, covered her face with her hands, turned, and went behind the tapestry, followed by her attending knights.

At the front of the room, Skjolden beckoned his own knights, before the throne, where they conferred, in low voices. Bryan slipped, unseen, behind the tapestry on his side of the hall, hurried to one of the store rooms, looking for a piece of parchment, found a scrap with a small map drawn at the top of the page, cut off the blank part with his knife, fashioned it into an envelope, slipped the blood stained gold ring with the green stone into the little pocket, tied a piece of silky ribbon around it, and sealed it with candle wax. With a quill from the tables ink well, wrote Germani across the front.

With as much stealth as he could muster, he slipped to the back of the room, and slid the package from beneath his tunic, to a small table. Anything there would be picked up by a page, and delivered to someone in the hall. Quickly, he hurried back to the front, to stand to the side of the throne; a good place to observe what was going on in the hall.

The Jarl, obviously angry, his face red, was speaking with emphatic, though quiet, bluster to his knights, gathered about the throne, listening nervously, their heads nodding in agreement, almost as vigorously as the Jarl's gestures.

Germani returned to the hall, accompanied by her guardian knights, and before long a page made his way to her to deliver the envelope. She turned it over and over in her hands, curious, puzzled, slowly breaking the wax seal, undid the ribbon, and shook out the contents into her hand, dropping the envelope to the floor, turning the blood stained ring over and over in her hand, her face paled, staggering backward, caught herself, straightened, and looked about the room to see who was watching.

Brian shifted his gaze to the throne, and the knights gathered there, beginning to feel rather pleased with himself; his little adventure, freeing the thralls, having just the affect he'd wished for. Glancing back at Germani, her scorching glare, directed at him, her rage obvious. He suppressed the temptation to laugh, as her knights turned in the direction she was looking. Raising an eye brow, tilting his head to the side, inquisitively, as if to say, "What?" smiled, nodding a bow; he would be dealing with them very soon. The Jarl dismissed his knights, and beckoned Bryan to his side.

"Yes, m'lord?"

"You heard what happened?" He asked Bryan.

"No, m'lord, everyone seems quite upset."

"The new shipment of thralls escaped, stole one of my long ships," He paused, "The guard at the barn, you knew him, captain of the pages, was murdered, as well as the men guarding the ship. We found their bodies floating in the fjord. The thralls could not have done this themselves there had to have been accomplices, the thralls had no weapons. If I find out who did this, I'll have him nailed to the barn, and peal away his flesh piece by piece, I swear by Oden. I can't believe it, those thralls were my means of financing the next group of Vikings, now both are gone. It'll cost a fortune to replace them."

"Yes, m'lord, I'm deeply sorry," lying so convincingly, with no feeling of guilt, just like the Dane. Thor had warned about him about that.

The Jarl continued, "The page captain was a bright young fellow, a shame, I've replaced him with Ivan, who knows my court well, and will keep things in order. The knights know him as well. You'll answer to him."

"Yes, m'lord." A thrill of joy rushing through him, his friend would stay.

"Please remain a while longer this afternoon, I'll be counseling with my knights, arrange to have food and ale served to them, send the petitioners away, tell them to return tomorrow."

"Yes, m'lord." Bryan bowed and stepped away.

He spotted Ivan, among the group of pages, gathered to the rear of the hall, while on his way to the kitchen. "Hello captain."

Ivan grinned, "Can you believe it?"

"At least one good thing has come as the result of our efforts."

"Guess so," Ivan said, "Time will tell."

"This will save you from going to Ireland, Won't it?"

"At least for now," Ivan said, unsure.

"Well, I'm happy for you, and for myself, wouldn't want to lose you to the Vikings," he said, "You'll still be able to help me, watch out for Germani, she likes to seduce page captains, you know."

"Yea, that'd be something, wouldn't it?"

"Get er to kiss you down there, might not be too bad," Bryan grinned.

"That bitch, I don't think so."

"Do me a favor?" Bryan asked.

"What's that?"

"Germani's body guards, their giving me the eye, I think she suspects I had something to do with it."

"Imagine that."

"Yea, imagine…, well I think that she's going to sick them on me. Would you send a page to my room to pick up my uncles sword. The Dane wants me to stay, and I'm afraid I could be caught unprepared."

"Consider it done. Aren't you afraid she'll say something to him?"

"She could, but I think she'd rather he didn't know what she's been up to with the boys. She'll try to take care of it herself, and I don't intend to come out on the wrong side of a fight."

"Ok, I'll have it to you right away."

Bryan ordered the food and drink, hurriedly dismissed the courtesans, set up the meetings with the Jarl. From the discussions, security was going to be much tighter. When Ivan showed up, he had not only Bryan's sword, but a fighting axe from the arena. "Be careful," He told Bryan, "These guys aren't playing games."

Bryan grinned, "Neither am I, my friend, neither am I."

It was well into the afternoon when the Jarl finished his business, and dismissed everyone. Bryan and the afternoon page, cleaned up the hall. He strapped on his sword, put the axe in his belt, picked up his walking stick, and pulled the cape over his shoulders.

Outside, a crowd remained gathered, gossiping, inventing rumors. He made his way through the courtesans, but, as he emerged from the throng, he was greeted by Germani's thugs, dressed in like uniforms, light gray tunics, and trousers with bright metal mail shirts.

"We need to have a word with you, page," the tall knight said.

"I've nothing to say to you." Bryan returned, defiantly.

"We think you do," the shorter one said, swaggering about. Bryan instantly disliked him. "We think you were the one killed the page captain in a fit of vengeance."

"I had no quarrel with him."

"You were jealous of the princess, hated him, because the princess preferred him to you."

"Princess is it, that's new. You really think I'd be angry with him because he's had his way with her, when she spreads her legs for any boy she meets," Bryan sneered.

"You impudent cur," the short man growled, through clenched teeth, as he pulled his sword from its sheath. A few years older than Bryan, and filled with conceit, he lunged toward Bryan, his sword drawn back.

Bryan brought his pole up quickly, its' end swinging close to the knight's head, flinching his head back, the sword struck out wildly. Bryan's training, proving its worth, he spun in the opposite direction, stricking the other side of the man's head, the hard metal pommel hit with a crack, snapping his head backward; he staggered, stunned stupid, and collapsed to the ground.

A rattle, behind him, a sword being drawn from its sheath, the tall knight stepped from the throng, and advanced, menacingly. Bryan threw away his stick and cape, and drew his own sword. The blows came hard and swift, Bryan parried, first one, then two blows, hard, powerful, but the man's untrained actions were awkward, clumsy, and inaccurate. Bryan backed away, making the man reach with his sword, missing, short, by a large margin; Bryan lunged, his blade coming down on the knight's fully extended arm, slicing through his wrist, like butter. Sword and severed hand flying through the air, in opposite directions, blood gushing from the stump, making him howl in agony, Bryan charged, brandishing his sword, the knight turned, and fled like a dog. The crowd roared with laughter.

While this was happening, the shorter man, recovering from Bryan's initial blow, advanced on him, more experienced, anger now mixed with his conceit, making him formidable. Dueling, Bryan, not wanting to dull the edge of his blade on the hard mail, repeatedly slapping him across the chest, with the flat of his blade, knowing its' sting would smart, aggravating, and humiliating the squat knight. A man with a hot temper was bound to make mistakes.

Shorter, but heavier, his blows were jarring, knocking Bryan backward, stinging his hands, pushing him back. Bryan striking back, the man easily parried his blows away. Then, somehow, Bryan wasn't sure, happening so fast, the little knight, got around behind him, and brought the pommel of his sword down hard onto Bryan's back, between his shoulder blades. He gasped, and fell to one knee, the air knocked from him. Out of the corner of his eye Bryan saw the blade coming, the little bastard was going to take his head off, he rolled to the side, heard the whistle of the blade, as it grazed his ear, the pain small, sharp, a warm trickle of blood ran down the side of his face. He scrambled away, getting back to his feet, and bringing his sword up, guarding against another attack, adrenalin coursing through his veins, the cords of his muscles warm with it.

For just a tiny moment, the knight let his guard down, Bryan sensing it, pounced, drove the point of his sword, with all his might, into the man's chest, penetrating hardly at all, separating a few links of mail, it stopped dead. The impact pushed the man back, off balance. Bryan, unrelenting, continued to thrust, his blade now stuck in the mail. He pressed upward, like a lever, forcing the man to topple, pulling back on his sword as the man fell; Bryan loosened it from the grip of the mail. The man hit the ground hard; Bryan stepped on his chest, and brought the tip of his sword to the man's Adam's apple, a trickle of red ooze ran down the side of his neck.

"Now," Bryan shouted, "Maybe the next time you accuse a man of killing someone on a whim, and the word of a trollop, you'll think twice about what you are saying, 'cus if you ever do it to me again, you'll not live to tell about it, get out of here, if I ever see you again, you'll regret it." He slipped the tip of his sword across the man's neck, opening a deep scratch, from his Adam's apple to his ear, flicked the man's sword away with his own, then took his weight from the man's chest, and kicked him in the ribs. The disgraced knight slunk away into the surrounding crowd, and like the other knight, was mocked with laughter.

Bryan sheathed his own sword, and swooped down to pick up the knight's. From behind the crowd, he heard someone applauding, loudly, making their way through the throng. Bryan turned to see the Dane emerge.

"Well done son," He said loudly, everyone could hear, "I'm proud of you, son. Tomorrow I want to talk to you about a little thing I have planned. I think there is a place in it for you. Well done." He slapped Bryan on the back.

Ivan brought up Bryan's cape and walking stick. The Jarl took the cape, and put it over Bryan's shoulders. Bryan handed the defeated knight's sword to the Jarl, who in turn handed it to Ivan.

"You should have a weapon of your own," he told Ivan, then turned to Bryan, bowed his head slightly, "Tomorrow." He turned away and returned to the Great Hall.

"Buy you dinner," Bryan told Ivan.

They ate fresh steamed cod and carrots with cardamom flavored flatbread topped off with tankards of strong ale, "You handled that situation like an experienced courtesan. The Jarl was impressed."

"You really think he was?"

"You'll find out for sure tomorrow, but I do," Ivan said. "If you had been beaten, their accusations would have carried more weight, but you sized them up, challenged them, and beat them, soundly, discrediting them and Germani with them; the kind of play the Jarl likes. You watch, tomorrow you'll get some kind of choice assignment."

"And we'll find some way to turn it to our advantage," Bryan said "I'm really happy that you got the captain's job, so you can stay here with me, maybe you'll get a chance to go visit your folks."

"We'll see."

"I was a little surprised, though that the Jarl chose you. I thought you said he wasn't happy with you?"

"He wasn't, but I think it was Vandel's influence that got me chosen, least that's what I hear."

"Interesting," Bryan said, "Didn't know he had that much influence, or interest in what goes on in court."

"Don't you know? Vandel is the Jarl's favorite, clever, quiet, sly, and he inconspicuously helps moderate some of the Jarl's rash decisions, but then you can never tell with court politics. Things can happen that are unexpected sometimes."

"Something the Dane said worries me a little," Bryan said. "He told me that the 'knights know you well,' His exact words. What does that sound like?"

"Who exactly was he talking about?"

"Didn't say. I was hoping you knew."

"No idea, curious, might be good, could be bad."

"Let me know."

The short summer of the north beginning to fade; next morning braking windy, rainy, and cool.

Chapter 13

Bryan was glad to have his cape to wrap around him as he made his way to the Great Hall. The huge drafty building, like all long houses, subject to a damp chill, penetrating every crevice; a stone hearth, would soon be built near its center, a fire would burn there, until spring, making the interior hazy with smoke, slow to rise, escaping through an inadequate opening in the roof, insufficient to warm the huge cavity of the hall, warming only those near it, others would wear heavy robes and furs, and huddle in groups.

For now, Bryan pulled his cape close over his shoulders, stomped his feet, and rubbed his hands as he busied himself with chores. At least the thick walls and heavy thatched roof insulated them from the damp wind howling outside, an artificial comfort.

The Jarl arrived with a flurry of activity, and commenced hearing his petitioners immediately, their number this day doubled, after being dismissed yesterday. They would plead their case, and he would pass judgment; the more profit offered, the more favorable the judgment, slanted by political intrigue. The vile politics, going on endlessly made Bryan edgy. Hours later with all of the petitioners heard, Bryan and Vandal were called to the throne.

"I've been cajoling the village of Sogndal across Esefjorden, and east on Sognefjorden to join us for some time now, but they remain stubbornly loyal to King Innver. They need to be taught a lesson. I want you two to put together a force to go over there and put things right." He turned to his knight, "Vandel, pick one of your knights, one who can gather a large enough number of men to take the village." He turned to Bryan, "I want you to go along as the knight's lieutenant, a chance for you to use what you've learned, experience how things are done. If we can extend our holdings in that direction we can take control of the fjord to the east, and increase our influence greatly. It is an important action, and Bryan, if the village is taken, the land, from Esefjorden to Sognadal will be yours to hold."

Bryan's mind raced, an opportunity, to possibly, somehow humiliate one of the Jarl's knights, set the Dane back, power and possessions inconsequential, they weren't part of his scheme.

"With your permission, m'lord," he said, bursting with enthusiasm, "I would like to try, one more time, to persuade the village to capitulate. If my effort fails I'll be more than willing to join your knight's forces."

"Well," The Jarl, taken back, "Don't we have a budding politician here? By all means, try what you will, but I can tell you, you won't succeed. Go ahead anyway, see what you can do. If you succeed, the land will become yours to rule over, same as if defeated by force." He turned back to Vandel, "Proceed with your task. Even if our young page succeeds, we will need a force to protect and expand our northern border. The time has come to begin expanding our military power."

"Sire," Vandel bowed, and backed away.

"Bryan, I'll have someone talk to you who has had contact with the village, someone who will be able to give you some pointers."

"Yes, m'lord. Might I pick someone, to travel with, for my protection?"

"From what I've seen, you'll not need protecting," he chuckled. "Let me guess, you want Ivan to go along with you?"

Bryan was amazed the Jarl knew of their friendship, apparently more perceptive of court activities than Bryan had given him credit for, probably knew of Bryan's brief affair with Germani, her liaison with the page captain, and her accusations, but, Bryan had vindicating himself, defeating Germani's knights.

Court had lasted well into the afternoon, and now that it was over Bryan left the hall and went to the bath, he was cold, and wanted to warm himself.

While washing him, the attendant whispered, "Wait in the bath until they leave," he tilted his head in the direction of the four men lingering in the tub, "I have some information for you."

The bathers recognizing him from the fight the evening before, showered him with questions; where was he from, how had he learned to fight like that, obviously not in court the day the Jarl introduced him. Bryan was pleasant to them, but preferred to keep to himself; the less others knew about him the better, he thought.

Besides, his thoughts were preoccupied with developing his plans.

When several more men joined in the tub, he got out. Ole dried him, directed him to the side, away from the tub, and as he dressed him, he whispered to Bryan.

"The Jarl is planning a raid on a village east of here, and you can guess the outcome will not be good for the village."

"He's already asked me to take part in the raid."

"Oh dear!

After Bryan told him briefly what he'd planned so far, Ole said, "Well…, I know someone who might be able to help."

"You do?"

"A trader, travels villages, selling wares, knows those people. When he's in town, you'll find him, most times, at the inn on the docks. Names Hager, little short guy, talks a lot, be there tonight."

Bryan headed to the inn, if the trader would help, was of the same mind, he might be of use. Darkness approached as he entered the Inn, the place, filled with dock hands, there for a strong drink before heading home, or for someone to warm their bed for the evening, it was crowded and noisy.

Not seeing anyone matching Hager's description, he took a seat, back where it was dark and private, to the rear of the pub, and offering a good view of anyone coming in or going out.

When the innkeeper brought him a brew, he asked if he knew Hager.

"Believe I know who you mean, haven't seen em for a while though."

"If he comes in, send him my way?" Bryan asked.

The innkeeper nodded and went away.

He sipped at the rich brew, and watched. In one corner, four or five men were engaging in a game of chance, toward the front a group of men, gathered around a story teller, spinning a tale with great enthusiasm, his audience approving loudly, and to the side, a couple of young men, speaking to two, rough and dirty, less than appealing, working girls. The boys, not much to look at either, likely little to offer other than money.

He didn't notice the little man, until he slipped into the chair next to him.

"You'd be Bryan?" The little man said, his voice like a squeaky hinge.

"That's me."

"Heard ye'r lookin' fer me."

"Might be, who're you."

"Hager – man of trade," he introduced himself. He was dressed in a brownish, thread worn, wool tunic. Clean, but well-traveled.

"The innkeeper send you over?"

"Inkeeper? Naw!"The man shook his head.

"What makes you think I'm looking for you?"

"A man in my line of work has to know things. I sell things, what people want, ta who wants it. I'd be a poor man if I didn't know things now wouldn't I," He said with a sly smile, a few teeth missing.

"If that's true you must know already what I need."

"Heard your looking fer information about Sogndal."

"T'is a matter of fact, one who knows the people there, is trusted by them, someone interested in their well-being, who can take me there and introduce me."

"I know 'em – been there," evasive, skeptical, "Wha'd the likes a you be interested in them?" The man asked, looking at the uniform, with squinting eyes.

"Cause the Jarl is sending an army to visit them, and intends to make an example of them, they'll lose their freedom, if not their lives."

"Why'd e send an army there?"

"He's asked them for their loyalty, they are reluctant."

"Can you imagine that?" The trader exclaimed.

"He's tired of asking, plans to answer with an armed solution."

"An 'oud you know that?"

"The Jarl asked me to help lead the army."

The man fell silent. Bryan excused himself, and went to get another ale for himself, and one for the trader. When he returned, the little man took a long quaff.

Still looking at him through squinting, suspicious eyes, "Why would someone in your position want to turn against the

Jarl? How do I know you're not just scouting out the village so's you can take your army in there?"

Bryan took a deep breath, looked around to be sure no one was listening. The young men were leaving, their girls in tow, the storyteller continuing to spin his tail. "The Jarl killed my uncle, I want vengeance." He told the trader his story. "Now, if you wish to help me, I'd be most grateful, if you have a problem say so, right now, nothing will be said." Bryan made his voice harsh and firm.

The trader took another swing of ale, not naive, with no illusions about nothing being said; if he refused, sure he'd be a dead man shortly after leaving the inn. At least that was what he believed. It was of no consequence, anyway, his sentiments lay with Bryan, "I'm your man then, I knows what he'd do ta those poor folk, thems my good friends, had to be sure of you, ya know. Not many close ta the Jarl are credible. But, you mussn't let anyone know of my part in this."

"Nor must they know of mine," Bryan replied.

"Then we've not got a problem, do we?" the trader said.

"What I want is for for you to take me there, introduce me to the leader of the clan, I told the Jarl I'd try to negotiate with them, one last time, he agreed. When do you think we can leave?"

"A few days, d'wana leave in too much of a hurry, rouse any suspicions."

"When you're ready, let Ole know, he's our go between, probably already your source of information," Bryan chided, with a grin; his humor waisted on the old man who ignored him.

They shook hands, Hager left the inn, Bryan a short while later, and went to the arena to practice, enjoying the exercise; he was able to his best thinking while sparing.

Eight days passed before Ole informed him the trader was ready. His position as Jarl's attendant, taken over by another page, he explored the shores north of Balestrand, hiked up into the hills, one day joining fishermen on a day's outing, and continued his mentoring with Vandel.

On the appointed day, he and Ivan met the trader, near the ferry launch, north of Balastrand where the waters of Sognfjorden, Esefjorden, and Fjaerlandfjord converged. Their crossing, to be made on a knarr; a merchant ship, special made to ferry trade to the other side. The trader, his two wheeled cart, already loaded, and the boatman, paid.

Hagar eyed Ivan with suspicion.

"Bryan introduced him, my accomplice," Bryan told him, "He is of like mind as we, and will be going along to help if there is trouble, two's always better than one," he joked.

Hager, hurmmphed, reluctantly satisfied with the explanation, motioned for the two to board. There were places for six oarsmen. Four men were at the oars, Bryan and Ivan took up the other two.

The knarr, short compared to its ocean going cousins, wide at the beam, like most merchant ships, in order to carry cargo. It didn't need to be fast, like the light, narrow, long ships used for war, and had a much deeper draft for stability.

A cool fog hung heavy over the fjord, chilling at first, but the work of oaring, even across the deceptively smooth surface of the water, quickly worked the chill from their limbs. Beneath that smooth surface, the deep, cold, waters of three fjords converged; causing violent turbulence where they met, their currents, hidden beneath the smooth surface, frequently caught the boat, spinning it off course. They pressed on, Bryan, reminded of stories, told by his uncles, of places in the fjord that never was a rope long enough to set anchor on the bottom. Anywhere on the fjord, water became bottomless, five feet from the shore, fostering stories of mystery, or monsters in the deep; Thor it was said, once battled one of them. The deep and frigid water not a bother to brave Norsemen, a good part of their lives spent sailing it, or fishing it, at peace with it, as long as they stayed on its surface.

They approached the eastern shore, and the boatman guided them into the dock. With great effort, they hoisted the cart onto solid ground, and the sturdy little Norse pony, Odie, walked the plank like a pro, obviously having done this, many times.

The trader harnessed him to the cart, Bryan and Ivan climbed into the back, Hager in the front, slapped the reins, and they were off. The road, but a rough path, full of ruts and rocks, heaving the little cart, to and fro, better than walking perhaps, Bryan had his doubts.

Monotony quickly setting in, Bryan's thoughts wandered; by the time this whole Sogndal affair was done, it would be time for the harvest feast. Afraid that it would be another bloody and deadly celebration, he had asked Ivan if anyone would be sacrificed, and Ivan assured him, only goats and an ox would be slaughtered. Soon after the harvest feast, Alfablot feast would be held in honor of the Elves of Vanir, or Elves of the Gods, one of Bryan's favorite celebrations, after which winter would soon be upon them.

As the day advanced, the clouds lifted, the sun burning away the mists over the fjord, reveling spectacular scenery; streams tumbling from towering cliffs, loosing clouds of mist, to drift gently away, in breezest scouring the cliff walls, grasses on sides of the path, now turned yellow, red, and orange, by the season, leaves on bushes and trees glowing yellow and red, and on the high mountains, a dusting of silvery white, insulated the deep blue sky, from the gray tundra below, the air crisp, cool, and clean to the nose.

Bryan shifted in his seat as the cart rocked to and fro, his buttocks becoming tender, walking would be difficult, by day's end. "How far to Leikanger," the first village on their journey, he called up to the trader.

"It's a ways," Hager said, turning his head to them, "We'll arrive there a while before dark, in time for evening meal."

"I don't know how much of...," he paused for a bump, "this I can take."

"Yer arse given ya fits?" The trader chuckled.

"It will be soon enough," Bryan answered. He moved to the front of the cart, and sat atop his pack. Ivan, rocking from side to side, smiled knowingly.

The suns light across the fjord, shattered into millions of shards of shimmering white light, the tiny, sparkling, flashes endless, mesmerizing, lulling him into a trance, his spell broken when he caught a glimpse of Ivan's cheeks, wet with tears, quieter than usual all morning, something was bothering his friend.

Bryan reached across, slapped him on the knee, "You ok?"

Ivan looked over at him, flashed an embarrassed smile, nodding yes, "It's so beautiful, reminds me of home," and turned back to look out over the water, "Sometimes it gets the better of me."

"Have heart my friend, soon you'll be free."

Ivan looked back at him, doubtful, searching Bryan's face for answers, "What do you mean when you say things like that?"

Bryan shook his head, "You'll know when the time's right, cheer up, we're on an adventure, have fun."

Ivan looked into his eyes, again trying to read his thoughts, then returned his gaze to the water, "You scare me sometimes," and fell back into the rhythm of the cart.

The trader halted, midday, on a grassy clearing, close to the Sognfjorden shore, climbed down, to eat some cheese, and have cup of wine. Ivan, still sullen, wandered down to the banks of fjord, and Bryan, never one to eat at midday, hiked up through the forest; the trees there, having never been harvested, extremely tall, and the ground beneath their massive trunks, thick and spongy with rotted needles. The quiet of the forest, away from the intrigues of the Dane, bringing him tranquility, a peace he'd not known in a while, where his thoughts could run free and wild, like back on the farm.

Still not sure he could pull this off; Up till now his adventures had been straight forward, simple, murder an easy answer, but, this was more complicated, requiring cooperation from the villagers, people he didn't know, and more than a little luck with Vendel's general, a knight he'd never met. The knights, on average, not overly smart, good fighters, leaders versed in tactics, might he be open to suggestion, but from a young farm boy. He fingered the miniature hammer, about his neck, wishing Thor would come to him, he had so many questions.

Halting at a high rock wall, he looked back out over the treetops, up and down the shoreline, Leikanger too far to be seen. There were clouds building to the west, blown in from the ocean, a good distance away. He headed back down to the clearing where Ivan and the trader were waiting.

Off again, the little horse trotting along, the cart bumping up and down, back and forth, endlessly jarring their teeth, bruising their back sides, Bryan vowed to himself, never to complain about riding a horse, no matter how sore he got, a far better ride.

Afternoon wore on, the clouds he'd seen earlier, slowly obliterated the sun, blanketing the sky with gray, and the air becoming cool. Rain could be seen falling west of them. The trader hurried his little horse along, but not fast enough; a light drizzle began to fall before they reached the village.

Liekanger was small; several longhouses, set in a row alongside the road. Hager turned back, "There's a family up ahead where I usually stay, has a room they hire out fer a small fee. They'll be glad ta put us up." He pulled the cart up to one of the longhouses, got off and went in.

"I sure hope this guy knows what he's talking about," Ivan said, half a grin on his face, pulling his wet blanket over his head, doing his best not to show his shivering hands and blue lips, his earlier gloominess, gone for the moment.

"You feelin' better?" Bryan asked.

"Yea, the weather's not so nice; takes my mind off of it."

"I'm going to need you the next couple of days. You need to pull it together." Bryan asked.

Ivan grinned sheepishly from beneath the blanket. "Had a few moments there, but I'm your man."

The trader immerged, "Ok, all set. Go on in and wait for me by the fire. I'll be there shortly."

They dragged their wet packs off the cart, and the trader led the horse and cart away. Inside, a warm fire burned in the hearth, the cavernous great room was warm and smoky, beckoning to them, come sit for a while, so much like his family home.

A rosy cheeked, healthy looking, older woman stood up from behind the hearth where she had been sitting tending a stew.

"Good evening," Bryan greeted, "How are you?"

"I am well, sire," she curtsied, "Thank you for honoring us with your presence, welcome to our humble home," she curtsied again, turned to Ivan, "And you sire, welcome." Again she curtsied and hurried away.

Bryan looked at Ivan, his eyes wide, a smirk on his face, they broke into laughter. "I wonder what Hagar told her about us. Obviously, she thinks us important or something."

"I hope we're not in any danger by it," Ivan said, "I doubt that the Dane's men are popular around here."

"Respected at least, hopefully, I really wish Hager wouldn't do that. We'll have to talk to him," Bryan said.

"Right this way men," Hagar's voice screeched from behind as he marched past into a side room. Picking up their sacks, they followed through several side rooms, past groups of people, going about their business; an occasional glance, the only attention they received.

The last room in that wing of the longhouse, a storage room, beyond a substantial gate lay stables, smelling of animals, but heat from the livestock made the room warm. Sacks of grain piled atop logs, racks of smoked fish hung from the ceiling, tightly bound wool filled one corner, and bins of various root vegetables lined one wall. Along the wall opposite the bins, an earthen ledge sleeping area, covered with hay, and a dry woolen blanket for each of them.

They hung their packs on wooden posts, and changed into dry clothes. The trader produced a length of rope, and strung it between two posts to hang their clothing and blankets to dry.

"Hagar, I need a word with you," Bryan said.

"Yes?"

"What exactly did you tell that lady about us? She treated us like royalty. If you represent us to these people as important members of the Jarls court we'll never get anywhere with them, not to mention possibly jeopardize our lives."

The trader, offended, his jaw muscles clenched, but remaining calm, "You chose me cuz you needed someone who knew the people."

"Yes."

"And you wanted me ta use my bilities ta help ya get dis thing done?"

"Yes."

"Then ya're gonna half ta trus me ta do what I know best. Or I can leave right now."

Bryan's face flushed with heat, he'd crossed a boundry he shouldn't have. "Sorry Hager, we need to trust each other, from now on you'll have mine."

The trader nodded, and they returned to the great room where the rosy cheeked woman served them fresh baked flat bread with bowls of boiled oxen stew with turnips; thick, and succulent, filling their bellies.

They went to sleep, that night, to the sound of wind, driving rain against the walls of the longhouse.

Chapter 14

Morning greeted them; bitter cold, wind wiped, freezing fog, swirling into a froth of gray, visibility, but a few arms lengths. Following the narrow, rutted road they climbed steeply to cliffs, high above the fjord, where frigid wind viciously ripped up shear rock faces, stingingly, raw, cutting into their faces. The icy cold mist froze into thick layers of frost on their blankets, wrapped tightly about them, futile against the cold. Hager huddled into a ball on his seat, the little horse, its coat covered thick with frost, followed the icy road, like a circus performer on a precarious tightrope. It was going to be a long, long day.

Colder, the wind becoming ferocious, frozen mist turning to snow, blanketing the road; the little cart careening this way and that, tugging the poor, stumbling horse, as he made his way along the narrow and now slick path.

Bryan, cold, shivering, huddled beside Ivan, their backs against the front wall of the cart, said little, suffering; their lives left to fate.

Finally, Hagar turned to them from his perch on the driver's seat, and shouted over the wind, "We're not goin' a make Sogndel afore night fall - Didn't think we would. There's a cave ahead, stayed there afore, better hole up there till mornin'. Be dark real soon, too dangerous ta travel at night with dis storm."

For Bryan, time meaningless, its perception lost to blinding wind and snow, the day seeming like several, hardly able to move, for the cold in his joints, disoriented, numb, and partially snow blind, he could do nothing but agree.

The cave, little more than a rock face over hanging a dirt floor, piled rocks at each end, put there by someone, perhaps the trader, on an earlier trip, to break the wind, offered a little protection. With great difficulty, they built a fire, to warm their fingers, and boil some dried meat. Bryan and Ivan huddled together under their combined blankets, and Hagar bedded the horse down, huddling next to it, under his blanket.

The savage wind, pounded the rocks, and whipped viciously through the trees, sounding like angry, howling beasts. Bryan hid his head under the blankets, hung on to Ivan, and prayed to Thor for warmth.

Dawn broke, gray, dark, bleak, the storm raging on. Shivering, uncontrollably, their blankets pulled tight about them, it crossed Bryan's mind that they might not survive, but if the trader, old, and weak, could be indifferent to the rigors of the raging storm, so could he. He banished the thought from his mind. They were soon on their way, the pony, covered thick with frost and snow led the way.

When finally arriving at Sogndal, the snow nearly knee deep, and drifting high, they went directly to the longhouse of the clan leader; the dark, smoky, warmth of the great room, welcome respite. Many of the clan chief's family, and clan members were sheltering together there, away from the raging weather, putting Bryan at ease; in his youth, his clan gathered like this, to shelter from storms, when they became unbearable; he was sure Ivan felt the same.

Hager greeted the chieftain, an old friend, of strong and sturdy, heavy build, face weathered, bearded gray, eyes deep pools of black, his once dark hair, braided back away from his face, and his clothing of the finest wool. After exchanging pleasantries, the trader turned to Bryan, "Chief Karl, I would like you to meet my friends, emissaries of the Dane; before you jump to any conclusions, I strongly suggest you listen to what they have to say. This is Bryan Thorson of Hoyanger, and his attendant Ivan."

The chieftain nodded wary recognition, offering a quick, short bow which Bryan returned. "What is it you have come so far, through this retched weather, to say to me, Emissary Bryan?" he said, his voice deep, full of authority, and with an unmistakable undertone of suspicion.

All the eyes in the room upon him, the silence palpable, squirming inwardly, Bryan wanted to turn away, run back out into the storm, but facing this man, necessary to complete his self appointed mission, what he'd come for, he cleared his throat, "I've come to you in most humble respect for your great clan, to offer you a proposal, I think you will find to your liking. But, right now, I and my friends are cold and hungry, my toes and fingers, like coals in you hearth, ablaze with fire, as they thaw. If we might have something to eat, be allowed to sit by your fire for a spell, I'm sure you will find my ideas worth the wait."

The Chieftain nodded. He stepped back, motioned to a woman, Bryan assumed the chief's wife, and she brought up a couple of wooden stools, set them by the hearth. Two young girls, brought bowls of stew, hot, steamy, thick with meat and vegetables. The older girl placed a bowl in Bryan's hands, extremely pleasing to look at, generous smile, slightly parted rosy lips, revealing clean, sturdy, white teeth, cheeks, pink, brown eyes sparkling in the light of the fire; looking deep into his eyes, she smiled, and then quickly retreated back into the shadows. Bryan watched; interest peaked; he'd not seen a woman like that even in the Jarl's court; in his chest, his heart lept with joy.

He consumed the warm, succulent stew, and a small, nutty loaf of flat bread, with a cup of warm mead, filling his belly; revitalized, the sizzling pain, gone from his toes and fingers, the chill in his bones waning, and feeling alive once again, he beckoned the chieftain, "I can talk now, but it would be best if we spoke in private."

The chief agreed, with a nod, motioned for Bryan to follow him. Bryan in turn, nudged Ivan to follow. They were led through a heavy wooden door, into a side room, a small fire burning at its' center, earthen ware lamps hung about the room, burning wale oil, their soft, warm light, a luxury, the clan well off to afford such extravagance.

With the wave of the chief's hand, the people gathered there, scattered away.

"Please have a seat," he motioned to furs on the floor around the fire. They took places across the fire from the chief and his entourage.

The chief introduced them to his son, Thorick, sitting next to his father, elegant, looking the part of a warrior, a few years older than Bryan, physically strong, obviously preparing to assume his father's place. His trousers and tunic elaborately embroidered in colorful thread, his eyes dark, fierce, like his fathers, his long hair unbraided, unlike the other warriors in the clan.

"We humbly thank you for your hospitality," Bryan began, "I know that times have been difficult for you. That the Jarl..., the Dane's knights, have visited you, without doubt threatened you, tried to intimate you into paying tribute, and swearing loyalty to Skjolden. He has told me of this, and further, I can tell you that he has told me of his intentions," he paused, "To send his knights with their armies to take your clan by force."

The chieftain exchanged a nervous glance with his son.

"In the past, when the Dane has done this, the men and old have been put to death, women and children taken, sold as thralls, villages burned, and the clan wiped out."

He had their attention; the chief stared at him, his hand on hilt of his dagger, glaring, angry, the fire dancing in his dark eyes. Bryan had to continue, or neither he nor Ivan would leave the room alive.

"I asked the Jarl for permission to come here, talk to you about capitulation, which I knew full well, to be a waste of time, as you are a justifiably proud man, with love for his clan, who would never betray its' loyalty. I come from such a clan myself. You see the Dane killed my uncle, head of our clan, sent my father Viking, so long ago, I barely remember him."

"My real reason, for my coming, was as a friend, to warn you of the treachery, to work with you, make strategic preparations, help you defend yourselves. I would very much like the Jarls' army defeated, humiliated, when it comes here. We must make plans."

The silence in the room was absolute, the chief motionless, contemplating, tension in the room, palpable, painfully uncomfortable, he pondered a long time.

Finally, nodding, "We shall plan" he said.

Turning to his son, he spoke a few words, his voice low, Bryan could not hear. Thorick got up, left the room, promptly returning with several men, introduced by Chief Karl as clan leaders, his best fighting men.

Through the afternoon and into the evening they worked out a strategy; home grown warriors, in tune with the lands about the village, having long planed a defense, as solid as their tough, hardened, bodies. Bryan was satisfied.

Returning to the great room, evening meal was served, the same stew they'd had earlier, along with a tankard of very strong ale, and while they ate, there was much talk in the room, about what was happening behind the heavy wooden door, prevalent with constrained optimism. Afterward, individuals drifted to their family rooms, Bryan and Ivan found space on the ledge at the back of the great room, among the villagers, for some warm and well needed rest.

He dreamed that night; Thor, sitting at the head of a grand table, holding a banquet, Bryan, the guest of honor. Four servants carried a large roasting pan, elaborately carved in runes, a polished silver lid, to the head of the table. The God gave Bryan his uncles' sword, asked him to carve the meat. Slowly, the servants removed the lid, Bryan looked inside, and rocked back in shock, and revulsion; staring up from a bed of cooked vegetables and fruits, an apple stuffed in his mouth, the Jarls' face stared out at him, with sightless eyes. His head spun with nausea, Thor laughed, a roaring belly laugh, "Take care, young Bryan that you are not the one served up at the Jarl's table." He laughed again.

Bryan woke with a start, nauseous, wet with sweat. The room quiet, except for the noise of sleeping people, Ivan, asleep beside him, breathing quietly, the fire burned down, no longer crackling and popping. Slowly the nausea subsided, and he fell back to sleep.

The sound of others, stirring about, roused him. The fire was again ablaze, and the young, rosy cheeked girl, greeted him, as he rubbed the sleep from his eyes. The same alluring expression on her face, in her hands a bowl of steaming porridge, cooked in milk, and covered in butter.

"Thank you, good morning," Bryan said brightly, then more softly, "My name is Bryan," He smiled.

She returned his smile, "And my name is Helgra," her voice, soft and demure, "Karl's daughter."

"Helgra…, indeed, you are very…, it was sweet of you to bring me…, could you bring me some warm milk to drink," he stammered, feeling foolish, his face immediately flushed with heat.

Her eyes twinkled, and she giggled softly, "Yes, Sire," she curtsied, turned and disappeared.

Was it desire, he'd seen, in those sparkling eyes, or was it self delusion on his part, sweet and young, perhaps a few years younger than he, was she flirting? Perhaps it was the uniform; or some naively imagined, romantic notion, about his position at the Jarl's court, the clan chief's daughter, he couldn't risk endangering his mission, or could he?

Returning with the milk, she said, "My brother was talking about you last night."

"He had good things to say I hope."

"He told me that you are going to help save the clan; very brave."

"Thank you for saying so," perhaps not as brave as you might think, he thought, uncomfortable in her adoration, yet not unwelcomed, her attraction powerful, his body becoming aroused, relieved when Thorick interrupted.

"Sister, I hate to disturb your conversation, but father would like to speak with Master Bryan."

"Of course, we'll talk later," she smiled, and backed away.

"My sister can be very forward at times, my father's favorite, and I'm afraid very spoiled, always gets what she wants," Thorick said as they walked through the door into the room.

"I can see that," Bryan agreed; Thorick was very perceptive.

The Chieftain had a map, drawn on the inside of a sheepskin, showing the points of their plan, and the landmarks, important to Bryan to carry out his role. Everything seemed in order, a plan, complex, with opportunity for things to go wrong, but these were experienced warriors, and it was not a time for second thoughts, he would have to trust their ability.

The chief wanted to speak with his warriors, and Bryan excused himself. Ivan not to be found, he decided to go outside, to check on the weather.

Cold, crisp, frigid air, hit his face, with its icy tongue. The wind no longer raged, light snow drifting from the sky; the soft sound, nearly imperceptible, of snowflakes landing atop the already fallen snow, a quiet sizzle. Across from the longhouse, a shed, someplace to go, he wandered across to it. Open in the front, in a stall just inside, a horse, large, light beige, its withers as high as his head, much larger that the small, sturdy Norwegian ponies. This was not a work horse, but a fine riding animal, from some far off land. The handsome beast came to him, nuzzled his hand, its nose soft as a baby's skin.

"Isn't she beautiful?"

Bryan jumped. He turned to see Helgra. How did she know I was here?

"You scared me, thought I was alone."

She giggled, didn't answer, and came to his side, ran her hand over the horses face, down over its neck, then took Bryan's hand in hers, silently led him back into the interior of the shed, around behind a wall, turned him around, his back to the wall, pushed him up against it, and kissed him hard on the lips. Her lips were full and her mouth warm, her tongue explored inside his.

He felt his insides explode, hot in spite of the cold, his hand when to her breasts, messaged without even thinking, feeling firm nipples through her dress.

His mind overwhelmed in a flood of confused thoughts, wanting her, his desire overwhelming, if they were found out, everything could be undone, what should, what could he do?

Helgra took his wrist; put his hand down between her legs, where her dress was pulled up. Feeling the smooth, soft, warm velvet there, by the god Thor, he wanted her, so soft and silky, and wet, she moaned lightly.

Fumbling about the waist of his trousers, she loosened the fastenings, and plunged her hand inside. Cold, but nimble fingers played with his scrotum then grasped his manhood. It felt wonderful; making her stop no longer an option. His finger slid inside her, and she moaned again, long, deep, satisfied.

She drew her hand from his trousers, grasped them at the sides, pulled them down, and pulled him to her, they kissed, roughly.

Bryan gasped for breath; things were happening so fast, his head spinning, passion consuming him, out of control, he turned them around, pushed her against the wall, took hold of himself, and pushed into her, penetrating deep, until his body was against hers. Arching against him, she pulled him to her, her finger tips digging into his buttocks.

For a moment he held her, so warm, soft, smooth, and moist inside; he began thrusting, their eyes locked, never was anything ever this good, never this passionate; he reveled in the pleasure, Bryan never imagining he could feel so good.

Responding to his every thrust, gasping for breath - a silvery streak of saliva, running from the corner of her mouth, her moaning loud, spurred him on. Both like wild, animals; their passion, frenzied, and Bryan pushing himself, until he felt he could go no longer, yet pressing on, his breathing wild, ragged; then not able to hold it any longer, with a long low urgent groan, filled her with his seed. Helgra's body spasmed in response, she cried out, louder. They held each other, tightly, contractions racking their bodies.

Then there was silence - except the whisper of light breeze through the cracks in the shed, and their heavy breathing, ecstasy, pumping through his veins, trembling, basking in their pleasure.

After long moments, he withdrew from her, and with shaky hands pulled his trousers up, smoothed her hair, and straightened her dress.

"Oh Helgra ...," her soft smile, innocent, beautiful, "You caught me off guard, so unexpected, and so, he stammered, I want to say I love you, you're so beautiful, but I hardly know you, I..."

"Shhhh," she put her finger to her lips. "This was my humble way of thanking you for helping our people."

"I don't deserve..., not this."

"Yes you do, you've come all this way, and offered us so much."

"But, I haven't..."

"You will, and when you do I'll be there for you again, ready to please, to give you pleasure."

"Helgra..., we muss'nt ..., muss'nt tell anyone about..."

"No, No one. This is our special secret, our little moment," smiling again, sweet, innocent, "You're so sweet, and handsome, and brave." She stopped, "I must go before I am missed," kissing him again, turned away and headed toward the long house.

Bryan watched after her, hardly believing what just happened, still shaky, deeply fulfilled, peaceful.

Waiting a while, before returning to the longhouse, and the warm fire, where Helgra brought him a mug of ale, smiling knowingly, aloof.

Ivan came over and sat beside him.

152

"What have you been up to? I was looking for you earlier," Bryan asked.

"Oh, I've found something to occupy my time," he said sheepishly. A young girl came up to him.

"Do you want something to drink?" She beamed.

"I'd like that," Ivan answered.

The two obviously knew each other; and the look on Ivan's face, a cross between a smile and ..., Bryan wasn't sure, Ivan was acting odd.

Thorick came by and told Bryan that the chieftain wanted to see him again.

After he walked away Ivan asked, "How's that going."

"We're almost done," he answered. "Want to come along."

"Na, I think I'll just set here," Ivan's thoughts were somewhere else.

Chief Karl sat cross legged next to the fire, "Our plans are complete, Bryan, go back to the Dane, and carry on as you promised."

"Very good," Bryan wished he had as much confidence as the chief, "Remember, the Jarl's men are well trained, skilled with their weapons, they'll be formidable."

"They've not met the likes of us," the chief said, "Our warriors are able to take on any Viking."

I hope so, Bryan thought.

Mugs of strong bjorr were served, followed by toasts, to success, and to the gods.

A feast was had that evening, Bryan thought it premature, but a sheep had been killed, and roasted over the fire. Roast mutton, plentiful and tasty, washed down by more strong drink. Sometime during the evening, Bryan noticed

153

Ivan absent, again, but distracted by Helga, soon forgot about it.

Morning dawned, time to begin their long journey back to Balestrand. The storm spent, leaving its blanket of snow, to Bryan's knees, would make travel difficult and slow, two days easily to Leikanger.

Bryan rode up front with Hager, at first, as they plowed through the snow, relying on the pony to find their way.

"So, you worked things out with the clan?" Hager asked.

"I think we did, seemed to understand each other, they're determined to defend their village."

"I know they were worried bout their future, things might not turn out well, but at least you've given em hope, sometimes hope's all ya need. T'are grateful to you fer that, I sure you."

"We'll see if they are still grateful when this is all done with." Bryan said. "We aren't going to make it to Leikanger today through this mess, are we? Is there any place besides the cave for shelter tonight?"

The trader was quiet for a while, then said, "There's a ol' cabin, a shack really, pretty dilapidated, if we get there for dark, we can clean out da snow, and shore it up with pine boughs."

"Ok, let's try that," Bryan said, slapped the old man on the back, got up, and climbed into the back of the cart with Ivan, still a little distant.

Bryan watched.

After awhile, unable to contain himself, Bryan shook his head, "A few days ago you were so down, I thought you might do yourself in. Now, you're…, I don't know, it's like you're…, I don't know." His voice dwindled off, "Happy. I guess?"

Ivan grinned, and gave a short little laugh.

"What?" Bryan asked emphatically.

"Nothing," Ivan shrugged his shoulders, and shook his head, nonchalantly.

They stared at one another, a suspicious smirk on Ivan's face.

Then Bryan asked, "Who was that young girl at the longhouse last night?" He watched, Ivan's face turned red, giving a broad smile, he giggled again, like a little boy.

"Her name is Sifa."

"And?"

"And she's the chief's youngest daughter."

Bryan looked at Ivan in disbelief.

"Isn't she sweet?" Ivan said dreamily.

"She is, and she's, well, young, very young."

"Yea, well, I think I'm in love with her."

"She's a baby, how can you be...," then Bryan remembered Ivan's absences, "no..., Ivan you didn't?"

"Didn't what?"

"Take advantage of her."

"No."

"Ok." Bryan said, relieved.

But there was more, "She took advantage of me..., quite a few times."

"Ivan, she's so innocent."

"Not any more she's not," Ivan shot back, the smile on his face broad and irrepressible. We just couldn't stop." Then he added, "By the way who was that rosy cheeked, sweet thing, all over you?"

"She's the chieftain's older daughter."

"Oooh?"

"And she's definitely not a baby."

Ivan knew exactly what Bryan meant, their gazes locked, Ivan began to laugh, Bryan, unable to control himself either, broke into laughter.

"You devil you," Ivan said, barely able to get the words out, for laughter.

"Oh, and look at you, Loki of the north," Bryan shot back.

They laughed, and exchanged teasing punches.

Ivan asked, "Are you coming back for her?"

"No," Bryan said, thoughtfully, "It was, just a momentary thing, very passionate, practically raped me, beautiful and sweet, I like her, a lot, wouldn't mind seeing her again, but I don't have any deep feelings for her." He wondered if maybe he was still smarting from the Germani thing.

"I think I'm in love," Ivan said, sure of himself, then denying, "Not sure, never been before."

They slogged along, through the snow, a long tedious day, nearly dark when they reached the cabin, if it could be called that, much worse than Bryan had imagined, full of snow, the roof largely missing. They cleared the inside, and tried to cut a few branches to replace the missing part of the roof, but it became dark, much too soon. Hager built a small fire, on the dirt floor, in the middle, which gave off no heat what so ever. Huddling together under their blankets they made it through the night. Thank the gods, there was no wind.

With great effort, the little pony made it on to Leikanger, where they stayed at the longhouse again, then on to the fjord crossing. When they arrived, the ferry boat was not there, and they had to wait overnight, till it came to pick them up.

Back in Balistrand, Bryan paid the trader handsomely, informing him that it was he, Hager, who, when the time came,

156

was to return to Sogndel, to warn Chief Karl, of the army's approch, and to be ready to leave on a moments notice. "I have no idea when that is going to happen," Bryan said.

"Tell me young Bryan," The Jarl's voice boomed, "What news have you for me from Sogndel?"

Chapter 15

"M'lord, the people's resistance is intractable. They do not bargain in earnest, never giving in to reason, agreeing to one thing, reneging as soon as they agree to another. I am sorry, m'lord, you were right; I was unable to change their minds.

"As I thought," his voice much softer, "Vandel has selected a leader for our little military visit. Get with him; lend him what knowledge you acquired from your journey. You will leave as soon as the snow is gone, and the ground dry enough for travel." He turned to Vandel, "Instruct your general to call his army, we'll show these insolent barbarians a thing or two. "You're dismissed."

"Oh, and Ivan."

"Yes, m'lord."

"Please, please return to your position. Your pages are out of control"

"Yes, m'lord, right away m'lord."

As they walked toward the rear of the hall, Vandel put his arm around Bryan's shoulders. "Your leader will be Lord Ansgar, not a bright man, but earnest, and a good fighter, with a small, well disciplined army. What plan of attack do suggest?"

"Storm the village, m'lord, like we would do any other, kill those who resist, when the rest see their best fighters defeated, they'll stand down and capitulate. They are farmers and fishermen, not prepared to resist, there should be no problems."

"There are always problems, son, those we anticipate, and make preparations for, and those things we cannot anticipate, and must respond to, as we can, when the moment arises," Vandel said, always teaching, "Experience, training, cohesion, give us an edge. You can learn a great deal from Lord Ansgar. He's seen a lot of battle."

Bryan's mentoring by Vandel, was fatherly, and Bryan felt him a friend, though the knight was unconditionally loyal to the Dane. "M'lord," he asked, "You are privileged to information I am not. I was wondering, have you heard anything of my father?"

Vandel paused, "Last we heard, he was in the Ire (Ireland), but I heard talk of trouble, a disagreement with one of the leaders. That's been some time ago, I've not heard anything since. I'm sorry son, that's all I know."

"Thank you, m'lord."

Lord Ansgar met Vandel and Bryan at the arena the next morning; a very large man, broad across the shoulders, and thick, strong muscular arms and legs, wearing iron mail, with doubled leather scale, fastened over its surface, and heavy leather protection on his arms and legs. At his side, a great decorated sword, and in his belt a broad axe. The man was a Jaugernaught.

Vandel said he wasn't smart, but by his speech, and his choice of words, Bryan knew he'd been schooled, and although the Jarl's man, Bryan took a liking to him right away, it would be regrettable to deceive him.

Taking no account how Bryan looked or spoke, direct and to the point, the knight wanted to spar with him, test him in combat; how well a man fought, was how this man judged others.

Bryan knew from his instruction, the size of your opponent was inconsequential, but this man was awfully big, well trained, and daunting. Thiorek had said, "He may be stronger, but you are faster and light footed, he is experienced, but you have brains. He feels pain like you do, bleeds like you do, and has emotions like you do." Bryan reassured himself, he could hold his own.

They selected appropriate dueling sticks, and squared off. The big man hunched into fighting position, and they began with a series of strikes and parries. Light on his feet, Bryan made the big man come after him, tiring him, allowing Bryan to make lightening fast attacks, delivering frequent blows to the knight's ankles and shins. But, Ansgar was fast enough, and delivered several stunningly powerful blows to Bryan's ribs. Pushed to his limits, Bryan fought on, his stamina challenged. The pleasure of sparing with such a skilled opponent drove him. Finally, the knight, relented, and stood tall, "Enough, are you as skilled with an axe?"

"Axe, spear, sword, makes no difference," Bryan bragged.

"He'll do," Ansgar told Vandel.

They took Bryan to the Knights Hall, a gathering place, for wealthy and powerful knights, for some nourishment, and to make plans. Porridge, rye flat bread, boiled eggs, butter, cheese, dried smoked salmon, soaked in ale and steamed, was the fair. Hungry from the morning exercise, Byran ate hardily, sipping judiciously at the strong brown ale they served up, by far the best he ever tasted, not wanting to lubricate his thoughts too much, and trip himself up in front of the knights.

Vandel spoke first, "Our young page just returned from Sogndal, he can tell us about the village.

"Oh?" Ansgar was skeptical.

Bryan described the road on the way to Sogndal, in detail; the climb onto the mountain side approaching the village, the narrow trial that ascends into the mountains when returning from Sogndal, that could be used to trap the fleeing villagers, reiterating that the village was made up of farmers and fishermen, not warriors, that should be no match for Ansgar's army.

Ansgar's plan, delivered without hesitation: "Any resistance will be put to the sword along with the old and sick. Young men and women bring good prices, they'll be captured and enslaved, we'll make a handsome profit." His casual, cold, calculated, manor sent a chill down Bryan's spine.

Regaining his composure, Bryan said, "We must hurry, winter is soon upon us; traveling there, we ran into three days of winter storm, had to slog through snow, knee deep. As soon as the ground is dry, we should be on our way."

"Agreed, an army will become discouraged if they spend much time fighting snow and mud, kills their fighting spirit," Ansgar said.

"How soon then can you be ready to move?" Vendal asked.

"Four, maybe five days?"

"You ok with that?" Vandel asked Bryan.

"The sooner the better," Bryan replied

"Good," Ansgar said, "It's decided then."

Bryan went to the inn hoping to find the trader, but Hager was not there. At the Great Hall, he exchanged gossip with the pages, and when Ivan proved busy, went back to the arena, to work on his skills.

Three days he searched for the trader without success, finally on the fourth, half drunk, slumped over a table, at the back of the inn, he found him.

"You said you'd stay in touch," Bryan said, angrily. "You've been paid well, yet you go off, and I can't find you."

"Well…, I'm here now, and you haven't gone off on your campaign yet, have you?" The old man's speech slurred, "So, what's the harm," he said with a cocky pretense of innocence.

"We'll be leaving tomorrow; maybe the day after, Chief Karl is depending upon you to warn them that we're on our way, if you fail, you'll answer to him," Bryan threatened.

Hagar's face paled, cocky smirk gone, the consequences of betraying Chief Karl, not something he wanted to contemplate. "I'm leaving right away," he stammered.

"No, wait until I tell you, otherwise they'll be waiting unnecessarily. You know this Hager. We went over this," Bryan was beginning to lose patience with the man.

"Right, I'll be right here…, waiting," Hager said sheepishly.

"And stay away from that drink, I want you ready to travel." Bryan tossed down a couple of coins on the table, "Get yourself something to eat."

"Eye, that I'll do."

Bryan wished he'd been more firm with the old man earlier.

As he headed back up the hill, still perturbed, a man from court, one of the Jarl's senior advisors, the man the Jarl had Bryan talk to about Sogndal at the very first, a scrawny, weasel of a man, saddled up beside, and walked with him.

"I heard you talking with Lords Vandel and Ansgar," his tone was sharp, accusing, "What'd you mean telling them that the people of Sogndel are not warriors?"

Bryan was taken back, how had he heard, surely the knights had'nt told him, he'd been eavesdropping, at the knights' hall, the little sneak.

"I told them what I saw."

"You and I both know it's a lie," the man accused, "I know that clan well, and those people are some of the best warriors on the fjord. Your little army is in for the fight of their lives."

"I've been trained well by Vandel, and disagree. Have you told the Jarl of you concerns?"

Bryan maintaining his composure continued walking, the man dogging him.

"You and I are going there now, don't know what your little game is, but we're going to have this out."

Bryan continued undaunted. Horiker, his name, Bryan thought, not sure, like a hound on a hare he was, determined to flush Bryan out, scurrying beside, huffing and puffing, trying to keep up.

Bryan took a path, back behind the bath house, like he was going to the kitchen, the man following. Behind the bath, a place dark and quite, were few ever ventured , Bryan stumbled, a fake, dropping his walking stick, stooping to pick it up slipped his dagger from his boot.

With mercurial speed, he spun; grabbing the man by the hair, jerking his head back violently, and just as fast, slit his throat, deeply, nearly decapitating him, so swift, the man hadn't time to yell out. Blood pumped rhythmically from the gaping neck. He was dead before he knew what had happened.

His body slumped, as his life passed, and Bryan let it slip into a pool of blood on the ground.

Quickly, he covered the body with piles of hay from a nearby stack, then ducked into the back of the bath, finding Ole stoking a furnace.

"Bryan!" Ole exclaimed, "What a nice surprise."

"Shhh...," Byran put his finger to his lips.

"Sorry," the boy whispered, "What ever happened!" his eyes wide at the sight of blood, dripping from Bryan's hands.

"You don't want to know, right now I need to clean up, quickly."

"Stay right here, I'll take care of it," Ole scurried off, a moment later returning with a bucket of hot water.

Byran scrubbing the blood from his hands, telling Ole, "There is a pile of hay, just outside your back door. Don't try to move it, and don't say anything to anyone about it."

"That hay has been there for weeks, haven't taken any notice to it," the boy caught on, "And I haven't seen you since you left for Sogndel."

"There's a good boy, someday I'll be able to repay you for all you've done for me." He slipped the clean dagger back into his boot.

Quickly, he walked to the kitchen, unseen, only then, noticing his hands and knees shaking, not from fear, but from the ecstatic pleasure killing gave him. Nasty business, this, he thought. Stupid bastard couldn't keep his mouth shut. He was more than a little irritated with himself, not anticipating the previous envoy hearing his lie, and calling him on it. His carelessness, needlessly, cost the man his life. Unable to eat the meat served him; he took a piece of bread and went to his room.

He met Thor that night, again in the form of a wolf, while walking in the forest, his dreams of the god, so real. "Remember, I told you, the closer you come to killing your enemy, the more like him you become." Thor said, "It would not trouble the Dane to kill the courtesan, to him it would be inconsequential."

"But, I can't put it out of my mind."

"Why not? You killed the page, and the men guarding the ship, when freeing the slaves, and didn't think much about it. In fact, seems, I recall, you quite enjoyed it."

"That was different."

165

"How so?"

"It meant freedom for those people."

"And killing the courtesan was any different? A man who could reveal your little scheme, been your downfall, preventing you from fulfilling your oath of vengeance," The wolf flashed a cunning smile, showing his teeth, a sparkle, in his piercing eyes. "Could you have tolerated that?" he laughed. "Besides, did you not experience great pleasure, when you killed him."

Bryan, stung with guilt, said, "Tis true," hanging his head in shame. "If being like the Jarl means not regretting the murder of someone, I will never be totally like him, that's not so bad, is it?"

The wolf smiled again, a knowing, slightly sinister smile, fading into the darkness, and from Bryan's consciousness.

Feeling better in the morning, he gathered his gear into a pack. Just after midmorning, a messenger found him, talking with Ivan, at the back of the Great Hall.

"Sir Ansgar's men are ready to move in the morning. They will assemble on the beach near the old boat house," the boy told him.

He headed for the encampment right away, stopping at the inn, where the trader waited, true to his word, though he'd again had a few drinks. The old man said he'd leave right away, and walked unsteadily out with Bryan, said, "Good- by," and left in the direction of the ferry on wobbly legs. Bryan touched his amulet, silently saying a prayer to Thor, hoping that the old man would get to the village in time.

The encampment was forming; men, tents, and horses, scattered in a haphazard state of organized confusion. At its center, Lord Ansgar, giving directions and orders.

"I came as soon as I heard, see you've gathered your men," Bryan said.

"Yes, and not any too soon. We'll be leaving at the crack of dawn."

"How many do you have?" Bryan asked looking about.

"About seventy five, ten on war horses, fifteen on Norse Ponies, the rest are on foot." He paused to answer one of his men. "You want to do some sparing later?"

"Sure," Bryan said eagerly.

"Meet me at the arena just before dark. We'll have a go at it."

"You're on," Bryan waved good- by, and headed for the Great Hall to say fare well to Ivan, got something to eat, returned to his room, changed to his military uniform, laid out his uncle's sword, and set a battle axe aside, then laid down to rest, before meeting the knight.

Lord Ansger, waiting for him when he arrived, sparred with him, with wooden axes for several hours. Then tired, both went to the camp, where the men were settling down for the night. Bryan spread his blankets, and was quickly asleep.

Chapter 16

The stirring army woke him, very early, darkness just begining to fade in the east, stars still studding the darkness above.

The knight's men were just beginning to assemble into rough formation when Lord Ansgar rode up on a great war horse, leading a black and white spotted, Norwegian pony, sturdy, strong, with a new, shaggy, winter coat.

"This is for you," He said, handing the reins to Bryan.

"M'lord, I can march with the others, there's no need to treat me special.

"You'll not march," the man growled, "You wouldn't be able to keep up. Besides, as my captain, you should not be on the ground, with common men. You'll lose their respect, now mount up, and ride at my side." The look on his face said, "Don't defy me boy. "

"Yes, m'lord," he lashed his pack to the horse, and mounted it.

They traveled north to the fjord crossing, which immediately became a massive bottle neck. Large knarrs had been fetched, but only three horses and a few men could be taken aboard for each crossing. A stiff wind drove the water to a frothy chop, making rowing difficult. After many crossings, and midday well past, the last of the army disembarked, and the march began.

With the mounted men taking the lead, Bryan soon realized why he had been provided a horse; while they cantered along, at a good clip, the foot soldiers ran behind, never falling back, never faltering, or stopping for rest, until they camped at sundown. "Thank you for the horse m'lord," Bryan began, "Your men are remarkable. I never would have

169

imagined them to have such stamina. You were absolutely right, I could not have kept up."

The big man looked at him and flashed a self satisfied grin. "They're very special men; some can run for days without rest, there are not many like these," He said proudly.

"I can believe it." Bryan said.

The knight smiled, "Their fathers, and their father's fathers have been in the service of my clan, a proud bunch they are."

Fires sprung up and meals cooked. Lord Ansgar's aid prepared a meal for him and Bryan. While they ate, Ansgar spoke, "We should pass through Leilanger tomorrow afternoon, and move well beyond before nightfall, to within striking distance of Sogndal, attacking early the next morning. We must be careful as not forewarn them of our advance."

"I may be able to help you with that," Bryan said.

"There's no need, my scouts will guide us to just the right spot."

"Scouts?" Bryan said.

"An army can't move without scouts. They're out there right now. They make sure we are on the right road, keep a look out for things."

Of course there would be scouts, why hadn't he thought of that? Such a simple thing, obvious; all Vandel's teaching, and still he'd missed a small detail due to his lack of experience. Would Chief Karl's warriors be aware of the scouts? And the foot soldiers also a concern; he'd not expected such strength - when he and the Lord Ansgar walked the camp, before the evening meal, they'd not seemed the slightest fatigued after the long march.

His night would be long; his mind churning, with worry, stiff from riding, the inside of his thighs, chaffed, his groin aching; a horse, better than running, and far better than a cart, but punishing.

Up and moving before dawn, the air cool, a light fog across the fjord, reflecting the sun's golden rays, as it broke over the mountains, quickly dispering the mist.

They passed through Leikanger at a fast pace, horses two abreast and foot soldiers four abreast.

"We want to impress and intimidate, so that they won't interfere with our business." Ansgar had said.

Carefully negotiating the narrow cliff road, they descended unto the flat and level shoreline, leading to Sogndal. Far ahead two riders approached, Ansgar slowed the column, and rode out to speak with his scouts, this was as far as they would travel today.

Lord Ansgar walked through camp, Bryan following along dutifully, like a puppy following its master. He sensed tension, almost undetectable, among men, preparing for battle. The knight talked calmly with them, giving instructions and advice, speaking of their families, and other personal things, soothing their anxiety.

Morning came all too quickly, a hardy morning meal, provided for all, while Lord Ansgar gave last minute orders to his men, and then gathered them into tight formations. The air, quite cool, little clouds of misty breath rose over their heads. In the east, a blood red sliver of sun, peered over the mountain tops.

At the knight's signal, they moved toward the village; Bryan's stomach tight. Arriving at the hill above the village, the foot soldiers separated from the group, moved silently to the left, in a flanking maneuver, and when in position, halted.

Day light seemed slow to come this day, the outlines of the longhouses down in the village, just visible, as Lord Ansgar drew his sword, and signaled. The two groups charged, in a sudden burst of noise and action. Bryan brandishing his uncle's sword, riding at the knight's side, everyone shouting and yelling, racing toward the sleeping village. The horsemen raced among the longhouses, turning at the other side of the village, and coming back, just as the foot soldiers, like so many ants, spread out through the buildings, entering inside, then - an eerie silence, for a few moments. Soldiers began emerging from the buildings, empty handed. The only sound was the rattle of harnesses.

"Empty," The men shouted.

"Where are they," Ansgar swore.

The knight, a look of horror and disbelief on his face, glanced at Bryan. Bryan shrugging his shoulders, and shaking his head, surprise on his face

"Spread out, into the forest, find them," Ansgar ordered.

The foot soldiers rushed into the forest, while the horsemen searched further among the buildings, everything empty, belongings gone, the fires a long time cold, abandoned.

Bryan rode up to the knight. "M, Lord, we should leave immediately, it could be an ambush, we're sitting ducks."

Ansgar thinking the same, panic taking hold, began calling his men back. "They must have figured you out, Sir Bryan," The knight mocked.

"Apparently, but I can't imagine how," he protested.

Ansgar, quickly reassembled his men, fear in his eyes, ordered them to, "Ride out." For him, not knowing was fear itself.

Charging back up the hill, back toward the sight where they camped the night before. About half way there, Bryan rode up beside Ansgar, yelling, "Stop."

"What is it?" The knight demanded.

172

"We should have burned it."

Ansgar halted the column, "Burned what?" he said impatiently.

"The village, we should have burned it to the ground so they can't return, and continue to defy the Jarl. You go ahead m'lord, give me twenty soldiers, I'll go back and finish the job, we'll catch up, when done. We cannot allow the village to stand."

Ansgar hesitated a moment, but Bryan's logic, irresistible, he nodded consent, "Pick out twenty men. Be fast about it."

Bryan broke formation, and rode to the rear of the column, detailed the last twenty men, and led them back toward the village, steeling his mind.

Arriving at the village, they quickly built a large fire, at the center of the village, and devised torches to carry the flames to the longhouses, suddenly, and without warning, from out of nowhere, the village was alive with clan warriors, making the noise of all holies. Fighting like furies, they pushed the soldiers into a core around the fire. From behind, Bryan was attacked, the braid on the back of his head pulled back, yanking him off balance, a gloved hand clamped tightly over his mouth, dragging him backward, helpless, someone powerful. The soldiers overwhelmed, began to fall, as Bryan was pulled behind one of the longhouses, forced down into the mud, rolled to his back to see his assailant, Thoreik.

Laying his weight atop Bryan, he spoke into his ear, "Lay here, don't move, till your soldiers are dead," then rolled Bryan to his stomach, in the mud, up against a wall, his face nearly buried in the muck; the sound of soldiers, being murdered, horrendous, going on and on, for a maddeningly long time.

Finally, Thorick returned, and helped Bryan to his feet. In the center of the village, dead soldiers scattered around the smoldering fire, the smell of death strong in the air. He felt sickeningly responsible.

"We can't thank you enough," Thoreik told him, "You had better be on your way, hurry."

Bryan mounted his horse, raced up over the hill, back toward the army, passing the place they had camped, approaching the the narrow road that began the climb into the hills, seeing one body, then another, the bodies of Ansgar's men scattered on both sides of the road, where the column backed up, trying to get up the narrow road, away from the murderous clansmen. The trail of bodies, continued off the road, up the side of the mountain, where the fleeing soldiers, trying to escape the fury of the village warriors and certain death, met their doom. Only after diligent searching, did he find Lord Ansgar, still alive, but severely beaten.

He washed the man's face, and gave him water; the big man, speaking nonsense, in and out of consciousness.

Darkness, closing in rapidly, Bryan built a fire, gathered blankets and food, from surrounding dead men's packs, covered the knight, and kept the fire burning through the night; the battlefield, eerie, with the smell of death, heavy in the air, he almost expected the Valkeries to sweep in, and take the bodies away to Valhalla. It was as if he were keeping an unintended silent vigil for the dead, whose deaths, he was responsible, a responsibility he felt acutely, though what he had wanted, only now realizing the enormity what he'd done.

Toward morning, Ansgar began to regain consciousness; Bryan made porridge, sat him up, and fed him. With the knight's senses returning, he noticed the bodies strewn about.

"Are there..., any alive?" He asked.

Bryan hung his head, "No m'lord, all dead."

"We should never have run from the village. They were waiting for us," Ansgar lamented.

"They were waiting in the village as well, my men fought bravely, there were too many, all of them were killed. I escaped by playing dead until I had an opportunity."

Ansgar looking him over, hair, face, and clothes, caked in dried mud, shook his head, "It's just you and me, dear mother of Oden," he muttered, "We'd better get moving, before they come back and kill us too."

"They'll be back to collect the spoils, you're right, we have to leave as soon as you feel like traveling."

The man tried to stand, staggered, caught himself, Bryan steadied him. He took a deep breath, and let it out slowly, "Dam that hurts."

Bryan went down the hill, found Ansgar's horse, picked up a skin of wine from one of the dead men, and took it to the knight.

"This might ease your pain some."

The knight drank the entire skin like it was water, mounted his horse with much moaning and groaning, and the two headed over the mountain to Leikanger. They detoured around the town, camping, that night, a short distance from the fjord crossing.

That evening, eating a small meal, sitting by the fire, Bryan asked Ansgar, what they were going to tell the Jarl.

"Tell 'em the truth."

"He'll be angry."

"He'll be furious, but what else can we do?"

"How did they know what we would do?" Bryan asked, needing to know the man's thoughts about what happened.

"They didn't. They just watched us, probably knew we were on the way, from the time we passed Leikanger. They watched, carefully emptied the village, knowing we would panic, fearing ambush, retreat, and all bunch up trying to get on to the narrow road up over the mountain, moving quickly, silently, through the forest, to ambush us. Probably something they've planned as their defense for years. When we split up, it made it that much easier for them. You and I are lucky to be alive. We underestimated them, and paid dearly for it."

It was a major tragedy for the knight; without his men, he would not be of much service to the Jarl, and being responsible to the soldier's families could mean financial ruin for him.

They sat in silence.

The next day, the ferryboat did not arrive till nearly midday. They went straight to the Great Hall after landing, but it was empty.

"We'll have to go to the Jarl's quarters," Ansgar growled.

"Dare we do that?" Bryan had never been to his personnel quarters.

"If we wait till tomorrow, he'll have our hides," Ansgar assured. The man looked so tired, his beating beginning to show; huge bruises on his arms, and the side of his face black, hunched over, from pain in his belly; Bryan felt sorry for him.

To the rear of the Great Hall, the Jarl's quarters, a longhouse with no side rooms, the door guarded. Ansgar told the guards the purpose of their visit, one of them entered, reappeared shortly, and ushered them inside.

It wasn't a palace, but very nice; at the center, a hearth, lined with stone, a low fire burning, the floor, covered with mats of woven marsh willow branches, unusual, even the floor of the Great Hall was dirt. Tapestries covering the walls, red, yellow and brown, probably from exotic places, far to the south, by way of Viking trade routes, through the Balkans and Rus, places Bryan had only heard about, through vague references, about this type of commerce. The furnishings, though few, were of the finest Danish craftsmanship. Small oil lamps provided soft yellow light, and the room smelled of spices and herbs.

The Dane sat, to rear of the room, speaking to a sparsely dressed woman, sitting on a stool, next to him. They turned to the knight and Bryan.

"Forgive our intrusion m'lord, we've only just arrived, and thought that you should know...," Ansgar's voice trailed off.

"Yes, of course Ansgar, you look ..., terrible," the Jarls said, looking both of them over. Bryan, still covered with dried mud, in his hair, clotted in his ears, and hardened like cement on his clothes. The knight's bruised body, clothing torn, ragged, and covered with dried blood, seemed to tell the story.

"M'lord," Ansgar's voice quaked. "We were ambushed in a hellish manner. My men, my best fighting men were all killed, slaughtered, Master Bryan and I narrowly escaping death ourselves. They were waiting for us." He went on to tell the Jarl the whole story.

The Jarl, clearly upset, his face red with anger, did not fly into a rage, as Bryan expected. His voice, slow, low, and deliberate, "Those people have been a thorn in my side long enough. It's late, and winter is nye upon us, no time for another campaign till spring. That will give you time to raise another army, see what men you are unable to obtain from your own lands, and you may borrow from other lords.

He turned to Bryan. "Get yourself cleaned up. You look and smell as if you've been sleeping with pigs.

"Yes, m'lord."

"And thank you for going along on the campaign," his voice softened, "Unfortunate as it may have been, there are lessons to be learned from the experience. I'm happy you survived." He smiled, "Continue your training with Lord Vandel so that you may be prepared in the spring to truly help lead the effort. Seek him out immediately."

"Yes, m'lord, thank you. M'lord." He bowed and backed away.

He knew then, his course of action was set; what had to be done, to avoid further aggression. After meeting with Vandel, he returned to the barracks, only to find someone standing in his room, looking at his belongings, back to the door.

Chapter 17

Bryan cleared his throat, "Beggen you pardon, I think you've found the wrong room."

The man turned around, slowly. "Damn boy, you look like shit, and smell even worse. Where have you been?"

Ari, a big grin on his slightly bearded face.

Bryan was speechless, tearing up, he threw his arms around him, and hugged his cousin, "Oh by the gods, it's good to see you, seems like years," holding Ari close, he inhaled his odor, so familiar, how odd, people have their own smell, he thought, you never notice till you haven't smelled them for a long time.

Ari pushed away, and held him at arm's length. "What happened to you?"

"Long story, when did you get here."

"Little while ago, went to the Dane's court, a page there, Ivan I think his name was, directed me here."

"Come on," Bryan said, "Let's get a hot bath, I'll tell you all about it."

Soaking in the bath, he told Ari what he'd been up to: the knight who'd been buggering Ivan, freeing the thralls, the champagne at Sogndel.

In turn, Ari told Bryan about things at home, "Your little brother is lost without you, and your mother weeps a lot," the words stinging to Bryan's heart, like shards of ice. Their uncles had worked out a leadership pact after some dissention, the crops were in, ready for winter. "And I miss you more than anything. I lost both father and you, within just a few days, I've been so lost, it hurt so bad inside," tears filled his eyes.

Bryan put an arm around Ari's shoulders, and they cried quietly together, for a long time.

"Being apart saddens me too," Bryan said, his voice shaky, "More than anyone will ever know, and worse, I don't know if we can ever be together again," he sighed.

After another long pause, and a deep breath, Ari asked, "What about you're plans for the Dane?"

"Not here, never know what ears might be listening."

Ole leaned over the edge of the tub and whispered, "You courtesan friend, back behind the bath, caused quite a stir while you were gone. Everyone's being very careful, avoiding dark, secluded places, for fear of the phantom, they call em. I hear tell the Jarl was beside himself. "

"Thanks for covering me there, friend."

After Ole walked away, Ari said, "That boy's strange."

"Yea, but he's a good operative, and a friend, I'll tell you about what he was talking about later."

They dressed, and Bryan took him to the Inn, telling Ari about killing the courtesan, on the way, "I had to cut his throat."

Ari stopped and paused a moment, "I have to admit, I didn't think you had it in you, cousin, how many men have you killed?"

"Scheming and treachery are a way of life here, to prove one's self, vanquishing your enemies is winning the truth; the vows we've made lend to violent solutions," Bryan said.

"I believe you, honestly, I do," Ari said, 'It's just that," he thought, "I guess I still think of you as you were when we were 10 years old, not capable of such, daring things."

Bryan shrugged, "Did what needed to be done."

Ari shook his head, "You've grown up."

"Thanks, maybe I was born into it, following in father's footsteps or something." Arriving at the inn, Bryan said, "We can talk here without nosy ears listening, and the ale's passable, I'll buy."

The inn, with winter coming on, seas more treacherous, limiting trade with the Ire, not as busy until spring. They ordered boiled lamb, swimming in gravy, with cabbage and onions, and loaves of flat bread, and butter. Neither having eaten in days, they downed the food, and ordered seconds.

"The Harvest Feast and Alfablot will be held in a few days. You'll stay for that won't you," Bryan asked.

"Sure, sounds like fun."

"As long as they don't get carried away."

Ari screwed his face in inquisitive curiosity, "Carried away?"

Bryan paused, "Last year, at Walpurgis, shamans sacrificed a boy, one of the pages, to the gods, along with goats, like some animal, made a big show of it. They butchered him, cooked him, with the goat meat, and ate him, got everyone very excited."

Ari's face paled, "By the gods, you ate him?"

"Not me, they did," Bryan added, "I been told, no one will be sacrificed during Alfablot."

"That's a relief," Ari said.

"Let's talk about the future," Bryan said, in a more serious tone.

Ari looked around, wary of anyone listening, and leaned close to Bryan, "I need to know your plans, King Innvik vows that he'll bring his army here, as soon as the Jarl is dead, I'll relay that to him."

Bryan was taken back, "You've been to Forden Torge? How did you get there?"

"On foot, this time of year it's the only way."

"And you're going back over the mountain again?"

"I would do it a thousand times to fulfill my vow," Ari came back.

"You're as impressive as your father was, cousin, take care in those mountains, they're fraught with danger."

"Not any more than you've faced here, my friend, now, tell me your plans."

"I think it best, if both of us take part in it. I said that before didn't I; after all, it was your father was killed. Our best chance will be in the spring, during Walpurgis, this next year it's going to be held over three days. By then sufficient time will have passed, to claim our vengeance, a good time for Innvik's men, crossing the mountains, and the best time for us to make our escape. " He went on to describe his plan.

He was just finishing, when Ivan came walking across the floor toward them.

"Ari, I'd like you to meet my friend Ivan, the one helped me with my little escapades."

After that their conversation became lighter, and livelier, aided by more tankards of ale.

In the morning, the three, took leave of Balestrand, and traveled on foot, north along the shores of Esefjorden. The sky clear, the air crisp and cool, finding joy in exploring the wilderness, fantasizing adventure as only young men can, sleeping in the open, watching the aurora dance its mysterious paths across the night sky, dazzling them with color; the promise of winter to come.

For three days, they frolicked and played; traveling north, crossing over a high mountain pass, leaving the fjord far behind, and descending into a valley, where they came upon a small village.

"Is this your home?" Bryan asked Ivan.

182

"By the gods no, my home is many leagues north, much easier to get to."

"I'm glad to hear that," Ari said as they walked in among the buildings.

Villagers watched apprehensively, Ari's clothing not identifying him, but Bryan and Ivan's clothing clearly betraying them as coming from Balestrand.

While Bryan and Ivan watched, Ari approached, engauging one of the villagers in a friendly conversation. Assured that they meant no harm, just seeking a meal, and shelter for the evening; the man, still wary, took them to the clan chief, who turned out to be an affable man, quickly striking up a friendship. By evening, the villager's apprehension overcome; the chief had a sumptuous meal served, drinking mead, exchanging stories, and news from Balestrand, to whom the town reluctantly owed allegiance, and generally having a good time.

Given a room to themselves, they huddled together, under their blankets; Bryan put his arm around Ari, and snuggled close to him, like when they were boys. He suffered their separation, of the last months, and dreaded even more, the separation he was certain to come, fearing that after that parting, they would never see each other again, a prospect too painful for him to contemplate, he shut it out of his mind, and went to sleep.

They headed back toward Balestrand, in the morning, after saying ado to the townsfolk, their frolic lasting three more days, ending in a long soak in the baths of Balestrand.

Their return conienciding with the Harvest Feast, a preparation for the Alfablot celebration; important families, bringing their homestead harvests, to the village, peddling them in the streets to other villagers, at stands, set up in front of their Balestrand estate homes. The three friends, dressed in their finery, Ari in clothes, borrowed from Bryan, enjoyed the day, tasting samples of pork, lamb, oxen, and goat, breads of every kind, with cheeses, fresh and aged, washing them down with luscious wine, boor and ales, and in the evening bedded down in the Great Hall, their bellies stuffed, and very drunk.

In the morning they helped set up the hall for Alfablot Feast, which brought all the food from the streets inside, for a feast in honor of the Elves of Vanir. Now Bryan didn't put much stake in the existence of elves, he'd never seen one in all the time he'd spent in the forest, where they were reputed to live. The Elves of Vanir, according the shamans theology, descended from the gods, acted as intermediaries with humans, enforcers of the laws of the gods, and were said to interbreed with humans, and were capable of bringing certain death or incredible wealth to humans.

At any rate, Alfablot was the feast of feasts, in their honor, a time of merriment, with meats of all kinds, sausages galore, breads, cheeses, vegetables, all washed down with liberal supplies of wine, boor, and ale, it was Bryan's favorite celebration. Everyone stuffed themselves again, and drank heavenly.

The following day, the three, along with everyone in the village, lay low, recovering.

Bryan said a tearful good-by to Ari, the day after.

In the aftermath of the celebration, winter fast approaching, and many of the courtiers gone, or preparing to leave, to their permanent homes, none bothering to attend court, the Dane was seeing the few petitioners plying him for favors, in his personal quarters. The Great Hall became a dismal place, a home for those seeking shelter from cold and snow. The northern night sky, flaming red and green, with the

Aurora Borealis, twisting and contorting, challenging the imagination of those brave enough to venture out into the darkness.

Bryan, along with the other pages, and a few of the knights who remained, began making their home there next to the hearth, away from their cold, drafty barracks, some nights sleeping in the bathhouse, next to the furnace.

The Yule celebration, a short reprieve, in the dreary winter routine, brought locals in to the great hall, to make a day of festivities. Women brought food and men their special dark, thick ale, brewed for the occasion. A great Yule log, burned at one end, as they celebrated winter, and the end of the year. Even the Jarl joined in the little party.

Snow came down, in the days following the Yule. It seemed as if it would never stop, drifting high, making walking from building to building difficult. Bryan stayed to the Great Hall most of the time, occupying himself, reading and studying, borrowed scrolls from the teacher's library, occasionally, sparing with the knights.

Weeks after Yule, during a particularly bad blizzard, lasting a number of days, Ivan came to him. "I need to talk to you," he said, with urgency in his voice.

Bryan followed him to a side room, Ivan closed the door, looked about to be sure no one was there, the room very cold, their breaths, hung frozen in the air, anyone would have to be desperate to be in there.

"What's all this about?"

Ivan half whispered, "The people we visited in the village to the north last fall are starving, some have died already, their food supplies given to the Jarl in tribute, and now, requesting help, have been refused. Turned away, some weeks ago, they arrived again today, in this blizzard, begging, only to be denied again." Ivan was beside himself.

"He has no conscience," Bryan hissed, his words freezing into frozen vapor. "Where are they now?"

"They're huddled in my barracks building, left their ponies outside of town."

"Ok," Bryan screwed his face, determined, "Go get some heavy clothes, and a weapon, meet me behind the bath house."

"What are we going to do?" Ivan asked.

"First, we're going to get dressed warmly. Then we're going to raid the Jarl's warehouse."

"But the warehouses are guarded?" Both he and Bryan had spent time standing guard there.

"Yea, well, the people will die if we don't, it's doubtful if the guards will be expecting anything, in this storm, we'll have the advantage, now, get moving."

Ivan's face went white. "You'll hang if you're found out."

"Then we'll have to be sure, not to be found out, won't we, now move it"

The fierce wind, an icy knife, tore at the flesh, penetrated even the heaviest clothing. It drove the snow sideways, stinging their eyes, sucking the heat from their bodies, and the breath from their lungs, drifting deep, clothing, quickly becoming caked white and frosty. Bryan lead five figures down the hill, through knee deep snow, toward the docks, then to the east, to the food warehouses. They struggled through the drifts and howling wind, to the shelter of a shed just outside of the warehouse. It wasn't much, but broke the wind and blowing snow a little, affording them brief glimpses of the storeroom entrance, when the wind dipped.

Watching the entrance intently, "There's just one guard," Bryan said. The figure huddled, close to the door, his back to the wind, miserably cold, Bryan knew t his joints would be stiff, and his brain numb with cold.

186

"There'll be more inside," He said, "They're taking turns outside, maybe asleep inside," familiar with the routine.

"Can we get to him?" Ivan asked.

"He keeps his back to the wind, I might be able to sneak up behind him, he won't be expecting anything. When I grab him, I'll need your help, as quickly as possible."

"I don't know how fast I can get there through the snow."

"I understand, just get there as soon as you can."

"What about the men inside."

"We'll worry about them after taking care of the one we can see."

Bryan made a long circle around and behind the guard, on all fours, wallowing through snow nearly covering his head, until close enough to reach out and touch the man's coat, standing to pounce; Ivan took that as a signal to attack, and rushed from his hiding place. His movement caught the guard's attention, who pulled his sword, much more rapidly than Bryan thought possible. Ivan was nearly half way to the guard, and Bryan needing to do something, quickly, reached out, grabbing the hand holding the sword, and with his opposite arm, long knife in hand, came around, from the other side. The guard, realizing the sudden danger, fought back. Bryan, able to still the man's sword, for the moment, began working his knife, through the layers of clothing, toward the man's throat.

Ivan reached them, clasped his hands about the handle of the sword, while Bryan wormed his knife inward, the guard's struggles becoming desperate. Bryan's knife, reaching flesh, began cutting. The guard's blood curdling scream, lost in the wind, as Bryan sliced blindly, blood began to stain the snow in front of them, the guard fought hard, Bryan burying his knife deep, the guard's throat open, mangled, taking forever, finally, his legs went out from under him, and his body went slack, Bryan let him to the ground, immediately removing the heavy coat before it could get bloody. Looking at the guard's face, relieved he didn't know him, he felt that familiar tingle in his groin, and cursed his pleasure.

He shouted to the villagers who came running. "Take the body away quickly. Bury it deeply so that it will not be found till spring."

He and Ivan covered the blood stained snow with fresh and tamped it in well. Then Bryan, the guard's heavy coat on, his head covered with the dead man's hat, pounded loudly on the door, with the pommel of his sword, "Stand back away from the door," He shouted to Ivan.

Through the door, he shouted, "Let me in, I'm freezing out here," no response. Again he beat on the door, still no response. He leaned his shoulder against it, with a creak it eased open, bracing for an attack that never came, pushing the door open enough to step inside; the cavernous room was dark, lit only by a few candles, stacked high, piles of onions, beets, cabbages, turnips, bags of barley, and great tubs of butter, the whole room fragrant, but quiet. Ivan following him in, they searched among the piles of food, for anyone hidden away.

Suddenly, voices outside, coming in.

"Sigrad, you fool, you're supposed to be standing guard, not hiding inside," the voice said, ever closer. The door swung open, four figures entered, silhouettes against the light of the open door.

Bryan lost track of Ivan, to the darkness. The guards, snow blind, unable to see well in the darkness, the leader berating Bryan, until he realized that Bryan was not the guard. "Who the blazes are you?" He demanded as he drew his sword.

"I might ask the same of you, abandoning your post," Bryan shouted, as intimidating as possible.

"Someone you'll regret you ever crossed paths with," the guard spat, "You're trespassing on the Jarl's property, a thief, who'll pay for your crime, right now."

Bryan held his sword on guard. From the darkness, behind the guards, Ivan appeared, sword drawn, making Bryan suddenly fearful for Ivan, not trained, he could be easily overcome. Quickly, he shook off the heavy outer coat.

The guard lunged, Bryan defended himself, a second guard stepped in to help, but Bryan, muscles on fire with adrenalin, fought both, ferociously, forcing both men back.

Ivan was fighting the third guard, he didn't know where the fourth man was. The second guard lunged at Bryan again. Bryan parried, striking viciously at the man's arm, cutting deeply, above the wrist, the guard dropped his sword, cried out, grabbing his arm. Bryan would have finished him, except the leader was on him, hacking wildly, blow after blow. Bryan defending himself valiantly, tiring the guard, who missed a blow by a wide margin. Bryan struck, it was quick, his sword tip swiped down, across the side of the guards face, sliced into his throat. Reeling back, his sword flying, choking on blood, trying to catch his breath, fell to his knees, and coughed, a shower of blood, shot from his throat, he collapsed face first, onto the dirt floor.

Bryan felt a heavy blow, to the back of his neck, stars burst in his head, his vision went black. 'What the devil,' he thought, staggered and turned, the wounded guard was standing over him, his right arm hanging useless, in his left, a large stick. Before Bryan could gather his thoughts, the man brought the stick down on his head. The dark room burst full of stars again, instinctively rolling away. He tried to focus his eyes.

Not knowing how much time passed, far away at first, a guttural sound, like a man vomiting, when his eyes focused, the man was in front of him, dropped to knees, a blank look on his face. Ivan stood behind him, his sword stuck deep into the guard's back, protruding from his stomach. Ivan, with a swift move, pulled the sword from the man, flicked the sword around, chopping into the side of the man's neck, he fell dead.

Ivan fought and killed the third guard, found the fourth man, cowering among the stacks and killed him.

Bryan's head spinning with throbbing pain, he sat, dumb on the dirt floor, trying to gather his toughs. Ivan had done all that, "Where did you learn to fight like that?"

"Watching you," Ivan answered a little smirk on his face.

"Well, I'm sure glad you did, lad was about to beat my brains out."

The villagers tied the bodies together, and hauled them away while Bryan & Ivan cleaned up the messy scene inside. They gathered the much needed food, loaded the ponies, each villager taking a pack on their back, and led the animals off into the storm, on their hand-made skis.

It was dark when they got back to the bathhouse. Bryan had not noticed the cold during the day in spite of the frigid wind, though the throbbing pain in his head remained, but now standing there in the warm bathhouse, with Ole washing him he began shivering, uncontrollably. He'd been telling about their exploits, but suddenly, he was overwhelmed with chill, coming from deep within his bones.

Ole noticed at once, "You're cold my friend, you've been out in this freezing storm for too long. Look at you, shaking like a baby." He poured a bucket of warm water over Bryan, helped him into the hot water to soak, sinking to his neck, in the warmth, heavenly, yet his body continued to be cold, what was wrong with him?

Ivan joined him, and they talked, "What do you think the Jarl will do?" he asked.

"He'll be furious; the Loki that's been a thorn in his side is still with him. He'll lash out at anyone he can, because he doesn't have a clue where the mischief is coming from."

"I'd say it was a little more than mischief," Ivan interjected.

"Suppose you're right about that. The snow should cover all tracks, and I rigged the warehouse door; the bolt fell into place, when the door closed, can only be opened from the inside, they'll have a good time, getting in. I hope the villagers hid those bodies well, wonder what they did with them?"

"Don't know, they didn't say," Ivan observed.

"With the guards gone, they may think that the lot of em abandoned the place." Bryan supposed.

"In a storm like this? I don't think they'd put much credence in that theory." Ivan reasoned. "I have to say, though, I didn't care for killing them."

"Yea, didn't get my usual thrill, my head still hurts like the blazes, had to feed the villagers though, they needed their share."

Ivan noticed Bryan's voice drifting off, kind of dreamy like. "Are you ok," A frown crossed his face?

"Yea why?" Bryan answered.

"You're shaking, like your sick or something, your eyes are blue around the edges, and you don't look so good."

"Let me hit you over the head, a couple a times, see how you feel. I'm just cold that's all," Bryan answered.

They soaked a while longer. When Bryan got out, he was a little short of breath, coughing a little. He went to the hall, and put on his heavy coat, covered himself with all the blankets he had, and slept.

By morning he was burning hot, the cold air, sent great, rocking chills through his body, his lungs were on fire, as was his throat, he coughed up foul tasting phlegm, and his arms and legs ached, worse than an old man's.

Ivan came, took one look at him, and said, "I'll be right back." When he returned, he had Ole with him. Bryan didn't know why, they seemed so excited, very concerned, he felt bad, but couldn't understand their anxiety, it was disquieting.

"You're coming with us," Ivan said firmly. They took him by the arms, practically drug him to the bathhouse, and laid him on a bench, in the back. Ivan brought him some warm broth.

For many days, the two cared for him, as he passed in and out of delirium, not knowing where he was, or what was going on. When he was awake, things were confusing; was he going to die, unable to fulfill his vows, cheating him of his chance of going to Valhalla. He was visited by his uncle Gunner, one night. They had a long conversation, but when he was gone, Bryan realized he hadn't asked the important question, what was it he quarreled with the Jarl about, what did the Jarl know that caused his father to leave to fight in far off lands?

He woke that night, full of fear, crying and yelling, Ole there to sooth his fear, and he quickly sank back into fever and delusion, dreaming of many beasts, a world of northern lights, the land of Thor, where the god, disguised as a wolf with sky-blue eyes, keen and intelligent, visited frequently.

By the time he regained awareness, able to rise from his bed; winter was nearly over, still cold, snow remaining on the ground, but the sky blue with promise. Ivan helped him to the kitchen, on weak, shaky knees, having lost much weight,

192

pale as freshly fallen snow, food having no appeal to him whatsoever.

"You're not much to look at my friend, but I'm glad to be looking at you at all. Honestly, I didn't think that you were going to make it through the winter," Ivan told him.

"I didn't think so either, but I was pretty mixed up for a while there."

"I know, it's going to take you a while to get back."

"I don't have a lot of time." Bryan said, an edge of panic in his voice.

"Well we're going to have to get to work on it then. We're going to start with daily walks, and you'll have to eat more." Ivan shoved another loaf of flat bread at him.

The loaf looked huge; it was going to be an effort.

Yesterday the attendant told him he was gaunt, no more than a skeleton, his hands and wrists thin, and the bones were obvious. He still coughed a lot, was very weak, feeling terrible.

Nibbling at bread and sipping ale, nothing tasted good; Ivan helped him back to the bathhouse, where he collapsed onto his bed and slept.

The days passed, and he struggled, with Ivan's constant insistence and urging, he walked a little further each day, and ate a little more of the tasteless food. Eventually, he was able to crawl into the hot tub, without the help of his friends. His improvement was slow.

The weeks passed, and the sun was beginning to shine with a little warmth melting the snow away. Getting around some, by himself, he even went to the sparing arena to practice for short periods. The time was approaching for the spring celebrations; he had to get himself back in shape urgently. Forcing himself to eat and drink; he was gradually gaining some weight, and he wasn't out of breath as much.

One day, the Jarl bumped into him in the Great Hall.

"Bryan," he said, surprised, "It's so good to see you out of your sick bed," trying to be sincere.

"Thank you, m'lord, I'm feeling much better now." Ivan had told him that the Jarl had visited him every day when he was very sick.

"That's wonderful, the last time I saw you we didn't think you were going to live. I'm so glad that didn't happen."

"Thank you, m'lord."

That evening they were eating, when Ivan said, "They found the bodies."

Chapter 18

"What bodies?"

"You know, the guards from the warehouse."

Bryan had forgotten about them, "When?"

"This afternoon."

"Where were they?"

"They were floating in the fjord just north of here in a little bay."

"In the fjord?"

"Yea, I guess the villagers hauled them up there in the blizzard, cut a hole in the ice, and stuffed them in; they really didn't want them discovered."

Bryan had to chuckle at the macabre way they followed his instructions during the blizzard.

Heavy winter weather gave way to spring, days warming, nights no longer frigid, patches of grass and spring flowers sprang from beneath the melting snow, the aurora no longer visiting every night sky, the sound of birds returned to the forest, and water birds gliding over the waters once again; another month, and Walpurgis would be upon them.

Bryan's health, returned for the most part, spells of coughing and weakness still plaguing him, his weight still not completely restored. He resumed regular training at the arena, spending many hours with Vandel, learning his wisdom and knowledge of politics and war, who the Jarl's allies were, who could be trusted, and who were untrustworthy. Bryan was frighteningly aware he was being groomed for leadership in the Jarl's court, amazingly having escaped suspicion, aware of partiality shown, and special treatment afforded him, by the Dane, adding to his now mixed emotions about, and the urgent need to finish his business with the Jarl, before given the commission to command a mission he did not want.

Fourteen days until Walpurgis, and Bryan, more edgy and anxious by the day, more secure when with Ivan, now occupied with his own duties, not always available. Heading to the Inn one evening, someone walking from the bottom of the hill, about to pass him, a bedraggled traveler; there was something about him, his gait, the angle of his shoulders, vaguely familiar; Bryan couldn't shake the feeling he knew this man, as they were about to pass he raised his face toward Bryan, it was Ari.

It took Bryan a second to fully recognize his cousin; it struck joy into his heart. Ari had matured; the expression of confidence on his face, presenting himself as someone other than who he was, without hesitation, his shoulders broad and powerful, his thighs strong, from walking over the great mountains, powerful like his great father.

In the dim light of dusk Ari did not recognize him. Bryan caught him across the chest with his walking stick, "Bow before your superior you sniveling karl," he commanded.

Ari straightened to his full height, defiance exploding from his face, with only a trace of recognition, he shot back, "I'll only bow if the swine deserves it."

Bryan quickly shot back, "You'll show respect if you're made to."

"And I suppose you think you're half man enough," Ari replied, his axe partially drawn from his belt.

Passers by stopped, the commotion drawing attention, as the two glared at each other, then broke into raucous laughter. Bryan threw his arm around Ari's shoulders.

"It's so good to see you cousin, let me buy you a drink, and something to eat, you must be starved, after your long journey."

Activity at the Inn was lively. They found Ivan sitting in a corner, and sat down to tankards of brightly fresh spring ale, told stories and joked around for a while, but the conversation turned serious when Ivan mentioned Bryan's illness.

"You've been sick?" Ari asked.

"Nearly lost him this winter," Ivan said.

"What," Ari exclaimed with concern.

"Bad cough, fever," Bryan explained, "Didn't know anything for a long time, took forever to get over it," making little of it.

Ari sat silently, looking at Bryan. It never occurred, to either of them, they might lose the other; he didn't know what to say.

"I'm ok now, really," Bryan assured him.

"Besides, if I weren't here, Ivan would be more than happy to take my place."

Ari glanced at Ivan. Who smiled and shifted in his seat; confident and cocky lately, although not really sure what they were talking about, confident it was something ugly.

"He's quite capable," Bryan added.

Ivan looked back and forth between the two of them, half expecting an explanation, which was not forthcoming, at the same time, trying to decide if they were joking or serious.

They left the Inn, walked slowly along the docks, brisk business going on; workers unloading, and loading ships, arriving in increasing numbers now that the seas had calmed, from the winter storms.

"Ivan, can you get away for a few days?" Bryan asked, "I'd like to go up into the hills again, just the three of us, like we did before."

"I might be able to have my understudy take over for a few days."

197

"Only three maybe four days, I need to get back as well," Bryan said reassuringly. "We'll leave first thing in the morning, early.

"You still have much to learn, Vandel objected, "After missing out this winter, every day is important. If you're going to lead men into battle you're going to have to know these things."

"It'll only be a couple of days, you won't even notice I'm gone, I'll catch up when I get back, you'll see," Bryan pleaded, knowing full well he was going no matter what the General wished.

Vandel finally gave in.

Off before dawn, the air crisp and cool, winding their way up through the forest, unto steep rocky trails, leading high up into the mountains. By evening, coming upon a lake, fed by a high water fall, and made camp, sleeping under their blankets and the clear star studded sky. Before sunrise, they were back on the trail, by the time the sun was overhead, reaching the cold, high, snowy ridges overlooking the fjord, a spectacular view, far up and down the fjord, boats, but tiny specks on the water, eagles soaring, far below. They made camp.

Cutting blocks of snow they built a wind break, protection against mighty winds, that would rip across the high peaks, that night. Afterward, the snares they set earlier provided hairs, to be roasted over a small fire, of burning branches, wood they gathered while still in the forest below. The sun slowly sank low to the horizon in the west, setting the sky on fire, orange and red, a single wisp of cloud, floating, golden, above the western horizon, dazzling them, with its incandescent, silvery brilliance. The fjord sparkled, reflecting the brilliant color of the sky, onto the mountains, it was spectacular; they sat in awe, silent, drinking in the splendor, watching the sky fade to the blue and purple of twilight. The moon made its appearance, climbing into the darkening sky, soon to turn black, sprinkled with stars, like sugar cast from earthly bonds by the gods.

They laughed and joked, told stories of youthful adventures, and tales heard in their younger years. Bryan and Ari shared many times like this in the past, and Ari and Ivan's friendship made him feel secure, avoiding thought of the future.

As if signaled by the rising moon, the icy wind roared down from the mountain tops, forcing their retreat to the shelter to huddle under their blankets, the evening interlude gone.

Across the tops of the mountains, the sun rose early, the wind, in turn, dying to a light breeze; mists flowed through forest valleys and crevices below. They set their course downward, into the trees, where it was warmer. They reverted to boyish games; sword fighting with sticks, chasing each other through the tall trees, when they became hot, striping off their clothes, and swimming in an icy cold lake, bone numbing, putting their teeth to chatter, and crawling out onto a huge rock, warming themselves in the sun; great fun, it was, to pretend to be young boys again, free of care.

They built a good fire, as evening approached, and roasted rabbits. Bryan began to talk as they ate, his mood suddenly serious, "This is our last night away from snooping ears. We must talk," speaking mainly to Ivan, "It is time for Ari and me to take our revenge, after we do, the kingdom will be plunged into chaos. War with the northern armies will ensue, reluctant villages will bolt, Balestrand will not be a safe place to be."

"Bryan and I will make a hasty escape, from the Jarl's knights. You too, Ivan, should leave as soon as you can, even before Walpurgis," Ari said.

"When is this going to happen?" Ivan asked.

"On the final day of the celebration," Ari answered.

"Does anyone else know?"

"No," Bryan answered, "I plan to warn Ole, so that he can escape, too."

Ivan stared down between his knees, for a while, and looked up, "I'll leave before the start of Walpurgis, and I'll not be returning home," he announced.

"Oh?" Bryan questioned.

"I'm going to go east, to Sogndal, to ask the chieftain for his daughters hand in marriage," Ivan said.

Bryan knew, Ivan had been thinking about it, since they had returned from the village, "You're going to do it aren't you? You know she may have already given birth to your child, and the chieftain may be after your head."

"That's a chance I have to take, can't help it, I love her," Ivan said, defiantly.

"I understand, I do, and I'll miss your friendship and bravery, but follow your heart, I envy you," Bryan said.

"Enough of this dour talk," Ari yelled, "I'm going to catch a troll," jumping up and running off into the darkness. Ivan looked up startled, mystified.

Bryan laughed, "Not if I catch you first," he yelled, and ran off into the darkness, after him.

Ivan, at a complete loss, trying to follow, not able to see in the dark, ran head long into Bryan with a yelp, knocking both of them to the ground, Bryan grabbed him about the chest as they fell; Ivan fought, struggling to free himself.

"Shh, shh, Quiet. Hold still," Bryan whispered urgently. Ivan stopped. "Come with me," Bryan whispered.

"You two are about as quiet as a heard of reindeer," Ari's voice echoed through the trees.

Bryan pulled Ivan by the arm, half dragging the poor boy through the trees.

"What?" Ivan whispered.

"Shh, come with me - be quiet." They ran in a wide circle, around the perimeter of the fire, Ari's heavy breathing coming from where they had just been, stopping. Bryan slowly walked Ivan back, away from the fire. Ivan stepped on a branch, it snapped, Bryan grabbed him by the collar, pulling him, zig zaging in a tangent away from the spot.

Ivan ran into a tree, dazing him. Bryan sat him on the ground by the trunk, "Stay here until I call you, if Ari comes near, don't move or say anything," he whispered, then disappeared into the darkness; Ivan was alone.

A few moments later, Bryan yelled something, from the far side of the fire, and someone ran past him, very close. It went on and on, like this, with hoots and hollers, coming from every direction, a crash, like someone hitting some brush, off to his left, another loud yell, sounded like Ari, then things went quiet, for a long while.

Ivan thinking they left him alone, became angry, and decided to make his way back to the fire, but not good at maneuvering in the dark, a branch caught his foot, he tumbled head over heals, something skittered on the ground to his left, a light breeze rustled the leaves over head, suddenly, in front of him, he wasn't sure, did he see something, was he just imagining things, something big, he thought, getting up slowly, there it was again, straining to see, his heart thumping inside his chest, wishing it would stop, sure it could be heard, he held his breath, panicing.

Suddenly, something huge moved in front of him, blocking the light of the fire, a deep growl, it towered over him. He didn't know if he let out a cry or not, but turned to run, taking a few steps, he ran into a - he didn't know what, hard, it gave a little, and grabbed him, in a vise like grip, he fell, it fell on top of him; screaming, fighting for his life, he felt something else on him too, tearing at his clothes, holding him down, his shirt pulled over his head, fighting harder, his trousers came off, his efforts, useless.

Coming to his senses, realizing Ari was holding him down, must be Bryan taking his clothes, he stopped fighting, began cursing, Ari released him, the two, laughing hysterically, ran off toward the fire, leaving him alone, naked, and feeling incredibly foolish.

The two cousins were sitting by the fire, talking, when Ivan returned to the fire side, from the darkness of the forest.

"Ivan, where are your clothes? Aren't you cold?" Bryan teased.

Ivan saying nothing, casually walked to the fireside, sat down, and stared at the fire, absently. After a long silence, Bryan began to giggle, Ivan himself, unable to hold back, started to laugh, Ari soon followed, all of them roaring with laughter.

"I've been had," Ivan finally said, wiping tears from his eyes, "How'd you ever think all that up?"

"That was an old game we used to play when we were young, you seemed so naive about it, after I caught Ari, we decided to see if we could give you a scare."

"We didn't expect you to come unglued; you're worse than a crazed berserker," Ari chipped in.

"I thought you were a bear or something," Ivan said, "How did you make yourself so large?"

"Ari gave me his shirt, and I held it up over my head, crude, but in the shadows, effective."

"Scared the Valhalla out of me," Ivan said.

"You fought like a banshee," Ari pulled his shirt up over his head. His stomach, chest, and arms were scratched and bruised like he'd done battle with a wild cat."

"Oh Ari, I'm sorry, I didn't know."

"It's nothing. Guess I deserved it," Ari said.

"Dam right you did." Bryan added.

"Who asked you?" Ari shoved Bryan off the log, into the dirt.

"My, aren't we touchy tonight?" Bryan came back.

Ari tossed Ivan his clothes, "Here, you're good looking, but you're turning blue, beneath a man of your station," he said, a note of sarcasm in his voice.

"Oh yea," Ivan exclaimed, "I've been having so much fun I'd almost forgot about my clothes."

In the morning, they reluctantly headed back to Balestrand, continuing the banter, teasing Ivan about running about nude.

"I rather like not having to wear clothes," Ivan claimed, "Might not wear any when I get back," He claimed.

"Yea the ladies in waiting would like that," Bryan said.

"I bet I could get some offers," Ivan claimed.

"I'd bet you could too, especially the ones you been poking," Bryan taunted.

"Ari don't believe a word he says."

"You mean you're head page, and you haven't taken advantage of the ladies?" Bryan questioned.

"I'd have to play their games, bitches don't offer up anything, less there's strings attached, and I'll not let them tie me down, just to get into their skirts."

"You don't like what's under those skirts?" Bryan ribbed him.

"Not those skirts."

"Oh, that's right, you fancy young peasant girls, don't you?" Bryan continued his chide.

"Just one," Ivan said, still pining for the chieftain's daughter.

As they neared Balestrand their talk dwindled, and they walked in silence. Bryan warily anxious about the next few days, he was about to turn his life upside down, become a fugitive, hunted wherever he went, his friends, family, and Norway would, in all probability, be lost to him for a very long time, if not eternity. His oath to Thor seemed distant, remote, abstract just now, yet he was bound to it, and the weight of its burden seemed very heavy.

Back in Balestrand, they headed for a bath and a decent meal.

They were devouring mutton stew when Ivan looked up, "Here comes trouble."

Brian turned to see Vandel heading their way.

Chapter 19

"You're late," the man shouted, irate, "You said you'd be back yesterday, now you're a whole day late."

"We ahhhh..., got lost," Bryan lied, "Sorry, M'lord, haven't eaten in days," more lies, "Got back as soon as we could. I'll resume my lessons right away, and I'll make up the lost time."

"See to it. I'll be expecting you straight way."

"Yes, m'lord."

The knight huffed away.

They looked at each other and snickered.

"Guess I'd better get going," He told Ari and Ivan. He'd let Vandel down, not his intention, and lying made him feel worse, the knight had been good to him, the only person in the Jarl's court he could trust.

"Well when you're finished with your 'royal duties' I'll see you at the inn," Ari said, "I'm going to enjoy a few brews."

The lesson seemed to drag on forever, his heart not in it, and the knight sensing it, not pleased, it was uncomfortable for them both.

Bryan found his friends, neither one feeling any pain. He would have liked to join them, but after a meal and a tankard, found he wasn't in the mood. Ari and Ivan struck up a lively acquaintance with some rather homely girls, who held no interest for him. Leaving his friends, to spend their money on the bawdy women, he walked out to the boat docks, sat there and watched seamen unload a newly arrived knar. Soft waves rolling in from the fjord, salt air invading his nostrils, a few birds circling overhead, searching for a last morsel or a sanctuary for the night, his thoughts wandered.

Faces of men he'd killed, burned indelibly in his mind, the smell of death in the forest, strewn with bodies, that eerie night near Sogndal, the guards in the storeroom he and Ivan murdered, the men the villagers stuffed under the ice, Ivan's rapist, the hapless head page, who's death ultimately lead to promotion for him, the Jarl's advisor, who died due to Bryan's own carelessness, and now, he was about to betray the Jarl, a man who obviously cared for him, and who's death would inevitably lead to death for countless people. He closed his eyes, trying to shut out the thought, to banish it from his mind, the oath was sworn, it had to be done.

But why, why was his father sent Viking, why had his uncle been murdered?

Morning came too soon, still listless, he went for a long walk, along the shore, on his return, he spotted the unmistakable broad shoulders, and muscular legs of Ari, far ahead, silhouetted in the morning light, standing on the shore, looking out over the water at nothing.

"What are you doing?" Bryan asked.

"Went for a swim to wash off, it's cold," he was shivering.

"Where are your clothes?" Bryan asked.

Ari looked down at himself, they were scattered over the shore, he stumbled toward them, obviously still drunk, Bryan steadied him.

"I'll get them; did you have a good time last night?" He asked.

Ari stopped to think, smiled, "Too good, she was a lot of fun."

"That's good, because she sure wasn't much to look at." Bryan added.

"Didn't need to be," Ari paused and smiled again, "Ivan sure had a good time, don't think he stopped all night, in the crib next to us, poor wench was crying for mercy." He chuckled, and almost fell down, hobbled by the trousers around his ankles. "That wench earned her money last night for sure, bet her back'll be akin' today, and she'll be raw as meat, down there this morning," he almost fell again, for laughing.

Bryan helped pull up his trousers, guided him back to the barracks, laid him out on the platform. "Don't you get sick in here, if you have to, go out to the street," He said. But, Ari was already passed out; Ivan was probably in a similar condition, somewhere.

He endured another long tedious day of grilling by Vandel, and when it was finished, went to the inn to see if his friends survived, finding Ari in a corner, drinking cider, nibbling flat bread, pale as a ghost.

"How you feeling?"

"Not so good," not moving his head, pointing to the door, "Better than him;"
Ivan, just coming in the door, walking funny, unsteady.

"You ok?" Bryan asked.

"Little stiff," Ivan said, "Used parts of me, hadn't been used in a while," he chuckled.

"And a little raw in places?" Ari chided.

Ivan blushed, "Kind a tender."

"No doubt," Ari added, "Never met anyone could get it up that much."

Ivan blushed, "Tell you my secret someday."

"All right you two," Bryan broke in.

"Jealousy speaks," Ivan shot back.

"Yea, well this morning, I was glad I hadn't joined in, carrying Ari back to my room," Bryan said.

"You're right there," Ari grimaced, "My head still feels like one a those big ole knights stepped on it."

207

Ivan shook his head, not any too vigorously.

Bryan had dinner, boiled eggs and salmon with a tankard of ale, as he watched the others pick at a bowl of stew. There was no celebrating that night.

The days passed painfully slow. He kept his sessions with Vandel, and tried to pretend to be interested, struck up a friendship with a lovely girl at court, would have liked to spend a night or two with her, but she was more interested in his prospects as a future knight, and always seemed to disappear as soon as court was over.

Walpurgis, only two days away, its eve would be a day of feast, in the streets, a happy time, followed by two nights of sacrifice and mayham by the shamans. The Hof made ready; the great oak cleared of previous sacrifices, wreaths, and dried flowers, the cauldron scrubbed clean, and piles of wood brought in to fuel the fire.

Skjolden was busy, making preparations, a time when he would speak with the gods, to ensure success in the coming year, when the knights would pay tribute to their leader, and receive commissions for the next season. The Dane would seclude himself in the Great Hall for two days and nights, very solemn and secretive.

During a break in his grilling by Vandel, Bryan found Ivan directing the pages at the rear of the hall. "Can I talk to you for a moment?" Bryan asked.

They found a quiet side room.

"What's this all about," Ivan asked.

"Ari needs a dark suit like the ones we have, but I don't want to have him fitted. It might look suspicious."

"I can see that," Ivan said.

"I was thinking that you could borrow one of the knight's uniforms, someone about Ari's size, someone who wouldn't miss it for a few days."

Ivan thought a moment then nodded, "I can do that." He paused, "Bryan?"

"Yes."

"I'll be leaving the night before Walpurgis eve."

"Won't they miss you?"

"No, the pages all have their assignments, won't be noticed till long afterward. They're going to be after <u>you</u>, remember?"

Bryan nodded, and said softly, "Yea …, I remember."

The evening before Ivan's departure, they met at the inn, a last meal together, a somber, emotion filled get together. Bryan tried his best to suppress the true meaning of the gathering, he was edgy.

"I've got a suit for Ari," Ivan handed a package to Bryan.

"Excellent," Bryan said, and handed the package to Ari.

Bryan had asked the inn keeper to prepare a special meal of roast duck, with carrots, radishes, and onions, they ate, and made small talk, afterward, Bryan ordered tankards of the inn's best ale.

Bryan cleared his throat, and steeled his emotions, "I have a few words for Ivan who is about to start a new life. I can tell you, I'm pretty choosy about who I call friends. But, Ivan, you are one of the best men I've ever met, don't come any better than you my friend, honest, true, and brave. I know that you will make that little girl happy, be a credit to your clan, and have many children, may happiness follow you."

They raised their tankards in a toast.

The next day, after Vandel finished putting him through his paces, Bryan met Ari and Ivan in front of the sparing arena.

Ivan, wearing heavy hunting clothes, a hefty pack slung on his back, a walking stick in hand, and his sword wrapped in cloth tied to the back of his pack.

Their good-by, lengthy, full of embraces and farewells; when Ivan headed off down the hill for the ferry, Bryan gave Ari a long sad look, sat down on the bench, buried his face in his hands, and wept, the emptiness in his stomach, beyond description. Ari at his side, arm around his shoulders.

After eating that evening, they went down to the docks to watch the sun set. Bryan wished he were one of the birds, free to fly away, to find Ivan, and frolic in the forest. But, he remained shackled to the earth, and the burden of his oath. He touched the tiny hammer tied to his neck.

Walpurgis eve day began with clear skies, bright sunshine, and warm breezes across the fjord. Spring was advancing, rapidly, summer soon to come, with its promise of afternoon thunderstorms, fresh crops, new food to eat, and adventure in every young man's mind.

People, all over the village, held feasts in the street, in front of their homes, while others paraded about town, in their finest attire. Strong drink of all kinds, specially made for the occasion, could be had everywhere, for the asking. There were dancing fools, performing acts of tumbling, juggling, and balance. Near the Great Hall, groups of courtesans gathered, politicking; making alliances, they hoped would bring profit and fortune in the following year. Shaman, priests to the masses, conjurers to the gods, soothsayers, makers of magic potions, and rulers of the spiritual world, roamed the streets, cajoling the crowds to attend the sacrifices.

Celebration was in the air and Bryan and Ari were going to take in as much of it as they could. They went to the bath house, only Ole was there. After a through scrubbing they soaked in the hot tub.

"Ole," Bryan called.

"Yes master Bryan," The attendant came trotting over.

"Ole, at the end of Walpurgis there is going to be great change. It will not be safe here, you must make your escape." Bryan warned.

The attendant looked worried. "I don't know if it is possible for me to do so sire."

"What do you mean?" Bryan asked.

The boy looked around, nervously. "I, I am not free to go, not a free man."

"You're not?" Bryan practically shouted, incredulously.

"No sire, I'm thrall to the Dane."

"Well I'll be." Bryan dumbfounded, got up out of the tub, backing the boy up against the wall, put a finger against his chest, "Now listen to me, after Walpurgis, you will no longer be indentured to that scum, I am giving you fair warning, Balestrand will not be a safe place to be, make good your escape while you can, Ivan's already gone, I don't want you on my conscience, so get out of here."

"Yes, master Bryan," He said meekly, unconvincingly.

Then Bryan softened, "You've been a good friend to me, helped when I needed help, I love you, Ole, I mean that, I want you gone from here."

Ari was out of the bath and standing behind Bryan in support.

"If I have to carry you out, with my bare hands, I will. Now, be brave, and ready yourself."

The boy lowered his gaze, and almost whispered, "Yes master."

"WHAT did you say," Bryan grabbed the towel from Ole's hand and began drying himself.

"Yes…, Bryan."

"That's more like it," Bryan said.

The boy hurried to Ari with a towel, but Bryan snatched it away from him and handed it to Ari. "We can care for ourselves; you've groveled before every man who came through that door for so long you don't know how to act any different. Ari and I are grown men, we can care for ourselves, you need to start taking care of yourself for a change."

The attendant gave Bryan a quick self conscious bow, and with tears in his eyes turned and left the room.

"Kind of hard on him weren't you" Ari said.

"Needed to be, shake him up a little, I'm his friend, he trusts me, it'll take him a while, but he'll break free," Bryan said, as much to reassure himself as Ari.

They were about to leave, when Ole came walking, from the back of the room, fully clothed, gone the gossamer fabrics, actually quite handsome, adult like, except for the distracting way of walking. Bryan was startled, then pleased. He hugged the boy and whispered in his ear. "You'll be ok, my friend," and kissed him on the cheek.

From there they went to the inn for a tankard of ale, and out to the docks, to exchanged friendly barbs with the dock workers.

One of the pages, a younger lad, happened by, recognizing Bryan said, "Master Bryan, how are you this fine day?"

"Quite well, my friend," Bryan couldn't remember his name, "What are you up to?"

"Just heading home, would you and your friend like to join my family in our celebration."

With little else planed, Bryan accepted, "We would be honored."

A friendly group, with good food and drink, who, after a good while, decided they should set out about town, to visit as many other celebrations as they could. After several hours, the group became quite rowdy, engaging in wrestling matches. Ari challenged some young boys to a foot race, winning handily, and was immediately challenged by older boys. Bryan found a few ladies to beguile, and before they knew it, darkness had fallen.

Piles of wood, in the streets, were set a fire, and people danced about, celebrating the arrival of spring, everyone confined all winter, finally free to be outside; their merriment continuing late into the night.

In the morning, they spent time sparing, went to the bath. Ole, still dressed in his uniform, refused to tend to them, "You can tend to yourselves," he said, "The soap is there by the tub, and here's a towel." Bryan was quite pleased, but the patrons who followed were rather indignant. Ole told them, "Go tell the Jarl if you don't like it." Bryan found it rather amusing.

Back in Bryan's room, and dressed; he in his military uniform while Ari made do with the knight's uniform, taking one of Bryan's smocks, the Jarl's coat of arms embroidered on the front, cut off the sleeves, slit it down the sides, making it into a bib to fit over the knights clothing, a sash binding it nicely at the waist. He looked elegant, and the two strutted about town like court dandies, having exactly the effect on the girls Bryan anticipated; the young women flirted, they flirted back, telling tall tales, and listening to the ladies own share of lies, a most enjoyable lark. They were fed well for their efforts, drinking plenty of fresh spring ale.

As evening approached, they headed for the Hof, to the spot on the wall near the Great Hall that Ivan took Bryan, a year earlier. The crowd, already beginning to swell, the shamans, in short time, entering in mass, parting the crowd, as they passed through to their place at the altar, putting the logs under the great cauldron to flame, bringing the water to boil, uttering incantations, passing bowls of wine about the crowd, and the chanting began.

The first goat was brought in, led through the crowd, blessed and slaughtered, its blood gathered, and passed about, the patrons smearing their faces with it, and drinking it.

The priests repeating the ritual again and again until six goats had been sacrificed, skinned, butchered, the skins, head attached, hung overhead on the poles, their meat added to the cauldron, and the crowd whipped into frenzy.

Late into the night, the air filled with the stench of dark clouds of burning flesh, Bryan nudged Ari pointing to the gate; a shaman just entering, leading a young boy, a rope tied about his neck, naked, about eleven years old, maybe twelve, not yet gone through puberty, his skin pale, unblemished, very youthful, with long, blond, curly, hair hanging freely to his shoulders, quite handsome, obviously drunken.

"What is this?" Ari said.

"Just watch," a shudder ran down his spine, knowing what was about to happen.

The boy was led through the crowd, who all tried to touch him; women especially, running their fingers over his face, through his hair, rubbing chest and caressing his genitals, the chanting frenzied.

As the shamans led the boy to the altar, Ari nudged Bryan, "Are they…?"

"Quiet, watch, we can't stop it," Bryan said.

"For the love of Oden," Ari recoiled in disgust.

The priests bound the boy's hands and feet, hoisted his feet high over his head, grabbed his hair, retched his head back, baring his throat, and slit it.

Ari cursed, closed his eyes, and turned his head; a great roar went up from the crowd. Blood flowing from his neck, the boy struggled, kicking a few times, and became still. If he left out a cry, none could have heard, for the cacophony of chanting and cheering, his body paled immediately. They hoisted the body to the alter and commenced skinning and butchering it, his hide and head, raised on a pole, and placed with that of the goats, his flesh placed in the cauldron.

"Byran, they are going to eat...," Ari pointed to the cauldron.

Bryan nodded.

"Surly not, how can the gods allow it," Ari said.

"The gods will have their way tomorrow night," Bryan said his voice dry and vengeful.

After dropping off their perch and exiting the Hof, they walked down the street toward Bryan's room.

"I don't believe what I just saw," Ari kept saying.

"The shamans hold great sway over the Jarl's kingdom," Bryan tried to explain, "He appeases them, and in turn, they help him control the kingdom. Terrible things have been done to control the people, like the murder of uncle Grunner, whole villages enslaved, they murder indiscriminately, starve the people, terrorize them, whatever it takes to keep them under their control," Bryan stopped, "We will change that."

Back in Bryan's room, they stripped off their uniforms, folded them, climbed onto the ledge, under the blankets, Ari on his side, Bryan huddled against him, placed an arm around Ari, who took Bryan's hand; a tender reminder of their vanishing youth, on what Bryan was sure, was their last night together, forever. Bryan cried, silently, until sleep carried him away, in its gentle hands.

When he woke, he was still snuggled against his cousin, like a groom with a newly wedded bride. He lay there a long time, listening to Ari breath; he was warm and his odor, a smell so familiar to Bryan, something he would miss. Today they would fulfill their oath to Thor, and embark on a new day, a new life.

He slipped from under the blankets, sat on the edge of the ledge, allowing the chill morning air to sting his flesh, reminding him he was still alive.

Ari stirred, rolled over, "What are you doing?"

"Waiting for you to wake up."

"I'm awake," he threw the blankets back, "Dam, its cold," He said, as the air struck his skin. He reached for his clothes.

"Let's go to the bath," Bryan said.

Ole met them, and set them up, and after they finished washing and settled into the tub, Ole took his clothes off and joined them, bold for the usually shy, timid boy.

"Someone might get angry with you Ole, aren't you afraid?" Bryan asked.

"Won't be any one in here today after last night," Ole said, rather proud of himself.

"You should pack and get ready to leave," Bryan said.

"Already packed, not that I have much, be gone shortly."

"Be sure you are," Bryan instructed.

Bryan sent Ari on back to his room to pack, "Ole and I have some private things to talk about."

When he was gone, they got out of the tub, dried themselves, Bryan pulled his trousers on, Ole had an inquisitive look on face, "What private things do we have to talk about Master Bryan?"

Bryan took the boy in his arms, pulled him to him, so thin and fragile, "You know I probably owe my life to you, you and Ivan, you've been such a good friend," he looked Ole in the eye, "I," He didn't know how to say it, "I'll miss you, I love you Ole."

"I Love you too Master Bryan, you are so strong and brave."

"I know you do Ole, perhaps in different circumstances, a different time we could be…, what you wanted us to be."

"Yes, perhaps, but to be your friend was enough," Ole said.

With a tear in his eye, Bryan bent his head down and kissed Ole on the lips, a long meaningful kiss, his tongue slipped into the boy's mouth, just for a moment. Then he released him.

Ole stood back and took a deep breath. "Thank you Bryan, I will always remember you," He turned and walked back into the darkness.

Bryan returned to his room, shaky and teary eyed, and packed his bag.

"You ok?"Ari asked.

"Yea, Ole was a good friend; it's hard to say good-by." He didn't care to share these particular feelings with his cousin; not even sure he knew what his feelings were, never having done anything like that, with another boy, that he was even capable of it, surprised him, though he didn't mind it, or regret it, he really meant what he did, though he probably would never do anything like it again.

.

The rest of the morning was passing tediously; in the afternoon he went to the Great Hall; waiting not one of his good points.

The guard standing dutifully at the entrance, Bryan told him, "You can go, I'll relieve you."

"But Master Bryan, It's not time yet, you have till evening," The young boy protested.

"I know, but I have nothing else to do, and don't like waiting around, you go ahead, enjoy your day. Is the Jarl still in there?" This was his third day of fasting and praying in seclusion.

"Far as I know, took a peek a while back, and he was up there reading and praying."

"Anybody else in there with him?"

"Don't think so, least as I saw."

"Ok, you go on then, have a nice afternoon."

Biding time was tedious and agonizing, but he found standing guard, better than sitting idle somewhere. He paced back and forth in front of the entrance, occasionally talking to passersby, trying not to appear anxious, monotony giving way to invention; in his idle mind rehearsing, in detail, the gruesome ballet he was about to perform, over and over, searching for mistakes, each time; the possibilities grew, along with his anxiety.

With evening approaching, Ari arrived, a loaf of bread in hand for Bryan. Nibbling on the loaf, Bryan gave instructions in a low voice.

"We'll go inside shortly, you'll shadow me, I can only stay a moment or two, when I leave, you'll stay, remove the smock, put on your mask, you'll be as dark as night, be absolutely silent, hide yourself somewhere close to the throne, and wait. I will be in after the first sacrifice. Stay concealed until I call you."

Ari nodded silently. Bryan wondered if his cousin was as nervous as he.

Slowly, quietly, he undid the latch, opened the huge door, enough to slip in, the hinges making a muffled, grating, noise, Ari following, stealthy as a ghost, Bryan eased the door closed. Ari removed his boots, setting them beside the door, put his mask on, and disappeared into the darkness. From where he stood, Bryan could see the Jarl, sitting on his throne, at the far end of the hall, the only light, huge candles, at either side of the throne, rivulets of frozen wax, caked their sides and bases. The Jarl was reciting something, in Danish, from a scroll. Bryan backed toward the door and slipped out.

Twilight, its dim colors of blue and purple filling the sky, brought with it the first of the revelers filing into the Hof. He stood nervously before the door and watched, wondering if Ole had made his escape, Ivan should have arrived in Sogndal by now; he said a prayer to Thor for his friends. Slowly the last light faded from the sky, the line of people entering the Hof increased, smoke from the freshly lit fire drifted into the street. The wait seeming interminable, at last the shamans led the first beleaguered goat into the Hof, the chanting began, reached a crescendo, then slowly dwindled.

When there was a quiet moment, Bryan slipped back into the hall, closed the door, bolting it from the inside, removed his tunic, except for his face, as black as night. Pulling Grunner's sword from its sheath, ever so slowly, not making a sound, and silently moving into the hall.

The Jarl sat illuminated, alone, surrounded by darkness, an actor on a stage, reading lines from a scroll, open on his lap; incantations to the gods, some in Norse, some in Danish, endlessly, without inflection, and probably without much understanding.

His uncle's sword, held close to his side, crossing the great expanse, one slow step at a time, not daring to make a sound, shrouded in darkness, nearer ever nearer, the Jurl's

219

figure, becoming ever larger, the walk taking much, much longer than Bryan had ever imagined, mind numbing; outside the people in the Hof beginning chanting again.

Bryan appearing from the darkness, as if by magic, but few feet away, the man jumped, frightened; nearly upsetting the throne.

"Bryan," he shouted, "What are you doing here? Why have you left your post?"

"I've come to avenge my murdered uncle." Bryan said, slowly, purposefully as he brought his sword, to the man's throat.

"What?" The Jarls said, clearly not comprehending.

"You remember," Bryan said, accusing, "you brought his dead body to our home, after you murdered him, then asked me to come to serve you."

"I've not murdered anyone," the Dane pleaded.

"You did, I saw you with my own eyes."

"How could you possibly, we found him dead in the road, I swear."

"My cousin, Ari and I were on the mountain, cutting wood, saw you argue with Grunner, watched your guards hold him, saw you kill him, stabbing him with your sword, and now, it's your turn to die."

"Bryan after all I've done for you; schooled you, promoted you, loved you like a son, how can you turn on me like this," the Jarl pleaded.

"I came to you, at your request, asked for nothing, giving you ample time, now vengeance is mine."

"I don't think so," a deep, calm, familiar, voice came from his left, a voice that shouldn't have been there; Vandel, the Jarl's forever loyal body guard, his sword drawn and pointed at Bryan.

The Jarl smiled, "Surly you didn't think me fool enough to rely on a single unproven and youthful guard."

"You know Vandel, I can best you in a fight." Bryan challenged, not taking his eye off the Dane.

"At your pleasure," Vandel accepted, "You can fight or drop your weapon."

Bryan remained unflinching, "I afraid I can't do that," a drop of sweat, trickled down the side of his face.

"Kill the fool," the Jarl said.

"Drop the sword, Now!" Vandel demanded.

Again, more magic, from the darkness, a long thin blade, appeared, from behind the knight, pressing against his neck. Ari's deep voice said, "I think not. Why don't you drop yours?"

Vandel hesitated, Ari pressed the razor sharp blade, causing a stream of blood to run down the knight's neck, "Drop it now," he said slowly.

The sword fell to the floor.

"Who in Oden's shit is this?" The Jarl demanded.

"You shut up," Bryan pressed the tip of his sword to the notch just below the Jarl's adam's apple.

"Shall I kill him?" Ari asked.

"No, Wait!" Bryan said firmly.

He carefully angled himself, close to the throne, pulled a sash from the legs of the chair. Vandel had been a friend to Bryan, taught him much, the knight should probably be killed, he would identify Bryan as the killer, but Bryan could not bring himself to it. He threw the sash to Ari, "Take him to the side and tie him securely. Gag him."

Ari well experienced, tying livestock, quickly bound and gagged the man.

Then returned behind the throne, reaching around the Dane, and flashed his blade before the Jarl's eyes.

"Ari here is fond of his long, thin blade, he's honed it to a fine edge, used it for killing pigs, like you, he finds it very efficient at cutting throats." Bryan said.

The Jarl very tense.

"Now…, Jarl Skjolden, this is my cousin Ari, Grunner's son. Ari and I are close, people call us brothers, Grunner a father to both of us, and we have some questions for you."

"Take this knife from my neck, and I shall consider it."

"Answer our question first," Bryan shouted back angrily, not in any mood to listen to this man's pander. Ari pressed the blade into the Jarl's flesh. "What did you hold over my father that made him abandon his family and go Viking?"

"Ask your father, he's probably too embarrassed to tell you, like he never schooled you how to service a women," The Jarl sneered.

"I think not, you worm, you've sent him to places even you know nothing of. Answer the question. Why did you kill Grunner, was it for the same reason?"

"Your father can tell you, of his cowardly tendencies, I will not, now get this scum off me," he demanded.

Bryan dropped his blade to the man's stomach just below his rib cage.

"Bryan you must stop this, this insanity," the Jarl beseeched.

"Insane it may be, but Ari and I have sworn an oath, to Thor, to avenge the murder of my uncle, be quiet now while I tell you a story."

The Jarl was sweating profusely, droplets running down his face. In the background the chanting in the Hoff went on and on.

"After swearing our oath, you invited me here, tried to woo me with power, prestige, the promise of adventure, but, as soon as I arrived, I began to press thorns into your side. It was I who eliminated your knight, for violating your pages, sins he paid for with his life, it was I who saw to it that your thralls escaped."

"YOU, you did that," the man shouted, his eyes bulging, red with fury, straining against Ari's blade, which cut deeper into his neck, blood oozed down over his smock.

"The defeat of your army at Sogndal, an ambush, arranged by myself and the clan's chief, how many died, seventy five? And your food stores, you could have given them to the starving villagers, but were too selfish to share, as you promised you would, I led the assault on the guards, and gave the villagers their supplies."

"You Loki, you'll die for this," the Jarl yelled.

"No I think not," Bryan's voice deep, and calmed now, "Thor has given this day to me, it's your turn to die," with that, Bryan thrust his sword into the Jarl's belly, up through his lungs.

The man let out a horribly loud, inhuman scream, at the same time Ari pulling his head back, drawing his knife across the taunt neck, cutting deep into the flesh of his throat. The man coughed up copious amounts of blood, through the new opening in his neck, that splashed down over his front, his eyes bulging, body shuddering, sucking air in through the opening, coughing it up again, blood spewing with every heart beat. Bryan again thrust his blade up into his lungs, shoving it to the side, the spasms stopped, his breathing ceased; his body went limp, and the gushing blood
slowed to a trickle.

Bryan pulled his sword from the body, stuck it into the floor. He placed his hands on the Jarl's chest, allowing blood to flow over them, raised his hands into the air, "Lord Thor here is the blood the Dane, Skjolden, our oath, fulfilled, as promised."

He fell silent, dropped his eyes to the gore of the dead man, the image burning into his brain, and the dead man becoming a vision, a raging bear, deep wounds on its bloody lips and tongue. Like a charge of lightening, he was bent over with orgasm, powerful, all consuming, taking away his breath, he stumbled backward, dazed, the spasms, incapacitating him, his brain bathed in pleasure.

"Bryan… Bryan," a stunned Ari called, not knowing what was happening.

Embarrassed, recovering, he stood up, slowly, trembling, his face flushed red, his trousers wet, hoping it wouldn't be noticed.

"Yes," Bryan stammered, "We must go," his head spinning.

"What about him?" Ari nodded toward the tethered knight.

"Go to the door, I'll tend to him."

Bryan walked to the rumpled form, on the floor, near the wall, and knelt down.

"M'Lord, according to my plan, I should kill you now, but you have been a friend to me, a good man, and I haven't the heart to put you to death, besides, what's the point? It won't take a genius to figure out who did this, please, don't think too harsh of me," their eyes met, Bryan patted him on the shoulder, "Old soldiers have to look out for one another, my friend."

He rushed to the entrance, unbolted the door, and pushed, with the creak of hinges, it gave way, they stopped, abruptly; Shamans, just a few steps away, were wrestling with an uncooperative goat, taking long anxious moments to move the animal toward the Hof, a few steps at a time. While they waited, Bryan rigged the heavy timber crossbar, to fall into place when the door closed, securing the door from the inside, he and Ari slipped out, pulled the massive door closed, the bar clunked into place with a loud bang.

Hurriedly walking down the street, past the Hof, to the barracks only to pick up their packs, past the sparing arena, to the Jarl's unguarded private stables, heading directly to the back where the Jarl's horses were stabled.

About half way, they came up short, "What was that?" He'd heard something strange.

Ari heard it too, "Came from back there," He pointed to the front of the building.

Quietly creeping toward the entrance, the noise almost inaudible, so soft, not sure they were hearing it, stopping at the first stall, they listened, there it was, subtle, faint, like the whimper of a baby; Ari turned the latch on the door, it swung open on its own, a single candle flickered, in the straw, on the floor, a boy, the same boy they'd seen sacrificed the night before. A cold chill ran up Bryan's spine.

Ari whispered, "What in the…, it's a ghost."

The boy looked up, in fear, his face wet with tears, naked, shivering. Bryan bravely reached out, touching his face, fair skinned, light curly hair, the face of an angle, exactly like the boy they saw killed in the ceremony.

"He's alive, no ghost," Bryan said softly.

"It's impossible, we saw them kill him, his hide still hangs in the Hof," Ari said.

Still for the longest time, Bryan's brain raced to understand, "Twins."

"What?"

"Twins, a perfect set-up, two boys exactly alike, on two nights of sacrifice, would set the crowd crazy," he paused, reached down, took the boys hand, and pulled him to his feet.

The lad began to sob, said something neither of them understood, a long sentence, foreign.

225

"Must be Rus or something," Ari said.

Bryan pulled the boy along, they hurried toward the rear, to the Jarl's horses, quickly saddling and harnessing the tall steeds, attached their packs, climbing up on their backs, Bryan reaching down, taking the youth by the arm, hoisted him up onto the saddle in front of him. Still crying and shivering, Bryan pulled him to his chest, wrapped his arms around him, he would need to find clothing for him, no time for that now. It would have to wait.

They rode quickly down the hill, though empty streets, to the edge of the village. Once clear, breaking into a run, till they were well away, then slowing to a canter. A beautiful crisp evening, full moon, casting long shadows, enough light to stay to the trail; the same trail Bryan traveled on his journey from Hoyanger to Balestrand.

About half way to Kvamme, Ari pulled up, "This is where I head north to meet Lord Innvik."

"And so we part again, cousin, with the heaviest of hearts," Bryan could not keep the sadness from his voice.

"Don't forget me," Ari said, moon light glistened from the tears on his cheeks, as he turned.

"Never, my brother," Bryan proclaimed.

"May Thor be with you," Ari whipped his steed, broke from the trail, and headed north.

Fighting back tears of his own, heart ache threatening to overwhelm him, Bryan urged the horse on at a dead run, the powerful animal closing the distance to Kvamme quickly, winded and in need of rest, by the time they arrived; Bryan pulled up at the cabin with the blue door.

The boy, still naked and very cold, no longer cried. Bryan lifted him from the horse, took his hand and gently led him to the door. He knocked.

The wait seemed forever, Bryan was nervous, the door opened, Gloa exclaimed, "What in the name of Furies can anyone want at this hour of the night."

"Gloa please, I need your help."

She paused a moment, then recognizing him, "Bryan, what's the matter, who is this poor lad with nothing on?"

"Remember I said I might need your help someday?"

"Sure, sure."

"Well, today's the day I spoke of, the boy's a thrall, about to be sacrificed to the gods, by the shamans; I only just found him, as we were escaping, there was no time to find clothes, he's almost frozen," Bryan explained.

"Escape, what were you escaping? And who are we?" Only then turning her attention from the naked boy, to notice Bryan, his hands and clothing still covered with clotted, dried blood, "Oh my goodness, look at you, what happened?"

"The Jarl is dead, my Cousin Ari and I killed him, thought perhaps you could find the boy some clothes."

She looked behind them, "Where's your cousin?"

"Riding north, to alert Innvik."

It took Gola a moment, to take it all in, catching her breath, she stared into his eyes, surprise and disbelief on her face, "He's really dead?" She whispered.

"Yes, he is. Throat cut, sliced through the heart, he's no more."

"Well, praise the gods for that."

"In a few days, Innvik will attack Balastrand, take over the Jarl's lands."

"Ok, O-K," She gathered her thoughts, "Clothes for this poor boy." She caressed his forehead, and wrinkled her nose, "And a quick bath, smells like a pig. You too, wash that blood from your hands, change your clothes, they're a dead giveaway." She stirred the coals in her hearth, had a fire

227

burning in no time, and placed a big kettle of water over the flames to warm.

Bryan took a bucket of water to the horse. When he returned Gloa was scrubbing the boy, standing passively in front of the fire. He looked up at Bryan smiling, such a lovely, handsome, youth, how anyone could think of sacrificing him, Bryan couldn't imagine.

He pulled off his blood soaked cloths, washed the blood from his hands and arms, put on dry clothes from his pack, and cleaned his uncle's sword. Gloa fitted the boy with a pair of her trousers, about the same height as the boy, but bigger around the waist, fitting them with a piece of rope, pulled tight, a heavy shirt, loose on him, fell to his knees.

"He say anything you could understand?" Bryan asked.

"Not a word."

"Spoke something, we didn't understand, when we found him, sounded like Rus."

"Well I wouldn't understand that."

The lad looked down at the cloths, then up at Gloa and Bryan and smiled. Bryan knelt down in front him, pointed to himself, saying his name, slowly, three times.
The boy nodded and said, "Bry – ann," heavily accented.

"Yes, yes, very good," Bryan exclaimed.

The boy pointed to his chest and said, "Uri."

"Uri," Bryan said. The boy nodded yes, with a big smile, his blue eyes sparkling with delight. Bryan hugged him; he could become fond of the lad in no time.

"Gloa, thank's for your help, I'd like to stay and talk, but we need to put as much distance between us and Balistrand as possible. I pray your help doesn't bring any trouble for you."

"You paid me already, bringing news of Skolden's demise, couldn't have done any better, knew it'd happen sooner or later, but never dreamed it'd be you."

She fed them, and soon as they finished they were back on the horse. Sometime, during the dark early morning, they quietly passed through Nessane, hopefully unseen, turned toward the mountain, and climbed into the peaks, with the light of dawn they crossed the snowy ranges, above timberline, Bryan keeping a wary eye open for the crazed bear, but the beast was not to be seen.

By late afternoon, they were down the mountain. Catching a glimpse of his families' homestead in the distance, sorely tempted to change his course, visit his mother, but fear, of leading anyone there, placing his family in danger, prevented it. Besides, a boat waited him, any delay could cause him to miss it, he pressed on, his heart aching, fighting back tears.

In Hoyanger, a large ocean going Karr, long in length, broad at beam, ballast of stone, loaded with cargo, was ready, the captain anxiously waiting.

"We expected you earlier," he shouted, as Bryan rode up; a big burly man, with a gruff voice, accustomed to giving orders.

"It's a long journey from Balestrand."

"Eye, I give you that, this the animal you're trade'n for your crossin'."

"It is, and this is Uri the Jarl's thrall. He'll be accompanying me, for Thor Bryanson, at the Jarl's orders. That's his own steed he's paying you with." Bryan waited, would the captain buy the story.

The man looked him over, suspicious. He ran his hand over the animals shinning white coat, feeling the muscles underneath, pried its mouth open, with strong fingers, and examined the teeth.

"Get yourself aboard then." He ordered, and handed the horse off to another man who led it away.

The ship's cargo, covered with planking, lashed down to make a deck, leaving room for rowing stations along the sides, where rowers sat ready. In the center of the deck, a single mast, rigged to hoist a square sail. Bryan sat on the deck, with the boy, near the mast. In short time, the knarr left the dock, on their way, in the early morning; they would be leaving the fjord for open-ocean.

Part II

Chapter 20

Ari drove the Jarl's, now his, beautiful white stallion, north along obscure mountain trails, up into the timber, and cold, rare mountain air. His mind troubled, the company of his cousin the past weeks had been immensely enjoyable. While taking particular pleasure in killing the Jarl, now he was not sure he would ever see Bryan again, being permanently separated; consequences that lay heavy on his mind.

He was physically bigger than his cousin, but not one able to easily show his emotions, unlike Bryan who was more outward going, ready to display his love, displeasure, left little doubt how fond he was of his cousin. Ari feared he'd not let Bryan know how much love he felt for him, or how much he was going to miss him.

He wiped the tears, with his coat sleeve, ripped his attention away from such thoughts, sucking in the icy air, and focusing on destroying what was left of the Dane's kingdom. Never had he felt pleasure, as sweet, as the feel of life leaving the Dane's body, no woman ever gave him such satisfaction, maybe he would feel it again, when the foreign kingdom was crushed, and he saw Balistrand burning to the ground.

He rode through the night and next day, entering Innvick's camp, in a high mountain park, surrounded by towering peaks, riding directly to the king's tent, in the center of the encampment.

"M'Lord," bowing on one knee, "The Dane is dead. I come to you my hand still stained with his blood," he raised his hands, "His kingdom will be in chaos, the time is ripe to destroy it now.""

"Your words are music to my ears my son," Innvic said; the king with no heirs of his own, treating Air as his own, "We will move on them straight away. You will remain with me here as my guest."

He slept that night in the comfort of the king's tent, on a wool mattress, under warm furs.

During the night, the army moved out, groups each taking separate trails, toward Balistrand. When Ari woke in the morning, the park was empty; he and Innvik followed the armies on horseback.

Three days later, early in the morning, the northern king's army appeared, like apparitions, all along the edge of the forest surrounding Balistrand, isolating it up against the water of the fjord, laying siege, throwing the citizens and soldiers of the town into panic.

Chapter 21

Ivan left Balistrand on Walpurgis eve, caught a ferry across the fjord and headed east to Sogndel. Shortly after crossing the fjord, he came upon a large encampment of the Jarl's soldiers, nearly half of the Jarl's army, grouped together there. Ivan, well known among the soldiers, passed without raising interest, but its presence concerned him. What were they doing there? None of the soldiers could answer his question.

He was welcomed, into the village, with open arms, the chief immediately accepting Ivan's proposal to his daughter, and she was ecstatic.

"She's done nothing but talk about you since you left, I'm quite tired of hearing it," the chief said.

They were sworn together, a solemn ceremony, that evening, and bedded down in the chief's quarters. Sifa's brothers and sisters, the chief and his wife, and others lay silent in the dark; waiting to hear Ivan consummate the marriage; Ivan didn't disappoint them, or his new wife, nor himself, their snoring started shortly after he finished; having satisfied his new family, he too fell off to sleep, happy.

In the morning, Ivan spoke to the chieftain, about the soldiers he'd seen.

"I'd not heard a word in court about this army coming together, their presence there is alarming." He went on to tell the chief what he thought Bryan's intentions were.

"Are you sure of all this?" The chief asked.

"As sure as anyone can be".

The chief pondered the news, and after the morning meal, called Ivan and two of his sons, Thorek and Val to him, "I want you to return to the army camp with my sons, investigate, keeping in mind, what might have happened in Balastrand."

Thoreck, in his early twenties, a tough young warrior, strong and dashing, with flowing long black hair, being groomed to take his father's place as head of the clan; made Ivan feel safe in his presence. Val however, reminded Ivan of his new bride; still youthful in appearance, his hair blond and braded, fair of skin, of slender build, seemed young to heft a weapon, but quite capable when tested.

Arriving at the camp, late in the afternoon, after the end of Walpurgis; Ivan went about the soldiers, gathering what information he could without rousing suspicion, while his new brothers remained inconspicuous.

"They know little," he told the brothers, "Their quite subdued, been told that court will not be held for several days, suspicious something is amiss, but they know not what, thinking that it does not bode well. We'll have to lay low, bide our time, see what happens."

The soldiers were restless, the following day; rumors flying hot and wild. Ivan and his brothers visited the soldiers, quietly keeping an ear open to their conversations. But, by the fifth day, the mood in the camp became seriously quiet, tension brewing, palpable. They'd received reports that court remained closed. "Something serious, has happened, we don't know what it is, or what is going to happen," a soldier told Ivan.

Just after mid-day, Thoreck came hurrying to Ivan, "Come quickly," he urged, a sense of urgency about the usually staid warrior.

"What is it?"

"Come, I'll show you."

Thoreck took him to the shore, pointing out to the water, a dozen transport Knarr lay in the water, several more approached, in the distance.

"Their getting ready to move," Thoreck said.

"Hum," Ivan considered, pensively, "There's no sign of preparation in the camp."

"Not yet," Val said, "Maybe tonight."

"Perhaps," Ivan's voice trailed off, thinking of Ari and Innvik's army. The Jarl's generals, aware of northern army's approach, in need of defense. "Let's go up there," he pointed, a low hill rose to a rock ledge, flat on top, to the rear of the camp, "We can rest, watch what happens, plan."

While they waited and watched, Ivan sharpened his sword, and the brothers played a game of bones, carved cubes, marked with runes, Ivan found the game unfathomable, thought they were cheating him. Unsure of the brothers, though they made some vague remarks about being with their sister, before the marriage, seemingly amused about it, smiling, giving knowing glances, not that it mattered, they couldn't possibly know, could they? Sure they were just teasing, he still wondered. He hoped he could rely on them in a fight, tough hard boys, good to have on his side.

The afternoon changed to twilight, with no troop movement, more and more ships came to anchor, by night fall, thirty or more were gathered. Thoreik came to him with a suggestion, a daring plan, difficult, challenging, adventuresome.

The night well advanced, and the camp slumbering, Ivan and his brothers crept silently to the shore. Thorick swiftly, stealthily, crawled up behind the guards, stationed at the ferry point, and slitting their throats. The three of them stripped naked, and slipped into the bone chilling water, quietly swimming out to a ship, boarded, and killed the men they found. Ivan's fear was running deep, as one by one, they visited each ship, till no one was left tending the vessels. With utmost skill, the two brothers, carrying torches, swam out and set each ship afire. By the time the conflagration was discovered, and an alarm sounded, they were out of the water, up to the hill, half frozen, glad to have dry clothes.

They watched the burning ships, masts toppling over on one another, something on one of the ship exploded; the entire armada was sunk, the conflagration spooking the army, turning it to turmoil.

A small boat arrived, early in the morning, bringing news to the already tense soldiers, of the Jarl's death. Their anxiety mounting, a second boat arrived, a short time later with news of the northern army's appearance at the forests edge.

Immediately the soldiers began to break camp.

"What are they going to do?" Vall asked.

"The only thing they can do, march around the fjord," Thorick answered.

After much confusion, and much wasted time, the army marched off to the north, their only route around the end of the fjord, would take all day.

Ivan now knew, Bryan's plan had come to fruition, and his new brothers had proven capable, and trust worthy; he was pleased. They lay low, waiting until the soldiers were gone, then taking one of the messenger's boats, crossed the fjord. The small boat barely supporting their weight; water coming very near the top of the gunnels, but Thiorek rowing skillfully, avoided rocking the boat while the others remained very still; they made the long trip without taking on much water. It would not have done, to swamp the tiny craft, in the middle of the frigid fjord.

In Balistrand, they found Innvik's army, in charge, the village already taken, the Jarl's army, those left to defend the village, lay dead and dying everywhere, villagers huddled in groups, terrified, fighting still on going, on the hill, near the great hall, which was ablaze.

At length, they found Ari, sitting on a rock, at the side of the road, dirty and exhausted, his sword bloodied, "What in blazes are you doing here Ivan? I thought you went to claim your bride," Ari said, his voice betraying his weariness.

"That I've done," Ivan answered, "These are my brothers Thiorec and Val, we've come to help."

"You're a little late; we're nearly finished here," Ari said, "Afraid a few of the Jarl's loyal knights escaped, to peruse Bryan, haven't been able to find them."

"You're not done yet, we've been watching a contingent of the Jarl's army, camped across the fjord, and think they were planning to cross the fjord, to flank you. We burned their ships, but they are on their way, on foot, around the end of the fjord, right now, you had better make ready."

Ari jumped to his feet, "By the gods Ivan, you are as crafty a devil as Bryan bragged you were, devious as he. Come, we must find Innvik, and prepare."

They found the old king consulting with his knights.

"M'Lord," Ari bowed, "These men are friends, from Sogndel, a clan who've remained loyal to you. They report seeing a large group of the Jarl's army on its way around the fjord, from the east, to make a surprise attack on us."

"And how have you come by this information?" Innvik asked.

"My lord, I ran across the army, camped on the other side of the fjord, we were suspicious, and have been watching it for the last seven days, they were planning to attack by water, but we were able to set fire to their ships," Ivan said,

"They left on foot this morning, headed north, to go round the head of the fjord, a full day's journey, should arrive toward evening, or possibly wait till morning."

"Hmm, tis good to have loyal friends, Eay, son," he slapped Ari on the back.

The shores of Esefjorden, just north of Balistrand, narrowed to a strip of grassy beach, running for several leagues, water on one side, a strip of dense forest on the other, running up against a vertical rock wall, not opening up until the ferry docks, a strip of land Ari, Bryan, and Ivan knew well from their adventures. Innvik's advisers believed the Jarl's men would try to pass through this narrow strip of land, to attack an unsuspecting Innvick, just before dark. The King's army would lay in wait, hiding in the strip of thick forest, and ambush them, pushing them into the fjord.

Ivan and his brothers joined in, for the long wait. The sun dipped, first below the trees, then dropped behind the western mountains, as dusk slowly took possession of the land. In the faint light, scouts, from the Jarl's army,no more than shadows, slowly passed by on horseback, carefully inspecting the area, in short order rode back, and after another long wait, the faint rattle of, harness and armor could be heard, soldiers marching, toward Balestrand. As the first solders reached the docks of the ford, a shout went up from the forest, Innvik's army, as one rushed forward, their bloody battle cry, terrifying the unsuspecting Jarl's soldiers, surprise and horror in their eyes; barely having time to draw their weapons, to meet Innvik's men charging downhill toward them; the two armies, coming together, with a horrific clash.

Ivan, with his brothers behind him, rushed forward, his sword held high, came down on the first soldier he encountered. The man countered with an axe, the jolt severe, stinging his hands, but able to maintain his grip, he countered, fighting savagely. The sound of battle, all about him, frightfully loud, deafening; sword and axe meeting each other, men, screaming, dying;   the Jarl's soldiers stumbled backward, pushed by the momentum of the attack, to the soft sand at water's edge. Ivan's opponent lost his footing, Ivan delivered a mighty blow, beneath the left arm, and into his chest, the cut severed the man's heart, blood, exploded, showering everyone close, and the man fell to his knees, his head dipping to his chest, Ivan brought his sword down on the back of his neck, he sprawled backward into the water, dead.

A cry from behind, drew his attention, he turned to see Val, wounded in the leg, still fighting, in serious trouble, quickly he stepped into the fight, defending his brother. The man was big, strong, Ivan defending himself against a series of blows and counter blows, the soldier advancing on Ivan, striking back in fear and fury, failing to still the advance.

Panic in his veins, he couldn't allow a mistake, or he'd be killed, his muscles stinging with fatigue, the blows kept falling, Ivan fell to one knee. The aggressive soldier, his sword raised, Ivan trying to shield himself, but, suddenly he was struck from behind, drenching Ivan in blood, the man's eyes focused on the sky, and he fell forward, almost on top of Ivan, behind him stood Thiorck, sword in hand, smiling.

"You ok?" He shouted as he grabbed Ivan by the arm, lifting him to his feet.

"Tired," He shouted back, "I think Val is hurt though."

Just then, another man attacked, thin, wiry, fast, avoiding Ivan's blade at every turn, fighting hard, Ivan's energy draining fast , the man kept striking at Ivan's legs, throwing him off balance, most annoying and tiring, suddenly Ivan realized, through the haze of exhaustion, the soldier was vulnerable when he swung low. He struck again at Ivan's legs, but Ivan, instead of stepping back, jumping into the air swinging his blade at the same time striking the man across his bare back, cutting deeply into flesh and bone. The man bent backward at a most peculiar angle, and crumbled into a heap on the sand, his back bone severed.

Someone nearby let out a loud blood curdling cry, and an axe flew over Ivan's head with a woop woop woop sound, Ivan never saw what happened, who cried out, or to who's army he belonged.

Suddenly, the din of battle died away, the few remaining soldiers left in the Jarl's army backed away, dropped their weapons, and raised their arms in surrender, with a collective breath of relief, everyone realizing they'd won, a cheer went up and down Innvik's line.

Ivan rushed to Val, bleeding badly, a gaping wound to his thigh, pale and weak, trying desperately to close the wound, with his hands. Ivan tore strips of cloth from his shirt, cutting the leg of Val's trousers away, packed the wound, and with another strip applied a tourniquet, above the wound. The bleeding stopped. Ivan lifted the boy into his arms, no idea where he was going, just away from there. At length he found a place, the wounded were being cared for, where Val's wounds were cleaned, and properly bound. Thiorek, desperately searching for his brother, finally found them.

With Val stable, Ivan and Thiorek went up to the village, obtained a cart, and bought a horse to pull it. Val rode without complaining, though the trip to Sogndel was difficult, arriving home, his wound badly infected, to be nursed him back to health, after many months, by Ivan and Sifa. He walked with a limp for the rest of his days.

Balistrand was pillaged, most of it burned. The Dane's people, those who survived, left back over the mountains, to their homelands.

Ari, for his part in defeating the Dane, and restoring the kingdom to Innvik, was knighted in the king's court in Torg. He returned to the homestead in Hoyanger to visit his family for a short time, but returned to Torg where he was cajoled by a wealthy father into marrying his daughter, with whom Ari had been having an on and off affair. He remained an important figure at Innvik's side.

Chapter 22

The rowers guided the knarr out into the middle of the fjord, after leaving Horanger, turning west, heading toward the open ocean. Bryan leaned against the mast, watching Uri, sitting on the little pack of clothes Gola gave him, fascinated, by the ship, the rhythm of the oars as they moved in the oarlocks, and the low musical sounds, the rowers made to keep their rhythm.

Darkness fell, the rowing stopped, and the boat stilled in the water.

"We'll wait here for the night, too dangerous to try to pass through to the sea at night," the captain said as he lit a lamp, its light quickly absorbed by the vast darkness, but providing a reference point, allowing the men to move about without falling off. The captain gave out small loaves of bread to eat, and they settled down to sleep.

Morning broke, skies crystal clear, a light breeze from the direction of the ocean. The rowers began their steady rhythmic labor, propelling the ship at a rapid pace, still a long way from open water. This was further west than Bryan had ever been. He'd heard stories, of many Islands along the coastline, dangerous towering rocky projections, perilous to any who approached, waves from the open water, could easily bash a ship against them, shattering the heaviest hull.

When finally, they did arrive, the coast was astonishing beyond his wildest imagination; waves rolling in from the ocean, crashing against sheer rock walls that rose to dizzying heights, roaring like thunder, and the Islands many, huge pillars, called skerries, like knife blades, jutting high to razor sharp peaks, the crashing waves churning the water to foam and spray, air smelling of salt and fish, untold thousands of sea birds, sreaking a constant chorus, seals resting on parlous perches, watching with curiosity as they passed.

The captain and the rowers, though the ship was tossed about like a stick, negotiated the turbulent waters, skillfully, breaking through to the open waters of the North Sea, where waves were, but ripples in the great swells. The bow would crash down, over the crest of a wave, spraying showers of water, into the air, blowing back over the ship, keeping them wet. Having great fun, Uri laughed and squealed. Bryan, on the other hand, found the motion exquisitely nauseating.

The captain laughed at him, "You'll get into the rhythm of it soon enough."

Bryan retched over the side of the ship, again and again; for him, it was a very long afternoon.

The long rays of the sun, lost their warmth, as evening fell, and banks of towering dark clouds, built to the west. The crew unfurled the sail, and tethered its lines to cleats on the gunnels, the wind pushing the ship hard, the rowers rested.

Near dark, the captain called Bryan to the stern where he tended the tiller. "Looks like we're gona be in for a blow," pointing to the black angry looking clouds, coming near, "Y'r might want a tie the boy and y'rself to the mast, while there's light to see, if it gets rough you'll not want a be washed overboard, that happens, there's nothin' we can do for ya."

Bryan tied a length of rope around the boy, wrapped it around the mast, and his own waist. Uri, tired, laid his head on his pack, and went to sleep. Bryan, edgy, from the events of the last two days, not having slept in that time, and uncertain about the captain's warning, didn't think tonight promised any rest, his stomach churned unmercifully.

Land left far behind now, towering stacks of mean looking black clouds loomed in the blackness, illuminated from inside by constant lightning, terrifyingly beautiful, The wind, tearing at the tops of the waves, clouds obliterating the rising moon. The rowers furled the sail, lowered the yard arm, and tied it vertically to the mast.

The swells grew rapidly, hitting the side of the ship, their impact thunderous, pulsating through the ships timbers. The wind building in magnitude; howling like banshees, sending shivers through Bryan who held on to the sleeping Uri.

A flash of lighting, reveled a gigantic towering wave, directly in front of them; the ship climbed up, up, up, hesitated, and then surfed down other side, again and again. Bryan threw up, his stomach empty, his head reeling, nausea so bitter it replaced the fear he felt.

Without warning a wave crashed over the ship, the captain yelling something, another wave swept the deck, pushing him away from the mast. He scrambled back to hold Uri. Another wave, he felt himself float off the decking, away from the mast, landing on his belly very near the side of the ship. A flash of lightening, Uri scrambling on the deck, toward the bow, a couple of arm lengths from the side of the ship, terror seized Bryan as he realized he had untied the rope, to go to the gunnels, to vomit; separated now, Uri was loose on the deck.

The ship rolled, Uri tumbled toward the water, Bryan struggled to find footing on the slick deck, he had to get to Uri, inching forward, the boat rocked, another wave, lifting Bryan from solid footing, suspending him there for agonizing moment, hitting the deck hard, straining to see in the dark, a flash of light, the deck bare, the boy gone. Terror coursed through his veins, paralyzing.

Turning to the ocean, a flash of light, there in the blackness, a patch of white, gripping the gunnels, he reached as far as he could, again and again, over and over, his hand hit something, grasping, finding the rope, he began pulling, still attached to the boy. He pulled the boy to the side of the rolling ship, caught his arm, and lifted him onto the deck, its loosely bound timbers, squirming under foot, disorienting in the darkness. He layed Uri's limp body on the deck, and not knowing what else to do, pushed on his chest, picked him up, shook him. Uri coughed, threw up, gasping for air, Bryan hugged him to his chest, edging cautiously to the mast, and once again securing them to its safety.

The storm eased some, waves no longer crashing over the deck, flashes of lightening, and roar of thunder, no longer constant. The wind continued to howl like a ferocious beast, the boat tossed about, like so many sticks, he held the boy tight, and slept.

Chapter 23

Bryan opened his eyes, it was day light, his mind rushing to remember where he was, the storm past, sail raised once again, catching a steady breeze, pushing the ship, fast across shallow waves, even the rolling swells tame.

The boy, still clutched in his arm, was not moving. Rolling him unto his back, skin pale and cold, his blue eyes stared, dull and lifeless, he was not breathing. Shock hit Bryan like a great hammer; he struggled to breathe himself, sinking to oblivion, his head spinning, he pulled the boy's body close, and wept, more alone than he had ever been.

The captain came, "Let me see the boy," his voice soft and gravelly, gently, he unbuttoned the boy's shirt with a course hand, and pressed his ear against his, cold, pale chest, held it there for a time, then reached up, closed Uri's eyes, and put a hand on Bryan's shoulder, "I'm sorry."

Bryan removed the boy's clothes; even in death, he was handsome. From the clothes, he sewed a bag, laid Uri in it, placed a stone, borrowed from the ships ballast, at the boy's feet, and sewed the bag shut. Remorse heavy in his chest; he lowered the bag over the side of the ship; it quickly sank out of sight, beneath the waves.

Uri gone, overwhelmed with emptiness, dispare gnawing at his gut; the man, he swore revenge upon, and to that end, drove his life for the past year and a half, dead by his own hand. The life he knew, gone behind him; his mother, cousin, friend Ivan, gone from his life, by his own action, and now the boy dead as well.

"Guess you'll have some explain'en to do to the Jarl," The captain said.

"Guess so, don't know what to tell him," Bryan said, glad at least he wouldn't have that to contend with.

"Don't suppose you could tell him anything that he'll understand, best bet is to catch a ship to Wales, maybe Ir'Ind, disappear, likely pursued by his men."

"They will for certain," Bryan said, though their pursuit would be for another reason.

The North Sea was much larger that Bryan ever could have imagined, vast and empty, endless waves, no sign of land. His travel companions, the rowers and captain, mostly wordless men, bent to their tasks, seemed not to notice that he was there, the day's endless rhythms of the seas, over rolling waves and swells. In his day dreams, he wondered what creatures might live beneath the surface; were there monsters like those told in legends of the gods, or more like fishes brought to port? Occasionally he saw a fin skim the surface.

They ate soggy smoked fish, stale, damp flat bread, drank water from an earthen container, its self stale and dank, there was no ale.

His mind, continuing to wander, numb and blank from monotony; what was the Isle of Man like, could it ever compare to the beauty of the land he left behind, would he find others to replace his family, what knight or knights would follow after him, how long would he have till they found him, could he defend himself against such warriors?

.

They were many days in crossing the North Sea, tacking back and forth into the wind. When finally they sighted land, it was far off to the south, Scotland the captain told him, then to the north far, far off, small Islands, the captain called Shetlands, a little line that floated above the waves then vanished.

Days later, land on both sides of the ship, still far off, traveling south now. The spots of land appeared, and faded away, until on the fifteenth day, land dead ahead, growing larger, as they approached.

The mood of the crew changed, beginning to joke among themselves. The captain barked orders, and the island grew larger, the better part of a day, till the ship put to port. A young lad, strolled onto the dock, shirtless, baggy pants, and bare feet, his upper body muscular, well beyond his age, a rope in hand, threw it, arching into the air, end over end, to the bow, where a crewman caught it and fastened it to the gunnels. The boy, single handed, pulled the ship to the dock, wrapped it to a pilling and snugged it, bringing it to a standstill. Bryan stepped to the edge of the ship, the boy reached down, took him by the arm, lifted him, pack and all, one armed, up from the ship, landing him on the dock.

"Welcome to Mann," his accent strange, Bryan barely understood.

"Thank you, I think," the earth seemed to move under him.

The boy laughed at him, "Ground try'n to move under ya?"

Bryan grinned sheepishly as the earth continued to move.

"You'll be look'n for da place to stay then," pointing, "Dar's an Inn just up ton the hill thar."

Bryan couldn't follow what he'd said, but he caught the meaning. "Thanks," nodded to the captain, "Thank you sir," and waved.

The isle was large, larger than Bryan had supposed. The village, Ramsey, a fishing village, reasonable size, buildings square, or rectangular, of stone with sodden roofs, much smaller than long houses, paths between them, winding

251

up the hill, crooked, coming together in no particular order. The 'Inn' was two story, quite long, added on to many times, patches of green paint, and red trim, long faded, and worn away, on the rock walls, high up on the hill. He imagined sailors, stumbling down the hill, from the inn, after too many ales.

Inside, it was clean, cozy, a little musty, with a bar and tables. From somewhere, food, cooking, filled the air; realizing how incredibly hungry he was, he ordered up a plate of lamb and turnips, much spicier than he was used to, but infinitely better than the ships fare, ale strong, and to his liking.

The innkeeper, a jovial working woman, seemed to do everything, from signing in guests to cooking, to serving up brew. Her daughter, waiting tables, was young, perhaps a few years older than Bryan, fair complected, red hair, long and curly, and freckles that tanned her face and neck, a sweet face, full lips and a delicate nose, her eyes as green as emeralds, and her breasts round and full, solid stocky build. Bryan pleased by her presence, having a hard time taking his eyes from her, feeling himself stir; seemed a long time since he'd oogled the ladies in Balestrand.

"You're new here," she struck up a conversation.

"Just got here."

"Saw the ship come in, just pass'n or going to stay a while?"

"Depends if I can find a place to stay, you know the boy down on the dock?"

"Strange one's hard to understand?"

"Yea, that's the one, what kind of accents he have?"

"Welsh I think," She smiled, "A thrall, killed his master, so's they say, somewhere down round sout Wales, never learned proper Norse tongue."

"Do you know where I might find some work?" he asked after deciding she was trust worthy.

"Well…, might ask me mum, always look'n for someone strong, to do the heavy work." She said, a smile and twinkle in her eyes, looking him over.

He tried to ignore the overture, not wanting to be premature, but couldn't help looking back.

"Should I wait till she's not busy?"

"No, gowan in the kitchen, she doesn't bite," the girl laughed.

He left his pack at the table, and walked gingerly into the warm kitchen.

"Beggin your pardon mame," she was bending over a pie she was getting ready to bake.

She stopped, looked up at him, eyes penetrating, could she see through his clothes, could she cipher his past, his skin crawled with selfconscious anxiety .

"I was talking to your daughter, said you might have some work for me," he cast his eyes to the floor, to show humility.

"What can you do?" She asked.

"Mame, I was raised on a farm." There was a long pause. "I'm strong, used to hard work, can do most anything."

An even longer pause, while she looked him up and down, mentally stripping him again, wanting to see how strong he was. "Ok then," she removed her apron, "Come with me, Sisi," she called her daughter, "Finish that crust, and put the pie in the oven, will you." The daughter's sly smile betrayed her delight.

She led Bryan into the dinning area, "You'll mop the floors, here and in the kitchen, the mops and brooms are in the kitchen." Then she led him to the trough in front of the Inn. "You get your water here; fill the caldrons in the kitchen and dining room from here. Each morning, take the cart down to the market, fetch me fresh vegetables. Once or twice a week, you'll go to the butcher's, and pick up meat for our guests. I'll have other chores when the occasion arises, your pay," she turned around, and led him back into the inn, up the stairs to the second level, showed him a small room, with a door, big enough to have a sleeping ledge, a little table, and a stool. "This'll be your pay, plus meals, and this," she placed two strange coins in his hand, "Every two weeks."

He didn't recognize the coins or know how much they were worth, but accepted them, "Thank you malady."

Never addressed in such a manner, she looked at him strangely. "Get settled in, then help Sisi with the evening meal," she sniffed, twitched her nose slightly, "There's a heated bath out back, you can use, when the guests aren't using it."

She needn't tell him more, fifteen days on the ship, there was an odor about him, he knew.

This new life would be different, mundane, reclusive.

Chapter 24

During the weeks that followed, settling into a routine, comfortable, he frequently complimented the innkeeper on her cooking, causing her to take a liking to him, and he and her daughter, Sisi, struck a friendly working relationship. She was most pleasant to the eye, arousing, erotic, perhaps her red hair, perhaps her healthy body; when she caught him looking, she would return a coy smile, and he would feel his face blush, wanting but not daring to bed her. At all times, he remained wary and watchful for any sign of the Jarl's knight's arrival.

Yearning to know more about this new land, he asked Sisi many times about the Isle, her answers, always short of his expectations. One day, after completing his morning chores, he set out to explore on foot. A road, if you could call it that, where a cart was occasionally driven, wandered north, slowly turned west, taking him away from the village, following the shore, above steep cliffs diving sharply into the sea, here and there a stretch of pebbly beach lying below. Rounding the north shores, and going further south, hills were covered with scrub brush and few trees, the shore line, to the south, craggy, and rough. On, over the top of the hills, past a few farms, carved from the scrub, and even further, he wandered up over the dome of the isle, where the land became densely forested, the trail sloped downward, to the west, crossed a clearing, were the trees were burned, providing a view south, across the isle; low mountains and deep valleys undulated, forming the back bone of the island, and running far to the south, a most difficult area for traveling. Deciding it would be wise to turn east, heading back toward Ramsey, through heavy timber, arduous to navigate, fearing he was lost, and about to lose hope, he came upon a road that seemed to run north.

He'd been walking along the road for a time, when a cart came up from behind, led by a shaggy, little Norwegian horse, its' wheels making a terrible clatter, over the rocks. The driver, a rumpled, plump, old farmer, perched on a board, across the front, a simple cloth hat pulled down over his ears.

"Hallo neighbor," the man greeted, "Ya like a ride," the local Celtic speaking people, tried to speak Scandinavian dialects, though not without a heavy brogue.

Bryan gratefully accepted.

The man looked him over, and asked, "Were ya from? Haven't seen the likes of you round these parts. With a brogue like that, tells a man ya'r not from round here," he chuckled.

Hardly understanding the fellow, "I'm Bryan, just arrived from Sognefijorden a few days ago," offered a hand, and climbed aboard, "Looking for my father."

They struck up a lively conversation, and Bryan, though missing much the man said, learned a good deal about the isle; the shore line north of Ramsey, to the tip of the isle, and south on the western side was lined with sporadic rocky beaches that rose steeply from the sea. South from there, around the tip, and back up to just south of Ramsey, with the exception of around the village of Douglas, was composed of rugged, rocky, cliffs. The mountains he saw to the south, the central backbone of the Isle, as he guessed, small by Norway standards, were sufficiently impenetrable to avoid Viking occupation. The inhabitants of the island used them for timber and water, and as refuge from the Viking warriors.

Unknown to the man and to Bryan, the Northmen easily conquered the Celtic people of the Isle, using it as a spring board for invasion of Ireland, they called the 'Ire', the Celts of the isle largely absorbing and adopting the Nordic and Danish ways and language.

Mid afternoon, the little cart descended into Ramsey, forded the river, and rounded into the dock area, stopping at a warehouse near the water. Bryan thanked the farmer, and wandered over to the docks to see what was going on.

The odd young dock hand spotted him, sauntered up, saying something Bryan didn't understand. When he said it again, Bryan realized that he was asking Bryan if he knew how to repair fishing nets.

"Of course I do, did it all the time back home," Bryan told him.

"Well the fishers er look'n fer a man to fix der nets fer yer interested," the boy said.

Bryan struggled to understand him. "Where?" He asked.

"Or on te shook," he pointed, a small shack, at the end of the dock, nets hanging on poles, a good distance behind it.

"Thank you," Bryan said as he headed that way.

"Telcum," The boy said; someone needed to help the poor lad, Bryan thought.

He strolled over to the shack where a ruddy looking man was repairing a rope.

"What can I do for ya," He said as Bryan walked up.

A sigh of relief; the man spoke Norse.

"Heard you're looking for someone to repair your nets."

"You any good at it?"

"Used to repair my uncles nets all the time back home."

"We always need repairs, can't pay much, but you can take a bit of the catch."

"I work for the lady up at the Inn, except for mornings and evenings, I can work on them"

"Show up tomorrow, and we'll see what you can do."

Bryan nodded and headed back to the Inn. From the shack he would be able to see ships arriving, watch for the chance arrival of men from Balestrand, and breathe fresh salt air, a vast improvement over the dank Inn, and after finishing his chores in the morning he headed to the docks, where the rough and ready fisherman met him.

"Morning to ya," he looked surprised, Bryan had shown up, "Come on round this way," leading Bryan to the other side of the little building.

"My name's Drest, this here is my brother Egan."

Egan was short, stocky, ruddy and tough like Drest. "Come on over here let's see what ya can do," his voice high, gravely, commanding, unfolding a large net, torn and full of holes. "Is amazing what the bottom can do to these things, big fish too"

Spreading the net out on the deck, and with some light cord, Egan handed him, similar to the netting, Bryan began weaving a patch in a hole. When he finished he pulled his knife from his boot, too long for the purpose, but sharp, and cut the line.

"Well I see ya been doin' this afore. We'll be letten ya be," Egan said, eyeing Bryan's knife. "You'll not be needen a blade like that around here. You'll find something handier inside. That cord I give you is all I have. There's materials to spin some more inside."

The brothers left soon after, their fishing boat, a practical, simple, adaptation of a knarr, somewhat smaller, with a square sale to use the wind, and oars when the wind failed, light and maneuverable , roomy enough to carry nets and a good take of fish.

Bryan busied himself, the brothers having neglected their nets a long time, leaving them in bad shape, insuring he would have work for a long while. He enjoyed being outside, in the sun, smelling the sea, the call of birds, making him feel alive, free for the first time since leaving the homestead, the feeling of loss, of his family, his uncle, his cousin, fading into the past.

"Tash dwork ter dably d wermens dun yating."

Bryan looked up from the net, the Welsh boy, not a word understood, an odd smile on his strange face. Again, to Bryan, he looked peculiar; his heavy muscular arms, shoulders and chest, made his head look small, his waist thin, and legs muscular, face not unpleasant, dark unruly hair long and curley.

"Hello, my name's Bryan. Come sit here next to me," he patted the top of a barrel next to him. To his surprise the boy understood, walked over and sat down. "What's your name?" He asked the boy.

"Em Wilgum," He said.

Bryan frowned trying to figure out what the boy said, "You mean William?"

"Ya."

"Well William, let's see, you're from Wales, right?"

The boy looked at him, suspicious, "Ya."

"How do you say your name in Welsh?"

"Bye 'dyn Nomie?" The boy replied.

"Say something else, in your tongue," Bryan continued.

"Ble 'dyn mi'n mynd? Ty tin en dy fi?" The boy replied.

Didn't make any sense, probably some form of Celtic, mixed with whatever other languages the boy came into contact with.

"William you can understand me quite well?" The boy nodded, "But, I can make out little of what you say. You've not learned Norse very well, have you?"

William hung his head, embarrassed, his face red.

"Would you like me to help you speak Norse?" Bryan asked.

The boy looked up, face still red, "Yud duit fer me?"

"Sure, while I'm repairing the nets and your idle we can work on it."

"William grinned from ear to ear, and rambled off a string of words totally unintelligible.

And so Bryan spent his days: chores at the inn, repairing fishing nets, and teaching William to speak Norse. The brothers and the folks at the inn thought him daft. "Your waistin' your time on that one," they said.

His friendship with the unfortunate boy grew: there was a lot of anger in the young man; treated well by few, parents killed by soldiers, made a slave by a landsmen, sold and moved from place to place, unable to learn an understandable language, and Bryan had no doubt, not cared for by anyone since his mother's death, having to fight for everything. At times raging against one person or another, from his past, Bryan would have to calm him. If he murdered anyone in his past it came as no surprise.   Sisi did'nt understand why he bothered helping the boy, maked fun of him, calling him an idiot, unteachable; but one afternoon, she told Bryan, "I spoke to that strange boy today, and I could actually understand what he was saying. You really are helping him."

Bryan felt gratified.

Late that evening, after he finished at the inn, tired and dirty, he went to the bath, scrubbing off, and soaking in the warm tub, then relaxing, eyes closed, nearly falling asleep. Something woke him, Sisi standing on the deck of the tub, a long white robe draping her voluptuous body, her red curls cascading over her naked shoulders, a sweet seductive smile on her face, alluring, flirtatious. Saying nothing, looking into his eyes, she opened the robe, and let it slip to the deck, naked underneath, beautiful, breasts round, perfect, firm and saucy, nipples pink and erect, waist narrow, hips wide, framing a perfect triangle of red hair, atop long strong, and shapely legs.

An instant charge of adrenaline shot through him, an amazing feeling, engorging his loin, his nipples tingling, shoulders and face set afire, at that moment wanted her more than anything he'd ever known.

She stepped down into the tub, toward him, he toward her; closing the distance taking longer than it should. Their bodies touched, her nipples brushing against his chest, their lips meshed. Caressing her lightly, running his finger tips up over her arms and shoulders, then down to the small of her back, around her waist and up her belly to her breasts, tasting her mouth, and exploring it with his tongue, holding her full breasts in his hands, gently running his fingers over her nipples, messaging again and again.

Slowly, he backed her, one step at a time, to the edge of the tub, and leaned his weight against her, possessing her, she relaxed. His hand followed the line between her breasts to her navel, then down between her legs, where her fiery bush felt soft and slippery in the water. His fingers eased between the lips of her labia, and messaged her there. She tried to move away, squirming at the strong stimulation, but he held her, dominating, afraid he was smothering her, unable to control himself, his will no longer his own, his passion burning strong, he would have her.

He drove his fingers deep into her womb, she moaned, a deep, carnal sound, her breathing ragged. Soft, smooth, wet, warm inside her, unable to stand it any longer, he pulled his fingers away, and taking himself, guiding it into her, past her soft red hair, between the delicate lips, deep into the dark, smooth, warm, wetness of her womb.

261

Gasping at the suddenness of it, then holding their breaths, drinking in the ecstatic nectar of lust, slowly savored, their bodies stilled one within the other. Slowly at first, pressing himself into her; rhythmic, raw rivulets of pleasure, coursing through his veins, pushing his desire higher and higher, his rhythm increasing, driven to attain greater gratification.

With each thrust, whimpers becoming soft cries, louder with the increase of his thrusts, tension building, finally gasping for breath, her time close.

He felt himself swell inside her, pushing him over the edge; orgasm, that strange, urgent, overwhelming feeling, coursed his groin, like a great dam bursting, traveling the length of his groin, he flooded her insides with his warm fluid, both crying out, clinging tightly, spasms washing over them, head spinning, pleasure pulsing through his veins, then peace. He nearly fell asleep, holding her in his arms, but roused himself, not wanting to miss any of this moment.

Limp in his arms, smiling, breathing heavily, humming ever so quite, looking deep into his eyes. For him there was a strange sense of purpose in what he had just done; what they had done together, for each other, to each other; deeply satisfying, so personnel, a gift from the gods.

She pushed him away, out of her, and sat up on the edge of the bath. He got up and sat beside her. She softly caressed his thigh, and played with him between his legs. He kissed her ear, and whispering, "That was wonderful."

Squeezing his manhood ever so gently, said "It was," leaning against him.

Putting his arm around her shoulders, and pulling her to him, they sat in silence for a long time.

Later, he lay on his bed, remembering until he fell into luxurious slumber.

In the morning, acting as if nothing happened, she went about her choirs. Expecting, he wasn't sure what, Bryan didn't know what to make of her, brushing if off as a woman's strange way, perhaps she didn't want to arouse her mother's suspicion. Whatever, when his choirs were finished he went on his way to the docks. Things were the same, that evening, and the next day, she did not approach him, or say anything to him, had he offended her?

Asleep for a while that night, he woke with a start, the latch on his door clicked, even in his sleep, ever vigilant. The door closing, the latch clicking shut, the room pitch black, he could hear someone breathing, close, he clutched his knife in his hand, then he smelled her, and whispered her name. In an instant, her lips clamped over his, she was naked, his passion raising instantly, the same fire in his loin as before.

"I tried to stay away," she whispered, "It was so strong the other night, you are so virile, I couldn't, I had to have more of you." She knelt between his legs, and took him in her mouth.

It was powerful, intense, something he'd not felt before. He lay back, allowed her to take him, the feeling washing over him, his face, chest, and arms flushed with heat, and sex. She must have done this before, it felt exquiste, but his desire overwhelming, wanting terribly to have more of her, to be inside her, he sat up, pulling away, taking her by her arms, laid her down where he had just been, and mounted her, ravaging her like an animal.

It wasn't quiet, patrons in the room outside his door heard, he was sure. He didn't care, taking what he needed to satisfy his passion and lust, panting, sweating, moaning, groaning. When they came, he heard himself call out, and her scream, as she dug her fingernails into his back, feeling so good, pure lust, pure sex, pure pleasure.

He collapsed on her, their bodies, wet, lathered, gasping, clinging to one another, they began to giggle and laugh.

"The guests will be sure to say something after that," he gasped.

"Let them go to Valhalla, that was incredible," she answered.

"It was pretty good, wasn't it?"

"We'll never have it like that again," she said.

"We can try," he said as he kissed her lips, caressing her between the legs, wet and sticky, he became aroused again, hot and ready.

"Oh, you nasty boy," she grabbed him.

They made love, this time, slow, leisurely, deliberately, again, and again until dawn when gathering her clothes, she was gone.

Bryan lay in silence, infinitely satisfied, exhausted, the pleasure taken all night long, like Ivan, bathed his body, smiling to himself at the thought. His wool trousers chaffed his groin, smarting, as he pulled them on. Leaving his room, one of the guests passed in the hall, giving him a rude look. He headed down the stairs, immediately feeling the sting of fire in his raw groin, aching in his testicles; it would be a long day.

He looked forward to sitting, working on his nets, avoiding the chafe of his trousers. The Welsh boy came to practice his Norse, by now just talking about everything and anything, taking his mind off his groin. The boy talked, sometimes at length, about how he'd been treated by people, and how he'd gotten back, his anger palpable, his sudden bursts of violence so near the surface.

That evening, Sisi was moving a little stiff, arching her back to ease stiff muscles. She smiled knowingly, when she saw the way he was walking. "How you doin'?" She asked.

" I can hardly move," he answered.

"Know what you mean," she said, "The price we pay."

"Do it again in an instant," he said, "How bout tonight?"

"Sounds adventurous," she shot back, passing him by, grabbing him between the legs.

"Owh!" He yelped, and grabbed himself.

She smiled back at him, the look of the Loki, "Maybe we should give it a rest."

A warm bath and a good night's sleep made him feel much better.

Next day, a merchant ship, not unlike the one that brought him from Norway, came to port. He watched as it passed by, on its way to the pier, nothing unusual about it. The shack, standing between him and the dock, hid him from view. Ships like it were coming and going all the time, maybe getting a little lax, he didn't pay it much attention until William came hurrying, a concerned look on his face.

Chapter 25

"What is it?" Bryan asked.

"A ship just came in from sea."

"Yes, I saw it."

"From Norway."

"They come from Norway all the time, William."

"There were men on it, big men, asking about you, they were."

"Me?"

"Yes, Master Bryan."

A cold chill ran through him, "What did they look like?" Bryan wanted to know.

"Big men, mail armor, big swords and axes. Are they a danger to you?"

"Possibly."

"They headed toward the inn, don't worry master Bryan, I'll kill them, wait till they sleep, slit their throats," the boy said, serious as a grave digger, brave as a knight.

"No, no don't, you will be the one killed, trust me, they are very dangerous," Bryan warned.

"I won't let them harm you."

"They won't," Bryan reassured, "Let me handle it," laying down the net and tools. "They went to the inn?"

"Yes, I come with you." The boys fear and excitement, taking place of common sense.

"No," Bryan insisted, "You must stay here, tend to business. If I need you I'll let you know."

Taking a circuitous route to the back door of the inn, hiding behind the wood pile, and watching, making sure no one would see him, then quietly, cautiously, slipping, unseen, through the kitchen, to a niche, behind a cabinet, to a crack in the wall, used often to observe the bar and dining area, unseen.

Sisi was talking to the three men, faces familiar from court, Skjolden's knights, henchmen, desperate, vicious, vile men, now landless, revenge on their minds. Her conversation with them, animated by gestures, most amiable; betraying him? He couldn't believe it, yet when he saw one of them, filling her apron pocket, with gold coins, drawn from his purse, Bryan knew she'd given him away. His heart sank, love betrayed again; illusions of romantic love dashed, their savage, physical sex, fantastic. Aroused, even now, just looking at her, remembering the way she enjoyed his aggressive love making, allowing him to dominate; her treachery disappointing.

He quickly, silently, slid from his hiding place, tip toed up the stairs, hurriedly put his pack together, retrieved his uncle's sword, and his axe from under the sleeping ledge, opened the shuttered window, sliding out onto the roof, jumped down to the wood pile. In a shed, behind the inn, from a hole, behind hanging bags of dried fish, he retrieved his money pouch, money he'd earned while with the Jarl, and the few coins he made at the inn.

Cautiously, he headed down the hill, toward the dock. The henchmen would, without doubt, have trouble recognizing him; he'd cut his hair short, grown a scruffy beard, and no longer in the Jarl's clothing, but he didn't want to chance it, one he might be able to handle, but three?

At the storehouses, next to the dock, he held back, until he spotted the Welsh boy, a short commanding whistle, catching the boy's attention. He came trotting over.

"When is that ship leaving?" He asked.

"Tomorrow morning, afore sunrise."

"Where's it going?"

"Place called Morecambe Bay, Jus nort of Wales, part a Saxony, but so far aways from the kings rule as to be a land of its own. Pretty wild country over there, it is."

"How can I get on it without anyone knowing?" Bryan asked.

"You need ta sow away?" The boy asked.

"No, I can pay?

"Then come wid me,"

The boy led him south, along the storehouse lined street, to a tavern. About to go in, Bryan stopped him.

William turned around, "What?"

"Make sure none of those men are in there," Bryan pointed, "If you come back out, I'll follow."

The boy nodded, and went in.

Bryan was patient, but the wait long, longer than he expected. Finally, he screwed up his courage, and went through the door. It was dark inside; a few candles providing little help, William nowhere to be found.

Approaching the man behind the bar, he asked "Have you seen William, the Welsh boy?"

The man pointed to a door at the back of the room. The room beyond, was even darker, straining to see, the moment the door closed, he was seized, a strong arm about his neck, dragging him into yet another room, it happened so fast, he wasn't sure what was going on.

Struggling to pull free, the arm tightened, pressing against his throat, choking him. He lifted his leg, and reached for the knife in his boot.

Someone yelled, "Watch, he's got a knife," grasping his hand, and confiscating the knife, while still another joined in the effort to subdue him. His instinct was to resist, but he quickly realizing the futility of his efforts; he was captured. Searching the room, who were these people? Would they turn him over for profit? How much was he worth? Brighter than the bar, William was standing across the room, a big man stilling him by the arm.

"Who are you? What do you want?" He demanded.

"Maybe we'd like to ask you the same thing," a large burley fellow stepped up. "We've heard a lot about you. Maybe you'd like to tell us why those Norsemen are hunting for you."

"And who are you?" Bryan demanded.

"I'm the captain of the ship that brought those thugs here. They made no bones that they were out to get you, and now you're wanting quick passage out of here. If I'm going to take you anywhere, I need to know why, and I need to know right now." He pushed the sharp point of Bryan's knife into the soft tissue beneath Bryan's chin. "An if the answer doesn't ring true, I could be turn'n the two of you over to them Viking Loki . Might bring a tidy sum, if you know what I mean."

"Take the knife away, it's not necessary," Bryan said.

Slowly, suspiciously, the captain lowered the blade.

"The Norsemen want me for revenge."

"And just whad you do that they want revenge on you for?"

"The men are knights. They want me because I killed their Jarl."

A murmur went around the room.

"Whad you do fool thing like that for?" The captain was incredulous.

"Revenge."

"Revenge, now this gets better all the time. Whad a youngin like you want revenge on a Jarl for."

"He murdered my uncle, our clan chief."

"Why'd he do that?"

"Don't know, He never did say why, even with a blade at his throat."

"An how would a boy like you go about killin' a Jarl."

"I was his personal page. He trusted me, was grooming me for something. I knew when he'd be alone. We..., my cousin and I did it, captured his bodyguard, slit his throat, and cut his heart in two. I was gone before they knew what happened. Once the Jarl was dead, the king whose land the Dane stole, sacked Balestrand."

"Balestrand?" The captain remarked.

"I heard something about it being burned," one of the men said.

The captain moved close, his face almost touching Bryan's, his breath warm on Bryan's cheeks. He stared into Bryan's eyes for what seemed an eternity.

"You got money for the passage?"

"Sir, I do."

Another long pause.

"Let 'em go," the captain finally said.

"Let me see the money. We keep your blades till you're a shore in Morecambe. You'll relieve my men at the ores when needed. Take it or leave it," The captain said.

Bryan dug in his pack for some coins, and put them in the captain's hands.

"It'll cost you a bit more 'n that, just for insurance."

Bryan gave him a few more gold coins.

"That's better," the captain said.

Bryan nodded to William, "You want to go too?"

"No sir, I'll not be settin' foot on Saxon soil again."

The captain chuckled. "They'd string em up on the highest tree they would," the men all laughed.

"When do we leave?" Bryan asked.

The captain glanced over at William, "We loaded yet?"

"By nightfall."

The captain nodded, "Be there just after dark, we'll sail then, that oughta save your skin."

For whatever reason, perhaps he didn't like the henchmen; the captain seemed sympathetic to his plight.

Bryan left the tavern with William. "I'll miss you Bryan," the boy said, "You've been good t'me, nobody ever treated me good like that b' fore."

"I know they didn't, but now you can talk now so people can understand you. Maybe you'll have more friends."

"Like the captain?" He paused, "Thought he was gona kill us both."

"Yea, well you hang around the wrong people. Maybe you ought a befriend someone more kindly."

"Maybe."

"How much work do you need to do on the ship?" Bryan asked.

"Quite a bit. Haven't got the old stuff out a there yet, an a whole load to put in."

"I'll help."

"No, Bryan they'll see you, ya ought a hide."

"I'll be ok, they're lookin' for a page, act like I'm your thrall. He undid his belt, removed his smock and shirt. "Let's get to work."

The work done, William told him, "Put your clothes on, an come wid me." He took Bryan to a pub and to a hardy meal, and when they left darkness was upon them.

They walked to the dock, the crew waiting; Bryan embraced the boy, said his good-bys, and boarded the ship. The craft moved out to the sea, and Bryan watched till William faded into the darkness; it seemed, he was always saying good-by to his friends; back at sea once more.

Chapter 26

The journey to Allithwaite, on Morecombe Bay, took two days. The seas were smooth, and he relieved the rowers, from time to time, working his muscles hard, rendering them sore and achy …, alive.

The evening before they arrived, Bryan sat on the deck, watching the sun slip beneath the waves. The gruff captain, not usually social, came and sat beside him, self-consciously cleared his throat, patted Bryan on the thigh, having something to say.

"A few years ago the Jarl, the one you killed, in Balistrand had me mother's right hand cut off out of sheer meanness, nothing more. Never met the man, but I tell you twas a good thing you did there, killing him, took a lot a courage ta do a thing like that. Never killed a man, myself, but I'd liked ta kill that one, sure. Didn't like those boys were after you atall, but had ta know you were on the up and up."

"When ya get to Allithwate, you'll be in for a hard time. Just to warn ya. They don't talk Norse, nor Dane, and don't like em either. You'll have your work cut out for ya." With that, he handed Bryan the extra gold coins he'd made Bryan pay to him, and went back to the tiller.

The fair sized bay, its sandy beaches, extending far out into the water, making the merchant knar, even with its shallow draft, anchor a good distance out, in ankle deep water, Bryan shouldered his bag and weapons, and waded ashore.

Walking into a different world, like he'd never experienced before; the houses small, mostly made of wattle and daub, topped with thatched roofs, richer homes, timber framed, wattle and daub filling the spaces between timbers, stone taking the place of wattle and daub in some, a few with white lime between the timbers, the thatched roofs rounded, instead of peaked.

They spoke gibberish, sounding much like William's broken language, he understood none of it. When asking directions, they looked at him as if he were a leper, saying, 'Nortic Nietenman', turning their backs, their distaste palpable.

He tried to buy something to eat; they were not helpful, rude. Dejected, tired, hungry, he wandered about, at the edge of the village. Sat down, nearly falling asleep, until a group of youngsters approached, shouting something he couldn't fathom, some of them threw sticks, girls running forward, spitting on him. He stood, they backed away, he stepped forward, they backed off a few more steps, became bold again, and advanced, Bryan reached to his back and drew his sword, they scattered.

Frustrated, humiliated, unable to understand, he went to the other edge of the village, and looked out over a bog covered with heather that rose gradually to trees on the other side, a cart path wound through the bog, and into the trees. He decided to go there.

The heather fragrant, millions of bees working the tiny flowers, their hum, almost inaudible, the sound comforting, the vegetation itself, damp, with the air blowing in off the sea, highly humid, spongy under foot,

He wandered up into the trees, sat and rested, out of sight of anyone coming along the path. Birds, in high tree tops, sang their melodic songs. Sunlight filtered through the trees, soft, peaceful. Feeling drowsy, he slid off the log, to the soft earth beneath, and fell asleep.

With a start, he woke to darkness, the forest silent, hunger gnawing at his belly. Stowing his sword and axe under the log, he cautiously made his way out of the trees, onto the bog. The village, in the distance, dark and quiet, hunger driving him on, the path barely visible. Nearing the village, muffled noises off to his left, he froze, kneeling, heart pounding, ears straining, the sound faint, realizing it was just young lovers having a roll in the heather.

Passing them by, quietly, entering the ghostly quiet village, going directly to the stand where the lady sold bread. Stealthy as a hunter in the forest, his hand explored the table top, then the shelf under it, finding two crusts, eating one immediately, and putting the other in his pocket.

Ever so carefully, not making the slightest noise, to alarm a dog, who's bark would bring searching eyes, he made his way where they were selling meat, mutton he thought, from the smell, finding a bucket containing a few scraps, fatty, rancid.

Having followed an old woman to a trash dump earlier in the day, he went there next, but impossible to tell what was what, in the dark, he sat down, and ate the rest of the bread and revolting, rancid meat, easing the craving in his belly. He made his way back, through the bog, to the trees, curled up under the log, and slept.

Opening his eyes with a start, nearly daylight, something woke him; listening, as his senses came to him, again, he heard it, a baleful baritone howl, echoing through the trees, a dog. On his feet in an instant, pack over his shoulder, running toward the bog. But, not fast enough; near the edge of the trees, he was surrounded by four hounds, their incessant baying, painful to his ears. Nowhere to go, nor long to wait, a horseman rode up, and dismounted, a bailiff or something, saying something in that hideous language.

"I cannot understand you, Sire," Bryan said.

The man looked at him strangely, and answered in more of the unintelligible tongue. Bryan realized this was trouble.

The man wrinkled his nose and spat words, "Okroesilegr Nordanverden dyr rekkr," In a most derisive tone, a demeaning insult, something like, 'filthy northern beast.'

The man called off his dogs, stepped up to Bryan, shoved him toward the bog, "Leodgrbraland, leaf," pushing Bryan again, "Leaf...nua...leaf," he shouted.

Bryan didn't understand the words, but got the meaning. The man wanted him out of the forest, calling Bryan some kind of beast. Running out onto the bog, he turned to see the man mounting his horse, calling his dogs, shouting something unpleasant in Bryan's direction, turning, and rode away.

Bryan was dazed; what kind of strange land is this.

Back in the village once again the villagers were no more pleasant, watching, glaring, suspicious, scornful, hateful. He went to the trash dump, finding nothing to eat. Back in the village, he watched the baker lady put out her, dark, long, fresh, warm, loaves, fragrant, and yeasty smelling, held out his hand to her, in his palm, several coins, worth more than all the loaves. She wrinkled her nose, like the man in the forest, and scowled, "Norlic alef, leaf," she pointed away.

Back out on the bog, he sat on a clump of heather, head in hands, dejected, hunger dominating his thought, not knowing what to do. The smell of heather filled his nostrils. He tried chewing on the pant, bitter he spat it out. The thick heather seemed to absorb all sound, except the hum of bees. Suddenly, be realized, he was hearing another sound, faint, soft, little voices; squeaks, mice in the heather? He searched beneath the thick, heavy foliage, and found little pathways running everywhere.

Quickly pulling his knife, he cut the bottom of his shirt off, unraveled the threads, he improvised tiny snares, like those he used to set for hairs, back in Norway. Before long dozens of snares were set, and not too much afterward he was chasing tiny squeals, one by one, collecting the tiny beasts, until he had a good lot of them.

Starting a fire of dried heather, he roasted them. Tasting of heather, from the fire they were roasted over, and the food the little animals ate, and not much to them, they made his belly feel better.

Deep in the bog he found a cavity, in the side of a hill, its walls lined in heather, big enough to shelter him when it rained. Each day he visited the village to check the bay for a chance ship that might carry him away from this retched place, and antagonize the hated villagers, inciting their rage in that ridiculous language, with delight.

A dozen days, one ship, going south, the wrong direction, and growing very tired of his diet, his weight dropping. One morning, on his morning routine; no ship, checked the dump, no food, then to the baker lady, not waiting for him to beg, launching into her insulting gibberish. He persisted anyway, offering coins. She was especially vitriolic this day, loud, and vicious. For some reason, he did not turn his back, instead returning her babble with a long, loud, string of Norse, liking her to the sea monster in the ledged of Thor, his anger rising, like a boiling cauldron, wanting to destroy her stand and her with his axe, to throw her to the ground and rape her, like the pig she was. He berated her and every person in the village with every vile curse he knew, his voice louder and louder.

"What is going on here?" A woman's voice came from behind him, so used to hearing language he couldn't comprehend, it took him a second to realize that it was spoken in Norse, he understood.

Chapter 27

Spinning on his heels, a lady, young, older than he by a few years, much younger than the fat old baker woman, dressed nicely, brown hair, hanging long about her face.

She said something to the old lady who spat out her usual vitriol.

"What is it you want?" She asked Bryan.

"I only wish to purchase a loaf. I've been trying for many days, but this witch refuses my money," he protested.

"She doesn't trust you. Give me your money."

He gave her his coins. She spoke to the woman, gave her a coin and picked up a loaf, and handed it to Bryan.

"I don't think she likes you very well either," she said, "Not you, but that you're a man of the north; they despise the Norse and Danes."

"Feelings mutual," Bryan shot back as he bit into the warm loaf.

"How did you get here?"

He liked the way her lips formed her words. "I came by ship from the Isle of Mann."

"When?"

He had to think, "Twelve maybe thirteen days ago."

"My, what have you been doing all that time?" She asked.

"Living out on the bog, pissing off old ladies," he glanced angrily at the baker.

"I see, well go get your things. You can come with me. I need someone strong to help on my farm, if you don't mind hard work, that is. You can stay there until you decide what you are going to do.

A place to stay, someone to talk to, a nice lady to look at, and perhaps good food, she didn't need to say anything more. He scrambled across the bog, retrieving his pack and weapons.

He threw everything atop her heavily loaded two wheel cart, pulled by an ass that followed her dutifully, as they headed out across the bog, along the path he'd taken days before, chased by the man with the dogs. He told her of the incident, leery of entering the forest.

"The forest belongs to the noble king; you were trespassing."

"But we're going there now."

"Traveling on the road, through the forest, and the keeper knows me, the locals don't think of me as Norse. You, they could easily identify as a Northman, as they called you. They despise Northmen, who attack them often, they're always telling stories of people, lost to Viking attacks. You're lucky, were they the killing type, you would be dead."

"What is the language they speak? I can't understand any of it."

"Celtic with a good dose of Cumbric from the south of Wales all mixed together after the Romans left."

"Romans, who were the Romans?" Bryan wanted to know.

"Oh my, poor boy, you are uneducated aren't you?"

"I know Danish history, and I can read and write ruins," Bryan said in defense.

"Good northern skills, for use among the Vikings, but these people are Britons, used to be under control of Romans, a Christian empire from far south, over the oceans. They once controlled all of the Brit, and much of the Carolingian Empire, very military they were."

"You're talking about a land south of the Danes?" Bryan asked.

"Very far south, I'll draw you a map later."

He liked her; she knew things, could teach him, not simple minded, unlike the courtesans in the Jarl's court, a little older than he, strikingly good looking; blue eyes, brown hair, tall, tending toward thin, agile, quite capable of holding her own.

"Since the Romans left, these folk have become independent," She continued.

"Like pigs," He spat.

"They hate you, of course."

"Rather evident, but why, I haven't done anything to them – yet," he complained.

"You're Norse. Northmen come from the sea, robbing them, pillaging, raping, and killing. Few have gone untouched. The way you dress, your language, your manner, your arrogance, to them you're a Northman."

Bryan walked on in silence, embarrassed, irritated. He could have taken a sword to any of them without a thought, the way they treated him. Was he barbaric for his resentment? Was he responsible for the way Vikings before him acted?

"Bryan," He said, not remembering if she'd told him her name, and sure that he hadn't said his.

"What?" She asked.

"Bryan, my name's Bryan."

"Oh! Hello Bryan, I'm Sorcha."

"Sorcha, what kind of name is that?" Bryan asked.

"It's Celtic, Gallic actually," she answered.

"What's Gallic?"

"From Ireland, my adopted name really."

They crested the top of the hill, a large grassy meadow ahead, bisected by the path, the forest resuming, on the other side, and once again the path climbing, finally emerging from the forest, near the top of the mountain; a group of buildings, across the distant end of cleared, planted, fields.

A large wood frame building, surrounded by smaller buildings, all white washed, very neat and orderly, other than the type of construction, reminiscent of the farmsteads in Norway, beyond the buildings, more fields, anyone approaching could be seen from a long way.

"Welcome to my home," She said, "I graze cows and pigs, grow gardens, raise crops, and run my hens as I see fit, without interference from anyone."

"All by yourself?" Bryan asked.

"Oh no, there's me, and Tyr, Helga, and now you. You did want to come work for me didn't You? Or would you prefer to go back to your bog," she smiled.

This was truly a Norse lady, bold, forward in the home and in business, presumptive, much like his mother, to resist would be fatal, for she would have her way with him, and his choices were limited.

"Of course, I will work, I grew up working a farm such as this," he answered.

They unloaded the cart, some things going to the home, he thought too large for one lady, the rest to a large storage area in another large building filled with all kinds of farm implements.

She set the burro loose, and led Bryan across the large open square surrounded by the out buildings to one containing even more farm things; at one end, partitioned off, was a living area.

"Tyr," She called as she approached a door in the partition."

A man appeared in the doorway, ducking his head to pass under the transom, massive, his face, baby like, framed by long flowing yellow hair, hanging to his shoulders.

"Yes, m'lady," His voice peculiarly high pitched.

"This is Bryan, speaks our language. He's going to be helping us."

The big man clapped Bryan on the back, smiling, "Sorely needed help, glad to meet you," taking Bryan's pack, "This way," he led Bryan into the living quarters.

The room spare, a window at one end, two beds, instead of ledges, rope lattice work, covered with a straw mattress, one at each end of the room, a stool and small table beside each.

"This one's mine," Tyr said pointing to the one by the window, "You can have the other."

"You get settled," Sorcha said, "Evening meal at the usual time, Tyr," She turned to leave.

"Uh, mame," Bryan said clearing his throat.

"Yes," She turned back.

"I wonder if I might impose to ask for a bath, I haven't washed since arriving at the bay."

"Of course, see to it Tyr."

"Yes, m'lady. Come with me," he said to Bryan.

Bryan grabbed his last set of clean clothing, following to the kitchen, behind the main house. A short fat lady, busy cooking something that smelled wonderful, looking up, smiling. "This is Helga," Tyr said, and here is the hot water. Bryan and Tyr each got a bucket full, and behind the kitchen, in an open lean-to they washed. Bryan, unbraiding his hair, cleaning the heather from it, and scrubbing the dirt from his skin, felt much better.

After dressing, he began to braid his hair.

Tyr looked at Bryan askance, "You're not very good at that are you?" Laughing.

"Always had someone else do it for me, but, I can manage."

"No, here let me," Tyr stripped out Bryan's crooked braids, and set about doing it right.

"What brings you here," he asked as he worked.

Bryan told a brief version of his story, leaving out his murderous role; he liked these people, but unsure of them, was cautious about placing his trust in them, yet.

Secretly, he was beginning to wonder about himself, the ferocity and brutality of his revenge, the thrill that those savage acts stirred inside him, the incredible pleasure he felt, dominating Sisi, what was it about him? Tranquil here, the peacefulness magnifying the violence of his past; he needed time to reflect.

Tyr, nimble of hand, seemed to enjoy working on his hair, and finished in little time.

"What about you," He asked Tyr, "How did you come to be here?"

"I came here with m'lady Sorcha; she and I lived and worked in a monastery, a long way north of here. Her parents came to settle here from southern Norway, both died shortly after arriving, she went to live with the monks. I was sent by my Norse king to fight with the Northmen, which I and they quickly found, I was not suited to. Tiring of me, they set me ashore, and finding my way to the monastery, I took work there. The Norse eventually sacked the place, but my lady heard of their approach, and together, we escaped, came here and built this place.

"You and she are...?"

"Lovers? No, kinsmen, we understand each other," he left it there.

Bryan put his dirty clothes away. He would find out about laundering them later. He laid his blankets out on the bed, and stretched out on them.

"Don't get comfortable, were going for evening meal straight way," Tyr said motioning him to follow.

"Where's that?"

"In the house, of course," Thy said incredulous.

"With Sorcha?"

"Yes, now come,"

The inside of the house was dark and cool, walls white washed, illuminated by numerous candles, set about the large square room. The ceiling low, beams held up by posts, supporting the roof. To the side, a large fireplace faced a grouping of furniture, and to the back of the room a long table, displaying a banquet: a great round meat pie, bowl of cooked turnips, greens, a plate piled high with fruit, and wine glasses of dark, fragrant, vintage.

"Be seated everyone," Sorcha called, entering from another room, wearing a long, plain, white smock, tied loosely at the waist, accenting her graceful body, stunning. The first time since leaving the Isle, he felt the deep stir of lust, drinking in her beauty, and savoring its affect. Breaking from the momentary trance, he assisted her to her chair. She thanked him as she sat down.

The cook seated herself beside Sorcha who introduced her, "Helga is my house manager. We have her to thank for this wonderful meal," she said, graciously, a twinkle in her eye, beaming toward the plump little lady, her voice like honey over fresh warm bread, "Let's eat."

Bryan, starved, the food so luxurious, having to use all the restraint he'd learned in the service of the Jarl to keep himself from gorging.

285

There was small talk as they ate; what Sorcha found at the village, how many eggs had been collected, which field needed to be hoed.

Taking advantage of a break in the conversation, Bryan cleared his throat, all eyes turned toward him. He asked, awkwardly, "What's a monastery, where monks live, and … who are monks," the question, burning in him since Tyr said the words?

The room went silent, he squirmed, not this uncomfortable since the Jarl last grilled him.

Sorcha began to laugh, they all chuckled, "Where did you hear that?" She asked.

"Tyr, he said you and he came from a monastery where you lived with the monks."

She nodded, and to the others said, "Bryan does not know of the Romans, we must take time to help him understand how they have influenced the lives of Briton," Turning to Bryan, "Remember, I told you of the Romans. They believed a religion called Christian. The monastery was a place where monks, men who were Christian, worshiped their god, not like the gods we know; Thor, Odin, Loki, and all. The monks were kindly men who did not marry, and were good to others."

"Thank you mame," Bryan answered.

She began to tell stories, of history, beginning with Britons, before the Romans, as much as was known of it. She told of the great Roman Empire, to the south, their invasion of Briton, how ancient cultures warred with the Romans, and how the Romans hunted down shamans who followed the ancient beliefs, killed them, and replaced them with Christian monks.

Helga and Try finished eating and excused themselves.

"Let's sit somewhere more comfortable," Sorcha said, and led him to chairs near the fireplace.

She told Bryan about Roman rule, their great halls, the baths, and the walls they built, nearly across the entire country, in an attempt to keep the northerners out. Bryan interested in their weapons, strategies and tactics, asked many questions. Sorcha answered as much as she could; however, Her knowledge was mostly political and social.

They talked long into the evening, she mesmerized him; exciting, bewitching, her intellect setting his brain on fire. He went to bed that night, his head full of Roman soldiers, and battles hard fought, and dreamed of Thor, doing battle with the monster of the sea, fighting with his hammer, a great battle of blood, sweat and guile.

The next day he and Tyr worked the vegetable crops, digging channels for irrigation, hauling wood, and carrying water, the air warm and humid, sweaty and tired at the end of the day. He enjoyed a hot bath, and another meal prepared by Helga.

Again the meal was a forum for conversation, led by Sorcha, and again they talked into the night, drifting from one subject to another. He learned of Viking raids in Ireland, Northman incursions into the Carolingian Empire, on the continent, across the channel from Briton, and attacks on monasteries on the northern coast of Briton.

During the days he labored in the fields, but night after night they talked, their conversations, lasting long into the night, far ranging, and included teaching him the Celtic tongue. She was fascinating, compelling, commanding, alluring, intelligent for her years, a lady who cared, about him, interested in his thoughts, and feelings, and he was like a sponge, soaking up the history he knew nothing about.

Finally, sucking up his courage, he asked of his father.

"Never met him, though he'd been to Allithwaite a time or two; the peasants speak of his visits with fear, awe, and anger. Gone off to Ireland, so they say, to fight for Thorgis in Dublin where they're determined to conquer all the north of that land," she said.

His interest peaked, though he didn't let on, he'd found a trail; perhaps she knew more, he could draw from her, later.

In time, fraught with fear, he told her about his treachery; the murder of the Jarl, arranging the defeat of the army and the death of its men; but instead of offending her, it seemed to peek her fascination, a pleasantly unanticipated reaction.

Attracted to her physically, her beauty a tonic for his eyes, but much more than her provocative sexuality, the spiritual connection he felt for her was something he'd not experienced. There'd been a spiritual attachment to Ari, and to Ivan, but she made his relationship with them paltry. Touching his sole, sitting close, talking, holding hands, he was falling in love. He wanted to think she felt the same, surly she must have some feelings for him, to spend soo much time with him, but, she was difficult to read, she gave few if any clues.

Tyr made some vague references to his late night activity, hinting at some romantic involvement, Bryan ignored him. The late night talks, lack of sleep, hard work, and emotional involvement were wearing on him.

Summer nearly over, the evenings cool, and due hanging on everything each morning, the cold cellar beginning to fill, fruit drying on racks, and sacks of it hung in the ceiling of the main house, its sweet fragrance a delight. The pigs were being readied for slaughter, and the sheep sheared, their wool ready to for carding and spinning.

One night, after finishing a conversation, in Celtic, about Britain after the Roman legions were gone, they sat quietly together, her eyes especially blue, the light of the fireplace dancing in them, making the edges of her hair glow golden. Her face, always radiate with the deep glow she held in her heart, she was angelic, her lips, red, luscious, perfect, alluring. Losing self-control, slowly, ever so slowly, he moved toward her, unable to stop, closer, their eyes locked, their lips met; like an explosion, all the fire in his sole unleashed, he pressed her to him, her breasts against him, his tongue, parting her warm lips, to taste her mouth, sweet like honey.

Then fearing he was being presumptuous, pulling away. Face to face, they stared into each other's eyes, like seeing into the depths of each other's sole.

"I've wanted to do that for a long time," she said softly.

"Why didn't you?"

"I was afraid I'd offend you."

"I've wanted you since the very first day I saw you, but you were so much smarter and a little older. I was afraid too."

"Please don't be," she said, her voice soft and soothing. She took his hand, stood, and led him into the shadows of her bedroom, her private refuge, her secret sanctuary, where he'd never seen anyone else go, a sleeping ledge to the side, a few chairs and chests along the walls, and in the center, on the floor, a large fur, padded by quilts underneath.

As they neared the rug, she turned to him, grasping his shirt, pulled it over his head, letting it drop to the floor. Her hands, caressed his shoulders, gently moved down, over his chest, stopping briefly, to run her fingers over his nipples, then downward over his abdomen, to his waist, loosening his belt, let his trousers drop to his ankles, and pushed him down, onto the fur, kneeling to removed his boots and trousers.

Standing, she undid the top of her gown. It flowed down over her shoulders and breasts past her flat stomach, slipping around her hips, dropping to the floor. Her naked body highlighted only by the soft light coming from the outer room, a thing of beauty, promising of satisfaction, for his longing, longing that tormented him since he'd fist laid eyes on her. She knelt down, and lowered her body on top of him.

It felt so good, holding her next to him; delicate, lithe, strong, naked, he loved her. Her tongue filled his mouth - he sucked on it, enjoying the fire flowing through his veins. Lifting her gently, he laid her beside him, then rose to his knees, between her legs, spreading them slightly, bent over to kiss and caress her breasts; soft, beautiful, nipples swollen, strangely firm, deliciously pliant to his lips and fingers. Then pressing his lips to hers, and moved himself down between her legs, feeling the moistness, within the triangle of soft fur, penetrating deep into the the warm, wetness of her womb.

She gasped softly.

Inside her, he felt himself swell with pleasure, her body holding him softly.

"You are so beautiful," he whispered in her ear as he eased his pelvis against her body, and began to make love to her; strangely different from his previous experiences, mysterious, lacking the usual urgent need to relieve himself; in its' place, soft, slow, luxurious, pleasure, a melding of their soles, her inner being touching softly on his brain, as tender as a morning breeze, yet commanding, like the passion and thunder of Thor. Higher and higher, desiring only to be consumed by her, giving her his very being, becoming one.

Aroused to greater and greater heights of ecstasy, beyond anything he ever thought possible. Softly, quietly, their orgasm billowed into all consuming physical and emotional ecstatic pleasure. Holding each other their bodies writhed in rhythmic convulsions, leaving them exhausted of all tension, luxuriously drifting in physical and spiritual fulfillment, like he'd never dreamed possible, in his wildest imagination; collapsing onto her, rolling to the side, and slipping into blissful sexual slumber.

When he awoke, she was staring at him, her fingers, playing with his braids, softly caressing his neck and ear. The burn of sensual blush still touching his face and chest; "Sorcha," he whispered, "Before this, before you, I've never made love before."

"Would you be offended if I told you I don't believe you?" she answered softly, "You certainly knew what you were doing."

"Oh…I've been with other women, lustful and physical, but never like that, so beautiful, magnificent, like you; you touched a part of me I didn't know existed."

She kissed him. They made love again. Eventually, he roused himself, dressed and went out into the night. The air cool and crisp, the stars were clear and bright as crystal in the sky. Standing, looking up, a shooting star flashed across the sky to the north, marveling he wondered if it was a good omen.

Retuning to his room near dawn, Tyr, already up and dressed, said, "Stayed longer than usual tonight."

"I did," Bryan answered.

Tyr said no more – there was no need.

Today Tyr would go the village and trade for supplies.

Bryan changed clothes, had a morning meal, and went to work on the crops. It wouldn't be long, the leaves were beginning to turn, the tree tops would soon be glazed with frost, and there was much to gather from the field that had not yet been harvested, winter was coming.

But, Tyr returned, the morning still young, hurrying across the fields, his cart nearly empty, out of breath, a worried look on his face, so excited, his speech garbled, they could not understand him. Sorcha calmed him so he could tell them what was wrong.

Chapter 28

"There are men in the village, Northmen, asking questions," Tyr said.

"I knew this moment would come," he'd been rehearsing it, over and over in his head. Stepping toward the forest where it met the trail, searching, as if he could already see the knight approaching.

"You didn't say anything did you?" Bryan asked, his voice low, his words slow.

"He didn't have to," Sorcha said, "The villagers will tell them plenty."

"One knight, no more will come, an insult to me, as if to swat a fly," Bryan said, almost in a whisper.

"I will help," Tyr said, bravely, "I've fought men before."

"No!" Bryan shouted, spinning on his heals to confront them. "You will not. You do not understand. These are battle tested warriors, skilled in what they do. They will slaughter you.

When they come, Tyr, you must take Sorcha and Helga into the forest. If I should fail, and be killed they will come after you as well, these are dangerous, vicious men."

Fear on her face, more precious to him than anything in the world, Sorcha; strong, resourceful, intelligent, with tremendous inner strength, dangerously frail, and vulnerable. He would leave, either before, or after doing battle, it would be unbearable, but to stay would bring certain harm to her. It would bring sadness beyond comprehension, pain deeper than the oceans that he knew would come, since first arriving here, like an arrow already launched, to pierce his heart; unavoidable.

His head bowed, and through eyes blurred with tears, he said, "I am very sorry to have brought this to you." Wrapping his arms about her soft, warm, trembling body, wraked with her sobbing, he rocked her gently. Tyr, his thoughts always difficult to read; on his face, obvious distress, and confusion as to what to do, his heart bleeding for them.

Finally, Bryan broke from Sorcha, brushing the tears from her cheeks with his hand, kissed her, and said, "I must go prepare now."

In his room, under his bed, he found his uncle's sword, and his axe. He sat at the end of the bed, gazing at Grunner's sword, battling his own fears, not far from the surface now; would the killing never end, the tradition of his Norse ancestors, the new Vikings, his father, and now him, it was his heritage. He fingered the figure tied about his neck, and said a prayer to Thor.

The Knight came in the afternoon, clouds rolling in, dark, threatening, a wind cold and stiff. A tiny figure, emerging from the trees, crossing the fields with a purpose, a Knight from Skjolden's court; a henchman who once reaped the Jarl's benefits, benefits now vanished, with the Dane'd demise, bent on revenge, the Viking 'Tradition', clad in armor; a shining helm, arms and legs in heavy leather, chain mail vest, a shield, sword at his side, and axe in hand.

Light rain began to fall, as the warrior closed the distance. The large, grizzled man halted at thirty paces, axe in his right hand, hanging to his side, sword hung at his left hip, the hilts of many knives sheathed in his belt.

"You," he bellowed, "We took you in, stood you at the Jarl's side, heaped you with the privileges of a warrior, the Dane's little prince; you turned on him, betraying him, murdered him, butchering him like a pig."

294

Bryan, not about to admit guilt to this barbarian, growled back, "The Danish cur murdered my uncle, leader of our clan, for no reason, brazen he was, enough to bring Grunner's body to our door step, as if a savior, a tyrant, enslaving innocents, maiming the poor, making war on defenseless villages, profiting from their enslavement, and calling it victory. He made profit of people's blood, spit on him."

"Enough," the warrior raged, "You'll now die for your murderous treachery."

Raising his axe, he advanced, the blade gleaming, even in the dim light, studded with rain drops, like millions of sparkling jewels, a glimmer of cool, quick, death.

Remembering Vandel's lessons about being intimidated by your enemy, he raised his axe to meet the onslaught.

Two blades met with a thunderous clash, sparks flying, Thore's hammer, forging his wrath in the heavens. The blow shook Bryan to the bone. The knight felt it as well. Not wise to reveal the effects of your enemies' assault, both remained stoic, a second blow quickly following, just missing Bryan's face. Following the knight's blade as it swung away, Bryan tried to use the back side of his blade to hook the warriors' axe, but the knight, quick to respond, snatched it away. Spinning, Bryan swung at the man's legs, catching the skin, only to scratch it above the armored knee. Countering, the brute struck out again, Bryan ducking back, the blade barely grazing his nose, the cold steel, so close, causing a chill to run down Brian's spine.

The knight struck out again and again, Bryan steadily backing away; defending each blow would sap his energy, tiring him much too quickly. Picking his next move carefully, he again attempted to hook the warriors' axe; a violent move he was quite adept at in training, quick and precise, the blades locked, the jolt shocking, wrenching the handles from each other's grip. The axes flew; linked tightly together in an iron embrace, end over end, singing a steely zing, in a high arch, away to Bryan's left.

Grasping his sword from its scabbard, the Knight mirrored his action. Bryan, sure the sword, lending an advantage to the lighter, quicker, fighter, would give him an edge, the knight quickly proving him wrong; though bigger and heavier, he was agile, and in short order put a gash in Bryan's left upper arm, stinging like a thousand bees injecting their venom; fighting back, delivering a jarring blow, staggering the big man, but sending severe pain through his arms and shoulders, the shock waves jarring his brain and spine. Fighting furiously for his life, inflecting superficial wounds to the knights' arms, and legs, a cut across the right knee, which bled profusely, the Knight returned a rapid volley of angry blows, slashing deeply to Bryan's right shoulder, warm blood, bathing his upper arm, and dripping from his elbow; Bryan began to fear the outcome,striking back quickly, to prove to the knight he was not injured, but fatigue was beginning to set in.

The knight made a series of vicious charges, Bryan continuing to back away, a good distance. His arms and legs aching; every movement was great effort; he made an attempted a lunge at the man's legs, caught the left knee, the point of his blade penetrating, feeling the crunch of bone and cartilage. The wounded man bellowed, limped backward a few steps, and turned toward Bryan, cursing.

Bryan, invigorated, charged forward, the knight clumsily defending himself, struck Bryan alongside the head with the flat of the blade, cutting his right ear deeply, slicing across his cheek and lip, leaving a gash above his right eye, his head reeling, sight narrowed; blinded by blood, he saw the knight limping forward at him, his sword raised for a fatal blow. With the last bit of effort left in him, Bryan blindly brought his sword up in defense. The knight stumbled, his wounded leg giving way, falling forward, sword descending, Bryan's blind thrust knocked the knight's sword aside, catching the knight beneath his chin, his full weight crashing down on Grunner's razor sharp blade, ramming the point upward through his throat, hitting the vertebrae at the back of his neck, crunching through the bone at the base of his skull, piercing his brain; dead before he hit the ground, his weight landing atop Bryan.

Unable to move, pinned, pain coursing through him, his world spinning wildly, vision narrowing to a pinhole, blackness.

Chapter 29

Opening his eyes, blinding pain exploding in his head, searing, burning in his arms, lying on the dining table, in Sorcha's house, Sorcha, Helga, and Tyr hovering over him, wiping his head with a cool wet cloth, trying to fight through the pain, remember, what happened, why was he lying there? The effort exhausting him, he faded to darkness again.

In and out of consciousness for, unable to tell, seeming a very long time, till able to part the foggy curtains, and speak. Sorcha hurried to his side, summoned by his struggle.

"Wha, what happened?" he whispered.

"You don't remember?" she answered.

"No," straining, shaking his head, immediately rewarded with searing pain, he gasped.

Sorcha looked down at him, the face of an angle, soothing, loving, making him, momentarily, forget the pain. "You fought the Northman," she whispered in his left ear, "you killed him."

"I did?"

"You suffered a mighty blow to your head, your ear nearly cut off, and face cut severely. I've sown you back together."

"My head hurts so," he said.

"I imagine it does. Your face will be swollen and discolored for a good while."

Struggling to remember, making it hurt more, his vision narrowed, and he slipped, once again, into unconsciousness.

When he again woke, the pain slightly dulled, lying on the ledge, in Sorcha's room, his clothing removed, he was bathed, and swaddled in blankets, like a child. The clouds in his head, beginning to clear; a horrific battle, he remembered, who had he fought, he'd killed the man, Sordha told him, but he couldn't recall. When did they fight? He tried to rise up, the pain in his head, he drifted away again, but woke when someone, Sorcha, entered the room.

Her face hovering over him, so beautiful, calm, peaceful, she called his name, her voice soft and soothing.

"Yes," he answered.

"Good, you're back with us," she answered, "You must be hungry?"

"No, not hungry." His thoughts were vague, he couldn't focus. There was something urgent, he couldn't remember.

"Sorcha?"

""Yes."

"Tell me, again, who was it I fought."

"You fought the Jarl's knight."

"Was I defeated?"

"No…, you killed him. You were badly wounded."

It began to come back to him, hurting, "How long have I been lying ill?"

"A day and a half," she answered.

A day and a half, he thought. Suddenly, the clouds cleared, his thoughts coming back to him, sitting upright, he hung his legs over the ledge, lightening sharp pain shot through his head, "Sorcha, you are in great danger. I must leave, Now."

"No you can't"

"Where are my clothes?"

"They were bloodied and torn, I threw them away," she said, anxiety obvious in her voice.

Like a knife blade piercing his head, throbbing, each step jarring, he began to walk, ignoring the shooting bolts of fire in his head.

Sorcha, becoming very excited, screamed, "You can't, you're naked, you're still sick, Bryan stop."

He walked past her, past Helga, through the great room, out into the square, each step excruciating, and bright sun light, slicing through his head like lightening.

"Bryan, stop, you can't," Sorcha was screaming, crying.

He kept going, across the square, into his room. Tyr came running to Sorcha's cries. Sitting on the edge of his bed, while they all came into the room, Sorcha ranting hysterically, Tyr wanting to know what was going on, Helga trying to sooth Sorcha, the noise, echoing from side to side, inside his head. He leaned forward, resting his head in his hands.

"SHUT UP," he screamed.

Silence.

Meaning well, they did not comprehend the gravity of the situation. "You do not understand," speaking slowly, deliberately, between his hands, to the floor, "When the knight does not return, they will come, all of them, after me and you. I cannot fight another, until healed. The dead man must be buried, not to be ever found, and I must be gone from here, as soon and quietly as possible, as far away as possible, as if I vanished. You must tell them, I've been killed, drug away by the knight. I will not have the ones I love slain. Now help me dress."

Sorcha approached quietly, her face streaked with tears, touched his shoulders softly with her cool fingers, whispering, voice soft as the wind, "Of course my darling, we understand, we are concerned about your safety, as you are ours." Gently draping a smock over his head, threading his arm through the sleeves, "We will help you. Please be patient with us," pulling his undergarments over his legs, then his trousers, finally tying on his shoes.

"Helga, go begin a meal for us, we'll be hungry when it is ready," back in command again, "You two, come with me, we will dispose of the knight."

They drew rope around the knight's body, tied it to a horse, and although strong and sturdy, the horse strained, pulling the heavey carcass, to the edge of the forest, as far away, as possible.

They dug deeply, Bryan's arms ached, where his wounds festered, his head throbbing, he worked on, until the hole was deep, tumbling the body in, along with his weapons, shield and helm, and the hole was refilled and packed so that there would be no settling; leaving no tell tale signs that the earth had been disturbed, the remaining soil scattered far from the site. As darkness closed in around them, they covered the site with brush, and carefully backtracked, scouring any trace of the body being drug in the dirt with branches.

Bryan, though anxious to be gone, his wounds still painful, after digging the grave, gratefully accepted one last feast, prepared by Helga, found Sorcha had been making her own plans.

"Tyr," she began, "As soon as we are finished eating I want you to go down to the village, scout out for any ships leaving to the west. You may have to wait till morning, but purchase a fair if you can, double the fair if you must, no one in the village is to know about it, and stay clear of the Northmen, as if I need tell you. It might take days before a ship sails, stay with it, and be as inconspicuous as possible. I will clean Bryan and tend to his wounds then take him to our camp."

"Camp?" Bryan said with a start.

"Yes, camp. Helga if the Northmen come, tell them we heard they were on their way, and escaped up over the mountain." Turning back to Bryan, "Long ago we built a small cabin about half way up from the village, well off the trail, hidden, for just such occasions," she turned back to Tyr, "Once you've obtained a fair, meet us at the camp. We'll make plans as the situation dictates."

Tyr, unexpectedly, returned; meeting them at the camp the next morning, out of breath, "You must hurry," panting, "There's a ship leaving for Dublin, the captain's waiting on you, I've never seen such luck, the northmen are nowhere to be found, villagers didn't know where they might have gone, probably don't care."

Bryan looked to Sorcha, "I have to go."

She nodded her head in understanding, reluctantly whispering, "I know," tears welling in her eyes. He took her in his arms, held her, kissed her forehead, smoothed her hair, and rocked her gently.

"We have to go," Tyr said urgently.

Bryan nodded. "I love you Sorcha, don't forget."

"I love you too," she whispered, choking back tears, "Take care of yourself," the words catching in her throat.

He nodded, his own eyes blurred by tears, pulling away, picked up his pack, stepped toward the door, and turned back toward her, their eyes locked, how could he be leaving her, the best thing ever happened to him, he had to, he knew, against every impulse in his body, he pulled away. "Good-by," he choked.

She smiled, sadly.

His downhill walk seemed an eternity.

Nearing the village, Tyr stopped and asked, "Do you want to take the back way, behind the dump, so no one will see you?"

Bryan thinking for a moment, "No...it would be better for us if the village were to see me leave," he paused, a slight change in plan,"That way the the knights will know for sure I'm gone." Pulling his sword from the back of his pack, and tying it to his waist, hooking his axe in his belt, said, "Let's go."

They paraded through the village, stopping at the butchers stand, bought smoked lamb, went to the bakers stand, and bought loaves of bread. The lady called him names, clucking until he told her in perfect Celtic, "Thank you, you miserable old witch," her face flushed, mouth dropping open, hutted, and turned her back to him. He laughed out loud, and left.

Stepping into the water, he turned to Tyr, put his arm around his shoulders, "So long friend. Take care of Sorcha well you, tell her I love her, if I ever can, I'll return," a promise he hoped not idle. Turning to the sea, wading to the ship, emptiness, pain, sadness, anger, and despair, beyond words; sitting on the deck, staring blankly into the waves, he wanted to be dead.

Once in open water, warming in the sun's rays, sea birds sailing free in the wind above, sea breeze breathing in his face, the sharp edge of pain dulling slightly, his thoughts turning to his fate, by the power of Thor, or otherwise, realizing, slowly, inexorably, he was being pulled toward the conflict in Ireland, where his father's trail led, and perhaps answers to the questions, troubling him.

"It's a few months since I've been there," the captain said in answer to Bryan's inquiry, "The Viking have built a sizable force, and the Irish king determined to throw them out, raising an army of his own, is marching on Dublin, 'll be a threat to the Northmen sometime in the coming weeks."

"And Thor Bryanson, have you heard of him?" Bryan asked.

The captain paused a moment, to think, "Heard talk of him, but not for long time, had a fearsome reputation, a favorite of Turgeis, Viking leader up there, had some falling out, I heard, not much talk of him since."

"How long is our sail to Dublin."

"Coupl'a three days or so, depending on the weather. Have to tack to the west till we find the coast then we sail north to find Dublin. You might as well relax – enjoy the ride."

Two men crewed the ship, serving as oarsmen, working the rigging. With a stiff wind from the west, little need to row. A smallish knarr, old, carrying a small cargo, decking lashed atop, seemed to flex with each wave, the decking shifting along with it, but it appeared to handle the sea with competence. With emptiness in the pit of his stomach, the warm weather, and constant gentle rocking of the waves, he settled into a sullen state of melancholy.

Very early, on the morning of the third day, he was jarred awake by a loud, deep, explosion, the ship trembled; pitch black, seeing nothing, the captain shouting commands. The bow rode the crest of a wave, tilted forward, came crashing down to the water below, a heavy spray of salt water blowing back over the ship, pelting the deck, icy cold, with the same heavy hallow thud that jarred him awake; heavy seas. A tremendous bolt of lightning, setting the world alight; terror gripped him; the sky, angry, billowing, swirling, black, ominous, the tormented sea, pitching, rolling, mountainous swells, in every direction, the ship straining against the waves, moaning as the timbers shifted underneath him.

"Not again," Bryan shouted, "What have I done to displease you Lord Thor."

Another flash, a huge, towering wave pitching forward, and crashing over the bow, with thunderous noise; the deck awash with water to his waist. He found a rope, and lashed himself and his pack to the mast. A second wave, and when Thor's hammer lit the sky again, there was but one crewman on deck. The captain screaming…, he couldn't hear what, over the rolling thunder, crashing waves, and howling wind. The ship shuttered and moaned as it crested yet another wave, smashing back into the sea.

Pushing through the tempest, moaning like an old woman, louder, waves higher, wind stronger, lightening more frequent, another wave, the bow plunged downward, burying itself into the trough below, its timbers straining. The next wave hit, with it the moaning changed; an explosion of creaking, and cracking, splintering. He felt the mast shift, quickly removing his lashings as it tilted, awkwardly. Another wave crashed over the bow. The whole decking moved, coming apart. Another wave, and another, he was in the water, he didn't know how, gripping to his pack, floating high in the water; by some twist of luck he'd remade it with oil cloth.

More waves, the ships timbers crunched together, splintering, and clattering, the entire vessel coming apart, waves full of timbers, he grabbed one, and paddled with his legs, away from the debris. Still, waves crashed over him, the ship gone when Thor's lightening lit the sky. Unrelenting, pounding, brutally punishing, gasping for air, at every chance, when the waves allowed, the water sapping his strength; cold, bitter in his mouth, blinding his eyes, up his nose, in his mouth, vomiting the salt water he swallowed, legs aching, so tired, so cold, so tired, blackness, sleep, peace.

Chapter 30

A sound, what was it…, Children? No, must be gulls. Numbing Cold, so deep, his head throbbed, pain coursing the length of his arms…, Freezing.

There it was again, children's voices, far away, coming toward him, eyes wouldn't open, unable to move, not his fingers, nor his toes, laying on something very hard and cold, stuck to it. Where was he? What happened? He could hear water; soft gentle waves, close, feel the warm rays of the sun on his skin. The children closer, adult voices too…, very close now, no longer laughing.

Forcing his eyes open, staring up at a young girl, a boy a little older, to her side, a man and a woman, coming into view, his mouth would not work, to say something.

"Is he alive?" the boy asked in heavy Celtic.

"I think, he's breathing," the woman said, "And his eyes are moving."

"Must'a shipwrecked in the storm," the man said, "Timbers all over here, and over there's his pack," his words heavy Celtic, too.

"Look at the sword," the boy said, admiringly, "Think he's a knight or something?"

The man kneeling bedside Bryan, put an arm around his shoulders, and raised him to sitting. The movement bringing burning, searing, pain, shooting through his muscles; looking down, his body, white, wrinkled, naked; what happened to his clothes? Still unable to move, or speak; "Help me," the man told the boy. Gently, picking him from the sand, to carry him to a cave, a fare distance; their home. Bathing him in fresh water, wrapping him warm blankets, and feeding him warm broth, the women and girl nursing him, over the next few days; heat returned to his body, movement along with it, and his remembering, without recollection of how he survived after the ship disintegrated, fortunate to be alive, the little hammer still hanging about his neck, the god must have looked after him those hours, unconscious, in the water, sending this family to rescue him afterward.

The man named Conall, spoke with him often; about the ship wreck, why he came to Ireland, about Conall himself, and his family; they'd moved down into the cave from the land above the cliffs to avoid Viking invaders. The cave was warm, protecting them from the elements, the sea providing sustenance, the Northmen never looking there. Poor people; Conall and his son Drustan went shirtless, their trousers worn thin and torn, cut off at the knees, offering little protection from the elements. His wife, Caiside, wore a simple wool dress, and her daughter Judoeus, her mothers hand me down, the little ones, having few items of clothing, fragments of old adult clothing, but for the most part, running naked.

Friendly people, clean, and strong, very thin, in a robust healthy way, "We eat shell fish we dig," Conall told Bryan, "Sometimes fish we are able to catch, and birds we can kill. The girls go up top to gather grain and wild plants. We eat well."

"How do you find wood for the fire?" Bryan wondered.

"We gather driftwood, and dry it. The ship wreck was a gift," Conall said. They had already gathered the timbers washed ashore.

"You didn't find anyone else from the ship?" Bryan asked.

"Only you, and your pack, there were a few bits of cargo, but nothing else."

"Pity their souls," Bryan felt sorry for them.

The women washed the clothing in his pack, laying no claim to the money in the sac that survived.

"What use is money to us," Caiside said.

When Drustan showed interest in Bryan's sword, he took it out and let the boy handle it, told of its history, minus some gruesome details, showing him how to defend himself with it; the boy, fascinated, delighted, romanticizing.

He decided to tell them of the knights hunting him, "They'll not find me here though. I'm certain they'll be looking for me in Dublin."

"Twas a good thing then, that your ship met its end at sea, and you landed here with us," Conall said with a smile.

Poor, honest, humble people, willing to help, even a Northman, if they could, nursing him back to health, providing meals and shelter, telling him of the strange Irish world; wee people scurrying about the undergrowth, and leprechauns dancing in the wood, creating magic and treachery, like the Nordic elves and fairies, and of kings who fought for their land, like Norsemen, and not the least of all, common people, poor as dirt.

Ten days passed, and Bryan feeling strong enough to travel, told them "I must continue on my journey, search for father, I owe you and your family my life, I am most grateful, perhaps someday I will be able to repay you."

"How will you go?" Conall asked.

"I'm thinking I would follow the shore north to Dublin," Bryan answered.

"The way by the shore is not clear," Conall told him, shaking his head, "There are places where sheer cliffs fall right to the sea. You cannot pass; have to climb around, difficult and time consuming. I'll have Druston guide you up off the shore, to a road on top, so you can find your way to Dublin."

The boy beamed, anxious at the chance to do the work of a man, with this Northman. The two setting out early the next morning; shirtless, barefoot, so young and full of energy, the boy led him up a tortuous trail, to the green surface of the island. For two days they traveled to the northwest, Drustan asking endless questions of Bryan; the boy, idealizing him, thinking him a great warrior, a knight. Bryan, flattered, accommodated him with stories about his time in the service of the Jarl, letting him carry the sword at times, but gently, letting the young boy know the inglorious business of killing a man, telling stories of betrayal and treachery among those in power, hoping that the boy understood, all was not glory.

At the end of the second day, they came upon a road, heading north. Drustan stayed with him that evening, saying good-by in the morning. Strong, smart, eager, naive; the boy had worked his way into Bryan's heart, becoming a good friend, someone he liked very much, with whom he was parting ways.

Traveling north, after another two days, unchallenged, horsemen, Northmen, over took him, three of them, surrounding him; a flashback of Vandal and his companions on the way to Balestrand, so long ago. "Where you headed, warrior, are you lost?" One of the men barked in Danish, dressed in leather armor, a polished helm with gold trim, a shield hung at the side of the horse.

"Headed for Dublin to join our forces there," Bryan answered.

"And what are you doing out here?"

"Shipwrecked, about ten days ago, I guess it was, landed on the beach south of here. Had to get my bearings, been walking ever since," Bryan explained.

"I remember the storm," one of the horseman said.

"You're lucky you weren't attacked by natives," the leader said, "Tis dangerous out here alone. Hitch a ride with one of them," he motioned with his head toward his men.

Dublin, situated up river a bit, east from the mouth of the river, a hodge podge of shelters; some old stone buildings left from the original village, some cloth and skin tents, rough timbered lean to structures, and a few smallish longhouses, Bryan assumed belonged to leaders, scattered about both sides of the river. Further up the river were open fields where horses grazed, and beyond, wetland marshes, willows growing up, along the river's edge.

The riders took him to a long house in the center of the town and dismounted.

"Wait here," the rider told him, and went in.

After a long wait, he returned. "Lord Turgeis will see you," he paused, "The lord is a great leader, and will be treated with due respect."

"I understand, thank you," Bryan said

One of the lord's guards approached him, "Follow me." He turned, and entered the longhouse, Bryan trailing behind the horseman into the interior darkness. In the dim light, Bryan made out a heavy bearded Viking seated on a bench, surrounded by at least a dozen well armed men. This was the great Turgeis whom Bryan had heard the Jarl's men talk of, leader of Vikings in Ireland and the Irish Sea.

"What is your name?" Turgeis asked, his deep, booming voice full of authority.

"Bryan Thorson, my lord."

"What business do you seek here?"

"I am a battle tested warrior," Bryan said, embellishing his status, "And wish to join my brothers in our venture here. I've heard much about you. It would be an honor to serve you, my lord."

"Probably much of what you've heard is lies," Turgeis laughed, "And you look battle tested," pointing to his face, still swollen and bruised from his battle with the Jarl's Knight. A chuckle rippled through the court. "Who do you serve?"

"Lord Innvik, my lord."

"So Lord Innvik chooses to join our endeavor now?"

"My lord, I doubt that Lord Innvik knows of my existence, however, I served in the court of the Dane, Lord Skjokden, until his untimely demise. In his absence, I became a subject of Lord Innvik.

"A maverick; some of your brothers were here a few days ago looking for your king's murder. You might try to join them if they are still about. Otherwise I would be most happy if you would join us." He turned to the horseman, "Take him to Yarvik, he was talking of a venture just the other day," dismissing them with a wave of the hand.

They found Yarvik in a lean-to on an extended fabric tent arrangement, closed in on the sides, filled with armor and weapons. Yarvik himself, a stocky, blue eyed man, bearded face, and yellow hair braided back without tails.

He frowned when he saw Bryan's face, "What the blazes happened to you?"

"Fight with a Welshman," Bryan lied, "They tell me he died, I don't remember though."

"The man winced, "I can see why," he said. "So you can fight, ever been in battle?"

"Yes sire, lost my axe in a ship wreck though."

"I see, well you can take your pick," he swept his hand over the sacked weapons, "Nice looking sword," He pointed.

"A gift from my uncle."

"Good to have such a generous uncle – have you any leadership experience?"

"I was trained in tactics in Lord Skolden's army, and helped lead an expedition."

"Successful, I presume.

"It was…, punishing," Bryan answered.

"I see, well we anticipate hosting an army of the Irish in the coming days. One of their kings' got 'em all stirred up. I need someone to lead fifty or so men, might be dangerous, if you think you can handle it?"

"You can count on me, sire."

"Good, now here's what I've got in mind…" he went on to explain the mission to Bryan. As he did, the man examined Bryan's face, intently, squinting his eyes, turning his head to the side; an odd one anyway, Bryan thought it just his peculiar way.

Finished telling of his plan, he asked, his voice full of curiosity, "You related to Thor Bryanson?"

"My father."

"Thought so, you look like him. Hope you have more of a stomach for battle than him, good fighter, fierce, but when it came to killing Irishers, lost his nerve. Sure hope you can do better."

Bryan's distaste for the man instant, "Haven't seen him in years, do you know where he is?"

"Left here some time ago, good riddens I say, no idea where he went, and don't really care." He was abrupt. "Stay close, we'll let you know when you are to embark." Telling Bryan where to find the men he was to lead, "You'll bunk with them till you go into battle. Prepare them as best you can."

The men, experienced, capable warriors, accepting of his leadership, understood what they were doing, needing little explanation. The more time he spent with them, the greater his respect for them grew. Why anyone thought they needed his leadership, he didn't know.

He explored the camp, warily inconspicuous, unsure if the Jarl's knights were still about. He observed ships, of all shapes and sizes, coming and going, mostly merchant knarrs, carrying goods to and from distant ports, ladened with treasure for various lords in Scandinavia, still others carrying human cargo to be sold at Spanish ports.

He did a double take, even at a distance there was no mistaking the familiar figure; broad bare shoulders, thin at the waist, heavily muscled legs, and trousers to the knees, bare feet, could be none other than William. He jumped from the piling he was sitting on, running along the dock, shouting, "William," rather loudly.

The boy spun about, not sure, the voice familiar, yelped when he spotted Bryan, running to meet him, they threw their arms about one another, William hoisting Bryan off his feet, hugged him tightly, and dropped him back to the deck.

"By the gods it's good to see you," the boy said, stepping back, a look of concern flashing across his face, "What in the name of Oden happened to you?" he said, touching his own face.

"Had a fight with one of the knights," Bryan told him.

"You beat him, didn't you?"

"I did, there are others though."

"Yea, they've been here, a few days ago, asking all kinds of questions, had to make myself scarce, didn't stay long though, once they found you weren't here."

"They were following me," Bryan said, "By a stroke of luck, the ship I was on came apart in a storm off the coast south of here, so they missed me. But, what are you doing here?"

"They stayed a long while on the Isle after you left, trying to figure out what happened to you. I left to avoid their suspicious questions, had to hide out, when they showed up here."

"Glad you didn't come to any harm on my account," Bryan said, "It's so good to see you. Are there any places to buy something to eat close by, where we can talk."

William took him to a little shack he knew, where a man sold them loaves of bread, a tankard of ale, and stewed lamb to put on the bread. Bryan told the boy of his adventures; the miserable Welsh people, living of rodents in the heather, Sorcha, his battle with the knight, the shipwreck, and the family who saved him.

"I have a favor to ask of you," Bryan said.

"Just say it," William answered.

"Would you let me know if the Jarl's knights show up again?"

"You'll know before they're off the boat," William promised.

Not long after, on a gray overcast day, the Irish king's army appeared, across the meadow, to the west of the Viking camp, now called Dublin.

Chapter 31

Unsurprised, the Vikings, long aware of the advance, having followed the great lumbering army for days, were ready for battle.

The Irish, at great advantage, positioned themselves, on high ground, the open field to their front, river to their left, the willow marsh to their rear, heavily reinforcing their right, positioned slightly forward to deflect any advance in that direction, avoiding being flanked in any direction, the field in front sloping down toward the Viking camp.

The Vikings, however, their plan prepared well in advance, showing contempt for the Irish, did not show themselves, to their front at least, allowing the Irish force a position with seeming tactical advantage.

Bryan received a summons to Yarvick's tent.

"Turgius has ordered our leaders to hear his plans for battle, we will go there now," Yarvick told his captains. Bryan and sixteen others followed their leader, through legions of Viking warriors, gathered in the narrow streets, between the various buildings, making up the western edge of Dublin, where Turgius gathered them in an open area, just inside the edge of the village, out of sight of the Irish.

He began, "We'll beat these Irish fools, surprise and deception, our advantage. We will attack where they think we cannot, not revealing ourselves until needed, they will not know our full strength, or from where we are coming. They will flee the battle, and we shall be free to pillage the land as we please, victory is ours to take."

His followers cheered, hammered on their shields, and rattled their swords. Bryan unsure, walked out onto the field, personally reconnoitering. The Irish line, long and deep, well armed, shields at the ready, strong, lean, men, ready to fight for their homeland. Would Turgius' plan work?

As mid-day approached the Irish sent forward two leaders, with flag bearers, and calvary at their sides. "Send us your leader," one of them shouted."

The Viking delayed a good while, eventually Turgius and two of his guards walked out on the field to meet them.

"What is it you want," Turgius demanded.

"Leave our land. Take your armies and be gone from here," they answered, "Do so and there'll be no trouble for you. Stay and we will expel you by force if not kill you, by orders of the king."

"To the contrary," Turgius yelled, "Tis our land now, take your army from our front and be gone with you, and we'll not pursue you, stay and you will face our wrath."

The Irish captains gave no answer. They rared their horses about, and rode back to their ranks.

Bryan made his way back to his men, and prepared for battle; they were to go with little armor, a small shield, knives, an axe, a sword, going nearly naked, a woolen smock their only protection, and leather shoes. At the river's edge, day light fading, rolling out its protective blanket of darkness, five small longships waited them. They made no noise, boarding the small ships, ever so quietly, launching into the river, moving up stream, poling instead of rowing, so not to make noise, past the Viking village of Dublin, past the open field where a thin line of Viking warriors now stood, slowly, quietly, within a stone's throw of the Irish troupes, inch by inch, not daring to breath too hard, they advanced.

Well past the Irish, they went ashore, among the willows, tall grass, and standing water. Slowly, ever so quietly, they crept from their boats, crawled through the muck and water, toward the Irish rear, until they could hear the enemy moving about, talking, restless in their lines. There they lie, waiting through the long, cold night; not daring to talk, or stand, sleepless, anxious, dawn, not revealing its dim light, in the east, for a very, very long time. As day light finally came, clouds lay low overhead, gray, featureless, a soft mist falling.

From their position, they could just see over the Irish lines. The Viking line was being reinforced; they could hear the faint movement in the distance.

The Irish, too, were beginning to stir; the low rumbling of voices, and clatter of weapons, drifting back over Bryan's group, laying silent, hidden, waiting, the morning wore on. Then there was movement in the front of the Viking line.

Rising up to see what was happening, "What the," one of his warriors whispered.

"Berserkers," Bryan whispered back; half a dozen men, naked, their bodies painted blue, were running about in front of the Viking ranks, screaming obscenities, brandishing swords and axes, threatening, menacing. "They're crazed; drugged by the shamans, with herbs, under a spell, cast by the priests, to put the fear of Oden in the enemy."

The crazed men ran and danced about, making fierce animal sounds, acting out what they were going to do to the enemy, cursing, their show going on and on, driving the Viking ranks to a frenzy of blood lust.

The anxiety of the Irish peaked; their warriors yearning to charge the Berserkers and kill them, or otherwise flee the field in terror, the time was ripe, the Berserkers charged the Irish ranks, followed by hordes of Viking warriors. The Viking line, not as thin as it had appeared, an endless line of warriors pouring from the village.

The two armies fused into a single mass, an explosion of yelling, screaming, dying, of metal on metal, metal on wood, wood on wood, confusion setting in, like great armies of ants, and the noise rose,thundering like a wave, rolling back over Bryan's company.

The rearmost ranks of Irish pushed slowly forward, compressing the ranks to their front.

Crawling on their bellies, through water and mud, Bryan's group advanced, closing on the rear of the Irish, uncomfortable wet and cold, within ten strides of the Irish, they could smell them. Bryan stood, his legs, cold and stiff, betraying him for a moment; staggering slightly, regaining his composure, ordered his men to charge.

Their axes dug deep into the backs of the Irish, their blood flowing freely, killing all too easy. The Irish, at first, unable to realize where the assault was coming from. Well into the Irish ranks; Byan, with limited battle experience, not prepared; the killing close, his muddy smock, now blood soaked, little room to maneuver, his axe less lethal, still killing, over and over.

The cohesion of his group lost to chaos, no longer knowing where his men were, consumed with terror and confusion, he fought on, the noise so loud he couldn't think, struggling, killing, killing.

Not the only one confused; the chaos spreading forward into the Irish ranks, believing they were being flanked, from the river side, they started running away to the right. Those to their left, now alone, panicked, and followed. The Irish warriors fighting at the front soon became isolated, no longer protected to the rear, panicking and running to their right, into their own lines, guarding the right side; confusion becoming the rule of the day, with astounding suddenness, the whole of the Irish army was running away, in full retreat, to be hunted down and murdered by the perusing Viking army, Bryan's group along with them.

Remaining behind, Bryan stood among the dead, the noise of battle fading. Numbed by noise, a dozen wounds to his arms, shoulders, and legs, covered in mud, soaked and dripping in blood, his own and others, the smell of death, blood, defecation, bellies split, intestines ripped open, urine, and sweat, hovering over the battlefield, like a blanket, heavy, sickening, filling his nostrils, he retched.

Slowly, the moans, soft and pitiful, pleading, began to enter his consciousness, and he bent drawing his knife, and stumbling over the bodies, found the poor souls still alive, and slit their throats, to end their misery.

Already there were men going about the dead gathering weapons and other valuables. Later, the bodies would be stacked into piles and burned; the battlefield a sobering place.

Chapter 32

Yarvik, taking full credit for success of the rear flank maneuver, had little good to say to Bryan. "You proved your ability to lead," he told him, "But, like your father, you lack aggressiveness, not joining your men in pursuing the enemy," ranting, full of derision, "As soon as you can put your men back together, I have another task for you, if you think you can handle it," he sneered.

Seething, Bryan left, bought bread, a roasted leg of lamb, and a bucket of ale, and went to the docks to find William.

They ate, Bryan complaining bitterly of Yarvik's slights.

William waited until he finished, then speaking softly, "Your father was gone when I arrived, but the gossip about camp at that time was Thor's leaving was the result of deep disagreement with Yarvik over the taking of slaves. Gone before they came to blows, he left behind a lot of bad feelings. I surmise that it made Yarvik look bad in the eyes of Turgis"

The following day Bryan led his men south on foot, to rout a group of Irish, held up in a hidden ravine, one of many campaigns solidifying the Viking victory. His orders from Yarvik specific, "Make it quick, charge into the camp, give them no warning, don't let any escape, kill them all."

Two days they marched, on the morning of the third Bryan's scouts returned with news that the Irish camp lay just ahead. Approaching carefully, avoiding detection, halting just outside the camp; a deep ravine, steep walls surrounding its only entrance, the floor, relatively flat, opening up, providing an area for huts. The sides of the entrance, heavily wooded; small trees, standing upright on the slopes, heavy scrub brush in the understory.

He waited and watched, his men, anxious to charge into the camp. Finally, focused intently on the entrance, he saw it, tiny flashes, the sun reflecting off metal: armor or weapons, on the hill sides.

Turning to his second in command, Oogar, "It's an ambush."

"Where?" Oogar asked.

Tilting his head toward the entrance, the hill sides are crawling with warriors, just waiting for us to enter, murder us, we can't go in that way."

"Master Bryan your orders were specific. Yarvic said to go straight in."

"I'll not lead my men in that way, it's an ambush, certain death for us all, call my scouts."

"Yarvik will be angered," Oogar warned.

"So be it. The Loki probably knew."

"Search the perimeter of the ravine for a path, no matter how difficult, to the bottom," he instructed the scouts.

Retreating to a safe site, hidden away from the ravine, they waited.

Nearly midday, the next day, the scouts returned, "We found a narrow trail, on the other side of the ravine, not much; it'll be chancy to get down there without being detected," they told him.

Near dusk, standing on the rim of ravine, the trail below narrow, steep, threading its way through the brush, the descent, to avoid being found out, would be made in complete silence.

"Master Bryan, we'll be in as much danger of being killed if discovered going down here as through the entrance," Oogar said.

"A chance we'll have to take, tell the men to wrap anything that might make noise in cloth, tie their shoes tightly, and be as sure footed as a Norse pony, we descend."

The climb, more difficult than imagined; slipping in the loose, gravely, soil, stopping, nearly impossible, and at the same time remaining inconspicuous, a constant chore. Darkness falling, half way down the slope, making travel unsafe, they slept where they were, and were headed down again, as soon as there was light enough to see their feet.

Mid-morning the head of the column, reaching the floor of the ravine, concealing themselves, waiting until the rest were off the slope.

Surveying the camp, a number of mud and wood huts, arranged haphazardly around an open area, a fire pit at its center. Warriors, here and there, busied themselves, others heading toward the gap at the entrance, relieving those who spent the night on the hill sides.

The rest of Bryan's warriors reached the floor, making, he thought, much too much noise, although the Irish seemed not to notice. Weapons were unwrapped and readied for battle.

"When do we attack," Oogr whispered.

"There are warriors heading out to relieve the men on the walls at the entrance. The men returning will be tired, and those just there will not notice what is happening to their rear, then we attack.

"Very well," Oogr said, "We're outnumbered."

"Maybe so, surprise is on our side, our men better trained, makes for an even match," Bryan maintained.

The Irish were straggling into camp, from their stations on the entrance, slowly, in ones and twos, Bryan waited, the sun rising, the air warming. When Bryan signaled his attack, they approached slowly, silently, taking the first huts, systematically killing, clearing most of the huts before alarm was sounded, surprise complete.

The Irish, finally realizing what was happening, fought back, mayhem ensued; warriors poured from the entrance, fighting viciously, desperately, defending their ground, victory tilting back and forth. The Viking warriors overwhelming them with ferocity, few escaped their murderous onslaught.

They camped outside the entrance that evening to lick their wounds, savor their victory, and avoid the stench of the dead. In the morning, after breaking camp, beginning the long walk back to Dublin, they met a contingent of warriors with a group of Irish, hands tied at their backs, bound at the neck to one another, dirty, nearly naked, clothing torn to shreds.

Among the captives, Conall, followed by his son, Drustan, Bryan's friend, and the rest of the family; temper flaring, blood running hot; his first impulse was to kill the Viking warriors, and free the prisoners, but he knew his men would not stand for that, nor did he have much stomach for butchering his Viking brothers. Quickly calming himself, taking a deep breath, he would find a better way.

"Nice group of thralls, you've captured there," he congratulated the Viking leader, where are you headed with them."

"Back to Dublin, ship them off to the south, then come back for more," the leader answered.

"Tell you what, we're finished with our business here, ran into a group of Irish rebels, eliminated the lot of 'em, heading to Dublin ourselves. You can join us," he paused as if to think, "Or we could take the thralls for you, you can return to capture more, save you a lot of trouble."

"They'll slow you down, but if you're willing to put up with 'em, I'd be happy to let you have 'em" the warrior said.

That night the two Viking groups had a meal together, drank some mead, and enjoyed each others company, in the morning going their separate ways.

Bryan led his group north toward Dublin; not looking at or speaking to the prisoners, throughout the day. In camp that evening, making sure the prisoners were fed, he set out sentries, and selected a guard for the thralls, someone special, whom he trusted, who would understand his instructions; Oogr.

When the camp was asleep, Bryan quietly crept away, to where the captives were sleeping, found Conall and Drustan, gently, waking them.

"Do not speak," he whispered, drawing a knife, cutting them free, gave each a knife, stolen from the stash of Irish weapons. "Free your friends, and go quietly, if you take the trail to the east you well not alarm the sentries. Be as far away from here as possible by dawn. If possible we will pursue you in the wrong direction."

Drustan wanted to ask questions, but Bryan hushed him, "There is no time, escape now while you can, you know I would never knowingly allow you to be made thralls, now go.

He returned to his bed.

In the morning Oogr sounded the alarm, and Bryan set out men to the south to search for the thralls, keeping his scouts under tight reigns, least they discover what direction the thralls actually went; in case he needed them elsewhere, he said.

Yarvick would not like what he had to tell him.

Chapter 33

"You can't even follow simple orders." Yarvik raged, " You endangered your men and the whole venture: Climbing down that sheer cliff, I told you clearly to surprise them, charge straight into that camp, but you didn't seem to understand that, did you?" His derision directed at Bryan.

Gathered outside Yarvik's tent were Yarvik, Bryan, Oogr, Yarvik's body guards, and a hand full of Bryan's men.

"It was an ambush," Bryan protested, "The hillsides at the entrance were crawling with warriors."

"And just how did you come to know that," Yarvik screamed.

"I saw them."

"You saw them?"

"The hills were crawling with them, their weapons gleamed in the sun, I could see them from where we were," Bryan answered.

"Your eye sight is that good," Yarvic mocked, "Or you imagined you saw them, and being the COWARD you are, were afraid to engage them," he paused, "Your eye sight was that good; yet you couldn't see the thralls escaping?" he laughed sarcastically.

Yarvic knew of the ambush; he'd sent them there to be killed, Bryan was sure of it the moment he surveyed the entrance. Why else would Yarvik have been so specific about his instructions? Threatened by Bryan; afraid the upstart, whose father he despised, would take his position?

"We saw them clearly," Oogar proclaimed loudly.

Yarvik jerked around to face the man, "I was not speaking to you – stay out of this"

"I chose to engage the enemy on my own terms," Bryan said, "Where and when we would have the advantage."

"Fact is, you disobeyed my order," Yarvik said, strutting back and forth, self absorbed, "And being too craven to carry out my directions, like you're father, I might add, not enough guts, no stomach for battle, and treasonous sympathy for the enemy, you sacrificed you're mission," Yarvik spat his words.

"I did not fail my mission, and my father is no coward, he's fought bravely for the Jarl, Skjolden."

"And how would you know that? You were back in Norway sucking on your mother's tits," Yarvik's vehemence was growing.

"Everyone knows of his valor in Balestrand. At least he went out and fought instead of sitting in camp, giving out orders he knew nothing about," Bryan accused.

Yarvik's face turned red, beads of sweat forming oh his forehead, nose to nose with Bryan, screaming, "I'll have you hanged you impudent upstart."

"Enough, yelled Oogar, "He successfully led us down into the ravine, suprised the Irish, defeating them. All Irish were killed but a few, and we only lost two of our own. It was not our fault that the thralls secreted knives to cut their ropes, and disappeared into the land that they know best. You should be pleased at our success. Maybe Turgius needs hear of this."

Yarvik pulled a knife, and turned on Oogar, "I told you to be quiet, I'll deal with this bastard traitorous coward, as I like," he lunged at Oogar.

Bryan's sword was out of its scabbard in a flash, carving an underhand arch, cleaving Yarvik's knife from his hand, peeling the skin from his knuckles. Yarvik let out a scream of pain, and leaped back. He drew his sword, his guards following suit. Bryan's men followed in kind.

Their men hesitated, not wanting to fight fellow Northmen, but Yarvik, enraged, struck out, recklessly, and mayhem ensued.

Bryan defended himself, Yarvik, more experienced and stronger, matching his every move, the duel raging long, advantage shifting, first in his favor, then in Yarvik's, each gaining then losing ground, each inflicting wounds upon the other, stinging, painful, bloody. Bryan stumbled, falling over his own feet, staggered backward, struggling to regain balance, Yarvik smelling victory, lunged forward, but Bryan somehow regained his balance, managing a defensive strike, grazing Yarvik's midsection. Bryan didn't think it a serious wound, but Yarvik stopped short.

Again, Bryan losing his balance, went down on one knee, parried a blow from Yarvik, noticing a good deal of blood staining Yarvik's midsection. Bryan, back on his feet, exchanged blows. Yarvik wavering slightly, Bryan thrust, Yarvik knocking his sword aside, inflicted a wound to Bryan's left forearm, pain, excruciating, sharp, shot toward his shoulder, blood, warm, red, from the wound, making his hand wet and sticky. Again Yarvik stuck, Bryan ducking, narrowly missed being struck again, stiking out desperately at Yarvik who, failing to put enough distance between them, took Bryan's blade deep into his abdomen.

Blood flowed, immediately, running down the length of Bryan's sword, soaking Yarvik's front. The Viking leader suddenly stopped, gasped, bending forward, trying to stop the flow with his hands, staggering, falling to his knees, dropped his sword, and collapsed to the ground, dead in a pool of blood.

Bryan backed away, his men, outnumbering Yarvik's guards, had quickly put them to the sword.

Catching his breath, he said to his men, "I'll be leaving this cursed isle straight way. Any of you who wish to follow me make haste to the docks. Otherwise, distance yourselves from here and create an alibi."

He turned and ran.

Chapter 34

Oogr followed closely, "I'm coming with you," he stated firmly.

"Gather your things and meet me at the docks," Bryan ordered.

"I have nothing," Oogr said, "I'm ready," trotting alongside Bryan.

They arrived at the dock, Byran carrying his pack and weapons, a dozen of Bryan's men, already gathered.

William, supervising the unloading of a large longship, the type the Viking used to invade seaside villages, noticed the unusual gathering, jumped ashore.

"What's going on, what happened to you?" he asked Bryan.

"I had an altercation with Yarvik. Where's this ship going?"

"Denmark, this afternoon," William told him.

"We need to take it," Bryan said flatly.

William called the captain of the ship over.

"Captain we are in urgent need of your ship," Bryan told him.

"This ship is reserved for one of Turgius' leaders. I have no room for you," the captain said, turning away.

"Captain," Bryan said raising his voice.

The man turned back.

"If you take us you will be amply rewarded," Bryan rattled his bag of coins. The captain hesitated, "And if you don't, we will take it anyway." Several of Bryan's men stepped beside him, their hands on the hilts of their swords or axes.

The captain looked the men over, still searching for excuses, "There's not enough of you, I need thirty men to row this ship."

Bryan turned to look as his men, "There are at least half that here, these men will easily each do two men's work, and if you can get a few more of your own, we'll have more than enough." He put his hand on the hilt of his own sword, and waited.

The captain clearly understood the futility of resisting, weighing the consequences; there were no alternatives. "Very well then, we must leave immediately."

The men boarded the ship and took places at the oars while William quickly acquired some provisions.

"I'm coming with you," he told Bryan.

"This could be a dangerous journey," Bryan told him.

"I don't care, I'm coming."

They left the dock, floated down the river, and were off.

Bryan counted eighteen men plus himself, William, Oogr, and the captain. The men who elected to come with him were experienced fighting men, smart enough to know that if they stayed behind they would be killed. There were some provisions aboard plus what William was able to throw in at the last minute, maybe enough to get them somewhere safe.

Making their way to open sea, Byran went to the stern where the captain manned the tiller. "Captain I hope our hostile takeover of your ship does not preclude our having a working relationship."

"Provided my bounty is adequate, and I'm not blamed for the taking of the ship, I should be fine. Your men told me what you did. I don't think I'm the one who has anything to worry about," he laughed, a cynical laugh, a rough seaman, not in the least stupid, "I suppose you are going to ask me to take you somewhere where they won't find you, some place safe."

"I was about to ask you that, yes." Bryan nodded.

"It depends on how seriously Turgius takes the murder of his captain. If he's determined to seek revenge I doubt there is any place safe from the men who will come after you, not to mention steeling one of his prize ships." The captain rubbed his beard, "The Isle of Man is too obvious, and Northern Wales up into the Scotts will be very unwelcoming, the Scotts, especially fierce people; it's doubtful if the likes of you would last long there." He was quite for a time, "We could go north to the Shetlands, a favorite place for fugitives and pirates. On the east side, the Isle of Noss. They'll likely look there eventually, but it is hidden away – might even be defensible."

"How long to sail there?" Bryan asked.

"Four, maybe five days if the wind is in our favor, the water calm, and storms stay away. We're heading into winter – North Sea can be precarious."

Bryan nodded, "That's where we'll go."

He made his way to where Oogr was rowing. "Captain recommends we head north to a place in the Shetlands. I think we can trust him, but I want you to keep an eye on him, of the direction we are headed, make sure he's not leading us into a trap. We're at his mercy; I can only hope that the lure of money and threat of violence will keep him honest."

Turning his attention to William, sitting at the bow, the wind blowing his long curly locks away from his face, "You deserve to know what happened," Bryan began, "Yarvik and I came to blows, he went after Oogr, we fought, I killed him, my men his guards."

William nodded thoughtfully. "I knew from the beginning that you two would come to blows, just like your father did."

"What actually happened between them?"

"They argued back and forth, about the taking of thralls, until Thor decided to leave before they came to serious blows. Looks like you didn't escape entirely unscathed yourself," he motioned toward Bryan's bloodied arm, still oozing, "Let me take care of that." Doctoring, he cleaned the wound with sea water that burned like the blazes, and bandaged it, the job not pretty, but stopping the bleeding.

While he worked, Bryan told him about the captain's suggestion, going north to the isles, asking William to keep an eye on the captain's directions. "I've asked Oogr to watch as well, but four eyes see more," he said.

Then Bryan looked the boy over, "Are you going to be warm enough?" Still shirtless, bare footed, trousers torn off at the knees, fitting for someone working on a ship, in a wind protected bay, "We're headed north on the open sea, with cold air in our faces."

"I'm fine," was the answer, hesitation in the boy's answer, as if there was something else he wanted to say. Bryan waited.

"Just thinking, I keep moving further and further away from my homeland, more and more on my own, and you've been the only one's treated me decent, been a friend. I would like to stay with you, serve you however I can."

"My servant?"

"Yes."

Bryan thought a moment, "I appreciate your loyalty, I really do, but I don't know what the future holds for me or you, for now - I welcome your company."

William nodded slowly, and looked out over the open water.

The sail was hoisted, and the ship made way across the water, headed north.

Chapter 35

This voyage, to Bryan's relief, they encountered no storms, only stiff head winds, producing turbulent seas, and cold air. At five days rounding the southern tip of the Shetland Isles, on the edge of the North or Noriegn Sea, the wind harsh, and the sea wild, the impressive longship cut through the water with ease, a craft far superior to the cargo knars he sailed previously.

William had come to him that morning, his skin covered in goose bumps, lips blue, shivering, asking for a shirt, Bryan pulled a shirt from his pack, offering the boy long woolen trousers, but William, perfectly happy, after donning the shirt, refused.

The sea quickly calming as they entered Bressay Sound, Bressay Isle to the left, a large island off the shores of the even larger main Shetland Isles, Noss a much smaller Isle to their east.

Noss faced the North Sea on its north side, with high sand stone cliffs, worn to treacherous crevasse, caves, and huge chunks of rock. The west, bayside, met the water with rocky shores, rising gradually to a bowl, the back side of the bowl rising to the upper surface, which gradually sloped upward to the cliffs on the east edge of the Isle, that top surface grassy and green. Below the bowl, on the flat, several small stone buildings, roofed in sod, appeared, from a distance, to be abandoned.

Making land with relative ease, they disembarked on wobbly sea legs.

Bryan paid the captain handsomely. "I would like very much for you to stay here with us," the captain had proven trustworthy and competent, "We will wish to leave this place in the spring?" Bryan cajoled, knowing full well the captain could not possibly leave without a full crew.

Bryan, with Oogr and William at his side, made his way to the buildings. An old man, sitting in front of one, stoop shouldered, grizzled leathery face, long gray beard, eyes as pale and gray as a dead man's, the only sign of life in him.

"Greetings, friend," Bryan began.

"Pends on what you want," his voice a dry and thin whisper, "Friendship's hard ta come by these parts.

"Is there someone whose leader here?" Bryan asked.

"No leader here, each to his own in this place," then with a long thin arm, and a bony hand pointed to one of the larger buildings.

The transom at the entrance low, bowing their heads to clear as they entered the darkness of a single open room, two small portals the only light; his eyes taking some time to adjust, but when they did, what he saw took his breath away.

Three men sat at a table facing them. Two, on each end, heavy fighting men, bearded, scared, clothed in wool, like that woven in Norway, and in the center, still partly blond, piercing sky blue eyes, short cropped beard, a younger looking warrior, muscular, strong, unmistakably, his father.

His breathing stopped, his heart exploding in his chest, he couldn't believe, hope beyond hope, a dream, not really thinking he would ever find him, yet there he sat.

Looking up at Bryan, curious recognition crossing his face, for the briefest of moments, not certain who he was looking at, "Yes?" his father said.

Bryan, fighting back tears, that voice, honey to his brain, "I am looking for someone, seeking sanctuary," Bryan said, bowing slightly in respect.

"And who might you be looking for?" his father said.

"Thor Bryanson," Bryan chocked out the words.

"And who might you be," Thor said still puzzled.

"Bryan."

"Bryan?" he questioned, searching Bryan's face intensely, trying to recognize, he stood, "Bryan?" a little more recognition.

"Yes, father."

"You're...," his voice drifted off as he motioned with his hand, indicating a small child, "Grown."

"Yes, father."

"What are you doing here, dressed like that, a warrior. You've been in a fight," he pointed to the wounds on Bryan's arms, clueless.

"I'm grown father; we have much to talk about."

"You shouldn't be here," Thor said, bewildered. He came around the table. He held Bryan at arm's length, his eyes taking Bryan in, beginning to tear up, finally pulling Bryan to him, "My young son, my son, what has happened to you."

"I brought some men with me," Bryan said, "We need sanctuary."

Thor went to the door to look over the men standing there, to the sea and the ship. Still bewildered, he turned back to Bryan, "What... is this all this about?

"We had some problems in Ireland father, much has happened, we need to talk."

Thor looked at the floor for a moment, thinking, shook his head in agreement, gestured toward the men he'd been talking to, who got up and left.

"I'm not suppressed you had trouble in Ireland, tis a troubled place, but how did you get there, and what are you doing with Gunner's sword?"

"Uncle Gunner is dead, father," Bryan whispered.

"No! Gunner dead, how could that possibly be?"

339

"There is much I have to tell you. It is soo good to see you. I've heard such great things about you, your valor, bravery, and great ability as a warrior. But, no one would tell me where you were, or what you were doing. Mother and I missed you terribly," Bryan wiped the tears from his cheek.

"I'm sure you did," Thor said meekly, "I'm sorry I wasn't there for you, it couldn't be helped. How is your mother?"

"I haven't seen her in almost two years now. She was well when I left, and Ari has told me that she is lonely.

Thor nodded, thoughtfully, "As am I, my son, as am I. Now what of Gunner?

"It was the Jarl, Skjolden, killed him."

"Skjolden! Are you sure?" Thor became agitated.

"I am, Ari and I saw him do it."

Thor slammed his fist on the table, "I'll kill that Danish bastard."

"You don't have to, I already have," Bryan said calmly.

"You?" Thors eyes went wide.

"Yes – sitting on his own throne during the Walpurgis ceremony. Ari alerted Lord Innvic what was to happen, and his army attacked Balestrand shortly after; the Dane's army has been defeated. " Bryan went on to tell Thor the entire story; how the Jarl's knight perused him to the Isle of Man then on to Wales, his fight with the knight, the ship wreck. "Then Yarvik accused me of cowardice, ridiculing you, we fought, I killed him too, and had to run."

"You killed Yarvik too?" Thor exclaimed, completely nonplused.

"Yes, I brought some of my men with me; those involved in the incident and wished to come along. I'm sure there will be a war party after us, and the Jarl's knights are still seeking revenge as well. I don't know if they'll be able to find me here or not.

Thor sat quiet for a long while, trying to absorb everything Bryan told him. Finally he spoke, "You've grown so much since I last saw you, you were just a young boy," he paused, "You make me so proud. It's true, Yarvik and I did not see eye to eye, we argued, I couldn't tolerate the taking of thralls, we were equals he and I, there wasn't room for the two of us, I left."

"There's something that's been bothering me," Bryan said, "Something I had to find you to ask. I've asked so many people, even the Dane, but no one would or could answer me." Bryan paused and took a deep breath; hoping Thor had the answer. "What was it the Jarl had over you to make you leave us, why do you think he killed Gunner. What was it?" Bryan pleaded.

Thor choked back a short cynical laugh, "You."

"Me?"

"Yes, my son – you, I don't know why he chose you, but he was fixated on you. He wanted to take you from us, to become his own son, your mentor, make you a great warrior, his successor," Thor paused. "I wouldn't allow it, so we struck a bargain; I would go Viking for him, and bring him riches, and he would leave you alone. Your mother knew of it, but I made her promise not to tell you. I'm certain that's what went on between Grunner and him; with me gone he probably thought he could get Grunner to relinquish you. With Grunner dead, he lured you anyway, not knowing that you saw him killing your uncle. Poor Ari, how is he?"

Bryan sat silent, unhearing, dumbstruck, he would ponder this, run it through his head, over and over, trying to sort it out, probably for the rest of his life; he was the cause, the reason his father left, the reason Ari's father was killed, the reason his mother was left alone, why couldn't he have seen?

His father calling him, he tore himself from his thoughts.

"Ari, how is he?" he wanted to know.

"Haven't seen him since the Jarl was killed. He took his father's death very hard, as you can imagine, but he's made himself a close ally to Innvik. He wouldn't say, but you know Innvik has no son, and I think the king is preparing Ari to take his place."

"Wouldn't that be something," Thor said whimsically, "Gunner's son, king." Thor smiled proudly. Then returning to practical matters. "We must make accommodations for your men. What about the ship, is it going to stay here?"

"The captain will stay, he's been paid, but he has no crew, other than my men, besides he'd probably be put to death even if he could get back."

In the coming days, Thor, having found a new reason for life, supervised the building of a longhouse, with rock, the readily available building material, searching far and wide, to find scarce structural roof material, trees being a rare item on the Shetlands, then cutting sod from the upper surface of Noss to cover the roof, reveling at the task.

The precipitous cliffs, bordering the eastern edge of the Isle, perfect nesting grounds for birds, though not the nesting season, thousands lived on the escarpments, a ready food source for the warriors. Fuel for cooking was rare, and they all had to forage extensively to find anything that would burn.

Thor and Bryan spend much time talking, in the evening before sleep, during long walks around the Isle, finding much in common, planning a return to Norway in the spring, to work the farm, rekindling a love for one another that had been lost during the years of absence.

The North Sea, a roiling cauldron, whipped by the wind, driving towering waves across the open water, at unfathomable speed, crashing into the rock faces of the east side of the Isle, in great explosions of white foam, providing, they thought, protection from detection, as the open water would be most difficult to negotiate.

Alarm rose, the morning the longship appeared, a long way off shore, in the protected, but still rough waters of the bay, after a long while, moving off toward the Isle of Bressay, vanishing below the horizon; speculation ran ramped, but Bryan knew, it was from Dublin, carrying men hunting him.

"This is not your fight, nor that of your men he told Thor."

But, Thor would have none of that, "You're wrong, my son, this fight is as much mine as yours, one I should have fought long ago, instead of leaving them bully me. If I'd fought then, Grunner would still be alive, and you would still be safe on the farm. We will fight."

Sentries were set out to watch, weapons made ready, and on the third day the skies cleared, the wind died, the seas calmed, and the ship approached.

Abandoning the stone structures, they climbed toward the upper lip of the bowl.

The Vikings beached the ship, charging straight up the rocky slope, Bryan counted eighteen. He was backed by twenty.

The hill slowed the assault, just before reaching the upper rim, Bryan attacked, his men charging downhill into the advancing warriors. The two groups meeting, the crash of metal, roar of male voices, the likes of which the little Isle never heard.

Bryan, his father at his side, backed by Thor's battle hardened men, were in for the fight of their lives, Bryan uttering to himself a quick prayer to Thor as he engaged a large knight. Victory demanded excellent use of weapons, and all the strength and luck they could muster.

The battle, working its way downhill, Thor dispatching a man, and quickly engaging another, while Bryan continued to fight a knight, a man deft with his axe, his weapon constantly in motion, Bryan continually adjusting , avoiding being struck. When the man seemed to tire, Bryan attempted to finish the battle, but the warrior, suddenly regaining his strength, stuck out, nearly slicing Bryan through his midsection. Smart move, Bryan thought, maybe trained by the same master, but leaping backward, avoiding the blade, tripping, fighting for his balance, in a heartbeat, on his back, the knight towering over him. From nowhere Thor appeared, and the knight backed off, Bryan leapt back to his feet, somehow able to cut the knights right wrist, in the next exchange, though it didn't slow him. Among the stone buildings now, Brian, finally, caught the head of the knight's axe, pulled it from his hands. The knight grabbed for his sword, but Bryan was fast on him, burying his axe deep into the armor; splitting his chest open, he fell back against a wall, blood weeping profusely from his lungs, slid to the ground to die.

Bryan pounced upon another warrior, out of the corner of his eye, catching a glimpse of Thor, backing a warrior into one of the buildings. Bryan's new opponent, one of Yarvik's men, not well trained, with little experience, took a blow to the head from Bryan's axe, knocking his helm away, stunned he stumbled backward; Bryan sunk his axe into the man's left side, near his heart. He screamed out in pain, and collapsed dead.

Another warrior attacked from behind, somehow sensing it Bryan spun around, caught the blow, deflecting it, turning him away, and sunk his axe into the man's back.

With suddenness that was stunning, there was silence; the only men standing were Bryan's or Thor's; each expecting an attack that never came. Looking around quickly, where was his father, calling, no answer, searching; unable to remember which building he'd seen Thor enter, the nearest building empty. He continued to call, running from one building to the next. Then there on the floor, grievously wounded, lay Thor, his opponent, one of Skolden's knights, dead in the corner, a great gash on the side of Thor's face, and blood oozing from his chest, his breathing heavy and wet.

"No, father," Bryan yelled, knealing beside him, he lifted his head. Thor opened his eyes, coughed, blood came to his lips, barely able to talk.

"Bryan my son, oh Bryan, I Lost my concentration for a moment there, and he got me, but I got him back." He laughed a cynical little laugh, and coughed. "Afraid this is it for me though," he said looking down, seeing the blood flowing from his chest, then back at Bryan. "I'm so glad I got to really know you, son," his voice gurgling, "I'm proud to have fought beside you, you've made me so very happy," he coughed again.

"I love you father," Bryan sobbed, "I don't want to lose you."

"My son, I thought you would have realized by now, as warriors we don't always get what we want," he smiled, "But, I'm going to Vallaha, and I always wanted that."
He coughed again, more blood, "Tell you mother I love her, that there was never another, I swear, she was – so kind to me, always, and don't let that woman you spoke of slip through your fingers, son," his breath short, and gasping, he was slipping away rapidly.

"I love you father, I love you," Bryan whispered, and wept as Thor was overcome with eternal sleep.

A hand grasped his shoulder, he turned, through teary eyes; William was at his side, a bloody sword in hand, his face and chest, smeared with blood.

"I'm sorry," William said, his voice soft, low, warm, and soothing, his hand stroking Bryan's back.

Bryan learned later that William had killed no less than four men, attacking from behind, while they fought.

A most painful victory.

Chapter 36

The warriors from Dublin, to a man, killed.

They weighted their bodies, including Thor, with stone, placed them in the second ship, rowed it to the center of the bay, and set it afire.

It burned until after sunset, before sinking to the bottom of the bay; an honorable and fitting end for Viking warriors.

Bryan's heart empty, yet heavy, through the long, lonely winter, in spite of his friends, William and Oogr, who stayed at his side, and gave their best to console him.

Plans were made, to sail for Norway, in the spring, to the homestead of Bryan's clan, when the captain deemed the seas safe to sail.

The cold winds, chilling to the bone, sea covered in froth, with nothing to burn, they tired of eating birds, raw, dried, salted, or otherwise, occasionally managing to catch a fish for variety, and as spring neared, stealing eggs from the bird colonies; their diet poor at best. It seemed spring would never come, and yet, finally, at long last, the wind died down, the sea calmed, and the days became warm. The captain, after surveying the sea from atop the Isle for days, thought navigating the open water, safe enough to sail. Wasting little time, they were soon at sea, headed home, to his family, and security; Bryan felt a great weight lifted from him, less despondent, looking to a future, less withdrawn, talking with the others, less remorseful; his uncontrollable grief eased, if just a little, taking part in sailing the ship. His mood change contagious, even the hardened warriors seemed happy to leave the dreary little Isle, with its cold dank buildings, and raw food of the last months, behind.

At the hands of the captain, now a close companion of Bryan and his company, the swift longship cleaving the waves with ease, his competence and skill, making navigating the North Sea, with accuracy, to the coast of Norway, just north of Sognefjorden seem easy. Finding land, they sailed south, to the mouth of the fjord.

Though Bryan had only seen this sight once, it seemed to him welcome and familiar; tall formations jutting from the sea, guarding the fjord's entrance, surrounded by towering rock monoliths, the foundations of great mountains, on each side; birds filling the air, their calls mingling with the sound of crashing waves, great clouds of salt mist billowing in the air.

As soon as they passed the entrance, the wind died, the waters calmed, they resorted to oars for propulsion, and after the better part of a day, reaching Hoyanger, arriving after dark, remaining off shore, sleeping on deck one more night.

As soon as light would permit, they sailed into the primitive docks at Hoyanger, and Bryan hired a man to take the party to the homestead by horse and wagon; their unexpected arrival causing quite a commotion among the members of the longhouse, not the least of which was his mother. Unsure at first, mother's instinct leading her straight to her son, tearfully holding onto him, refusing to let go. Introductions were made all around, and it wasn't long until the women were preparing a feast. The men bringing Buckets of fresh ale from the granary, the rest of the day spent eating and drinking, one thing the Norse did well.

Toward evening, Bryan, not feeling any pain, made his way up the hill to his uncle's tomb, where he fell to his knees, said a prayer to Thor, then in private, quietly told his dead uncle of all that had happened.

In the morning, gathering his family, mother, brother, and sister about, and while eating porridge and bread, told of his adventures, some of which they knew from stories told by Ari. He told them of his encounter with the bear on the mountain, his escape from Balestrand, the storm crossing the North Sea, his time on Mann, and his escape to Wales, of his love for Sorsha, the Irish family who saved him, his difficulties in Dublin, and finding his father.

"You found him alive," his mother exclaimed.

"Yes on the Isle of Norr in the Shetlands. He fell out of favor with the same leader I fought and killed. I pirated one of their ships to escape, and they sent men after me along with the Jarl's warriors who were already on my tail. Father and I fought them, and father was killed.

"Oh my, I so feared that," his mother said, sadly.

"He fought valiantly, defending me, and his last words were, 'Tell your mother I love her," Bryan paused, "He was a great warrior, mother, known for honesty, bravery, and great skill in battle."

His mother, always the stony one, wiped the tears from her eyes and cheeks. "We heard of your bravery too. Ari told us much about what you did in Balastrand. You know he is Innviks second in command, destened to become king when the old man dies."

"I didn't know, but am not surprised; my cousin will make a great king."

"And your brother is betrothed to Godheim Karlson's daughter. He will become leader of their clan, and strengthen ties between our clans."

"Congratulations brother," Bryan turned to his not so little anymore brother, who blushed deeply, the sparkle in his eyes betraying his enthusiasm about the arrangement.

"And your sister is to be wed to Godheim from the Helgi Clan."

"Really," Bryan turned to her. She beamed all over.

"He is very handsome, strong, and smart. His clan has one of the largest heard of cattle in the valley. I'm sure he will one day lead our clan," she grinned.

"And produce strong healthy babies," her mother pronounced, making his sister blush even more red than her brother.

His sister looking at him, "Of course, you will be next in line as chief of our clan.

Bryan made no reply to her pronouncement.

"We must go fishing," his brother said, "The stream is teaming with fish this spring."

"I would love that," Bryan told him, glad to change the subject from his sisters last pronouncement, "Perhaps tomorrow, there are some things I need to tend to today."

"Well, Master Bryan, you are full of surprises, as always," came a familiar voice from behind.

He spun around to see the boy from the bathhouse in Balestrand, no longer dressed in exotic sheer, wearing a smock and woolen trousers, like a common villager.

"Ole what are you doing here?" Bryan exclaimed, pleased to see his old friend.

"I didn't know where else to go, and remembered you telling about your family. They've been very kind to me."

"Ole has been very helpful," Bryan's mother said.

Bryan embraced the boy, "It's good to see you, old friend, you look different, healthy, you're filling out."

"Family life has agreed with me," the boy said, "Looks like you could use some tending to those wounds."

"You should let Ole take care of those injuries," his mother ordered.

"Perhaps, later," Bryan said, "I must attend to some things," excusing himself, "I'll be back later."

In the great room, Ole in tow, where William was waiting, Bryan introduced the boy, "William this is Ole, an old friend."

"We've met," a sound of delight in Ole's voice, Bryan thought.

"William and I are going to the village to take care of business, is there a horse available?" Bryan asked the boy.

"In the stable," Ole answered.

"Good, we'll catch you later."

There was only one horse that looked capable of making the trip with any haste, which they harnessed and saddled, Bryan climbed up to the saddle, reached down, and pulled William, shirtless and shoeless, up behind him. William wrapped his arms about Bryan's waist and they were off.

"How do you know Ole?" William wanted to know.

"He was in charge of the baths in Balestrand, a thrall to the Jarl, had a lot of contact with Skjolden's men, privy to their talk, information that he passed along to me. We became friends.

"Nothing more?" William asked.

"That was enough, we helped each other out," Bryan explained, "Why?"

"Just wondered."

Meeting the ships captain at the dock, they took him to the town chief, authority for Innvik in the village.

"The captain is experienced and skillful; his ship seaworthy, and for hire. I'm sure Lord Innvik would find good use of him," Bryan told the chief, hoping the leader, aware of his escapades in the Skjolden court, and role in the Jarl's death, would be influenced by Bryan's recommendation.

"It'll take some time to get word to Innvik and receive his response which I'm sure will be accepting," the chief said,

"In the mean time I'll give permission to sail and trade on the fjord, and I'll see if I can put a crew together for him to train."

It was more than Bryan expected, and the captain was delighted.

"I also have a group of men, experienced warriors, would like to join Lord Innvicks army, and some may wish to join the captain," Bryan told him.

"Good, good," the chief said, "Send the ones who want to crew the ship to the captain. The rest must go to Forde Torg, to your cousin there, who'll welcome them I'm sure."

Bryan returning to the dock, retrieved the horse and William, and while walking to the edge of the village they encountered a couple of young girls, young and fresh, their smiles inviting, who offered fresh flat breads and butter. They spent time exchanging pleasantries.

Leaving the village, Bryan turned back to William, "There you go."

"What?" The boy said, nonplused, from the back of the horse.

"Those pretty girls, didn't you see how they were looking at you, liking how young and strong you are. If you look em up latter, I'm sure one of them would love to - a - entertain you, if you know what I mean."

William chuckled self-consciously.

Bryan went fishing with his brother the next day in the rushing water of the stream running along the western edge of the farm. Cool and clear, full of fish, it brought back memories, fishing and playing with Ari, after working hard, on hot summer afternoons, they would run to the stream, strip down, and plunge into icy water, making their skin tingle, unimaginable pleasure, and now enjoying camaraderie with his brother, who stepped up after his leaving, becoming mature beyond his years, now planning marriage; this brother, who made him proud, to just be friends, relax with, without worry, feeling more at ease and secure than he'd thought possible in the last few years.

In the evenings, Bryan, his brother, and their uncles, reveled in hearing each other's adventures, sitting around the fire in the great room, drinking their own dark brewed ale; Bryan was at last feeling at home, comfortable.

Two weeks later, a change in the weather; over night, the blue spring time skies turned gray, icy cold wind blew out of the north, and by mid-day the heavens opened up, and cold rain, driven by the bone chilling wind, soaked everything, by nightfall, freezing, then turning to blinding snow.

Bryan was in his usual place, by the fire in the great room, when suddenly, his mother staggered through the door, from outside, carrying buckets of milk, nearly collapsing on the floor. He ran to her, and wrapped her in his arms; dripping wet, caked in snow, her lips blue, face pale, shivering, coughing, gasping for air. He swept her off her feet...

Chapter 37

In his mother's room, Bryan laid her on the ledge, removed her wet clothing, his aunts at his side with blankets, rubbing her down, feeding her steaming tea. Responding; her cheeks reddened, color coming back to her lips, and her breathing easing some; she was hot, feverish, sweaty, and a rasping gurgle, deep in her chest, rattling with each breath, her consciousness blurred.

Through the night, he sat at her side, holding her hand, brother and sister beside him, giving her sips of warm tea and honey. Her breaths becoming laborious, shallow, wet, cough more frequent, weakening, with the first rays of sunlight casting their light across the land she became very pale, and her breathing stopped.

Bryan removed the amulet, the one she gave him, from his neck, and fastened it about her's. They wept. Bryan's head spinning, weak, helpless, lost, sadness beyond anything he ever experienced; his father, his mother, gone, he hardly knew his brother and sister, Ari gone to a faraway place, distance and time over the past years alienating him from the rest of the clan. All through the next days, the preparation, burial, morning, and after wards, none of them, not his brother or sister, or William, or Ole could console his loneliness and isolation, eating him up, so deeply, so completely; he needed someone to hold, to share his sadness, warm him, to understand. He needed Sorsha, and knew what he had to do.

A few days after the burial, sitting outside the longhouse, talking to William, having just announced his intention to go back to Wales, the sun shining brightly in the air chill, providing no warmth, the boy shirtless and bare foot, as usual, basking in its rays. Two of his beautiful young cousins emerged from the long house, leaving, heading home after paying their respects; lively, rosy cheeked, full bosomed, long, brown, braids flowing down their backs. They stopped by to say farewell to Bryan, and especially William to whom the two had paid particular attention during their visit.

As they walked away, down the path, Bryan teased, "There you go again," pointing to the girls, "You should be chasing after that. I'll bet one of them would be happy to wrap themselves around you, keep you warm at night. "

The boy gave him a short, self conscious, laugh, smiled, then said after a pause, "I'm sure they would, but," he paused, "I've never been one for the ladies." He fell silent, as if in deep thought.

Then after a few moments, he asked Bryan, "I would like to come with you to Wales, Do you think I could?"

It caught Bryan off guard, surprised he said, "I suppose. Do you think it wise; I mean would it be safe for you, going back there, I recall that thug on the docks in Mann saying they'd hang you if you went back?"

The boy thought for a moment, "Its far enough north of Wales, be odd to find someone there knows of my trouble that far away. Still it's close enough to feel a little like home, besides, you'll be there. I always feel safe around you."

Byran chuckled, "As much as trouble seems to follow me around, you still feel safe, I should be flattered, I guess."

That afternoon he and the boy hitched up a cart, needing to go into the village, and arrange for their voyage.

"Can Ole come with us?" William asked.

"Ole?" Bryan said, odd, he thought, William would want Ole to go, "Sure, I guess so," he shrugged, "There's plenty of room in the cart."

So down the road the three of them went, bumping along over the rough road, a merry group, telling jokes, and reminiscing.

Arriving at the docks, a couple of workers, sitting on casks talking, directed him to a little shop, "Boddi'd know about that," they said.

Old Boddi, a man remembered from his youth, unchanged but for grayed beard, hair the same color pulled back, and braided, furrows on his face, so deep they resembled fields ready for planting, his voice dry and gravely as dirt.

"Bryan," the old man groaned, "My you've grown since last I saw you. Heard you were back. Had a little tiff with that scoundrel Dane, and I'm pained to hear about your dear mother, there's a woman's had a hard time of it, she did."

"Yes," Bryan said sadly, "Not much here for me anymore. I'm looking to go back to Wales, and was wondering if you knew of anything going that way."

"Wales, thas a far piece, but know what you mean, life has a way of changing one, a man has to move on sometimes," said a man who'd spent his whole life in one village. "Nothing moving that way for a few weeks to a month now, I'd have to let ya know when it comes up - just you?"

"Me and William, here."

"Ah, Bryan," William cleared his throat.

"Yes," Bryan turned around.

"Ole would like to go too," his face suddenly red, oddly embarrassed.

"Ole?" Bryan looked at the lad, "I thought you liked it here with my family?"

"Well I do, but I ahh..."

"He would like to be with, ah.., me and him, we ..." William stammered; the two exchanging nervous glances.

"You see we..., we, kind of...," William's voice drifted off.

Like a bolt of lightning, it struck him, the clouds in his mind parting; William had been trying to tell him, "You two are," Bryan knew..., lovers.

"Yes," William said, blushing red over his neck and chest.

"I'm sorry, William," Bryan finally said, "You tried to tell me, I didn't understand."

He turned back to Boddi, "That'll be passage for three."

The old man shook his head, confused. "You'll only get passage to the Isle of Mann, from there, you'll need to arrange your own ship."

"Of course," Bryan understood, "You'll send a messenger to the farm when you know?"

"Not a problem," the old man promised.

The next weeks drug on; Bryan and William helped plant crops, while Ole worked milking cows and goats, and making butter and cheese.

Half way through the third week, a boy from town came to the field.

"Are you Master Bryan."

"I am," Bryan answered.

"Well, Master Botti sent me to tell you, there's a ship leaving for the Isle, day after tomorrow, said you better take it cus it looks like there won't be another for a month or so, and the weather looks good for sailing."

"Thank you, boy, tell Master Botti thanks, and we'll be there straight way," Bryan, dug into his pocket, and gave the boy a shiny silver coin.

"Thank you Master Bryan, I'll tell him," and was gone in a flash.

The morning of the second day, Bryan's uncle driving a wagon, on their way, to the village to meet the ship, he and Bryan, sitting together at the front, talking.

"We wish you would stay, Bryan, your youth and strength would add much to the farm, and you'd be able to continue your father's line."

"I understand, uncle, but my brother and sister will do just fine passing Thor's blood on to the future, and you and the rest of the family are quite well off as you are. If there is trouble, I'm sure there's Ari to step in and help."

"Have you seen your cousin," his uncle asked.

"Not since the night we killed the Dane," it stung to even say that, "But we knew, even then, we were not likely to see each other again. I love him deeply, and miss him, but Wales is where I left my heart. I must return there and, fulfill my love. My life wouldn't be complete otherwise."

His uncle was quiet for a long while. "I understand, a man isn't complete without a partner, one whom he loves," he paused, "Do you think you'll ever go Viking again?"

"I can't imagine anything that would cause me to, though I'd kill anyone who tries to stand in the way of myself and Sorsha."

"Never killed anyone," his uncle said.

"There's not as much glory in it as some would have you think, uncle," Bryan said.

The village came into view.

At the docks, a large Knar, loaded with cargo, mostly food stuffs, grain, dried fish, and the like, waiting for them. Botti met them, Bryan paid him, and they said their good-bys. The ship left the dock that afternoon.

A bright, warm, sunny day, the sky blue, a breeze out of the east, fresh and cool; they passed through the mouth of the fjord, waves crashing against the rocks, nesting birds soaring, their calls echoing form the rocks; heading into the waves, they were on their way.

The second night out, the captain woke them in the early morning hours to see a rare and glorious aurora of green, red and yellow that danced about the northern sky, mysterious, and incomprehensible.

"Thor's glory," Bryan said.

They passed the days talking, napping, playing games of chance, and watching the waves roll, in endless succession, to the horizon, meeting the clear blue sky. Bryan, marveled as he watched William and Ole interact with one-another; their conversations private, different from other men, uncomfortable in society, finding much needed friendship in one another, obviously caring greatly for each other.

His heart ached to see Sorsha, thoughts of her, her home, her farm, her eyes, her hair, her smell, the food she prepared, lying close, her skin, so soft to the touch as his fingers passed over it, occupied much of his time, the longing never ending.

It seemed forever until, at long last, they sailed into the Isle, unchanged from last he saw it, except the dock hand, a gruff man, tolerant of little.

The crew, wasting no time, started immediately to disassemble the decking, preparing to unloading the cargo, the place chaotic; distracted by the activity, he didn't notice what really happened, but all at once, William had the dock boy down on the planks, a knife at his throat, screaming like a bezerker, the man was going to be dead in another moment.

Bryan leapt over several men, grabbed William by the waist of his trousers, lifted him, screaming from the man, with one hand, immobilizing the knife with the other.

Squirming, still screaming at the top of his lungs, "Let me down, I'll kill em," his face and shoulders red with rage, "let me go, let me go," fighting.

Bryan managed to disarm him, wrapped the boy in a bear hug, holding him until he calmed, finally collapsing into tears. Ole, stood by, also in tears, trying to console the boy.

"I want em outa here," the old dock boss, now on his feet, shouted, very agitated, coming at William.

In a flash, Bryan's hand went to his boot, his knife point at the man's throat, the deck hand stopped abruptly.

"I've slit other mens throats for much less, and I won't think twice about doing it again, unless you calm down," Bryan said through clinched teeth.

The man backed away.

"Now, we're not looking for trouble, just passing through, only be here a few days," Bryan said, "You go about your business, and we'll go about ours."

The man raised his hands, shook his head, and turned away.

"Come on," Bryan said to his friends, a hand on William's shoulder, turning him away. "Where'd you get that knife?"

"My knife!" William quickly turned back, found it on the deck, and came back with it.

"Where'd it come from?" Bryan wanted to know.

William smiled, pulled the waist of his trousers open, and slid in down into a sheath concealed between his groin and leg.

"You've had it there all this time?"

"Yes."

They walked up the hill toward the inn.

"What happened back there?" Bryan wanted to know.

"The son of a dog, said some nasty things to Ole," William said.

"Shouldn't of paid him any attention," Ole said," I've heard it all before."

"Not while I'm around," William said.

"Well, in another blink of the eye, you'd have killed the man," Bryan said.

"You can bet your ass, I would have," William said, then muttered, "I've done it before."

"You killed several up in the Shetlands, I know, and I heard rumors…," Bryan said.

"They're true, what they said, them rumors, I killed my master, never said it out loud to anyone before, told me my parents sold me, think he killed them, and he did things to me, when I was too young to say no, or fight him off. When I grew old enough to say no, he beat me till I give in, and when I couldn't take the beating any longer, I killed em in a rage – with this knife – and ran."

"You and Ole's the only ones ever treated me like I was worth anything. I love you, you know, and I'd do anything for you, even kill," his eyes flashing with anger, then filling with tears that ran in streams down his cheeks. He wiped his nose with the back of his hand.

Bryan motioned for them to sit down on a stone wall beside the road.

"What you did was a long time ago; no one would blame you, knowing what he was doing to you." Bryan's voice, soft, low, soothing, "But, you are much older now, William, an adult, that kind of rage can only bring you sorrow. If you had killed that man they would have hanged you. Think about what you are doing. If you must seek revenge, wait, plan it out, so you will not be made to pay, that's the way of the Old Norse, the wise way. I've killed men, the gods will attest, not in anger,

362

but revenge, not a pretty thing, and had to defend myself, but I'm still here to tell you about it."

He paused, reflecting; always the guilt, the shame he felt, about the indescribable, ecstatic, thrill, he experienced with each man what he'd killed, every time, even to the last man in the Shetlands; hanging his head, in quite shame, he couldn't tell even William or Ole about.

"Ole and I, we love you William, we don't wish to lose you, try not to kill in anger, you'll live longer.

The innkeep looked at Bryan with big eyes, "Well, look what the cat drug in, left here in kind of a hurry, now, didn't yee – girl friends gone too, I'm afraid, ran off wid one a those so called knights was chasin' you," she laughed, obviously not missing her daughter much, the lady had a way of cutting through to the truth. "They still chasen' ya?"

"Chasin'? Not anymore their not." Bryan answered.

"What? You killed em all, I suppose," she said sarcastically.

"As many as were there to kill, had some help," he nodded toward William.

The woman looked at William with doubt in her eyes. Bryan thought it good people underestimated the boy.

"What can I do for you today," she finally said.

"Roof over our head, and a couple of meals a day for a few days," Bryan answered.

"There's some mutton stew for ya right now, if ya wish,"

"That'd be good, and a tankard each."

"Uh, you left rather unexpected like first time you was here, no disrespect, but I'd like three days in advance, ya don't mine."

Bryan paid, and took his companions to a table. Good to eat real food, they were silent until finished, and their thirst quenched. Then Bryan moved his chair over next to William, put his arm across the boy's broad shoulders, and said, "There's something I want you to do, Billy boy."

William looked at him, startled, Bryan had never addressed him that way.

"You remember that pub you took me to when you were helping me leave the Mann."

The boy nodded yes.

"I want you to go there, if that's where you need to, don't mess with the deck boy, and find out when the next ship to Morecombe Bay will be, and how much they want for us to go there. You think you can do that?"

"Sure," William said.

"And stay out of trouble, ya hear."

"Yes, Master Bryan,"

While Bryan and Ole laid claim to places in the loft, William made his way to the docks, where the men, including the man he'd fought with, were still unloading the ship. Skirting behind warehouses, avoiding contact with them, he entered the tavern, still a seedy place, were, for a price, almost anything could be bought. The man behind the bar, unfamiliar to William, didn't recognize him, and was unpleasant.

"Is Vikarson in?" William demanded.

"Who's askin?"

"Tell em William from Wales, he'll know," William said, belligerently.

The man when into the back room.

Vikarson ran the waterfront with a strong arm, his thugs, the same who threatened Bryan when he needed escape from the Isle, helped him extort fees from the ship captains, shippers, anyone else on the ships, and the dock workers.

The bar man returned, motioned with his head, and begrudgingly said, "Go ahead."

364

William went through the door, across the dark room, and through the second door. Vikarson sat on a stool on the other side of the room, his henchmen, one on each side of the room.

"Well, look whose back. Suppose you're lookin' for your old job back, even after you left me in the lurch," the man said.

"Don't imagine I left you in too much of a lurch, but lookin' at the boy you got out there runnin' things right now, I can guess you're interested. But no, I don't want your job. I'm looking for passage for three to Morcombe Bay."

"Morcombe again, what's in Morcombe that's of such interest? Sides, you'll get strung up going back there."

"Chance I'll have to take, its personnel business."

"Personnel business, those Skjolden thugs still after you?"

"Their screwing Valkeries with Oden in Valhalla," William boasted.

"You don't say, well why didn't you ask about this passage with my dock boy?"

"He and I aren't see'n eye to eye," William said.

"Heard you had an altercation with em."

"Boy has a big mouth, needs to learn to keep it shut," William said.

"And you were going to teach em?"

"Would a done it permanently if it hadn't been for Bryan."

"Always were fast with the temper," Vicarson said, "Hear he had something to say about your girl friend."

"Don't tempt me, you bastard," William ground his teeth.

Vickarson laughed a loud mocking laugh, "Calm down Billy, I'm just kidding, could care less."

"When do you think we can get a ship outa here?"

365

"You in a hurry?"

"Not that much, but sooner would be better than later."

"You Payin'?"

"Bryan is, but it has to be reasonable."

They bartered back and forth, and reached a fee William thought Bryan could accept.

"When can we expect to set sail?" William wanted to know.

"Tell you what; you always were one of my favorites. That ship out there, the one you came in on, isn't leaving for a while. I can have er ready to set sail, first thing in the morning. You can pay my men; I'll send em out to meet you in the morning."

Bryan was very pleased, "You are remarkable, William, a man of many surprises."

The praise, music to his ears, delighted William.

They had a good meal that evening, a few drinks, Bryan paid the inn keep, and they retired to the loft, and slept.

William was first to rise, and woke the others. "I'll meet you at the dock as soon as you can make it," he told Bryan, and headed for the stairs.

"Where are you going?" Bryan shouted after him.

"Got some business to attend to," he said as he headed down.

"Well if he doesn't want to eat, I do," Bryan told Ole. They enjoyed a hardy meal, then headed to the docks, meeting William, talking with Vicarson's man. He had new trousers, freshly cut at the knees, strange.

Bryan paid the men, friendly enough, met with the captain, boarded the ship and were off. As the ship pulled away from the dock, Bryan noticed something floating in the water beneath the dock, behind the pilings; looking again, more closely, a body, the old dock boy, face up, naked from the waist down, his neck cut open, floating, the water red with blood.

Bryan drove a quick glance at William, who flashed him an odd grin, and turned to Ole, to continue what he was saying.

The voyage to Morecombe Bay, the waters calm, uneventful, the hull empty of cargo, the ship floating high in the water, and fast, able to sail right onto the shore, upon reaching the bay. They said good-by to the captain, and headed for the village.

Excitement building within him, he went directly to the dreaded bread lady, who looked him over, dismayed.

"I would like three of your best loaves," he said politely in his best Celt.

She curled her lips, looking his companions over.

"Please mame, three of your best loaves," he repeated.

"I don't make bread for you, you Northman dog," she spat.

Bryan started to draw his sword from its sheath, "You will or I'll slice you in two, you Welsh pig," Bryan seethed.

William stepped forward, placed his hand over Bryan's, easing the sword back into its sheath.

"My lady," he said, his voice calm, and soothing, "Please, I am not a Northman, but Welsh like you, we only want some loaves to make our dinner with. Our money is good. I know you are a good woman, in your heart. We mean you no harm, just three loaves," his voice so soft and humble, she could not refuse.

They walked away with the loaves in a sack.

"You truly are surprising; I had no idea you had that in you Billy Boy, you've a silver tongue. You would have no problem getting into the ladies skirts."

"I told you," William shot back, "I'm not one for the ladies."

"He's pretty good with the boys though," Ole added, thoughtlessly.

They all chuckled.

Bryan bought a leg of lamb, and they started up the mountain.

Nearing the top of the mountain, something moved up ahead, stopping quickly, the others piled into his back. It was coming toward them on the trail, at a trot, a dog, no, a wolf, as it got near. Stopping just a stone's throw from them, its ears erect, eyes blue as the sky, gray fur trimmed in black; for a long time, they gazed at each other. Quitely, Bryan said, "Its Thor." The wolf lowered its head, sniffing their scent, then turning its head slightly to the side, smiled as only a canine can, then cantered off into the forest. "He approves," Bryan said.

Midafternoon, they emerged from the forest, across the fields from Sorsha's home, and headed toward the buildings. Tyr, walking across the square, noticed them, stopped, looking intently curious, not sure, who they might be, then thinking he recognized the way the big one walked, began yelling, "Sorsha, Sorsha, come quick, come see who's here," his exuberance uncontained, running toward them. Sorsha emerging from the house, trying to figure out what was going on, searching, not recognizing, until she heard Tyr yell out Bryan's name, "No..., Bryan?" screaming, running toward them.

Bryan broke from his friends, caught Tyr in a hug, braking from him he ran to Sorsha, threw his arms around her, lifting her from the ground, spinning her around, their lips met, they embraced.

"Oh Bryan, I never, I didn't think I'd ever see you again."

"I told you I'd come back."

"What about the knights?"

"All dead; I found my father, and together with his men we killed them all," he paused, "I brought two friends, loyal, good workers," he hesitated, "They're ... ah, lovers."

"Should fit in well with Tyr," she smiled, "I can't believe this is real."

Helga began preparing the lamb for a feast, while Bryan showed William and Ole the barracks. They would have to share a bed, his old bed, until another was built, they didn't object. Tyr was ecstatic, dancing about, and helping when he could.

Bryan made William wear a shirt to dinner. The conversation lively, Bryan told his stories, and Sorsha updated him on what was happening on the farm, the food delectable, the wine sweet, enjoying each other, a new found family.

William, Ole, and Tyr left for the barracks, and Bryan and Sorsha, sat and talked till late, then went into her bedroom. After making love, lying naked beside her, wrapping her in his arms, so in love, home at last.

About the Author

William Jay Taylor, actively retired, holds Bachelor Degrees in Business from Penn State University and Nursing from Beth El College of Nursing, University of Colorado, Colorado Springs, and has been a student of history since high school. Extensively traveled, he enjoys delving into obscure, little known cultures and well written fantasy. Emulating authors of excellence like Ken Follett, J.R. R. Tolkein, Christopher Paolini, Frank McCourt, and Khaled Hosseini he attempts to capture historical accuracy and entertaining fantasy in his writing.